PRAISE FOR MATTHEW FITZSIMMONS

PRAISE FOR *DEBRIS LINE*

"Matthew FitzSimmons writes the kind of thrillers I love to read: smart, character-driven, and brimming with creative action sequences. If you're not yet a fan of FitzSimmons's Gibson Vaughn series, strap in, because you soon will be. *Debris Line* is tense, twisty, and always ten steps ahead. Don't miss it."

—Chris Holm, Anthony Award–winning author of *The Killing Kind*

"Matt FitzSimmons continues his amazing literary feat of creating an ensemble cast of troubled heroes and shooting them through page-turning thrillers with his latest, *Debris Line*, continuing the fast-paced adventures of Gibson Vaughn and his crew as they battle to stay alive and find some measure of justice in this unforgiving world. The Gibson Vaughn Series is on its way to being a classic franchise of thriller fiction, with a unique voice and an unusual approach that keep the stories as appealing as they are entertaining. Highly recommended."

—James Grady, author of *Six Days of the Condor*

"*Debris Line* doesn't waste a word or miss a twist. It's always smart, always entertaining, and populated top to bottom with fascinating and unforgettable characters."

—Lou Berney, author of *November Road*

PRAISE FOR *COLD HARBOR*

"In FitzSimmons's action-packed third Gibson Vaughn thriller . . . fans of deep, dark government conspiracies will keep turning the pages to see how it all turns out."

—*Publishers Weekly*

"*Cold Harbor* interweaves two classic American tropes: the solitary prisoner, imprisoned for who knows what; and the American loner, determined to rectify the injustices perpetrated on him. It's a page-turner that keeps the reader wondering—and looking forward to Gibson Vaughn #4."

—Criminal Element

"There are so many layers and twists to *Cold Harbor* . . . FitzSimmons masterfully fits together the myriad pieces of Gibson Vaughn's past like a high-quality Springbok puzzle."

—*Crimespree Magazine*

PRAISE FOR *POISONFEATHER*

An Amazon Best Book of the Month: Mystery, Thriller & Suspense category

"FitzSimmons's complicated hero leaps off the page with intensity and good intentions, while a byzantine plot hums along, ensnaring characters into a tightening web of greed, betrayal, and violent death."

—*Publishers Weekly*

"[FitzSimmons] has knocked it out of the park, as they say. The characters' layers are being peeled back further and further, allowing readers to really root for the good guys! FitzSimmons has put together a great plot that doesn't let you rest for even a minute."

—*Suspense Magazine*

PRAISE FOR *THE SHORT DROP*

". . . FitzSimmons has come up with a doozy of a sociopath."

—*Washington Post*

"This live-wire debut begins with a promising lead in the long-ago disappearance of the vice president's daughter, then doubles down with tangled conspiracies, duplicitous politicians, and a disgraced hacker hankering for redemption . . . Hang on and enjoy the ride."

—*People*

"Writing with swift efficiency, FitzSimmons shows why the stakes are high, the heroes suitably tarnished, and the bad guys a pleasure to foil . . ."

—*Kirkus Reviews*

"With a complex plot, layered on top of unexpected emotional depth, *The Short Drop* is a wonderful surprise on every level . . . This is much more than a solid debut, it's proof that FitzSimmons has what it takes . . ."

—Amazon.com, An Amazon Best Book of December 2015

"Beyond exceptional. Matthew FitzSimmons is the real deal."

—Andrew Peterson, author of the bestselling
Nathan McBride series

"*The Short Drop* is an adrenaline-fueled thriller that has it all—political intrigue, murder, and suspense. Matthew FitzSimmons weaves a clever plot and deftly leads the reader on a rapid ride to an explosive end."

—Robert Dugoni, bestselling author of *My Sister's Grave*

DEBRIS
LINE

ALSO BY
MATTHEW FITZSIMMONS

The Short Drop
Poisonfeather
Cold Harbor

DEBRIS LINE

THE **GIBSON VAUGHN** SERIES

MATTHEW FITZSIMMONS

Text copyright © 2018 by Planetarium Station Inc.
All rights reserved.

Published by Thomas & Mercer, Seattle

www.apub.com

Amazon, the Amazon logo, and Thomas & Mercer are trademarks of Amazon.com, Inc., or its affiliates.

ISBN-13: 9781503951648 (hardcover)
ISBN-10: 1503951642 (hardcover)
ISBN-13: 9781503901124 (paperback)
ISBN-10: 1503901122 (paperback)

Cover design by Rex Bonomelli

Printed in the United States of America

First edition

When building sandcastles on the beach, we can ignore the waves but should watch the tide.

—Edsger W. Dijkstra, *The Tide, Not the Waves*

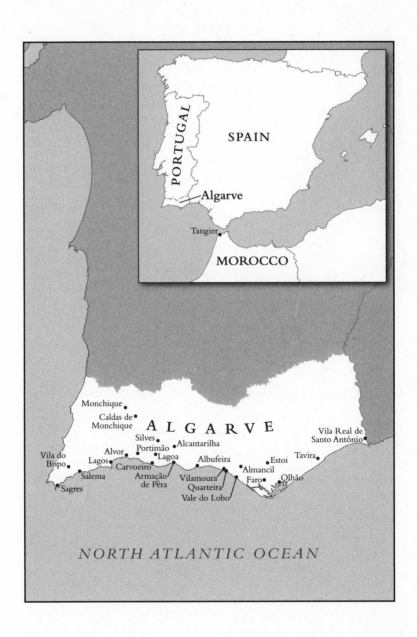

CHAPTER ONE

João Luna steered the *Alexandria* south and west into open waters. At his back, the towns of the Algarve that lit the horizon dimmed and faded from view as the trawler churned its way out into the Atlantic. The *Alexandria* had been in his family for thirty years. A modest boat— she wouldn't win any beauty contests—but solidly built and reliable. Twelve meters from bow to stern with a crew of five. João had grown up on board, fishing the sardines that swam in immense schools along the coast of Portugal. At night, the sardines rose to the surface to feed on plankton, and ordinarily, the crew would have already begun to prepare the nets. But not tonight. Tonight, the crew of the *Alexandria* had another job ahead of them.

The ocean was unusually calm. Hard to imagine a storm was on the way. But the maritime forecast promised gale-force winds and heavy rains in a few hours. It wasn't the season for such weather, but the seasons no longer meant what they once had. João knew better than to flout the forecast. He meant to be done and on the way home before the worst of it hit. In stories, the sea often mirrored the emotions of sailors. João knew that was only the poetic license of writers who had never worked a day on the water. The ocean didn't give a good goddamn for the concerns of men like him.

The accursed device beeped. The black box with its sleek modern contours looked out of place on the old wooden console. João glared at it but adjusted course, keeping the blinking red dot in the screen's crosshairs. The device filled him with an unfamiliar dread. He would have thrown it into the ocean had he dared. Had his father not explained why that was impossible.

The device beeped again. They had to be close now.

João had dreamed of captaining the *Alexandria* since he was a young boy. Since that first night when his father took him out with the crew. He couldn't have been more than seven. His father stood him on a crate so João could take the wheel. Feeling the hum of the engine, the camaraderie among the crew, all other ambitions had died in him that night. School became a meaningless torture. None of its lessons applied to fishing, not even the vocational training that his father insisted upon. All that had ever made sense to João was the ocean, and all the education he would ever need came from his father and the men who crewed the *Alexandria*.

The way he'd imagined his life unfolding, he would work beside his father on the *Alexandria*. Perhaps meet a woman, court her as best he knew how, and marry. A small home. A son or daughter to follow in his footsteps. Years from now, his father would retire, and João would carry on in his place. It would have been a good life. The diagnosis had changed all that.

It was still hard to accept, because his father looked as healthy as ever. The doctor warned, however, that cold nights on the deck of a fishing trawler would accelerate his decline. Always a decisive man who kept his own counsel, João's father had retired suddenly and without fanfare. João had learned the news over a glass of port. He'd never cared for the taste but, sensing the importance of the moment, drank it seriously.

I'm finished, his father had said simply. *You are captain now.*
I'm not ready.

Perhaps not, but life is ready for you.

And like that, at nineteen, João found himself the captain of the *Alexandria*. His life's ambition realized, and he didn't want it. Not under these circumstances. But he'd done as his father asked and become captain. That had been six weeks ago. There had never been any question of the crew following him. João had worked on the *Alexandria* for more than a decade and knew every inch of her. Things had gone on as they always had. He had simply done what his father had always done. Until yesterday morning.

His father had met him unannounced on the docks at Olhão, where the *Alexandria* berthed. It had given João a bad feeling. He'd feared that his father's health had taken a turn for the worse. They had walked to their favored café at the old fish market. That was where his father had told him about the debt.

Seven years earlier, the family had almost lost everything. Poor hauls, lower market prices, and unforeseen expenses had pushed his father to the brink of bankruptcy. Then the engine of the *Alexandria* had failed. João remembered it well. His father had been as withdrawn and somber as João had ever seen him. What João didn't know was that Baltasar Alves had come to his father with a proposition: he would finance the overhaul of the *Alexandria* and replace the engine. The trawler would remain in João's family, but four nights a year she would belong to Baltasar Alves, their new patron. The *Alexandria* and its captain.

Tonight was one of those nights, and his father had come to the docks that morning to pass the responsibility on to his son. And to entrust him with the black box that was charting the *Alexandria*'s course. At first, João had been angry at his father for getting them involved with a man like Baltasar Alves, angry that his father had concealed the truth all these years. But then João saw shame in his father's face and fell silent. His father was an honorable man; João saw he had only done what had to be done to take care of his family. How could João do any less? He took the device and asked what needed to be done.

On the console, the device began beeping incessantly. João cut the engines and scanned the ocean. To starboard, a blue light strobed in the darkness. He brought the *Alexandria* alongside, and the crew used hooked poles to bring the mysterious packages onboard. Each was perhaps two meters wide, two meters tall, four meters long, and bound in heavy plastic—impossible to tell what might be inside. João was curious to open one and find out, but his father had warned him above all else never to tamper with Baltasar Alves's cargo.

Instead, João ordered the crew to stow the packages in the hold. He wondered how many other boat captains were working for Alves this night. He hoped not many. If the stories were true, then once a man was in Baltasar Alves's debt, he never left it. João pushed the thought aside and went to help the crew. It would raise suspicions with the maritime police if they returned to Olhão entirely empty-handed.

CHAPTER TWO

The streets were all but deserted at this hour. Like the pale, peaceful face of an old drunk sleeping off a night of poor choices. After the night's last tourists had staggered home from the nightclubs but before the morning's first tourists stumbled out of bed to stake claim to a rectangle of sand. Before the sun climbed to its perch in the cloudless Mediterranean sky. When the street cleaners emerged to sweep up the broken glass and wash away the blood and the vomit and the urine. A dull reset before the good times rolled again.

Gibson Vaughn's favorite time of day.

The morning before the morning. Alone with his thoughts.

Mercifully, he never remembered his dreams—hard memories of home—but he felt them in his body when he woke. Sore muscles and knots in his back like cigar burns. By six a.m., when he could no longer pretend that he might doze off again, he took a long run down to the beach. When he'd first arrived in Portugal, Jenn Charles would join him. They'd run side by side, talking and shooting the shit. That had tapered off after a few weeks, and they hadn't run together in months. He missed her company.

For the last six months, home had been a small house on the outskirts of Albufeira, a beach-resort town in the Algarve region of

Portugal. Jenn had the bedroom at the top of the stairs. The smallest of the three. Gibson went by it quietly, carrying his shoes. There was no need. Her door was open, bed unslept in. Probably out with her boyfriend, or whatever it was they called each other. She wasn't saying, and Gibson wasn't about to ask.

Dan Hendricks's bedroom door was closed, but Gibson didn't bother to knock. Hendricks had settled into a comfortable routine and wouldn't be up before noon. Just in time for his afternoon siesta. Besides, Hendricks took a dim view of running unless he was being shot at.

The house was owned by an old associate of George Abe's named Baltasar Alves—the criminal boss who ran things in the Algarve. He owed George a debt. The exact nature of the debt, Gibson didn't know, but whatever it was had been enough for Alves to grant them all sanctuary. No small thing, given they'd fled the United States under a cloud. Gibson and Jenn were both wanted by the FBI in connection with the events at Dulles International Airport. And as far as they knew, Titus Eskridge, the head of the private military contractor Cold Harbor, was still out there with a score to settle. So far there hadn't been any strings attached to Alves's hospitality, but Gibson was wary of the benevolence of criminals. However, the problem with not having any options was that it didn't give you an option.

Out on the front steps, Gibson laced up his shoes by the light of a streetlamp. Setting off at an easy jog, he picked up his pace quickly. He couldn't help himself. It had taken months to rebuild his stamina, and it felt good to be able to push himself and for his body to respond. The CIA had held him for eighteen months in a windowless cell. It had taken its toll on his mind as well as his body, and he was only now beginning to feel like his old self.

He charted a winding route through town. Past the traditional white homes capped by orange clay-tile roofs. Thirty years ago, Albufeira had been a sleepy Portuguese fishing town. Legend had it that Paul

McCartney had written the lyrics for "Yesterday" while on vacation here in 1965. Even then, it was the perfect place to hide out when the world was looking for you. Gibson could still see the outline of that way of life beneath the garish bars, restaurants, and nightclubs that had built up like plaque on porcelain teeth. As best as Gibson could tell, Portugal and Spain now served as the Florida of Europe. Northern Europeans owned vacation homes here, and each year millions of tourists flocked south to the Algarve region to enjoy their holidays in the sun.

The crush of tourists had made hiding in plain sight that much easier. August was high season, and Albufeira was currently overrun with sunburned visitors from Germany, France, Holland, and the British Isles. The menus were printed in languages other than Portuguese, and everyone who worked in the tourist trade spoke some English. Irish pubs served a traditional breakfast while musicians strummed guitars and sang "Molly Malone." English pubs served pints of Carling and Strongbow and advertised Premier League matches on curbside chalkboards. The perfect vacation for people who wanted to travel without all the unpleasantness of experiencing anything new.

Gibson understood the appeal of southern Portugal. He'd spent time at Pendleton and knew that San Diego liked to boast about its perfect weather. It had nothing on southern Portugal. Up until last night's storm, it had rained only once since June. There was hardly ever even a wisp of a cloud in the sky. It was a seductive way of life. After six months, they'd all gotten comfortable here. Maybe too comfortable. Gibson understood that. It had been a difficult few years for all of them. The search for Suzanne Lombard had extracted a heavy price, and for two years they'd all absorbed the repercussions.

They had deserved the rest. Needed it. They were beat up—physically, emotionally, and spiritually. Still, Gibson couldn't help but fret. There was a point after which rest turned to rust. Instincts honed over years lost their edge. It was okay to pretend they were civilians for a while, so long as they knew that, in the end, they weren't. They were fugitives. How long could they afford to stick their heads in the sand? They were all but penniless and needed work. They needed a plan for the day when Baltasar Alves decided his debt was paid. But whenever Gibson raised the subject, Jenn shut him down. Somewhere along the line he'd become the nagging killjoy putting a damper on the endless party. He didn't relish the role, but sooner or later the universe would present them with the bill. They would need a way to pay.

Gibson ran on, winding his way through the narrow streets of Old Town. Past shops and stalls that sold all the same trinkets at all the same prices. The approaching dawn warmed the rooftops. Hating to miss the sunrise, he coaxed himself into a sprint. His lungs burned while the quitting part of his brain offered compelling excuses for walking the rest of the way. He did his best to tune out everything but his feet, focusing instead on picking them up and laying them down, as his drill instructor on Parris Island had commanded in the South Carolina heat.

Gibson rounded a bend onto a cobblestone side street. Built in a time before automobiles, it was no wider than an alley, and a row of cars parked tight against a tall brick wall took up nearly half the roadway. Animal masks decorated with plastic jewels and gaudy feathers littered the cobblestones. As if a Mardi Gras parade had passed this way and spontaneously decided to reveal its true face. More likely, one of the nightclubs had thrown a theme night. The street sparkled, and the masks crunched beneath Gibson's feet. He glanced down to avoid stepping on too many of them.

Maybe that was why he didn't see the car lurch out of the parking spot. Gibson heard it and looked up, expecting the car to slow, but instead it leapt forward crazily. It accelerated toward him, hugging the row of cars on one side and the closed shops on the other. With nowhere else to go, Gibson flung himself onto the hood of a parked car. He felt an impact, felt himself spin in the air, bounce off the hood of the car, clatter off the brick wall and back onto the hood. He sat up on the car in a daze. His foot throbbed. He was missing a shoe. His sock was bloody, which didn't bode well for his ankle. He'd skinned his elbow, and his forehead hurt. Otherwise, he couldn't complain.

He slid off the car, testing to see if his ankle could take the weight. It hurt, but nothing seemed broken. Had the driver and passenger been wearing Mardi Gras masks too? He'd only caught a glimpse through the windshield, but he remembered an elephant and a rhinoceros, like two themed henchmen working for a zookeeper supervillain. Gibson sighed. After everything he had been through, it would be fitting somehow if he got himself killed by some raver wacked-out on ecstasy. His missing shoe wasn't anywhere in sight. He knelt to look under the parked cars.

"Senhor?" a woman called to him. She had his shoe in one hand, a broom in the other. One of the street cleaners. She looked him up and down with a shake of her head. He crossed over to her.

"Crazy tourists," she said.

Gibson couldn't tell if she meant him or the driver.

"Obrigada," he said.

The woman smiled. He'd already spoken more Portuguese than most tourists to the Algarve bothered to learn. She seemed to appreciate the effort and handed him the shoe.

"Obrigad-o, senhor. Only the ladies say *obrigada.* You don't look like a lady to me."

"Obrigado," Gibson said sheepishly. He'd learned one word of Portuguese since he'd been here and had been saying it wrong all this time. That was what going soft looked like. Not bothering to learn enough of the local language to hold even a basic conversation. What if the car had hit him? What if the doctor didn't speak English? Of course, if he were taken to a regular hospital and they ran his information, he'd have bigger problems than a language barrier. It would be like shooting off a flare for anyone hunting them to see.

It reinforced how tenuous their position here was. They weren't on vacation and needed to stop acting like it. They'd gotten away with it up until now, but they were one slipup—one car accident—from being blown. Jenn might not want to hear it, but too bad. She was going to listen. Not thinking about the future didn't stop the future from thinking about you.

It was time.

He winced as he pulled on his shoe, then limped down the hill toward the ocean. After his morning runs, he liked to finish with push-ups, sit-ups, and chin-ups while the sun came up. He wasn't that hurt, he told himself again. But after a hundred yards, he downgraded his optimism. His ankle could use a day off. And if he was being honest, his shoulder felt a little hinky too. He soldiered on anyway. He could still watch the sunrise.

The small fitness park was deserted at this hour. So, for the most part, was the street that overlooked Fisherman's Beach. In the old days, before being displaced by tourists, this was where the boats had brought in the haul. Down below, Gibson saw signs of last night's storm. The debris line cut a jagged path across the beach, the high-water mark of the storm surge.

His father had spent his childhood summers on the Outer Banks and had always loved the ocean. Sometimes he would take Gibson on long walks along the beach near Pamsrest, Virginia. Duke had liked beachcombing the debris line after storms to see what had been tossed ashore. Said it helped to clear his head. Mostly all they found were shells, seaweed, and broken branches. But every so often they'd stumble across a treasure. Gibson remembered finding a Peruvian license plate half buried in the sand. He'd spent hours studying his father's atlas, imagining its improbable journey around the southern tip of South America to the ledge above his bedroom door. Duke told him that nothing was ever lost forever. That it was the nature of lost things to be found. Just not always when and not always by whom you hoped or expected.

Gibson powered on his phone and looked at the most recent photograph of Ellie. Nicole, his ex-wife, had pleaded with him to stay away.

One of Gibson's enemies had burned her house to the ground to send him a message, so as much as Gibson hated it, he accepted the necessity. For now. It helped that Nicole e-mailed him pictures of their daughter now and again. Ellie had apparently given up on soccer and was now a green belt in aikido. The idea of Ellie standing still long enough to learn martial arts brought a huge smile to Gibson's face. He was working up the nerve to ask Nicole for a video. More than a little afraid to push his luck. He scrolled through her pictures from the past few months. His little girl wasn't so little anymore and looked more and more like her mother. Lucky girl.

His phone vibrated. He'd missed a call from Fernando Alves, the only son of Baltasar Alves. What could he possibly want at *this* hour? Gibson didn't have any interest in finding out. He wanted a quiet breakfast. But when he looked up at the row of restaurants overlooking the beach, he saw Fernando sitting alone on a bench waiting for him. Not that Fernando paid him any mind. Instead, he studied the ocean and sipped a coffee. His legs, stretched out before him, were crossed at the ankle. He sat with the languid confidence of a man aware he was wearing a tuxedo and you weren't. His shirt's top two buttons were undone and might well have begun that way. He was the kind of man who would go to the trouble of putting on a tuxedo and draping an untied bowtie around his neck simply because he liked the look. For Fernando, it was always the end of the evening.

Behind Fernando rose the Hotel Mariana, which he operated on behalf of his father. The hotel had been named for Fernando's mother, who died when he was a boy. It was also his home. He lived in an enormous suite overlooking the Atlantic. Fernando liked to joke that it was his life's ambition to live on room service. As far as Gibson could tell, Fernando had already achieved it.

"What on earth happened to you?" Fernando inquired. Baltasar had sent him away to England for school, first to Eton and then to Cambridge, and his English carried an aristocratic inflection.

"I got hit by a car."

Fernando looked him up and down. "Are you sure? You don't look like someone who was hit by a car."

Nonchalance wasn't recognized as a world religion, but if it were, Fernando would have been its messiah. He never offered any hint about whether he was serious or joking. It made for awkward pauses that Fernando seemed to relish. Gibson was glad he didn't work for him. But they'd gotten to know each other over the last six months, and Gibson could appreciate Fernando's dry sense of humor and the sly smile that played on his face when he thought no one was watching.

"My foot," Gibson said by way of explanation.

Fernando stared at Gibson's bloody sock, one eyebrow arched slightly. "Was it a very small car?"

"I don't remember, but a rhinoceros was driving."

Fernando chewed on the implications of a rhinoceros being involved in an early-morning accident. "Did it have insurance?"

"It didn't stop."

"They are very territorial animals. Perhaps you startled it." Fernando held out a bottle of water beaded with perspiration. "You look thirsty."

Gibson drank it gratefully.

"What are you doing up so early?"

"Late, not early," Fernando corrected. "My father is looking for you. You weren't at home or answering your phone. I told him I knew where to find you."

"It was off. What does he want?" Gibson asked, wary of what their Portuguese benefactor might want at this hour. He'd had an audience with Baltasar Alves when he'd first arrived, but this was the first time Alves had ever wanted to see him. Instinctively, Gibson didn't like it. He didn't like being beholden or coming when called like a dog. It felt like the penny was about to drop.

Fernando shrugged. "As if he would tell me."

While Fernando was in England, Baltasar had decided that his only son would play no part in his criminal concerns. Fernando had told Gibson the story once between dirty martinis, his words gin slurred and eyes like unpaved roads.

He could see the devil in me, Fernando had said with a wink.

The arrangement had worked for a time, but eventually Fernando graduated and returned home, a well-educated, aimless delinquent. He'd kicked around the Algarve for months, getting into trouble and making a nuisance of himself. One night, he'd found himself in a nightclub owned by his father.

A real toilet, Fernando had called it.

Over the course of his career, Baltasar had amassed an array of legitimate businesses and real estate through which to launder his money. The crime boss, however, had no interest in overseeing businesses he considered little more than fronts. As a consequence, they'd been poorly run and left to rot. Fernando had called his father from the nightclub and offered to run it for him. Out of desperation, Baltasar had agreed, hoping it would keep his son out of trouble. The next day, Fernando had fired the entire staff. Within six months, the club had turned its first profit. Now, seven years later, Fernando oversaw his father's entire real-estate portfolio. He had knitted it together into a thriving operation, completely segregated from Baltasar's other interests.

"Come, I'll drive you." Fernando stood and buttoned one button of his tuxedo jacket.

"I can call a cab."

"It's better if I take you. My car's just there."

Ordinarily Fernando would have been happy to accept Gibson's out. "Errand boy" didn't suit his disposition. That he hadn't taken it made Gibson nervous all over again, but he played it off. "Well, you're the best-dressed cabbie in the Algarve."

"Am I?" Fernando asked, looking down at himself with interest. "How do cabbies dress?"

CHAPTER THREE

The sun woke Jenn long before she would have liked. They'd forgotten to close the curtains last night as they'd stumbled into bed. The giant remote on Sebastião's side of the bed controlled everything in the room, including the curtains, but it might as well have been in Indiana. She slapped feebly at the bedding in Sebastião's general direction and asked him to shut the curtains. No response. Lifting her head, Jenn confirmed that she was talking to herself. She'd never slept in a bed large enough to lose track of who was in it. It had to be almost twice as large as a king. Custom built like everything else in this house, it had a Marie Antoinette level of decadence. Jenn had lived in apartments smaller than this behemoth.

It was dangerously comfortable, though. She dragged a pillow over her face and tried to fall back to sleep. Nothing doing. Her head ached. Her mouth was brittle and dry. And despite the air-conditioning, it seemed about a hundred degrees in the bedroom. She kicked back the covers and lay there like a sponge left to die on a rock in the hot sun. She ran her tongue over her front teeth and considered the glass of flat champagne on her bedside table. *How bad could it be?* Best not to find out. Besides, she really needed to pee.

Jenn rolled over, and rolled over again, until she found the edge of the bed and swung her legs over the side. Sitting up seemed an important beachhead, and she sat there for a full minute contemplating the bathroom door, angry at the sunlight. Last night she understood, but it ticked her off that Sebastião hadn't shut the curtains when he'd left this morning. Not that it surprised her. That was vintage Sebastião. His needs were a full-time job. Even with two assistants, an agent, a personal trainer, a chef, a maid, a valet, and a platoon of lawyers, he couldn't be expected to think of anyone but himself. At least it made it impossible to misinterpret the nature of their relationship. That was what appealed to her most about him. Well, that and his body.

Standing shakily, Jenn stretched until her back cracked like someone forcing open a stubborn dead bolt. She padded naked into the bathroom, flipped down the toilet seat, and sat, staring sleepily at the ornate Portuguese tile between her feet. She had intended to meet Gibson for a run this morning. Actually, she'd been meaning to do that every morning for the last two weeks, but evenings with Sebastião usually took a blowtorch to her good intentions. Not for Sebastião, of course, who had the metabolism of a gazelle. He could party all night and still be up before sunrise, bright-eyed and raring to go. The drawback of sleeping with younger men. One of them anyway.

She washed her face in one of the bathroom vanity's three sinks. That had always struck her as profoundly arrogant. Sebastião would only wink and say, "Sometimes you need three." Smug son of a bitch, but she had no doubt that sometimes he did. Sebastião Coval lived a three-sink kind of life. She bent and drank right from the faucet, which had all the effect of pouring water into sand. She fumbled open a bottle of painkillers and spilled half of them on the counter. She picked out five—it was going to be a five-pill hangover, she could feel it—and swept the rest into the sink. She winked in the mirror.

"Sometimes you need five," she told her reflection.

Jenn scouted the bedroom for her clothes, then remembered she'd left them out by the pool along with her judgment. Sebastião's bathrobe wasn't hanging from its usual hook, so she borrowed one of his sports coats and went down the wide marble staircase. The staff wouldn't arrive until eight, so at least she'd be spared that awkwardness. In the kitchen, she found a note from Sebastião saying he'd driven up to Lisbon for the day. He hadn't mentioned anything about it last night, but she knew why he'd gone. His team and many of his doctors were there. His right knee had more doctors than a pediatric ward.

Sebastião was superstitious about discussing his rehabilitation with anyone. As if acknowledging it was a sign of weakness. It had been a gruesome injury—"a horror-show tackle," the commentator had called it on YouTube—and she'd only watched it once out of morbid curiosity. Knees were not supposed to bend in that direction. Sebastião's recovery had been slow going, but the doctors estimated he was 90 percent of the way back. He'd been cleared to begin running again. She'd never seen anyone so joyful in her life, or more beautiful. Sebastião was made to run. Scheduled to rejoin the club next month, he was like a child at the prospect. But she also knew that he secretly feared that he would never be the same player again. Sometimes after a few drinks, he would smile ruefully, rub his knee, and say to her affectionately, "*Meu bem*, I am become an old man." He was twenty-nine years old. It was those tiny glimpses of humility that helped her not to throttle him when he was in a more Sebastião frame of mind.

When he did rejoin his team, that would be the end of whatever this was. No doubt Sebastião had a woman tucked away in every corner of Lisbon. Jenn was his flavor of the month. Part of his rehabilitation. That was all right, he was part of hers too. She'd miss him, but it was time. Gibson was right about that much—this wasn't her world. Jenn looked at a framed photograph of Sebastião kissing an enormous silver trophy, surrounded by teammates in the throes of celebration. From what she could tell, he had kissed a lot of trophies in his time. The entire house was a shrine to his storied career. Jenn found it all a little over the top, but she also knew that he needed it. Needed to be surrounded by reminders that he was Sebastião Coval and that he would make it back. She envied him his certainty and wished she had a house full of mementoes to help her remember who she had once been.

On the counter beside the note lay a rose. Before leaving, he'd gone out to the garden and cut her a flower. That was Sebastião to a tee—nailing the romantic gesture, flunking at closing the curtains. At least he'd left her some coffee. She poured herself a cup and topped it off with whiskey. Glad to be alone so she didn't have to sneak it. Besides, it was only a splash to even her out. The painkillers weren't making much of an impression on her headache.

She took her coffee and her rose and went outside, hoping some fresh air would help. Evidence of last night's festivities lay scattered around the pool like a crime scene. How had two people made such a mess? She started to tidy up the empty bottles of champagne, but her head reeled the first time she knelt, killing any impulse toward housekeeping. The chaise lounges beckoned invitingly. She curled up on one, stared out at the dawn, and sipped her coffee.

If the height of the sun was any indication, Gibson would be down at Fisherman's Beach in Albufeira. Hanging from a chin-up bar, if she had to bet. He'd found his discipline right about the time she'd misplaced hers.

That had been part of his rehabilitation. He'd been a wreck when she'd found him in Virginia—talking to ghosts and crying in his sleep. But he was as tough as anyone she'd ever met and had come a hell of a long way in six months. Sometimes when you let the body heal, the mind followed. That approach hadn't worked for her, and she'd taken refuge here instead.

At this point, Gibson and she hadn't run together in so long that he'd stopped asking her. That stung her pride. Not enough to motivate her, but enough that it bothered her that it hadn't. One more way that Gibson Vaughn had been driving her crazy lately.

He had also been arguing for some time that they needed to move on. That they weren't safe here. At the root of it, Gibson didn't trust Baltasar Alves and didn't like being at the mercy of his whims. He was right to a point but, true to form, was taking it too far. Their circumstances might not be ideal, but they were the best that they could manage for now. She agreed that they would need to relocate eventually, but not now. They weren't ready. More to the point, George wasn't up to being moved. She didn't know how many more ways she could say it, but once Gibson made up his mind, it was made. Every time she thought she'd won the argument, a week would pass, and he'd be right back in her ear, chewing it off.

It had been two weeks since their last fight, and they were due to go another round. He had that disappointed look again, and Dan Hendricks had warned her that Gibson had been trying to recruit him to his side. She wasn't looking forward to another argument, but the longer she put it off, the worse it would be. The thought of it made her want another cup of coffee and the whiskey that would sweeten it. But it had to be done, so once she was back in an upright and locked position, she'd see if Gibson wanted to have lunch. Or maybe dinner. She could use a night off from Planet Sebastião.

Behind her, someone cleared his throat to announce his presence and said, *"Senhorita?"*

Jenn jerked upright. A lot more quickly than she would have liked. She hadn't heard anyone coming, and that startled her even more than the voice itself. Two men stood a polite distance from her. The older of the two she recognized. His name was Anibal Ferro. One-third of Baltasar Alves's inner circle. A short, wide-hipped man, perhaps fifty years old. His hair was crankshaft black, but his thick mustache looked like freshly plowed snow. He held a flat-brimmed *cañero* sombrero in his hands like a shield.

The other, barely more than a boy, she didn't know. But the shotgun he held? She knew that well enough, though it puzzled her. In the six months since she'd arrived in Portugal, it was the first time she'd seen any of Alves's people openly armed. The organization had no natural predators in the Algarve, and Alves preferred a low profile. The whole gentleman-gangster routine. A foolish pretense, as far as Jenn was concerned—it wasn't a gentleman's business, and to imagine otherwise was inviting trouble. Still, Baltasar liked the image it presented, so whatever had caused them to strap up, it couldn't be good. Not so bad that the shotgun was pointed her way, but in her experience with armed men, that had a way of changing without much warning at all.

There was also the matter of how they'd gotten in. Sebastião's villa came equipped with walls, a gate, a security system, and its own private rent-a-cops who patrolled his neighborhood. Yet they had apparently waltzed in like they were invited guests. Perhaps they were. Baltasar had known Sebastião since he was a boy, and Jenn still didn't understand the nature of their relationship.

She glanced around, assessing possible escape routes. Something that she had once done as autonomically as drawing breath, wherever she went. If she had to flee, she could go for the pool. They would hesitate to follow her in, and she could cross faster than they could circle. Over the fence and down the hill. The empty champagne bottle would make a serviceable weapon if it came to that. She thought she'd try talking her way out first. George and Gibson would be so proud.

"Something I can do for you fellas?"

The boy said something in Portuguese to himself that Jenn didn't catch, an odd look on his face. Anibal studied the hat in his hands, turning it over and over with great interest. Jenn remembered she was wearing nothing but a sports jacket. It had fallen open when she sat up. She ran her tongue across her front teeth but made no move to cover herself. It was too early and she was too hungover even to feign modesty.

The boy kept on staring.

"Having a good time?" she asked and sipped her coffee to mask her irritation.

Anibal saw the boy ogling her and cuffed the back of his head, knocking off his cap. The boy protested, but when he knelt to retrieve it, Anibal slapped it out of his hand. All while lecturing the boy in Portuguese too fast for Jenn to follow.

"Por favor, aceite minhas desculpas," Anibal apologized for the boy, who stared sullenly out at the ocean.

"Por que você está aqui?" she asked.

"Senhor Alves asks that you come. He wishes to see you."

"Now?"

"Sim," Anibal said with a nod.

She couldn't imagine what Baltasar Alves wanted with her at this hour. Any hour, really. They had been his guests here in the Algarve for six months, and this was so far out of the norm she didn't have a word for it. Something was obviously happening. What she couldn't gauge was whether it was happening *to* her.

"What's this about?"

Anibal glanced up questioningly and looked away in embarrassment. The boy smirked. Neither answered her question. She wasn't even sure that he'd heard her. As if a glimpse of her body had muted her voice. A man could see a thousand naked women and still greet the next with the wonder and fascination of a blind virgin. But you saw one naked man, you'd seen them all.

"I need to take a shower. *Tomar banho de chuveiro,"* she said, translating.

They shook their heads in unison, as if the idea were madness. Anibal said, "I am sorry, *senhorita.* You must come now."

Either they were on a clock or they'd been ordered not to let her out of their sight. She didn't see any option but to go with them and find out. She told the men to turn around. Anibal turned away gratefully. He had a reputation as a hard, serious man, so she found it almost endearing how flustered he'd become. The boy, on the other hand, was slower to react. She cocked her head and made a spinning gesture with her finger. His free show was over. Grudgingly, the boy turned and faced the other way while she found her clothes among the ruins of last night's party.

She might not retain much of her dignity this morning, but she drew the line at yesterday's underwear. She slipped them into the pocket of her jeans. Damn, she really wanted that shower. Her hair felt starchy and tangled, but there was nothing to do about that now. When she finished dressing, the two men led her out to a car and held open the back door for her. Nothing like taking the proverbial walk of shame to see a gangster.

She remembered the hairbrush in her purse, which she spotted poking out from under Sebastião's pants. She'd probably lose half of her hair trying to get the knots out, but at least she wouldn't walk into Baltasar Alves's home looking like her head had been used to clean a nightclub bathroom. She'd have killed for a hair tie. The only saving grace was that Gibson wasn't here to see. She could only imagine how amused he would be by all this.

Thank God for small favors.

CHAPTER FOUR

Baltasar Alves lived beyond Lagos, a town on the Atlantic Ocean forty-five minutes west along Portugal's southern coast from Albufeira. Fernando made the drive in under thirty. Whether Fernando was a bad driver or simply didn't care that someone had taken the time to paint lines on the road, Gibson couldn't say. It made no difference. Fernando handled a car as if he'd learned to drive on a video game with a shoddy physics engine. He took blind turns at reckless speeds, drifting across the divider into the path of oncoming traffic. Fortunately, they hadn't encountered any oncoming traffic.

Miraculously, his driving didn't attract the attention of the GNR—the Guarda Nacional Republicana. Not that it would have mattered. There wasn't a cop in the Algarve foolish enough to ticket the son of Baltasar Alves. Top down, the red Porsche roared unimpeded down the N125, wind coursing in and around the vehicle. Portugal preferred roundabouts to stoplights. Most drivers slowed as they approached; Fernando accelerated gleefully, pulling g's like an astronaut in a centrifuge. Fernando's bowtie snapped at his neck. He took both hands off the wheel, steering with his knees while he removed it. There had been a time when that would have stressed Gibson out. Now it was just one more thing beyond his control. At least the wind was airing him out.

Gibson had wanted to stop by the house for a shower and a change of clothes. The idea of turning up at the home of Baltasar Alves in sweat-soaked workout clothes didn't appeal, but Fernando had vetoed any extra stops. If his father was in that much of a hurry, it must be serious. Gibson wondered if his fears had come true and one of their enemies had found them at last. If so, they would need to move quickly. This could very well be their last morning in Portugal.

"You were spotted in Buenos Aires," Fernando said.

Fernando had discovered the conspiracy website AmericanJudas and felt it his responsibility to keep Gibson up to date on the latest rumors and theories about him. AmericanJudas had been concocting theories about Gibson for some time, but hijacking a plane and making the FBI's Ten Most Wanted list had turbocharged Gibson's infamy. And it wasn't only AmericanJudas any longer: theories about Gibson's presence in Atlanta two years ago had proliferated into the mainstream media. The suspicious nature of Vice President Benjamin Lombard's suicide had garnered national attention, and Gibson's name never trailed far behind. He'd become a boogeyman for a certain kind of politics that saw conspiracy in coincidence. Not that Gibson's presence in Atlanta had been coincidental.

Fernando found the whole thing hilarious, and his favorite quote was from an article that had dubbed Gibson a "digital-age Lee Harvey Oswald." A label that only served to remind Gibson that he would probably never see home again.

"Did I look good at least?" Gibson asked.

"You were begging on a street corner and ran away when confronted."

"Sounds about right," Gibson said.

Baltasar Alves's estate was surrounded by a high stone wall. Trees, planted in a tight row, overhung the wall to provide even more privacy and mask the barbed wire. The Porsche roared to a stop at a gate of dark, polished wood that gleamed in the morning sun. Fernando, unaccustomed to waiting, leaned on his horn and snapped his fingers at the security camera for them to open the gate. Security cameras were ubiquitous in the United States and in much of the European Union, but Portuguese courts had sided with privacy concerns over security, making surveillance cameras a rarity here. Another reason why lying low in Portugal had made sense.

Off to the side, a door opened in the stone wall. Four armed men emerged and surrounded the car. Fernando protested in Portuguese, but the leader explained that he would have to radio up to the house to clear Fernando and his guest through. He said it would only take a moment, then disappeared back through the door. The remaining men kept their weapons trained on Gibson. From the beginning, none of Baltasar's people had cared for the four Americans in their midst, tolerating them on the boss's orders. So Gibson was accustomed to a degree of animosity. This was something else entirely. An edge that hadn't been there before. Had Fernando and his easy smile led him into a trap?

"This will only take a moment," Fernando finished translating for Gibson, his eyes wide in mock seriousness. No one and nothing touched Fernando Alves. He was protected from on high and could afford to be cavalier. Gibson couldn't imagine what it must be like not to have a care in the world. It was probably incredibly liberating, but Gibson didn't think he'd want to live that way. Caring had given him a reason to choose sanity. Caring had kept him alive. Still, it seemed to work for Fernando. After all, he wasn't the one who'd get shot.

The call came back, and when the gate opened, Fernando didn't stick around to say thank you. The Porsche darted off like a greyhound. Situated on fifty acres, the house remained a half mile distant. The Algarve was an arid region, and Gibson could only imagine how much it cost to water the lush, green lawns. The curving driveway was flanked on either side by neat rows of tall cypress like a mandible full of razor-sharp teeth. Through the gaps, Gibson saw men with rifles patrolling the grounds. The compound was on high alert. Up ahead, fronted on three sides by cliffs, the central black turret of Baltasar Alves's home rose above the trees. A modern, medieval watchtower keeping vigil for invaders from land and from sea.

Automobiles choked the driveway for fifty yards, jammed together every which way like vehicular Tetris. Fernando wedged his Porsche into a gap between an old Peugeot and a white panel van. It didn't make the row disappear, though, and Gibson had to climb over the door and shimmy sideways between the two vehicles.

A second car pulled up midshimmy, joining the scrum of vehicles. Two of Baltasar's men got out. The younger of the two cradled a shotgun like he'd just found true love. The older man had no need to compensate. He ran one of the territories in the Algarve and had an easy, jaded confidence that couldn't be faked. He appeared half asleep; a cigarette, more ash than tobacco, dangled from between his lips. But his lazy demeanor masked a taut alertness. Anibal Ferro saw everything from beneath his flat-brimmed sombrero, which he pushed back at the sight of Fernando and called out a greeting.

"*Olá*, Anibal," Fernando answered, then pointed to the house. "Why aren't you in with Peres and Silva?"

Baltasar Alves had three lieutenants: Carlito Peres, Branca Silva, and Anibal Ferro.

Anibal puffed out his cheek in dismay. "I was. It is not good. All I can say is I am content to be driving errands."

"Out of harm's way," Fernando said with a wink.

"I'm not sure such a place exists today," Anibal said.

"Don't worry, I'll look after you," Fernando said with a tone that betrayed how much he enjoyed Anibal's discomfort. On the surface, everyone was friends. All smiles and warm camaraderie, but beneath, Gibson saw the tension between the two men. There was no love lost between Fernando and any of Baltasar's lieutenants. He didn't belong in their world, but because he was Baltasar Alves's son, they had to feign respect. Fernando rarely returned the favor.

Gibson asked what was going on, but Anibal ignored the question. Not a surprise. He had been around Anibal perhaps a dozen times, and they'd never so much as made eye contact. Anibal's young associate stood off to the side and sneered at Gibson. That feeling of being unwelcomed returned.

An unsteady Jenn Charles emerged from the back seat like a movie star cornered by a horde of paparazzi. Much like Fernando, Jenn appeared to be dressed for entirely the wrong time of day: heels, jeans, and a short bolero jacket over a racerback tank top. But while Fernando still somehow looked ready for his close-up, Jenn's eyes had all the luster of Times Square on New Year's morning. She caught sight of Gibson and froze for half a second before looking away. He saw her jaw set.

Good to see you too. He couldn't think of anything he'd done to piss her off. Recently anyway.

Fernando caught sight of Jenn and smiled broadly. Never a good sign. He took an unhealthy pleasure in poking any bear that crossed his path, and Jenn was one of his favorite targets. "*Bom dia*, Jenn. And don't you just look a picture this morning."

Jenn said nothing but found her sunglasses and slipped them judiciously over her eyes. Gibson braced himself; the quieter she became, the larger the eventual blast radius. Fernando didn't appear to notice, or noticed but didn't care.

"We were disappointed that we didn't see you last night. You promised me a command performance. Very naughty." It had been Fernando who introduced Sebastião Coval to Jenn. Sebastião and Fernando were childhood friends, and Baltasar Alves had sponsored Sebastião's development early on, bringing him to the attention of professional team scouts when he was only eight years old.

"We stayed in," Jenn said.

"Sebastião is a wise man to keep you all to himself. How is he? How is his knee?"

At the mention of the knee, Anibal and the younger man gathered around, ears up. Sebastião Coval was a star midfielder for both the Portuguese national team and Benfica, a club based in Lisbon and one of the powerhouses of Portuguese football. Gibson knew this because it was a constant topic of conversation. He also knew that Sebastião had suffered a catastrophic knee injury last season, spawning endless speculation about when he would make his return. Would he still be the same box-to-box intimidator that he had been? He was hailed lovingly by the Portuguese media as Dom Sebastião, named for a sixteenth-century king killed in battle. His knee was often discussed in similar terms, but the media still held out hope of a resurrection.

Sebastião was idolized in the Algarve and kept a home in Vale do Lobo, where he spent the off-season. The house where Jenn spent most of her nights. He had grown up in poverty, escaped it to become a wealthy superstar, but had never forgotten his roots. And they had never forgotten him. His charity work supported programs for children throughout the region. Fernando—who didn't have a philanthropic bone in his body—oversaw the charities on Sebastião's behalf, working his magic on them the same way he had his father's business interests.

"The knee is strong. He feels good," Jenn said with all the conviction of a spokesperson reading from talking points. Sebastião was notoriously tight-lipped about his rehabilitation, so Jenn often found herself in the uncomfortable position of fielding questions about the knee. The men all nodded seriously at this unexpected bit of good news and lapsed into animated Portuguese as they threaded their way through the parked cars toward the house. No doubt debating the implications for the upcoming season. Jenn and Gibson trailed behind.

Gibson realized he'd misread her. She wasn't angry, only embarrassed to be seen like this. She had spent the last two years at war with Cold Harbor—the private military contractor that had held George Abe captive following the death of Benjamin Lombard. Gibson knew she was having a difficult time transitioning back to peacetime. It was a hard thing for a strong person to admit, and she'd done her best to hide it. Gibson would have liked to tell her there was no need. She'd seen him at his absolute worst and hadn't blinked. Far as he was concerned, she could do no wrong. Or at least no wrong that he wouldn't accept. He would have told her all that, and more. He owed her no less. Problem was, telling her would've only made matters worse. So instead, he asked her if she knew what was going on.

She shook her head. "Only that I couldn't take a shower."

They walked on.

"Anyone ever tell you that you talk too much?" he said.

She cracked a smile and bumped his shoulder with hers. "That's me. Won't shut up, can't shut up. How was your run?"

"Got hit by a car."

"I know just how you feel," Jenn said, misunderstanding.

Up ahead, they heard angry voices. Men came out of the house and squared off trading insults. They stood toe to toe, taunting each other—their loyalty divided between Silva and Peres—while the guard at the front door attempted to play peacemaker. None of them seemed inclined to give peace a chance. Anibal spat on the ground and strode forward, stepping between them before the men came to blows. Reluctantly, both sides shrunk back from him, but not fast enough for Anibal's liking. He slapped one and shoved the others roughly away, berating them.

Jenn and Gibson traded a look. Twenty years ago, the Algarve had been divided between four rival syndicates. Baltasar had controlled one, Anibal another, Peres and Silva the remaining two. Then in 2001, Baltasar had bound them all together into a single organization in a bloodless coup that had become legendary. Anibal, Peres, and Silva had become his lieutenants, but they each maintained control over their territories. The peace had held since then, but it didn't bode well for the "Pax Algarve," as it had come to be known, to see infighting among the factions on Baltasar Alves's doorstep.

Anibal sent the men packing with a final stern reprimand. He watched them get into their cars and drive away, clearly troubled. Fernando watched it all with a smirk and looked almost disappointed when a fight didn't break out. When he caught Gibson watching him, he shrugged as if to say, *Can you blame me?*

At the front door, Anibal questioned the guard before turning to Jenn and Gibson. "The other Americans are already inside. They are waiting."

"How many guys did you lose rousting Hendricks out of bed this early?" Gibson asked, a failed attempt to lighten the mood.

Anibal ignored him again.

When Fernando moved to enter the house, Anibal's young associate blocked his way, fingering his shotgun with the eagerness of someone who'd never fired one before. Fernando took a step around him, but the boy stepped with him as though the two men were practicing a dance neither knew well.

A smile crept onto Fernando's face. "Who is your young friend?" he asked Anibal.

"Tomas. My nephew," Anibal said with an apologetic shrug. "He is still learning."

"The golfer? What happened?"

"It didn't work out," Anibal explained diplomatically.

"Couldn't cut it, hmm?" Fernando asked and switched to Portuguese, smile never wavering. The boy's face colored and his hands tightened around the shotgun. Anibal sighed apologetically and switched back to English to shield his nephew from Fernando's insults. At least ones that he would understand.

Anibal put a hand on Fernando's shoulder. "He means no disrespect."

"But it comes so naturally to him. Perhaps he is a prodigy?"

"You know how young men are. He hopes to make a good impression."

"Well, he is lucky to have you for a role model."

Anibal took a deep breath and let the slight go unanswered. "He is only following orders."

"Orders?" Fernando asked without breaking eye contact with Tomas.

"Your father asked that you not come inside today. Only the Americans," Anibal said.

Gibson saw anger flash in Fernando's eyes, disappearing so quickly that he questioned whether he'd seen it at all.

"It's for the best. Trust me," Anibal said.

"I am fortunate to have you looking out for me," Fernando said coolly.

The front door opened, and a woman stepped out onto the threshold. Her name was Luisa Mata; the men called her Senhora Mata; Baltasar Alves called her his niece and right hand. She ran the criminal arm of his empire in the same manner that Fernando ran the legitimate side. Although Baltasar had not officially anointed a successor, it was expected that she would assume control when he died.

Luisa was a tall reed of a woman. She never wore heels but still towered a good five inches over Gibson. As was her way, she didn't speak immediately but stood quietly, taking in everything. She looked each of them over, pausing to consider Jenn Charles with considered disdain. With her long nose and disappointed eyes, Luisa reminded Gibson of a crane in shallow water choosing its next meal from among the hapless fish darting around her ankles.

"Thank you, Anibal," she said.

Anibal took his hand off Fernando's shoulder. Tomas stepped aside.

"Cousin," Fernando said. "Come to my rescue again?"

Gibson didn't know the entire history but could hear the simmering tension in the question. Both their mothers—sisters, twins, and best friends—had died in a car accident returning home after a night out celebrating their birthday. No one knew why neither had been wearing seat belts, and it had been impossible to say which sister had been driving. Only a last-minute emergency had kept Baltasar from being in the car himself. Everyone said that it was a turning point for Alves, who took in Luisa and raised her as his own. Luisa had been eight, Fernando six.

"Thank you for bringing the Americans," she told Fernando, ignoring his question.

"American," Fernando corrected. "Anibal informs me that I'm not welcome inside."

"It is an unusual day. Your father wants to maintain your distance from this morning's events."

Fernando played it off, but Gibson could see his disappointment. "That's very thoughtful of him. A shame, though. I am dressed impeccably. Perhaps I could be of some help."

Luisa didn't answer immediately. Finally, she said, "Actually, there is something. Dani Coelho."

"With the computers?" Fernando asked.

"Yes. With everything happening, we need him somewhere safe. Out of sight. Will you take him to the hotel? Keep him under wraps?"

Even a fool could see Luisa was giving Fernando a graceful out. Taking a menial task and dressing it up to let her cousin save face. Fernando was accustomed to being the one doing the patronizing, so it was impossible to predict how he would react. To Gibson's surprise, he chose to take it seriously.

"Yes, that's a good idea. No one would think to look at the hotel."

"Exactly my thought," Luisa said.

"I'm on the case." Fernando winked at Jenn and clapped Gibson on the shoulder. "You're on your own, my friend. If you live, let's have drinks tonight at the hotel. I have another woman I want to see you embarrass yourself in front of."

"You're a dick," Gibson said.

"And you are like a nature documentary about an endangered species."

And with that, Fernando left them at the door and strolled back toward his car.

Gibson felt immediately exposed, as if nothing terrible could happen so long as Fernando was there.

Luisa cleared her throat to get their attention. "My uncle is waiting."

CHAPTER FIVE

The wide entry hall of Baltasar Alves's home had an exacting, minimalist feel. Tasteful if "nothing" happened to be your taste. The French limestone floors gave way to tall ebony walls and ceiling. A block of text in a large, bold font had been chiseled into one wall. It quoted Portuguese poet Fernando Pessoa: "Any wide piece of ground is the potential site of a palace, but there's no palace till it's built." Seemed fairly self-evident to Gibson, but it made sense for a man who had built himself up from nothing. Though why a Portuguese gangster would want an English translation of Portuguese poetry on his wall, he had no idea at all.

As they entered the house, a familiar figure stepped out from the shadow of the door and fell in behind Luisa. He was powerfully built with a trowel for a nose, thick forearms, and fingers like sewage pipes. His head was shaved, and a prominent vein at his temple pulsed like a river swollen after a storm. Gibson guessed his age to be between forty and fifty, but fifteen years as a super middleweight had dulled the edges of his face, making it hard to judge. All that was important to know was that where Luisa went, he followed. His name was Marco Zava, but the men called him *"Fera"*—the Beast—and most would have begged for a bullet before going five minutes alone with him.

With nowhere to sit, the dozen armed men in the entry hall milled about. One even sat cross-legged, cleaning his pistol on the expensive limestone tile. All seemed dour and restless. Hard men acting hard because they didn't know what else to do. They reminded Gibson of soldiers awaiting an emergency deployment. The higher-ups never told the grunts what was going on until the last possible moment, which kept everyone on edge. Rumors would spread like a virus among the rank and file. Whispers and conjectures about where they were going and what they would do when they got there. And just to get your hopes up, there was always the chance that the whole thing was a preparedness drill and everyone might be turning around and going home instead.

But this wasn't the military, and it was definitely no drill. Jenn and Gibson wouldn't be here if it were. As Luisa Mata passed, the men fell silent. She paused before the man sitting on the floor and looked down at him. Zava stood placidly at her side like a leashed dog. It said something about Luisa that the man on the floor never so much as glanced at the Beast at her side. When Luisa spoke, it was in Portuguese. Gibson didn't understand it, but the tone was of a concerned mother speaking to a child. Calm and even, but its condescension showed on the pale face of the man, who climbed hastily to his feet.

Under her breath, Jenn, who spoke enough Portuguese to follow the conversation, murmured, "Goddamn." Only minutes earlier they'd watched Fernando do much the same thing to Tomas. It was easy to forget that Luisa and Fernando had grown up together. They looked nothing alike, and on the surface, couldn't have been more different. Fernando was all elegant, polished surfaces where Luisa had the awkward depth of a philosopher. But Baltasar had raised them together under one roof, and you occasionally saw that shared bond in their mannerisms, and in their cruelty.

Luisa ushered Jenn and Gibson through the house. It hummed with activity. In each room they passed, men were busy working the phones or typing at computers, voices low and serious and determined.

They turned a corner and found two men practically at each other's throats. They stopped at the sight of Luisa, offered perfunctory apologies, and hurried away in opposite directions.

"Something is not well in the house of Alves," Gibson whispered to Jenn.

"Getting that feeling myself."

"That's the second fight we've seen since we've been here."

"They're scared of something," Jenn said. "Discipline's always the first thing to go."

Luisa stopped, then turned slowly back to face them. Ordinarily, she was nearly as unflappable as her cousin, but Jenn had clearly hit a nerve. "I am so glad Sebastião's whore dragged herself from his bed to evaluate my men."

Gibson, caught between them, thought invisible thoughts and prayed for a foxhole. Luisa, who was also close to Sebastião, had never masked her contempt for Jenn. Although until now, she hadn't said so in quite such explicit terms.

Jenn didn't reply immediately, only nodding to herself as if she'd received confirmation of some inconsequential detail. "Believe me, I'd rather be in bed. It's a really nice one."

"We all feel the same," Luisa said.

"Then what are we doing here?"

Luisa hesitated as if Jenn had scored an unexpected point. "I don't know," she admitted.

"Well, then quit wasting our time," Jenn said. "And take us to someone who does."

The two women lingered a moment, neither willing to be the first to break eye contact. Gibson didn't know what to make of the fact that Luisa didn't know why they were here. She and Baltasar were fused at the shoulder, and one always knew the other's mind. The men joked that if Baltasar had an itch, Luisa scratched. So, what did it mean that Luisa didn't know why Baltasar had summoned them?

Baltasar's living room was as wide as an African savannah. In keeping with the minimalist décor, hardly any furniture broke up the floor plan. It could comfortably have hosted a party for hundreds. There weren't nearly so many now. Only a handful of underlings who lurked in the margins of the room, deferentially out of earshot of Baltasar Alves, who stood holding court with Peres and Silva. The air felt poisonous. At Baltasar's back, a wall of glass offered sweeping views of the Atlantic. While the lieutenants talked, Baltasar glanced out at it wistfully.

Gibson couldn't make out what was being said, but he knew an argument when he saw one. Without a word, Luisa and Anibal peeled off to join Baltasar; Zava remained behind to chaperone the Americans.

Baltasar greeted his niece with a relieved nod and stepped back, leaving her to wrest control of the debate from Silva and Peres. It quickly turned heated, but Baltasar kept his back to the room, gazing out at the ocean again. In his Bermuda shorts, he looked more like a tourist than a gangster. His floral-print shirt was unbuttoned to his navel, accentuating the long vertical scar that cleaved his chest in half.

Five years earlier, he had barely survived his own lifestyle. Food, drink, chain-smoking cigars, and a pathological avoidance of physical exertion had left him obese. The predictably massive heart attack should have killed him, would have killed him, had it not been for the cardiac surgeon dining at a nearby table. Five hours of surgery and a pacemaker later, Baltasar had emerged a changed man.

The story went that he had awoken from surgery to the sight of Fernando, Luisa, and Sebastião—who had flown in from a match in Italy—gathered around his bed. In a trembling voice, Baltasar had sworn off all of his vices. Then, with the help of Sebastião's trainers and chef, he'd crafted an entirely new lifestyle. To everyone's surprise, Baltasar's most of all, he had followed it faithfully ever since. Since the heart attack, he had lost more than 150 pounds. The transformation was nothing short of miraculous. However, it had not left Baltasar glowing with good health. His gaunt, weary face always looked hungry, and his skin didn't fit anymore. It hung off him like an old, stretched-out sweater.

Baltasar's recovery had also marked the beginning of his stepping back from the organization that he'd created. From what Gibson could tell, he was more or less a figurehead at this point. The symbol around which the peace orbited. His was still the final word, but it was Luisa who did the heavy lifting now. Anibal and the other lieutenants reported directly to her, and Baltasar no longer involved himself with day-to-day operations. Another indication that today was out of the ordinary.

The door opened, and George Abe and Dan Hendricks were ushered inside. George wore his trademark jeans, crisp white oxford, and sports coat. Not a wrinkle. Not so much as a hair out of place. Even his jeans looked like they'd been pressed. So close to the old George—the six months had been good to him—but all the dry cleaning in the world couldn't conceal the limp. Any more than the plastic surgeons had been able to erase the damage done by Cold Harbor during George's two-year imprisonment. Gibson had known him since he was a boy, when George Abe and Duke Vaughn had both worked for Senator Benjamin Lombard. George had always had an ageless quality that made you question whether he was forty or sixty, but Cold Harbor had shattered his youthfulness. Gibson doubted whether he would ever be whole again.

The more immediate mystery was how Hendricks, who never rose before noon, was wearing a suit and looked like he'd been up for hours.

"Way to dress for the occasion," Hendricks said.

"How the hell are you so put together?" Gibson demanded.

"Excuse me for taking pride in my appearance."

"I was jogging."

"Hmm?" Hendricks said as though the word were unfamiliar to him.

"Seriously, when did you buy a suit?" Jenn asked.

Hendricks shrugged and spread his hands noncommittally as if Jenn were inquiring about one of the great mysteries of the universe. He didn't look like a twenty-two-year veteran of the LAPD, much less one of the most efficient detectives in the history of the department. He was a short, slight man—perhaps 160 pounds if you fed him a steak dinner first. The last few years had aged him beyond his fifty-one years, as he'd been forced to live a cloistered, paranoid existence, waiting for Calista Dauplaise's killer to return and finish what they'd started in Atlanta. The stress had played havoc on his vitiligo, and what had once been small white patches at the corners of his mouth and eyes had been plowed into wide, pigmentless tracts across his black skin. It gave him a clown-like appearance, but you would be making a grave error to treat him like one. Hendricks didn't suffer fools gladly and gave the impression that he found himself surrounded by fools most everywhere he went.

"That's enough," George said sharply, and the banter ceased.

Once upon a time, Jenn and Hendricks had both worked for George at Abe Consulting Group. The business bearing George's name had long since ceased to exist, but George still commanded their loyalty. Gibson, whose history with George had never been fully resolved, didn't feel the same devotion to the man. But he knew that George was a talismanic figure, especially for Jenn. She needed the idea of his leadership as much if not more than the actual guidance he provided these days. Truth was, Jenn had been calling the shots for a long time now, whether anyone cared to admit it or not. Or maybe it was George who needed to feel valuable, and deferring to him was an act of kindness by Hendricks and Jenn. Either way, Gibson was content to play along.

"What do we know?" George asked.

The four compared notes, but none knew anything the others didn't. George asked for hypotheses, and they speculated that the FBI could have found them. But that didn't explain the obviously heightened security or the presence of all three lieutenants.

"How often are they all in the same room together?" Jenn asked.

"Rarely," George answered.

"I don't think this has anything to do with us," Gibson said.

"And yet here we are," Hendricks said.

"Here we are," Jenn agreed.

Luisa quashed whatever objections the three lieutenants harbored. Neither looked pleased, and Gibson had the impression they were choosing their words with the utmost care, while Anibal remained silent.

Satisfied, Luisa went and whispered in Baltasar's ear. He looked in their direction and nodded. With a single crooked finger, she beckoned them to join him.

Hendricks muttered, "This is how cattle get led to the slaughter."

For once, he and Gibson were ordering from the same side of the menu.

CHAPTER SIX

Baltasar greeted George, ignored the others. The two men shook hands and shared a meaningful embrace. "Thank you for coming, my friend," Baltasar said, voice full of gratitude, as if he'd given them any choice in the matter.

"Of course," George replied with a relaxed smile, all traces of concern tucked safely away.

Baltasar took the seat at the head of an enormous conference table, Luisa to his left. When Baltasar had unified the Algarve under his control, Anibal had been the first to join him. That broke the standoff between Baltasar and the syndicates—Peres followed suit a few days later, leaving Silva, the lone holdout, no option but to bend the knee. Consequently, Anibal took the seat to Baltasar's right, second only to Luisa. Silva and Peres took the next two seats. Then George, Jenn, Hendricks, and Gibson at the far end.

From a distance, Baltasar Alves had looked much as Gibson had remembered. Sitting across a table from him, however, Gibson saw how much he had wasted away in only six months. He reminded Gibson of a drawing on an old chalkboard that had been half-heartedly erased. The lines of his face looked blurred and indistinct. His eyes were set back in hollow craters like pinpoints of black water at the bottom of a quarry.

"How are you and your people?" Baltasar asked. "You have everything you need?" It was less a question than a reminder of all that Baltasar had done for them.

George said, "You know how grateful we are for the hospitality you've shown us."

"It was the least I could do. You've always been a true friend."

That was the second time Baltasar had called him "friend." Gibson watched the dance between the two men with fascination. Not one honest word had been spoken, but the nature of their lies told the story to anyone who knew how to read it. Baltasar was softening George up for something.

Baltasar said, "We have a bit of a situation this morning. As I'm sure you've noticed."

"Security does seem a little stepped up," George said.

"Simply a precaution. You are in no immediate danger, I assure you."

Somehow, Gibson didn't feel reassured.

"Why are we here, my friend?" George asked.

Gibson saw Luisa shift subtly forward in her seat. She'd been telling the truth—she was as much in the dark as they were. The three lieutenants too. What did that mean? Gibson wondered. Why was Baltasar playing this so close to the vest, even keeping it from his own people?

"Early this morning, one of our shipments was hijacked," Baltasar said, underlining the word "shipment" with his tone. "Ransom demands have been issued."

Gibson didn't like the sound of "shipment." Until this moment, he'd had the impression that Baltasar's operation was fairly minor league. Or perhaps it would be more honest to say that he'd allowed himself to hold that impression so he wouldn't have to think too hard about the nature of the man granting them safe harbor. He willed George to ask what kind of shipment, but Baltasar was being intentionally vague, and either George was too diplomatic to press or already knew the answer.

"These hijackers were very good. Well planned." Baltasar looked at Luisa and his lieutenants before continuing. "Too well planned, I think. I need fresh eyes on this. You and your people, I need you to be my eyes, old friend," Baltasar said, leaning hard on his last word for a third and final time.

A wind-tunnel silence enveloped the room. Gibson felt Luisa staring at them, felt a swirl of anger beneath the surface of her gaze. But she hid it carefully, like a suspect disposing of the murder weapon.

"*Tio,*" Luisa said. "Perhaps if we could speak in private?"

Baltasar looked sternly at his niece. "There is no need."

She tried to switch into Portuguese, but Baltasar kept the conversation in English. Gibson found that interesting too. Baltasar wanted the Americans to understand.

Frustrated, she said, "What can they tell us that we don't already know? We know who is responsible."

"The Romanians? You don't know that for certain."

"Who else could it be? What other enemies do we have?"

"A question I have been asking myself all morning."

"*Tio . . .*"

"So what would you recommend?" Baltasar asked his niece, although Gibson got the impression he already knew exactly what she would say.

"Drive them out of the Algarve. Back to Romania where they belong. As we should have done two years ago, before they took root."

Gibson saw from the lieutenants' body language that although they agreed with Luisa in principle, they didn't like hearing it put in such stark terms. Anibal looked as if someone had switched on the stove with him in the pot.

Baltasar's face darkened. His niece had crossed an invisible line that Gibson couldn't see. Some old disagreement over these Romanians, whoever they were.

"So, war?"

"It was a mistake to let them stay."

"Careful," Baltasar said.

"*Tío*—"

Baltasar cut her off. "Do you all feel this way?" He directed the question at his lieutenants but didn't wait for their answer. "Do you have any proof it was the Romanians? Anything concrete?"

Luisa shook her head.

"I'm not prepared to go to war on your hunch. War is our last resort, never our first."

"It's the only language these people understand. And there isn't much time."

"I know exactly how much time we have and what is at stake. This is my decision. I have known George Abe a long time. He and his people can help us do better than a hunch."

"How? They can't even help themselves," Luisa said.

"Mind yourself. Do you know what these people have done?"

"I don't care what they've done, only what they are now." Luisa turned to the four of them and cast a disappointed glance their way. "Do you remember when Fernando was little? How he flung his most expensive toys from the roof of the house? They shattered on the rocks below, but you wouldn't get him new ones and forced him to play with his broken toys until he learned his lesson."

"I remember."

"These people remind me of those toys. Perhaps they were something once, but they've been thrown on the rocks. Look at them. A cripple. A crazy man. This one sleeps all day. And a drunk."

After the confrontation in the hall, Gibson expected Jenn to explode. Instead, she went stock-still. The effort at self-restraint turned her alabaster, but she held it in. Gibson could tell George was offended, by the way he interlaced his fingers and rubbed the palm of one hand with his thumb, but it would take a microscope for anyone to see it in his face. A visibly furious Hendricks stood to leave, but Jenn put a hand on his arm. Reluctantly, he sat.

For his part, Gibson found he couldn't muster all that much indignation. He'd been making much the same case to Jenn for the last couple of months and couldn't find fault in Luisa's assessment, cruel though it might be. As individuals and as a unit, they were far from their best. You needed no further proof than the fact that only Hendricks rose to defend himself, and even then, only weakly. The old Hendricks would never have let himself be hushed by Jenn that way. They were all meek, pale shadows of themselves. Baltasar had to be truly desperate to turn to them for help.

Baltasar shouted for his niece to show some respect, and the table devolved into a yelling match, with the three lieutenants joining the chorus of angry voices. The scar on Baltasar's chest throbbed angrily as he chewed his niece out. Only Luisa reined in her temper, waiting until the others had had their say before speaking. When she did, her voice was low and full of feeling and commanded the room.

"*Tio*, our organization has thrived for decades. The organization that you built. It was your vision—your genius—that made us what we are and brought the peace that we have all prospered from."

The three lieutenants nodded in agreement.

"It hasn't always been easy, but we have met every challenge. Today will be one of those days. I know that, but it is an insult to our people to bring these Americans into this. They can do nothing to help us. This matter must be handled internally. I am more than capable of taking care of this."

When she finished, Baltasar gathered his thoughts for a moment and then delivered the dagger. "If you were more than capable, niece, there would be nothing to take care of."

That stopped Luisa cold. For a moment Gibson could see the little girl who had grown up idolizing her uncle. He doubted whether many men could hurt Luisa Mata with mere words, but Baltasar Alves was one of them.

That's when it dawned on Gibson why Baltasar had summoned them without giving his people an explanation: he suspected the hijacking might be an inside job. That's what he'd meant by it being too well planned. He'd orchestrated this meeting to provoke his own people. Asking for George's help was a curveball that they could not have predicted. He'd brought them all together so that he could gauge their reactions, perhaps sniff out a traitor. It was a shrewd, calculated move. Baltasar might be a figurehead, but he was still a dangerous player. And now he'd flung Gibson and the others into this mess like chum in the water, waiting to see what predators might rise to the surface.

CHAPTER SEVEN

Before the debate could flare back to life, Baltasar dismissed Luisa, his lieutenants, and all their lackeys from the room. When they moved too slowly for his liking, Baltasar roared at them to get out. When they were finally alone, the old man's entire demeanor shifted. Anger and disappointment disappeared as abruptly as a summer storm. Or more accurately, as Jenn saw now, it had never been there at all. He looked pleased with himself.

"Not bad," Baltasar said. "I should have been in movies."

"They looked convinced to me," George said.

Baltasar buttoned his shirt thoughtfully and took a sip of water. "So, what do you think?"

"Anibal is with you."

"The hijacking occurred in his territory," Baltasar said.

"Even more indication that he had nothing to do with it. If he was going to betray you, he wouldn't draw attention to himself that way."

"Yes, I see what you mean," Baltasar said. "What about Silva and Peres?"

"Not guilty," George said.

"What then?"

"Doubt."

"In me?"

George nodded. "You know as well as I do what signal this morning sends."

"That I am old. Vulnerable. That I was naïve for not moving against the Romanians when they first arrived."

"That will be the takeaway," George said. "I don't think Silva or Peres betrayed you, but that doesn't mean they aren't evaluating their options."

Baltasar frowned. "So, I'm auditioning for my own people's loyalty?"

"You didn't buy their loyalty; you only rented it. They'll be watching to see if you can still afford it."

"And Luisa? I've lost my objectivity where she's concerned."

"As if you ever had any," George said.

Baltasar acknowledged the truth of what he said. "What did you see?"

"Not a chance."

"Good. Thank you," Baltasar said, although he still sounded troubled, almost as if he were disappointed that Luisa hadn't betrayed him. Jenn wondered why. Luisa ran the Algarve for her uncle. If she hadn't betrayed him, then it meant the shipment had been hijacked on her watch. As with Anibal, Baltasar was torn between his niece being treacherous or incompetent. Either option had consequences that left him looking weak.

Baltasar rubbed his temples. "Do you think I should take Luisa's advice? Hit the Romanians?"

"I didn't say that, but your people are looking for reassurance. If you don't give it to them, they'll seek it elsewhere."

"You really know how to cheer me up."

"What happened two years ago?" George asked.

"Crackdowns," Baltasar said. "For the last fifteen years, government crackdowns have driven Eastern European gangs west. They've settled in France, Greece, Germany, Spain—where the police are more restrained in their tactics. These gangs are uncivilized and amoral. An invasive species. Two years ago, a group of Romanians arrived in the Algarve. They settled in Quarteira and then came to me, asking to become partners in some new business. I declined, but they were respectful and offered to pay for protection. The city of Quarteira is of minor importance, so I allowed them to remain."

"Luisa disagreed?" George said.

"Perhaps she was right," Baltasar said. "Perhaps I have become so accustomed to peace that I've become afraid to risk it. If the Romanians are behind the hijacking, then I've doomed us. You know what will happen if I don't get the shipment back."

George nodded. "The ransom? How long do you have?"

"Midday tomorrow."

As the conversation unfolded, it dawned on Jenn that George had conspired with Baltasar. That she and the others had been paraded in front of the room so that the two friends could evaluate the reactions of Luisa and the lieutenants. It wasn't the move itself that bothered her. It was a smart play—the threat of involving four American outsiders would be unexpected, and the unexpected often caused people to make mistakes. No, what bothered her was that George hadn't confided in her. She'd been in his shoes enough to know that the reason you left people in the dark was that you didn't trust them to play their parts.

That stung. She would take it up with George later, but Gibson might not wait that long. He'd recognized the same thing and looked furious. That didn't bode well. Even Gibson would admit that he had a righteous streak that he couldn't always keep in check. She caught his eyes and pleaded silently with him to stay calm. He mouthed, "Did you know?" She shook her head. His eyes narrowed, and she shook her head again. This time he accepted it and turned his glare back on George.

"What would you advise?" Baltasar asked.

"Pay. If you believe they'll hold up their end."

"Won't that only succeed in making me seem even weaker to my people?"

"It isn't ideal, but anything would be preferable to placing a call to Mexico."

Baltasar nodded grimly. "Agreed, but it's not possible. Having put a gun to my head, the hijackers have demanded a sum that I cannot raise. And they have been unreceptive to negotiation."

"I see," George said. "Then your only hope is to find the hijackers. Why does Luisa believe it was the Romanians?"

"If the shipment's lost, my Mexican partners will be in the market for a more reliable partner. The Romanians would be happy to offer their services in my place, and the authorities will go with whoever can keep the peace."

"That would be a bold gambit," George said.

"Agreed, but it's either the Romanians or else I have a traitor inside my organization."

"But you have no proof the Romanians are involved."

"No, but they are the only ones with a motive."

Baltasar drifted off into thought. George took that as his cue to leave. "I hope we were of some help." George put out his hand. Baltasar did not take it.

"I'm afraid I need your help a little longer."

George's smile remained, but its warmth vanished. "I don't know what else we can do."

"Just what I told Luisa. I need you and your people to be my eyes. Get my shipment back."

George faltered, his hand falling back to his side. "Although I might not have phrased it as colorfully as Luisa, I have to agree with her. What can we possibly offer that she can't? Especially if you only have thirty-six hours."

Baltasar checked his watch. "Twenty-eight, now."

"We don't know the lay of the land, the people, nothing. We'd be starting from scratch."

"Then just go through the motions. Perhaps your involvement will force the hijackers into a mistake."

"I agreed to play along this morning, but this is not part of our arrangement."

"No, this is true, it is not," Baltasar said. "Just as it wasn't part of any arrangement that I allow you to hide here under my protection. Because there was no arrangement until we made one. Until you came to me in your hour of need. Then I took you in, you and your colleagues. And that became our arrangement."

"I know, and we're grateful. But—"

"Understand me, George. If I do not recover the shipment, then you and your people will need to find a new tree to hide beneath. Because the Mexicans will prune me, chop me down, and make a bonfire of my remains. You know what these people are capable of doing."

No one spoke. Jenn didn't like the direction this was heading but held her tongue. Baltasar was manipulating them, and George was wise enough to play out the string without angering their host. At least not while still a guest in his house. Baltasar, recognizing he'd put his friend in a difficult position, switched modes and became reasonable and accommodating.

"Let Luisa take you to Olhão and show you the shipment. See what you see. After that, we can discuss further."

"Show us? I thought you said the shipment was stolen."

"No, I said it has been hijacked."

"What's the difference?"

"Go and see."

Reluctantly, George began to acquiesce, but before he could speak, Gibson interrupted.

"A shipment of what, exactly?"

Every set of eyes in the room turned to Gibson, surprised, as if he'd teleported there in a puff of smoke. Baltasar gazed at him levelly, for the first time acknowledging anyone but George.

"Gibson, please," Jenn said.

"It's fine. The boy has questions," Baltasar said without taking his eyes from Gibson. "I am in business with a Mexican concern to assist in the importation of their product."

Gibson blinked in disbelief. "Jesus fucking Christ. Are you trying to tell us you're a drug dealer for a Mexican cartel?"

"It's complicated," Baltasar said.

CHAPTER EIGHT

As they left Lagos and drove east across the Algarve, the land turned increasingly arid. The sun, still climbing in the morning sky, beat down on their convoy of vehicles. Even through the heavily tinted windows of the SUV, Jenn could feel its power. Pockets of green scrub brush dotted the landscape, but the dominant hue was a dehydrated brown the color of stale bread. A solitary horse standing near a tree watched the convoy pass. It made Jenn sad. Why didn't the horse stand in the shade?

George hadn't spoken more than two words since leaving Baltasar Alves's home. In the old days, he had preferred to meditate before offering his thoughts. When he finally broke his silence, he'd usually have a solution to whatever problem they faced. Jenn had always found that comforting. It pained her to admit that she didn't hold out any such hope now.

Dan caught her eye and inclined his head toward Gibson, who had said even less than George. Unlike George, Gibson didn't practice silence. Ever. Usually when Gibson had something on his mind, Jenn couldn't shut him up. She leaned forward and put a hand on his shoulder.

"You all right?"

"No," he replied, staring straight ahead.

"Let's have it, then."

Gibson turned in his seat to look Jenn in the eye, searching for something there. Mind made up, he leaned forward and asked Baltasar's men how much farther.

They looked at each other, and then back at Gibson. *"O quê?"* the driver asked.

Smiling, Gibson described their mothers in crude, degrading terms that reminded Jenn that he'd been raised by the Marine Corps. The driver shook his head apologetically. Satisfied that they couldn't understand English, Gibson turned back to Jenn.

"What's bothering you?" she asked.

"Besides consulting for the local crime lord on his hijacked shipment of Mexican narcotics? Because other than that, I'm pretty fucking swell."

"We're just going to take a look," Jenn said.

"So 'just the tip'?"

Jenn ignored the crude comparison.

"And then?" Gibson asked.

"Then we're done."

"And you actually believe that?"

Jenn didn't have an answer—not one that she believed. "It's complicated."

"You're just going to roll over, aren't you?"

"What other option do we have?"

"We get gone. Before we get mixed up in whatever this is."

"And go where?"

"It doesn't matter where. Not here."

"You're not thinking this through. It takes money to stay hidden. We're low on funds. Where can we go that we'll be safe?"

"What about this situation strikes you as safe?" Gibson asked.

"It's not ideal. I know that. But playing ball is our best move. At least for now."

"So . . . what? We're just going to live in Portugal now and work for a drug dealer? Is that what we are now? Mercenaries?"

It was the strangest argument Jenn had ever had. They were both smiling and talking in friendly tones for the benefit of Baltasar's men. It made the whole thing feel surreal.

"Gibson," George said. "These are special circumstances."

"They're going to get a hell of a lot more special if we do this," Gibson said. "You know it won't ever end, right? We do this, and Baltasar Alves decides we're useful, then he'll own us. He'll never let us go."

"He's a friend," George said.

"He's friendly. It's not the same thing. You really trust him?" Gibson paused, but George wouldn't go that far. "We shouldn't have stayed here this long. We should have moved on."

"I'm not in the mood for I-told-you-sos," Jenn said.

"Hey, I stayed too. So, I got none for you. None of us wanted to think about this moment, but now it's here. And I'm wondering what we're going to do. And why we're going to do it. I've done some messed-up things in my life. I'm not proud of all of it, but I've always tried to have a good reason."

"We're just investigating the hijacking. Nothing more. Everything's not as black and white as you always paint it," Jenn said.

"Helping a drug trafficker is as black and white as it gets. Hendricks, back me up."

In a previous life, Dan Hendricks had been a detective in Los Angeles for twenty-two years. He'd started in narcotics and finished in homicide. Didn't talk about it much, but he would have been a star if he hadn't proven so difficult to work with.

"Hey, don't look at me," Hendricks said. "If it was up to me, I'd decriminalize the works."

"What does that mean? We should do this? Go to work for a criminal?"

"Wouldn't be the first time," Hendricks said, meaning Calista Dauplaise.

Jenn winced—Hendricks should know better than to go there. Calista had been George's silent partner at Abe Consulting Group, and most of what had befallen them in the last few years could be traced back to her door. Not long after they'd arrived in Portugal, Jenn and George had sat up late into the night, talking. He'd wept over his guilt for involving them with Calista Dauplaise.

"Yeah," said Gibson, "but we didn't know that at the time. And I like to think that maybe we learned our lesson." He paused and looked squarely at George. "What do you think? Did you learn your lesson?"

"Easy now," Hendricks said softly.

"What's wrong with you?" Jenn said.

Gibson said, "Don't tell me that you aren't pissed about that dog and pony show back there at the house. Or did you enjoy getting played like a pawn in George and Baltasar's little chess match?"

"There wasn't time," Jenn said without conviction. It had bothered her, but her protectiveness of George made it hard to admit.

"That's bullshit, Jenn."

They glared at each other over the seat back.

"I want to apologize to all three of you," George said. "I should have made time to brief you. It was an error in judgment."

Gibson didn't look mollified. "Well, we have time to kill now. What else don't we know? Help me understand why this is a good idea. So I know what we're going to be about. Maybe start by telling us how you know Baltasar Alves. Really."

"It's complicated."

"Yeah, so I've been hearing. But we're pretty smart people, George. I think we can handle complicated."

Resigned, George nodded. "I met Baltasar in 2001. I counseled him through his consolidation of the Algarve."

"You worked for this drug dealer?" Gibson said.

"As I said, it's complicated. But, yes, in essence. Did you know that, prior to 2001, Portugal had one of the worst drug problems in Europe?

More than one percent of the population was addicted to heroin. HIV-related deaths were at epidemic proportions."

"What happened in 2001?" Jenn asked.

"The Portuguese government took Dan's suggestion and decriminalized possession of all drugs intended for personal use. You can look up the statistics for yourself, but by every measure, it's been a spectacular success."

"And what? You helped Baltasar take advantage of the new laws to cash in?"

"Quite the contrary," George said. "We went to the Mexicans and offered them a deal. For a fee, Baltasar would serve as middleman. Four times a year, he would oversee and facilitate the importation of Mexican product, repackage shipments, and send the narcotics on their way to markets throughout Europe, far from the Algarve."

"Why did Silva, Peres, and Ferro agree to that? That must have slashed their profits in half," Jenn said.

"It did. However, after Baltasar struck his deal with the cartel, we went to the GNR. Once the authorities understood that Baltasar meant to keep drugs out of the hands of Portuguese children, they agreed to turn a blind eye to his other less destructive criminal activities."

Hendricks said, "Lower profits but less risk."

"Precisely. It took time to convince the syndicates that it was in their long-term interests, but eventually they all came on board."

"So you're telling me there are no drugs in the Algarve?" Gibson said.

"No, of course not. But it's tightly controlled and mostly recreational drugs aimed at tourists. Nothing schedule-one. I don't claim that it's a perfect solution, but Baltasar Alves brought stability and calm to a region wracked by drug use and violence. The region has enjoyed peace for over fifteen years."

"And then this morning happened," Hendricks said.

"Precisely. How do you think the Mexicans will react to the loss of one of their shipments?" George asked. "Even if Baltasar does get this shipment back, he will be under the gun to repackage it and get it on the road to its destination on schedule. What do you think will happen to the peace then?"

Baltasar's men interrupted to announce their arrival. It halted their discussion, but the issue was far from settled. Jenn knew that stubborn look on Gibson's face. Her real problem was that, in principle, she didn't disagree with him. They really shouldn't be doing this. However, when principle collided with the real world, taking a stand could get you killed. Gibson had always had a hard time accepting that.

They drove into the town of Olhão along the Avenue 5 de Outubro, which commemorated the establishment of Portugal's first republic on October 5, 1910. It ran parallel to a long, natural harbor formed by a series of barrier islands that shielded Olhão from the Atlantic. Sailboats and other pleasure craft bobbed sleepily at the docks, but this was a less touristy part of the Algarve.

Passing the old fish market on their right, they followed the natural bend of the road and came to a second, human-made harbor. Here the boats were all commercial vessels, mostly small fishing boats and a few larger coastal-control ships. The surrounding buildings were more industrial— warehouses and a shipyard with all manner of boats in dry dock.

At the far side of the harbor, a pair of low buildings rose up behind a chain-link fence. Large chemical tanks joined by convoluted piping flanked the main building. The smaller structure looked like a vehicle depot. There wasn't a soul in sight. Small eddies of dust danced across the empty parking lot. A dirty sign read: "Fresco Mar Internacional"—it was a sardine cannery. Jenn didn't know what to make of that. As the convoy pulled to a stop at the red-and-white traffic barrier, she picked up movement all across the compound as men stepped out of the shadows. All were armed.

"Must be some expensive goddamn fish," Hendricks observed.

Up ahead in the lead car, Anibal Ferro rolled down his window and barked at his men to raise the gate. Since Olhão was part of his territory, he'd been dispatched by Baltasar to assist the Americans.

The convoy circled around to the far side of the property and parked at the loading docks. Three men stood guard at a metal roll-up door. Anibal followed Luisa up the ramp; Marco Zava had been sent on a separate mission. As they disappeared inside the building, Tomas and the other men stood beside the SUV to make sure their American guests didn't wander off. The driver killed the engine, and they sat there for fifteen minutes in the baking sun.

"This is how dogs get brain damage," Hendricks said, loosening his tie.

"Suit doesn't seem like such a bright idea now, does it?" Jenn said.

"At least I'm already dressed for my funeral."

Anibal returned to collect their unwanted charges. Hendricks mopped his brow. Jenn took off her jacket. Gibson was a puddle, but he was still in his running clothes and didn't care. Only George seemed unaffected by the heat. Not for the first time, Jenn wondered if her old boss even had sweat glands.

Luisa, from the top of the loading dock, looked down at them pityingly. "As my uncle requested, we're going to show you inside the cannery. Please touch nothing."

The "please" surprised Jenn. Luisa had been different since Baltasar chastised her. Muted. Still digesting that she, too, was under suspicion. It had clearly rattled her. Jenn didn't much care for Luisa but couldn't find it in herself to take any pleasure in it. She couldn't imagine how she'd react if George questioned her loyalty. The danger of looking up to someone was that their words could come whistling down.

"And whatever you do, stay outside the circle."

"What circle?" Hendricks asked.

"The yellow one," Luisa said curtly. "If by some miracle something significant should occur to one of you, tell me and no one else. If you need anything, tell me and no one else."

Hendricks raised his hand.

"Yes?"

"Who do I tell if I gotta take a leak?" Hendricks asked, lighting a cigarette. "Would that be you too?"

Luisa nodded, a tight grimace on her lips. "Anibal's men are on edge and are not as forgiving as I am. Come, we have much to do." Luisa strode up the ramp, followed by Anibal and Tomas.

Jenn came up alongside Hendricks. "Remind me why it is you never made sergeant?"

Everyone gathered at the top of the loading dock while the roll-up door rumbled open. Without waiting, Luisa ducked under and in. A welcome blast of cold air greeted them along with the overpowering smell of salted fish. Behind them, the door hiccupped and began to close again.

Jenn fell in beside George to keep one eye on him in case he needed her help. He did his best to mask his limp, but she saw the strain on his face. The doctors had done a good job of breaking and resetting his bones, and George had worked diligently at his physical therapy, but this was still a long way for him to walk. And he was too proud to use his cane. Jenn offered him her arm, but he declined with an appreciative squeeze of her elbow.

Luisa led them down a wide hall that opened into an enormous refrigerated warehouse. Thick concrete pillars spanned its length, and lazy, unfocused fluorescent lights hung in wide rows. Around one of the center columns stood a mountain of coffin-size blocks wrapped in plastic. Other than that and a hastily assembled security station, the warehouse was empty.

"What's that?" Jenn asked, meaning the mountain.

"That," Luisa said, "is the shipment."

"The hijacked shipment?" George asked. "I don't understand."

"Hate to brag," said Hendricks, "but I think we solved the case. Who's buying the first round?"

"If only it were that simple," Luisa said.

CHAPTER NINE

The hijackers had painted a thick line of canary-yellow paint around the shipment. The painters had done a sloppy job. Fat droplets of yellow lay splattered everywhere. A roller on a pole, a paint tray, and several empty paint cans lay discarded at the circle's beginning and end. A yellow brick road leading nowhere.

Staying outside it meant that no one could get within fifty feet of the shipment. Heroin, unless Jenn missed her guess. Maybe cocaine. The Mexican cartels had a hand in both.

Gibson peeled off from the group and walked to the edge of the circle for a closer look. Since the argument in the SUV, he had lingered on the periphery, which Jenn found encouraging. She went over and stood beside him.

"What do you see?" Jenn asked.

"Paint."

"Don't be difficult."

"Yellow paint," Gibson said and walked away.

This was why she didn't believe in olive branches. People had a habit of sharpening them to points and using them as weapons.

"Gibson."

He stopped and turned back slowly, arms folded across his chest. When she was a child, Jenn had always wanted a sibling. A little brother or sister. Someone to share the loneliness of growing up with a grandmother who had treated her more like a burden than a family member. Gibson made her grateful to be an only child. Caring about people was exhausting.

"Are you with us?" she asked.

"I'm here, aren't I?"

"But do I have to worry about you?"

He considered the question. "I'll make you a deal. I'll play ball if you promise that when this is over we decide what our next move should be. Start making plans. Can you do that?"

"I can do that."

"I mean it, Jenn. No more putting it off."

"I said yes, goddamn it."

"All right, then," Gibson said and walked back to the group.

Jenn took a deep breath and counted to ten. It didn't help. Why, if they'd reached an agreement, did it still feel like they were arguing?

Luisa and Anibal led them on a slow circuit around the perimeter of the circle. They walked side by side, but distinctly apart. A suspicious cancer was growing between the two old allies. Jenn had watched it metastasize since leaving Baltasar's estate. Both recognized that the existing status quo had changed, but neither yet saw how they fit into it. For now, Luisa gave the orders and Anibal followed them, but there was a touch less certainty in Luisa's voice. And Anibal seemed a step slower in responding.

Luisa walked backward, as if giving a guided tour of a historic monument. "There. And there. And there. Do you see?" Luisa pointed out black bundles that dotted the shipment at regular intervals. They paused so George could study them through the binoculars they'd borrowed from the security station. Jenn glanced back at Gibson, who trailed behind the group like a recalcitrant child in a museum.

"You're sure those are explosives?" George asked, handing the binoculars to Jenn. "It could be a bluff."

"They look real enough from here," Jenn said.

"No, we're not sure," Luisa said. "But this is as close as we can come without tripping the motion detectors."

"And the motion detectors are real?" Hendricks asked.

"Yes, of that I'm certain," Luisa said and stepped across the yellow line.

From the center of the shipment a Klaxon blared. Luisa took a second step, and the horn sounded twice more. She took a third and final step toward the shipment, and a mechanical voice began a countdown.

"*Cinco . . . Quatro . . . Três . . .*"

Luisa retreated back behind the line. The countdown stopped, and the Klaxon shrieked one last time, sounding almost disappointed. The warehouse fell silent once more.

"Well, that was dramatic," George said.

"As you can see, we've no option but to take the hijackers at their word," Luisa said. "For now."

"What about IMS? Ion-mobility spectrometry," Hendricks elaborated. "Do any explosive detectors work at this kind of range?"

"We're making inquiries with our sources in the GNR, but it will probably take time we do not have."

"And I assume there's no coming up from beneath or dropping in from the roof?" Jenn said.

"The foundation is solid concrete, and the motion detectors cover the airspace above the shipment."

"It's kind of ingenious when you think about it—stealing something without actually stealing it," Hendricks said admiringly. "Cuts out transportation, storage, security. Then they just sit back and wait to get paid or else blow it into orbit."

Jenn saw Gibson's head jerk up as if Hendricks had given him an idea. He took the binoculars and stood at the yellow line, studying the shipment. This time she decided against joining him. Better to let him work.

"So, as you can see, we're in a difficult position. I am open to suggestions," Luisa said, the admission clearly painful for her.

"Why is Baltasar so sure it's an inside job?" Gibson asked, cutting to the chase. The question had been on all their minds since leaving the house, but Jenn hadn't planned on asking so bluntly.

Luisa's eyebrows raised. "Did he tell you that?" she asked. "What did he say?"

The reason Jenn hadn't asked Luisa directly was because it raised this exact question. Baltasar wouldn't appreciate them exposing his deception to Luisa.

"He didn't say anything to us," Gibson said. "He didn't have to."

"Then what makes you think that?" Luisa demanded.

"Because we wouldn't be here if he didn't," Jenn said, covering for Gibson.

Gibson nodded, picking up on Jenn's misdirection. It felt good to be on the same page, if only momentarily.

"Only reason to bring us in is if Baltasar doesn't trust his own people," Gibson said.

"So, why doesn't he?" Jenn asked.

Reluctantly, Luisa laid out the situation. "Because the hijackers had information that they should not have had. We receive four shipments a year from Mexico and never use the same location twice. The exact date of each shipment is a closely guarded secret. Our own people aren't told until the last possible moment. And my uncle owns a dozen warehouses and facilities."

"And yet these guys knew when and where," Jenn said.

"Yes," Luisa said. "More than that, they knew our security and how to breach it. If it wasn't an inside job, then the hijackers have turned at least one of our people."

Anibal looked pained but said nothing.

"And you have until noon tomorrow to pay?" Jenn asked.

Luisa said, "Yes, but we cannot afford to wait that long."

"Why is that?" George asked.

"Because if I do not have this shipment in transit within seventy-two hours, the cartel will want to know why, and they're not the kind of people who forgive. If we can't guarantee the safety of their shipments . . ." Luisa paused, calculating the implications as if it was too terrible to consider. "They will move in. We will resist them, but they are bigger, stronger, richer. They will wipe us out.

"Perhaps you think to yourself—so what? What difference does it make if one group wipes out the other? We are all just criminals. Perhaps we are. But it's not only we who will suffer. The cartels are a plague, and Baltasar is all that stands between them and the Algarve."

Jenn had to hand it to Luisa—it wasn't easy to make a crime boss sound like a social worker. Next time she should get some bunting and fireworks. Throw a parade. Or maybe that was just Jenn's cynical black heart talking. Good for Luisa if she thought her uncle was the second coming of Robin Hood.

Luisa said, "That is why—"

Gibson cut her off. "Is that where your people left the shipment? Or did the hijackers move it?" He shivered in his sweat-stained T-shirt and shorts.

"No, the hijackers moved it to the center of the warehouse to give their motion detectors more operating room. Why?"

Gibson took out his phone. "Is this place wired for Wi-Fi?"

Luisa stared at him with a mixture of loathing and triumph, as if he'd proven everything she'd argued to Baltasar. She cursed in Portuguese. "For what? So you can check Facebook?"

"Noon tomorrow," Gibson said, underlining the urgency of the situation. "Maybe just answer my question, huh? Is this place wired for Wi-Fi?"

"Yes, of course, this is a business. Why are you asking?"

"I'm just curious what that camera is connected to."

"What camera?" Luisa asked.

Gibson pointed to the shipment. "That camera there."

Jenn didn't see anything. She took back the binoculars and trained them where he was pointing. It took a minute, but she finally saw the glint of the lens. How the hell had he seen that?

Luisa snatched away the binoculars to see for herself.

Gibson said, "They've been watching us the whole time."

Luisa cursed in Portuguese.

"What are you thinking?" George asked.

"Not sure," Gibson said. "I need my equipment. Everything in my laptop bag. It's under my bed."

Luisa nodded at Gibson. "I know where it is."

"Well, that's damn creepy," Hendricks muttered.

"Can we make that happen?" George asked.

Anibal nodded and made a call. Gibson jogged away and made a lap around the shipment. Jenn noticed he had a slight limp and a bloody sock. What had he said about getting hit by a car? He returned and confirmed the presence of cameras at regular intervals that would give the hijackers 360-degree coverage of the warehouse. Gibson had a funny smile.

"I thought you weren't interesting in helping," Jenn said quietly.

Gibson shrugged. "That was before. This is cool as hell."

"Okay, but don't put it that way to Luisa?"

Gibson made a sinister face and winked at her.

Great.

"What do you suggest?" Luisa asked.

"That we talk outside. If they've got cameras, I wouldn't bet against them being wired for sound."

Luisa turned a color that a clever interior designer might dub midnight murder. In silence, they left the warehouse. This time George did take Jenn's arm. They reconvened outside. Anibal said Gibson's gear would be here within the hour. Luisa pressed Gibson for his assessment, but he resisted and said he'd know more soon.

Anibal's and Luisa's phones both rang simultaneously. They looked at each other in concern and stepped away to answer.

"What do you have?" Jenn asked Gibson.

"Nothing for sure until I get my equipment. How much do you know about ransomware?"

"A bit. What does ransomware have to do with it? This isn't a computer hack."

"You're thinking about it the wrong way," Gibson said.

Before Jenn could reply, Luisa hung up and barked at Anibal for her car to be brought around. For once, Anibal didn't hesitate.

"What's happening?" George asked.

"We have a development," said Luisa. "Maybe a lead. My uncle wants you to be there, so I'll need you all to accompany me." She turned to Gibson. "Except for you. I would like you to stay here and wait for your equipment. Finish your evaluation. Anibal will stay behind and provide anything you need."

Hendricks asked, "This development of yours, it happen to be a crime scene?"

"No, one of our men missing since last night has turned up alive."

"That's a good thing," Jenn said.

"Not for him," Luisa replied.

Hendricks said, "All the same to you, then, I'll stick around and keep Gibson company. I want to take another look around."

Luisa agreed that would be acceptable. Her car pulled up, and she got in the back. George got in beside her and left the front seat for Jenn, mostly to keep her from having to sit beside Luisa. That was why she loved him. It was the little things.

CHAPTER TEN

Gibson stood on the loading dock and ran his fingers through his beard, scratching at his neck, deep in thought. The whiskers drove him crazy, particularly in this heat. He wasn't really a beard guy and would kill to shave it off. But the beard hid the scar that ran across his throat from one ear to the other. A souvenir from the time he'd been hanged in the basement of his childhood home.

Something Hendricks had said about stealing without stealing had given him the crazy idea that hackers were behind the hijacking. But he'd be damned if it didn't look like a ransomware attack. Ransomware attacks had gained prominence in the mid-2000s, but the first such crime actually dated to 1989. The attacks had become much more sophisticated in the decades since, but the principle remained the same: Malware would encrypt a person's or company's computers, rendering everything on them inaccessible. The victim would pay a ransom to get the digital key to their own data. A hijacking without actually physically taking anything. Like ransomware hackers, Baltasar's hijackers had "encrypted" his shipment. He still had physical possession but couldn't get near it, and he would need to pay a ransom to regain control.

Hendricks snapped his fingers in front of Gibson's face. "Hey, Coma Boy. What are you cooking on in there?"

"Nothing. Just tired." Gibson wasn't ready to answer that question. His theory was still loose change in his pocket. He preferred to wait until he knew exactly what he had before sharing his suspicions.

"Don't even. I've seen enough movies about genius white people to know when you all are having your big thoughts."

Gibson had to laugh. "What movies?"

Hendricks shrugged. *"Rain Man."*

"Zing."

Hendricks flicked the butt of his cigarette off the loading dock. It tumbled end over end and landed in the dust. "So, what do you actually think? What made your head pop out of its gopher hole?"

"I don't think this was an inside job," Gibson said.

"Interesting," Hendricks said in his least interested voice.

"And there's at least one American involved."

Now Hendricks gave him a dubious look. "And what color are his eyes?"

"How the hell would I know?"

"You wouldn't. Just making sure you aren't Sherlock Holmes–ing me." Hendricks turned serious. Well, more serious. "Tread lightly, all right? Don't go overboard being helpful just because you found something shiny. We could be screwed here either way, but let's not do it to ourselves."

"Jenn is pretty adamant that if we don't help Baltasar, we get squashed," Gibson said.

"Maybe. But help too much, and we get squashed another way."

"Like a bug," Gibson agreed.

"Like a bug."

"I mean, that's a lot of heroin in there."

"How would you know what a lot of heroin looks like?" Hendricks asked.

"Trainspotting."

"I need for that to be the last time you talk."

"What? I thought we were doing movies now," Gibson said.

"I'm going to walk the scene. See what I see."

Without his equipment, Gibson didn't have a lot to do. He didn't feel like waiting out here with Anibal eyeballing him. "Want company?"

Hendricks paused, something caustic on the tip of his tongue. But then he shook it off. "Why not?"

"Really?"

Hendricks walked away without another word. Gibson took that as a yes and followed him inside. Together they made another lap around the yellow circle. Anibal's nephew Tomas strolled along behind with his shotgun like a bored chaperone. No one spoke, conscious that they were under surveillance. Gibson stopped dead in his tracks.

Five gray network cables snaked up the central column in the middle of the shipment. Gibson had missed it the first time. Virtually unnoticeable. Whoever had run the cables knew their business. It was clean, meticulous work. But why go to all that trouble? The hijackers had clearly been on a tight timetable—they'd thrown down the yellow paint so sloppily it was practically a lost Jackson Pollock. But not the cabling. That they'd taken the time to do right. Gibson traced the cabling across the ceiling until it disappeared discreetly into a cable tray that bisected the warehouse.

What didn't they want anyone to notice?

Gibson followed Hendricks the rest of the way around the circle. It gave him time to process. His first hunch had been that the cameras and motion detectors protecting the shipment were using the cannery's Wi-Fi to communicate with the hijackers. That's why he'd asked for his equipment. To see if he could break into their traffic and get a sense of what he was up against. But if they'd taken the time to hardwire themselves into Baltasar's network, then Gibson would need to do the same. There was also the possibility that they'd set up their own network. He'd eliminate that possibility first.

Back out on the loading dock, it became clear that Hendricks had seen something too. He pulled Anibal aside. "I need someone to get the paint cans and bring them out here. But not you or Tomas. Get one of the men who've been here all morning. Real casual. Okay? Throw it all in a garbage bag like they're just cleaning up a mess."

Anibal dispatched one of his men back into the cannery. Since Gibson's equipment still hadn't arrived, he thought he'd see if he could figure out where the cabling terminated. It was either a server closet or the roof. While he was waiting for his equipment, he'd start with the roof.

"I need to go up top. Check something out."

Anibal said that was fine as long as Tomas accompanied him.

The roof was accessible by an exterior fixed ladder. Gibson went up first. Tomas fumbled around at the bottom, trying to work out how to climb a ladder while holding a shotgun. It was pretty damned comical. Finally, he rested the shotgun against the wall and followed Gibson up.

"I don't see any bandits," Gibson said, patting the young man on the shoulder. "I think we're safe."

Tomas gazed longingly down the ladder.

The roof was dominated by a series of large white air handlers and air-conditioning plants to cool the cannery below. Pipes and conduit snaked everywhere like weeds in the cracks of a sidewalk. The sun reflected crazily off every surface, blinding in every direction. Gibson squinted and shaded his eyes. Nothing leapt out at him.

He circled the roof, looking for anything that didn't belong. If the hijackers had set up their own wireless network, then it would need an exterior antenna from which to transmit. With all the existing equipment up on the roof, anything they'd set up would blend right in. No one would even notice unless they knew what they were looking for. Gibson did. On the northeast corner, he found it.

At first glance, he'd dismissed it as a security camera. An easy mistake to make. Pole-mounted on a pan head, its curved white cover and glass front looked the part. He almost walked away but then hesitated. He hadn't seen cameras anywhere else at the cannery. And it was a strange place for one—pointed aimlessly off at the horizon. Plus, there was no way a sardine cannery would have a laser bridge on its roof. Except this one did.

Gibson walked around the device like he'd discovered life on another planet. A laser bridge was fairly state of the art. The US military and businesses used them to transmit large quantities of very low-latency data. They had a range of about a mile and a half and required line of sight but were all but unhackable. That kind of security didn't come cheap. This model probably ran twenty-five thousand, not including its paired twin. Gibson smiled—now all he had to do was find the other end.

The smile melted from his face. There was rust on the mounting bolts. How could there already be rust on the mounting bolts? Gibson knelt and looked carefully at the cabling. It was sun-faded. That wasn't right. This laser bridge had been here a lot longer than twelve hours. More like twelve months, judging by the grime that had accumulated in the corners of the roof mount. Probably longer. Unless the hijackers had set this job up a year or two ago, the laser bridge had nothing to do with it.

He stood up and dusted off his hands. Tomas looked at him questioningly.

"There's rust on the mounting bolts," Gibson explained.

Tomas looked at him uncomprehendingly.

"Right? That's exactly what I thought," Gibson said.

It had been a good theory. Gibson couldn't imagine why Baltasar would need a laser bridge, and didn't want to know. It wasn't relevant to the task at hand, and it was probably best if he forgot he'd ever seen it.

Gibson finished his search of the roof but found nothing else of interest. Whichever way the hijackers were communicating with the shipment, it wasn't via the roof.

They went back down the ladder, where Tomas was reunited with his shotgun. Damn touching scene. Hendricks was on the loading dock, sorting through paint cans. Tomas went over to talk to Anibal in Portuguese. Probably telling him about their tour of the roof.

"Where's the network closet?" Gibson asked Anibal, who looked at him uncomprehendingly. "Small room? Computers?"

Anibal nodded that he understood. "Near the main offices. But I can't let you in."

"Why the hell not? I thought this was your territory."

"You would need Luisa's permission," Anibal said, and Gibson could tell that it hurt to admit.

"Then get it."

"And we would need Dani Coelho. He runs the computers. No one goes in there without him."

"What the hell kind of sardine cannery is this?"

Anibal shrugged.

"Well, where is he? Can you bring him here?" Gibson asked.

"No, he is at the Hotel Mariana. Luisa wanted him kept safe."

"Then I need to go to him."

"Your equipment will be here soon."

"It's not much good to me if I don't have access to the network closet. Will you make a call?"

"I will make a call," Anibal said, sounding mightily put out.

Gibson and Hendricks watched him walk away before exchanging a look.

"Like this chump is doing *us* a favor," Hendricks said.

"No argument," Gibson said.

"Come take a look at this," Hendricks said. He'd laid the paint cans out in a row. "What do you see?"

Gibson looked at the empty cans. All the stickers indicating point of sale had been scraped away. Hendricks saw that he understood and nodded approvingly. He flipped the last can over. A receipt for the entire order was stuck to the bottom. It had gotten wet, and peeling it off would destroy it, but the address of the store where the paint had been purchased was still legible. The date was only two days earlier.

Anibal returned to say that Luisa had okayed a face-to-face with Coelho. He leaned in to get a better look at what Hendricks and Gibson were discussing. The receipt caught his eye, and he picked up the can excitedly, as though he'd spotted something that they'd missed.

"There's an address," Anibal said.

"No . . . really?" Hendricks said.

"Yes, on the bottom of this can. We should investigate."

"That's some good thinking, boss."

Anibal didn't catch Hendricks's tone, too busy shouting for Tomas to fetch the car. Hendricks stood and dusted off his knee while Anibal called Baltasar to announce his discovery. It was an opportunity to remind Baltasar that he was indispensable, and Anibal took full advantage of it.

"This shit is exactly why I retired," Hendricks joked. "Boss man always swooping in to take credit where credit ain't due."

"What about the hotel?" Gibson demanded when Anibal got off the phone. "I need to see Dani Coelho, remember?"

Anibal dismissed Gibson with a wave of his hand. As if Gibson were a selfish child for putting his own needs ahead of the interests of the group. The receipt was real. An actual lead, and all Gibson could think of was the cannery's computers.

"Then I'll stay here and wait for my gear," Gibson said.

"No, you come too," said Anibal. "Both of you."

CHAPTER ELEVEN

A quarter mile from the Faro Airport, the old hotel seemed like a last-ditch option for those on a budget holiday. It rose out of the ground and sloped sleepily to one side. Jenn felt sure that if God reached down, he'd be able to wiggle the hotel back and forth like a loose tooth. Over a low wall, trash floated in a dingy pool. The only guest in sight was a man sprawled in a lounge chair that sagged almost to the ground. Empty beer cans lay scattered around him. His skin was the red of a fresh slap and covered from neck to ankles in curly chimney-black hair. Jenn doubted that image would be going in the brochure.

The hotel lobby wasn't much of an upgrade. The waiting room of a used-car dealership offered more ambiance—linoleum floors the color of a coffee stain, backless metal benches lining the walls, and a pair of vending machines that served as the hotel restaurant and bar. Luisa's men outnumbered the hotel's staff so badly, and looked so out of place, that the guests took one look into the lobby and left the way they'd come.

Marco Zava hustled over to Luisa and updated her in rapid-fire Portuguese on their missing man. Luisa halted him with a raised palm and made him switch to English for Jenn's and George's benefit. She might not want them there, but Luisa was obeying her uncle's instructions to the letter.

"Is he still up in the room?" Luisa asked Zava.

He confirmed that no one had been in or out.

"Good. And where is the manager? Is he here yet?"

"I'm right here, cousin. Relax." Fernando, still in his tuxedo, strolled over. "You're upsetting the guests."

"What are you doing here?" Luisa said, even as she put it together. "This is one of *our* hotels?"

"They can't all be five stars," Fernando said with a shrug.

"This *puto* is hiding out in one of our hotels?"

"You have to admit he's got style."

"I'm going to skin him alive," she said, neither a threat nor a boast, but the casual decision of a woman picking her entrée.

"Feel free. I doubt it will ruin the décor."

"What room?"

"A312. He booked the room a week ago. For one night. Paid cash and checked in under a false name—Willie Sutton."

George gave Jenn a look, and she raised an eyebrow. The name meant nothing to Luisa or Fernando, but as Americans, they both recognized it. Willie Sutton had been one of the most successful bank robbers in US history. All while carrying an unloaded pistol. When asked why he robbed banks, Sutton answered famously, "Because that's where the money is." As he'd been dead since the 1980s, it seemed an odd pseudonym for a Portuguese to choose.

"And his real name?" Luisa asked.

"João Luna," her man said. "He is the captain of the *Alexandria*, one of our boats."

"I thought Abílio captained the *Alexandria*."

"This is his son. Abílio retired."

"Ah, yes," Luisa said. "So yesterday was his son's first run for us? He has some balls."

"I doubt for long," Fernando said.

Luisa did not dispute it and turned to grill Zava about security. He assured her that every exit was covered and that João Luna would need a cape to escape the hotel. Satisfied, she praised his quick work securing the hotel.

"Thank you, Marco. You've done well."

Since this morning, Jenn had seen signs that the hijacking had eroded morale. A moment's recognition from Luisa wouldn't magically fix that, but it did help settle her man. It was smart leadership. Jenn didn't care for Luisa Mata, and it forced her to question her assumptions. Disliking someone didn't mean they were incompetent.

"You have the room key?" Luisa asked her cousin.

Fernando held it out as if offering a treat to a waiting puppy. Luisa plucked it from his hand and told him to wait in the lobby. "Better yet, go back to the Mariana. You shouldn't be here."

"Try and keep the noise down?" Fernando called after her. "It's a family hotel."

Jenn and George packed into a coffin of an elevator with Luisa and Marco. It had an old, manual gate that Zava had to wrestle closed. The elevator jerked into motion, pausing momentarily at each floor as if working up the will to go on. Luisa had wanted to take the stairs, but George couldn't manage it. She stared up at the slow blinking floor lights through narrow, impatient eyes. Jenn had been a lot of things in her life, but the weak link had never been one of them. It made her thirsty.

She tried to push the thought out of her head, but now she'd had it, she couldn't think of anything else. She'd been drinking too much; she knew that. But she'd told herself that when the time came she could control it. A voice of golden honey asked, *Why would you want to fight something that feels so good?* Problem was, she didn't know that she did.

At the third floor, Luisa was first off, Zava on her hip. George and Jenn followed behind like forgotten children. Down the hall, two guards flanked the door to A312. They dropped their cigarettes at the sight of Luisa and crushed them out in the carpet. Fernando was right—it didn't affect the décor any.

When they were all in position, Zava took the key while everyone formed up behind him, Jenn and George at the rear. Luisa told them, "Stay back, say nothing, do not interfere."

Jenn didn't know what options that left them.

Zava eased open the door and listened. The hotel room was silent, air heavy and stale. Jenn flinched, aware of how tightly grouped they were around the door. If it had been booby-trapped, they'd have all been dead. *Use your head,* she chided herself. *Don't prove Luisa right.*

Zava slipped inside, gun drawn. The two guards and Luisa followed while Jenn and George hung back in the hall. Methodically, they cleared the hotel room. First the bathroom, then Zava slid along the short corridor and peered around the corner into the main room. He looked back, nodding that it was safe, and waved everyone forward.

João Luna lay sleeping on one of the room's two twin beds. He was fully dressed and hadn't bothered to pull back the covers. On the nightstand, an old flip phone rested atop a passport. A plane ticket jutted guiltily out of its pages. On the other bed sat a leather satchel. Zava brought it over and, lifting aside a layer of clothes, showed Luisa the bundles of euros at the bottom. Luisa thumbed through the bills and arched an eyebrow at Marco.

"Wake him."

There was no need. At the sound of Luisa's voice, the captain of the *Alexandria* sat bolt upright in the exaggerated way people woke from nightmares in movies. Unfortunately for him, this was no dream. Disoriented, he looked back and forth between the six faces crowded around his bed. He didn't look much like what Jenn imagined when she heard "fishing boat captain." She'd envisioned someone older, weathered, with a thick beard. João Luna was young and gangly, no more than twenty or twenty-one, almost pretty in a boyish way. If he owned a razor at all, it was a sharp one. He mumbled a question in Portuguese and then made a panicked break for the door without waiting for an answer. Zava backhanded him across the face and sent the boy crashing against the wall like a Ping-Pong ball. Luisa tsked at Zava, who shrugged apologetically.

The two guards hoisted the dazed boy by his armpits and set him on a chair. He sat rubbing his cheek in a daze. Zava searched the bed and found a pistol under the pillow. He held it up to show Luisa, who pulled up a second chair and sat facing the boy. For all her threats of violence, she looked calm and relaxed. It would be tempting to think the storm had blown itself out, but Jenn sensed that they'd merely entered the eye. Luisa spoke softly in Portuguese, and one of her men went to the bathroom, wetted a hand towel, and gave it to the boy, who held it against his face.

"Do you speak English, João?" Luisa asked, smiling.

She got no answer, so Luisa asked again in Portuguese. The boy shook his head. Luisa glanced back apologetically at Jenn and George before continuing in Portuguese. Jenn understood most of what followed—and George's Portuguese was better than hers—but standing in the doorway, neither felt sure of their roles beyond witnesses. Leery of what they might be about to become complicit in.

"It's been a busy morning," Luisa said. "Did you sleep well?"

"What?" the boy asked, confused by the question. "Why am I here?"

Luisa smiled patiently. "Do you know who I am?"

He shook his head.

"My name is Luisa Mata. Do you know who I am now?"

He paled and nodded.

"Tell me."

"You are the niece of Baltasar Alves."

"Good. I'm glad. That should save us considerable time. And saving me time is our only chance of becoming friends. Would you like us to be friends?"

Luisa reached into a pocket and took out a travel alarm clock. She wound it and set the hour and minutes, then placed it where they both could see it. João Luna looked like a scared kid, lost, and way out of his depth. If it was an act, it was a hell of a good one.

"My time is valuable, João," Luisa said. "I must account for every minute of every day. I cannot appear to waste time while my men work hard. You captain your own boat, so you know how important it is to set a good example for your crew. To take time out with you? That is an extravagance I cannot afford. So much is happening today that I should be attending to, but instead here I am. It is unfortunate." Luisa stopped so that João could consider exactly how unfortunate it truly was.

"I'm sorry," João said simply to fill the silence.

"I appreciate that. I do. I don't like to feel taken advantage of. It gives me a bad feeling, you know? Here," she said, tapping her heart.

"I'm sorry."

"So, to help make things right between us, I will need you to compensate me for my time."

"Compensate?"

"Every five minutes that I do not have the answer to my questions, you will pay. The longer you drag this out, the more you will owe. Do you understand?"

"Pay with what?"

"With whatever you have that is worth something to you," Luisa said and made it sound almost tender. "Do you have anything that you value?"

João looked on the verge of tears as he nodded that he did.

"Good," Luisa said. "I would hate to charge you more than is absolutely necessary."

"Answer to what questions?"

Luisa held up the plane ticket. "Why are you going to Brazil?"

João's brow furrowed. "What?"

Luisa pressed on as though he'd answered to her satisfaction. "Who hired you to betray my family?"

"What?" João said again. "No one! I would never do that."

Luisa nodded, but she didn't raise her voice or even repeat her question. She didn't badger João with the evidence stacked against him or pretend to commiserate with his situation. She didn't threaten him or offer him an out. There were dozens of tactics a seasoned interrogator could choose from to soften up an uncooperative subject. Luisa didn't try any of them. Instead, she looked over at the small clock. João followed her eyes. Together, they watched the time pass. Jenn could see the tension building in his body and on his face. He began to babble helplessly that he didn't know what she wanted. Luisa continued to stare impassively at the clock.

Jenn had worn several hats in the CIA, including spending long stretches in Afghanistan as an interrogator. Taliban responded poorly to women in control, and that had given Jenn an edge over her male counterparts. Luisa might be unorthodox in her approach, but Jenn admired her technique. She had established control of the room. Given the boy simple parameters for his continued survival and let her reputation work on his imagination. Jenn guessed that when five minutes had passed, Luisa would escalate the stakes and give João something more to fear. The anticipation of torture could be more productive than the act itself.

Still, something about this didn't sit right with Jenn. One of her interrogations in particular kept coming to mind, and it wasn't one of the dozens that she'd conducted for the CIA. Instead, her mind went back to a storage locker in Pennsylvania. During the hunt for Suzanne Lombard, she and Dan Hendricks had taken a suspect who they'd both been sure was their man. Kirby Tate. They'd found both circumstantial and hard evidence linking him to the girl's disappearance.

At the time, you couldn't have talked Jenn out of his guilt. He was her guy. She had felt it in her bones. She'd gone to work on him with a righteous fury, the memory of which ate at her to this day. She'd crossed lines she never thought herself capable of crossing, and, in the end, although the man had been far from innocent, he wasn't guilty of anything to do with Suzanne Lombard. He'd been served up to her on a platter, and Jenn had swallowed the setup whole.

That was what bothered her now. How neat this all was—the money, the plane ticket, the gun. All laid out for Luisa to find. So perfectly staged. Jenn knew what Luisa must feel. Her desperation to show Baltasar progress—emotions clouding her judgment. The need to prove herself to the father figure who had placed so much faith in her. Luisa was beating on the wrong door, but Jenn didn't know how to stop her. Diplomacy wasn't her strong suit. She was more of a breaker than a fixer. Putting aside the fact that Luisa despised her, she really had no idea where to begin.

"I don't like this," she whispered to George.

"You read my mind."

"This kid doesn't look like a thief to me."

"Remind me what those look like again?" George asked.

"How did they know he was here?"

"If he was under an assumed name, you mean? What do you want to do about it?"

Jenn didn't have an answer for that. Unlike Gibson, she didn't want to openly defy Baltasar's request for help. That would not end well for them, and she still saw value in Alves's hospitality. It didn't mean, however, that she intended to go out of her way to involve herself. Gibson wasn't wrong that proving useful might be dangerous in its own right. Baltasar Alves was a pragmatic man, and if he came to see them as an asset, then Gibson's paranoia might prove prophetic.

Five minutes came and went.

Luisa turned her dark eyes back to the boy in the chair.

CHAPTER TWELVE

By the time they pulled up at the paint store, Hendricks was having second thoughts about the receipt.

Now, positivity was not Hendricks's natural state. Gibson had once called him a pessimist, to which Hendricks had retorted, *I'm not a pessimist. I'm black.* Whatever the reason, Hendricks wasn't often wrong. They didn't see eye to eye on much, but Gibson had learned to listen up whenever Hendricks got a bad feeling. Anibal hadn't learned that lesson and dismissed Hendricks's concerns.

"What's up?" Gibson asked.

"You know how in movies where the police scour every square inch of a crime scene and find nothing. Then later, the hero breaks in and finds a clue that all the cops overlooked?"

"Doesn't happen in real life?"

Hendricks shook his head sourly.

"Well, Baltasar's crew aren't exactly trained detectives."

"No, that's not even what I'm talking about. Criminals don't make *one* mistake, see. Either they make none, or they make all of them. There's either a million fucking fingerprints or the scene is pristine. There's no middle ground. Either criminals know what they're doing, or they don't. Take these hijackers. Would you say they have their act together?"

"I would."

"Yeah, they're pretty slick. Thought of everything, so it seems. Planning was meticulous. Knew when. Knew where. Tiptoed past security. Cameras, motion detectors, explosives. In and out like ghosts."

"Except for the receipt."

"Three gallons of bright-yellow paint. Kind of a memorable purchase, wouldn't you say? So why wait until two days before the job to buy it? Increase the chance that someone remembers. And why leave the cans lying around, with or without a legible receipt conveniently on the bottom?"

"So, what are you thinking?"

"Man, this is nothing but cheese. And we're the damn mice."

"You think it's a trap?"

"Don't know, but one thing it ain't is a lead."

"So why are we here?"

"Well, this is Anibal's show now. Personally, I'm kind of curious to see what happens. It'll tell us more than any receipt will, that I guarantee."

"Think I'll stay in the car," Gibson said.

"Not the worst idea you ever had."

Hendricks followed Anibal inside the paint store. Gibson watched through the store's floor-to-ceiling windows, which glinted in the sun. Tomas opened the garbage bag of empty paint cans and set them in a row on the counter. Anibal went looking for the manager while Hendricks wandered through the back of the place as if shopping for paint. Didn't look like much of a trap.

The store sat on a solitary stretch of road. To the east stood a broken, weathered building. Only the layers of graffiti, like the rings of a tree, gave any hint as to how long it had been abandoned. Other than that, Gibson didn't see much in either direction apart from the café next door. Gibson's stomach growled. It was like Portugal had passed a law requiring X number of cafés per capita. In busier neighborhoods, you couldn't throw a stone without hitting three or four. And even on a desolate stretch of road like this one, there'd still be one bright, hopeful café. The mystery Gibson hadn't solved was how they all stayed in business when he almost never saw any customers.

This one was no exception. Empty tables stood guard outside on its narrow patio. Gibson remembered the ten-euro note still tucked into his sock. After his morning run and workout, he'd meant to have breakfast in Old Town but never got the chance. He fished out the crumpled bill and smoothed it on his thigh. It had blood on one corner, but ten euros was ten euros.

The owner of the café, a gray-haired man with a jet-black mustache, greeted him in Portuguese. Gibson asked if he spoke English, but the man shook his head. As you got away from the resort towns, English fell off quickly. Gibson fumbled his way through ordering a sandwich and a bottle of water. It was the height of the day, and the patio offered no respite from the sun, so Gibson sat at a table inside and sipped his water. The owner disappeared into the back.

Across the courtyard, Gibson could see Anibal talking to the store manager. Didn't look like the receipt had produced the big break that he had hoped it would. Judging by body language, that upset Anibal a lot more than it did Hendricks, who leaned against a counter and listened disinterestedly.

Gibson finished his water but was still thirsty. The shopkeeper was busy in the back, so Gibson left money on the counter and took another bottle. He hadn't gotten used to European servings sizes—a large was smaller than an American small. He'd have killed for a Big Gulp right about now. A shadow passed behind him. Gibson turned to see a white panel van pull up to the café, blocking out the sun.

The side door rolled open. A man crouched inside. He held a gun in one hand and, even when he jumped lightly down from the van, he never stopped pointing it at Gibson. Outside, from the direction of the paint store, gunfire and the sound of shattering glass erupted.

Hendricks had been right again. Gibson hoped that whatever the ex-cop learned was worth it.

"Put this on," the armed man said and tossed a black cloth to Gibson. He had a Portuguese accent but spoke the English of someone who had lived out of the country.

Gibson caught it, saw it was a hood, and dropped it like it was radioactive. The light pixelated before his eyes. His skin went cold, and he was hyperventilating. The last time someone had put a hood on him, he'd wound up in a windowless cell for eighteen months. He'd lost his mind and everything he cared about. This son of a bitch was living in a fantasy world if he thought Gibson would willingly subject himself to that again.

"No. Fuck no."

"Pick it up. Put it on. I *will* shoot you."

"So shoot me," Gibson said and meant it. "I'm not putting that on."

The man gave him an exasperated look, as if Gibson were screwing up a basic social convention. Don't talk in movie theaters, hold the door, wash your hands after using the bathroom, and when the guy with the gun tells you to put on a hood . . . put it on. Gibson estimated the distance between himself and the gunman. He wouldn't get two steps, but he preferred a bullet to another hood. However, before he could put his death-by-kidnapper scheme into action, someone clipped him across the back of the head and sent him sprawling to the ground.

A knee dug into his spine. Gibson struggled anyway, but when the hood went over his head, the strangest thing happened. He felt himself go limp as if he'd been drugged. Almost peaceful. Was this what happened to a horse wearing blinders? He allowed himself to be handcuffed and bundled into the van. A crazy thought entered his mind—he was going home. He felt relief, which scared him more than the gun. The last six months had given him confidence in his reconstructed sanity. He no longer talked to the dead, and more importantly, the dead no longer talked back. But it was discouraging how quickly he'd gone docile under the hood—like he had some switch in his head waiting to be flipped.

CHAPTER THIRTEEN

The beating that Marco Zava put on João Luna verged on the balletic. Most big men relied on brute strength, but the bodyguard worked João over like a butcher carving filets. Zava didn't touch the boy's face but focused instead on the torso. Jenn could tell he was pulling his punches, but every blow landed with precision and purpose. The purpose being to make him hurt but not break him. João twisted and turned, trying to squirm away out of reach, but the guards held him fast to the chair.

Luisa read a list of names from a small black notebook, intoning them with ecclesiastic contempt. The names meant nothing to Jenn, but they meant something to the boy in the chair. As the blows continue to fall, he wept and begged Luisa not to harm his family. Unmoved, she kept up the recitation until her voice, the thud of the blows, and the boy's cries blended together in a sinuous music. All they needed was an organ, Jenn thought, and this would be her grandmother's kind of religion. *Hallelujah, amen.*

She blanked her mind so that, although she could see and hear, she wasn't watching or listening. A little trick she'd learned as a little girl at the hands of her grandmother, then perfected on forward operating bases in Afghanistan. João Luna stopped being a real person to her. She pushed the little hotel room into a distant corner until it was as abstract as a history book. A tragedy but nothing to do with her. Jenn felt bad for the boy in the chair, but he had made the mistake of working for criminals. He would need to find his own way out. Same as the rest of them.

It wasn't abstract to George.

He'd spent two years being tortured and beaten by Titus Eskridge's people. A scapegoat because Eskridge couldn't punish Jenn, who had put a bullet in Eskridge's son at the lake house in Pennsylvania. Seeing it happen to another person clearly brought it all back to George. He began to shake, breath coming in tight hitches. Jenn saw it too late. Tried and failed to hold him back, but he stumbled toward the boy in the chair and bellowed for them to stop.

Zava froze midpunch, fist floating in the air as if someone had pressed "Pause." All eyes turned to George. The two guards drew their weapons and drove him back. One pressed the muzzle of his gun against George's temple, twisting his head sideways, pinning it to the wall. The other covered Jenn and looked to Luisa for instructions. Jenn raised her hands and looked imploringly at Luisa. Neutral was no longer an option.

"Please," Jenn said. "Don't."

Luisa showed no signs of empathy. "What's the matter with him? I don't have time for this."

"He's innocent," George spat.

"You have the wrong man," Jenn said. "He had nothing to do with the hijacking. Please."

Luisa looked at the boy cowering in the chair, then at the satchel of euros, the gun, the plane ticket. The overwhelming case against him. Wheels turning. Jenn could see she had doubts of her own. Doubts that she'd silenced because putting a face to the faceless hijackers had finally given her an object for her anger. Jenn understood exactly how seductive that felt. And how hard it was to talk someone out of it once their mind was made up.

"Tell me why," Luisa said but gave no order for her men to holster their weapons.

"How did you find him?" Jenn asked. "He checked in under an alias."

Luisa narrowed her eyes. "He turned on his phone. We tracked his GPS."

"How long ago?"

"Ninety minutes."

"Seems pretty stupid."

"Criminals *are* stupid. Trust me on that, I have a lifetime of experience on the subject."

"Perhaps, but this one seems pretty well prepared otherwise. He knew enough to switch his phone off. Check in under an alias. Pay cash. So why turn it back on and fall asleep? Why not get a burner phone? He has everything else."

"Criminals are stupid," Luisa repeated with a little less enthusiasm than before, so she tried another tack. "He hadn't slept. The stress of running for his life. He is tired. He makes a call and then a mistake. He falls asleep without switching it back off."

It was a reasonable interpretation. Entirely within the realm of possibility, but Jenn still didn't buy it. An idea occurred to her. It was risky but might push Luisa in the right direction. Only if she was right, though. Otherwise, João Luna really was on his own.

"Who did he call?" Jenn asked, taking a tentative step forward.

"What?"

Jenn said, "Check his ingoing and outgoing calls. Check his texts. I'll bet you that satchel of money there that he didn't talk to anyone in the last ninety minutes."

Luisa gestured for the phone, and Zava brought it to her. She asked for the passcode. João gave it to her without hesitation. They all watched Luisa scroll through the phone's history. Jenn could tell from her expression that the call wasn't there.

"He could have deleted it," Luisa said without conviction.

"So he was smart enough to delete the call from his history, but too stupid to turn the phone back off? Come on, Luisa. You can't have it both ways."

Luisa stared at her for a long moment. "What the hell is happening here?"

CHAPTER FOURTEEN

In the end, Gibson didn't know if they'd driven for ten minutes or sixty. Whether they'd traveled in circles or in a straight line. An old Robert Redford movie about a team of hackers, a favorite of his father's, had given him an idea. In one scene, Redford had been kidnapped by goons, thrown in the trunk of a car, and driven to the boss's hideout. After his release, Redford's team reconstructed where he'd been held based on what sounds he'd heard from the trunk. It was a cool concept, but it didn't take Gibson long to realize it was impossible. Not when the world didn't offer geographically distinct sounds every few miles to serve as audio landmarks. Lying on the floor of the van, Gibson only felt the vibrations from the road and the monotonous rumble of passing vehicles. Not much to go on if he ever managed to get free.

So, what did he know for sure? Not a great deal. Was Hendricks dead? Gibson hoped not, but from the sound of it, his abductors had gone full automatic on the paint store. They'd taken Gibson alive, though. He took that as a good sign. Unless his abductors wanted to take their time killing him. It would explain why the gunman hadn't bothered with a mask. A disheartening thought. Gibson didn't want to die in running shorts.

When the van finally lurched to a halt, the men dragged Gibson out unceremoniously. Strong hands stood him upright and led him up a flight of steps. Cool air buffeted him as they passed through a doorway. The men deposited him onto a hard-backed chair, removed the handcuffs, and yanked off the hood like he was the main course at a great feast.

Gibson rubbed his wrists and examined his new accommodations. He sat in the center of a windowless room painted the color of burned pancakes. The only furniture aside from his chair was a rectangular folding table against the far wall. On the table, a laptop in a docking station connected three oversized monitors. Speakers played an old Nine Inch Nails track. The volume gradually rose, and the lyrics—in oversized type—scrolled down the center monitor.

Gibson didn't need the prompt. He knew every note and word. Back in high school, NIN had been on heavy rotation while he was learning his way around computers. This particular track had been a personal anthem for his hack of Senator Benjamin Lombard. One of the damning articles written about him after his arrest had pointed to his taste in music as emblematic of the degenerate hacker culture that he supposedly represented. If your child listens to Korn, Rage Against the Machine, Linkin Park, or NIN, then he might be an antisocial hacker too. The classic idiocy that certain music led to a life of crime. The article had specifically referenced NIN's "Head Like a Hole," so hearing the track now felt pointed. A message being delivered: *Hello, Gibson Vaughn, I know who you are.*

Gibson doubted that very much.

The song ended and the center monitor faded to black. Someone had an overly developed sense of the dramatic. Gibson looked forward to the smoke bombs and laser show. After a moment, text appeared on the monitor.

Why is the back of his head bleeding?

One of Gibson's abductors stepped forward, clearing his throat embarrassedly. "He wouldn't put on the hood." The man's English was good, but the accent was Portuguese.

Gibson touched the back of his head. His fingers came away wet. Whoever was typing could see the back of his head. He glanced around and saw cameras circling him. Someone really didn't want to miss a thing. It reminded Gibson of the hijacking at Fresco Mar . . . And like that, he knew they were the same people who had taken him. The problem was, he couldn't decide if that was good news or bad.

He wouldn't put on the hood, so you cracked his head? the monitor typed, followed by a frowny-face emoji.

"We didn't have time to negotiate with him," the man explained. "Alves's people put up more resistance than expected."

Gibson hoped Hendricks had given them hell.

The monitor asked, Well, is he ok? Did you break him?

"You know," Gibson said, interrupting, "I'm sitting right here."

Apparently not, the monitor concluded. Good. Everyone can wait outside.

His abductors filed out, locking the door behind them and leaving Gibson alone with the monitor.

Gibson Vaughn, the monitor read. This is a trip.

"Do I know you?"

No, but I'm a huge fan. The BrnChr0m, the monitor read, using Gibson's old hacker handle.

"It's not all true," Gibson said.

> It never is. But between you and me, did you pop
> the vice president down in the ATL?

Gibson set his jaw and tried to keep the anger from his face. He doubted he was successful. The inherent asymmetry of this interrogation placed him in a weak position. He or she or they could see his face and hear his voice all while safely obscured by monochromatic typeface. It was like playing poker with a machine. Still, Gibson would bet that whoever was typing on the other end was an American. He'd had that sense looking at the setup at the cannery, and the monitor's word choices cinched it.

The monitor continued, No need to be modest. You altered an American presidential election. Swung it from one party to another. That's the brass ring, man. Do you not see how epic that is? The man in the White House is only there because of you. You're a kingmaker.

"Do I look like a damn kingmaker to you?" Gibson snapped. The last thing he was in the mood for was to listen to someone mythologize his past. Spin his life into a narrative. Turn him into something he never was and never would be.

A significant pause followed. Have it your way. So I guess you're wondering why you're here.

"You hijacked Baltasar's shipment."

Another pause.

Have to tell you, the old jaw about hit the floor when I recognized you in the cannery. You were NOT on our radar. At all. Believe me, we are going to do a complete overhaul of our procedures. I'm not going to sleep until I know how we missed that Gibson Vaughn was in Portugal working for Baltasar Alves.

"I don't work for him."

Semantics. So how did you wind up here? That has to be some story. After the whole Dulles Airport

thing? Someday you have to tell me what really
went down.

Gibson was fast wearying of the monitor's pretense that they were
buddies simply because they were both hackers. As a rule, he found most
people in the "community" to be arrogant assholes. There had been a
time that Gibson fit that description himself, but the last few years had
done a good job of humbling him. The person behind the monitor didn't
seem to be an exception to the rule. Time to cut to the chase.

"Are you going to kill me?"

Why would we kill you?

That "we" again . . . Gibson assumed he didn't mean the gunmen
waiting outside. The people behind the monitor had clearly subcon-
tracted local muscle. Probably anonymously. Explained why those
men hadn't concealed their faces—they couldn't lead back to anyone
in charge.

Gibson said, "Because you're running a real-world ransomware
attack, and I'm the only one that can actually stop you."

YES!!! the monitor responded enthusiastically. See? I knew you
got it. This is what I'm talking about.

Not the reaction Gibson expected.

What else do you know? the monitor asked.

"Not much. Your boys grabbed me before I could make any headway." Gibson waited, but the monitor made no reply and remained
dark. "Is this the part where you say you don't believe me and bring in
the interrogator?"

No, the monitor finally responded. This is the part where we offer
you a job.

Definitely not the reaction Gibson expected. "A job?" he asked
dubiously. "A job doing what? Because I can't do anything that's going

to jeopardize my people. So if you're thinking of buying me off so I lead Baltasar in the wrong direction, it's a nonstarter."

No, nothing like that.

"Then what?"

We want you to stop us.

Gibson sat there dumbfounded. "You want to hire me to stop you?"

If you can.

"Thing is, I've already been asked to do that."

True, but you're not entirely enthusiastic about it.
We want a motivated Gibson Vaughn.

Gibson sat back in his chair. He'd been offered some strange jobs in his life, but this might be the topper. Someone had gone to considerable risk to put Baltasar's shipment in play. Why would they want him to . . . ? The answer was obvious. They were conducting a dry run against Baltasar Alves's operation. Prepping for something bigger.

"You're running a beta test," Gibson said.

That's right.

"You're taking one hell of a risk."

There is only so much you can learn from simulations. Eventually you have to do a live-fire drill.

Gibson filed the use of US military jargon away in the profile he was building of the person behind the monitor. His suspicion that he was dealing with at least one American continued to solidify.

> Baltasar Alves is small-time. Why do you think we chose his operation? It's inconsequential.

"Not to him."

> Kind of the definition of inconsequential, don't you think? However, the drawback of picking Alves is that no one in his organization is equipped to understand what they're seeing. No one with a realistic chance of punching holes in our setup. The outcome is a foregone conclusion.

"So, why do it?"

> It gave us a real-world operation to plan. A chance to evaluate how we run things on our end. But when I saw you at the cannery this morning, I realized what an amazing opportunity had been presented to us.

"So you want me to pen test this operation of yours? Figure out a way to stop you."

> Precisely.

"And if I succeed? Am I supposed to keep a lid on it? I don't know if I want to be at ground zero when Baltasar Alves loses that shipment. That won't go well for any of us."

Understood. No, if you are able, you are welcome
to give Alves back his shipment. Thwart away. You
have our blessing. All we require is that you also
share it with us. Everything you learn.

"Must be major," Gibson said. "Whatever you've got in the works."
The monitor remained dark.

"Let's say I agree. What are you prepared to offer?" There was risk
inherent in working for anonymous computer monitors, but if Gibson
could get five or even ten thousand euros, it would serve as a down payment toward convincing Jenn to begin extracting the team from under
Baltasar. Was "team" the right word for what they were? he wondered.

The monitor said, We will pay one hundred thousand euros for
a complete breakdown of our operational flaws, vulnerabilities, and
weaknesses.

The figure made Gibson immediately suspicious. It was too much.
Way too much. The kind of money to tempt a desperate man into
throwing caution to the wind. He forgot that they were watching him,
and something in his face must have betrayed his distrust.

It sounds like an awful lot of money. You think that
when the time comes, we won't hold up our end.

"Something like that," Gibson said.

We'd be foolish to cross someone with your
reputation.

"All that money and a hand job too. This is my lucky day."

How about a retainer? A convincer of our good
intentions.

"What did you have in mind?"

There's a duffel bag under your chair. Open it.

Cautiously, Gibson reached down and dragged a tan duffel bag out from between his feet. He unzipped it. Stacks of five-hundred-euro notes filled the bag. He looked up at the monitor questioningly.

One hundred thousand euros.

"That's not a retainer, that's payment in full. How do you know I won't take the money and run?"

You already have the US government after you, among other motivated parties. We think you're smart enough not to add us to the list.

"And all you want is a report?"

A thorough report. Also, under no circumstances may you reveal our existence, or this meeting, to any of Baltasar Alves's people. Doing so will void our arrangement and give you a new problem to worry about. Do we understand each other?

"What do I call you?" Gibson asked.
There was a pause. Dol5, the monitor said.
"Dol-five?" Gibson asked.

NO. Dol-fin. Dolphin. Come on, man. You know how a five-dollar bill is called a fin?

"No, I never heard that."

Well, it is.

"Whatever," Gibson said. "So what are you planning, Dolphin?"

That's not any of your concern, the monitor read. Do we have a deal?

"I don't know. Is Dan Hendricks dead?"

I don't see how that's relevant.

"It's relevant if you want me to work for you."

Well, why don't we take a look, then.

The leftmost monitor flared to life. It showed a video feed of the inside of the paint store. It looked like a platoon of Marines had used it for target practice. Anibal and Hendricks stood in the rubble, talking silently.

"This is live?" Gibson asked.

Give or take a millisecond.

A worrisome thought came to mind. "What about Jenn Charles? George Abe? They were on the way to check out a lead. Was that bullshit too? Are they all right?"

Ah, well, that's a bit of a different story.

The right-hand monitor turned on to reveal the interior of a hotel room. There was no audio, but Gibson didn't need it to see the situation was dire. A gunman had a pistol pressed to George's temple while Jenn pleaded with Luisa Mata.

A tense scene, the center monitor said. About to get a whole lot tenser.

"Don't."

Well, that's kind of up to you, now isn't it?

Gibson watched the left monitor as Anibal and Hendricks took out their cell phones and made calls. On the right monitor, Luisa and Jenn reacted to their phones ringing. Gibson watched both sides of the conversation. Luisa snatched Jenn's phone from her hand. They began arguing again. Gibson could see Luisa's frustration building. She began searching a badly beaten young man and his belongings. She lifted up a satchel and dumped bundles of euros out on the bed.

Now watch this, the center monitor said. This will be interesting.

Luisa flinched. Gibson couldn't tell why, but all eyes in the hotel room turned to the satchel.

"What do you want from me?" Gibson demanded.

A yes. I want to hear an enthusiastic yes.

CHAPTER FIFTEEN

When Luisa's phone rang, it interrupted their argument over João Luna's guilt or innocence. In the quiet of the room, Jenn could hear the alarm in Anibal's voice on the other end. Whatever he told Luisa caused her eyes to widen.

Jenn felt her own phone vibrate. Hendricks. When she answered, his voice sounded incredibly faint, as if he were calling from deep underwater.

"I can barely hear you," Jenn said. "Are you hurt? Where are you?"

Hendricks made an effort to speak up, but his voice was still little more than a whisper. "We're at a paint store out on N125. We just got lit up."

"Paint store? I thought you were at the cannery."

Hendricks explained the receipt he'd found on the bottom of one of the paint cans. Apparently, they'd gone to investigate.

"Who was it?"

"They didn't formally introduce themselves."

"Anyone hurt?"

"Miraculously, no. Although this store's going to need more than a fresh coat of paint."

Jenn could hear something in his voice. "But . . . ?"

"Vaughn is missing. He was outside when we were attacked. Lost track of him in the firefight."

Luisa took the phone out of Jenn's hand and tossed it to Marco Zava.

"My people were just attacked at a paint store," Luisa said.

"So were mine."

"No," Luisa corrected. "One of your people was attacked. The other decided not to come inside."

"So, what? Gibson knew the attack was coming but left Hendricks in harm's way? Give me a break."

"He has been openly antagonistic about helping my uncle from the beginning."

"You've been openly antagonistic about our assisting your uncle from the beginning. Believe me, if Gibson was working the other side, you'd never see him coming. This isn't his style."

"And what about you? Protecting this man." She pointed at João Luna slumped in the chair. "What does he know that scares George so much?"

"George isn't scared of what he knows. He's scared the boy doesn't know shit and you're going to beat him to death for nothing," Jenn snapped back. "You honestly think we're all in on it? This morning I was a drunk whore. Now suddenly I'm a mastermind running an elaborate con? Why don't you make up your mind?"

Luisa didn't answer. She looked from Jenn to George, who still had the muzzle of a gun pressed to his temple. Finally, her eyes settled on João Luna. She asked him how he knew Jenn and George. He shook his head, not understanding, but that wasn't good enough for Luisa. At her direction, Zava pinned him down and began searching his pockets. Luisa flipped through his passport, looked carefully at his plane tickets. Tossing them aside in frustration, she lifted up the satchel and dumped the money out on the bed. Hunting for anything that might help her make sense of the situation.

From inside the satchel, they heard an electronic beep and a click like a mousetrap snapping shut. Everyone froze. Slowly, Luisa turned the satchel right side up. With one finger, she opened it wide enough to see inside. Her face paled. She looked up at Jenn then back down into the satchel.

"What is it?" Jenn asked, although she was afraid she knew.

Luisa raised one hand and pointed to the door. Her eyes never left the satchel. Her men backed carefully out of the room. Jenn didn't move. When the men were gone, she approached Luisa and peered inside the satchel.

The explosive device wasn't large, but in the small confines of the hotel room, it wouldn't need to be. If it went off, anyone caught inside the room would be turned to paste. Why hadn't it already? The device had triggered when Luisa overturned the satchel—a tilt fuse of some kind. Jenn had heard it. They'd all heard it. So why weren't they dead? The question coiled around Jenn's throat. She swallowed hard, but it did nothing to lessen her thirst. How badly she wished she were already on her second drink.

"Why aren't we dead?" Luisa asked.

"Maybe it's a dud?"

"You really think so?"

"No, but it's nice to have dreams."

Luisa laughed dryly. "So, what now?"

"Give it to me," George said. Jenn had been so fixed on the satchel that she hadn't noticed he had remained in the room.

"Sir, no," Jenn said.

"Give it to me," George said, using both hands to support the weight of the satchel.

"Why?" Luisa said but didn't let go of the handles.

"How about you get out of the room," George said. "And you can ask me from there."

Gibson watched the monitor without realizing he was bouncing nervously in his chair. Or that he was sweating.

Luisa had the satchel by the handles; George cupped the bottom with his hands. Jenn was visibly upset and was imploring George not to do whatever he was doing.

This is exciting stuff, the center monitor said.

"What's in the bag?"

I think you know.

"What's in the goddamn bag?"

The central monitor played a GIF of a thermonuclear explosion. It cycled over and over. Almost hypnotic. Almost beautiful.

"Why are you doing this?" Gibson said. "I'm enthusiastic, all right? Enough."

Just making a point.

"It's made."

And now I know who to hurt if you cross us up.
Always good to know where a man's soft spots lie.

"I won't."

So we have a deal? the monitor asked.

"Yes. We do. We have a deal. Now deactivate it."

It was never active.

The monitor showing the hotel room went dark. Gibson slumped back in his chair.

Need me to have the boys bring you a defibrillator? the moni-tor asked.

"Funny."

Don't be grumpy.

"What happens now?"

We give you an e-mail address to deliver your report. You put the hood back on. Our people will drive you out of here. Then you get to work.

"I don't really like hoods."

For a hundred thousand, you can get over it. I don't think we trust each other enough that I believe you won't peek.

Gibson couldn't argue with that. What he needed was a plausible explanation for where he'd been since the attack on the paint store.

Being out in the fresh air felt good. It helped flush the adrenaline from Jenn's system. On the nearby chaise lounge, the furry belly of the sleep-ing sunbather rose and fell. He hadn't stirred and had no idea that the hotel had narrowly escaped a bombing. Jenn found that oddly calming. Life went on.

George sat beneath an umbrella at a poolside table. She couldn't put her finger on it, but he seemed more present. As if he'd woken from a long nap and rubbed the sleep from his eyes. He put a hand on her wrist and squeezed lightly.

"Are you okay?" he asked.

She nodded. "I'd be better if I knew what the hell just happened. Explosives don't typically disarm themselves."

"Agreed," Luisa said, emerging from the dark of the hotel. She joined them at the small table. "It was wired to a cellphone. Someone decided to spare us."

"Why?" Jenn said.

"My question exactly."

"Where is the boy?" George asked.

Luisa grimaced at the mention of João Luna. "He's fine."

"He had nothing to do with your hijacking."

"He has something to do with it now," she said.

"He goes free."

"That's not possible."

"He goes free or we're done here," George said. "The boy was only there to lure you into that hotel room. Or do you think he was a suicide bomber?"

"No," admitted Luisa. "But why? What purpose did it serve?"

"The same purpose as the paint cans," Jenn said.

"A diversion?" Luisa said skeptically.

George said, "How much time did we just waste? They gave you thirty-six hours to pay up, and they have you chasing dead ends all over the Algarve. I think they picked up your fishing-boat captain sometime this morning, drugged him, planted him in this hotel, and then switched his phone back on so you'd track him here."

Luisa thought this over. She clearly didn't like George's reasoning, but that didn't mean she disagreed with it. "We are being toyed with."

"We should be cautious about following any more easy leads," George said.

"Why didn't the bomb detonate?" Luisa asked.

No one had a good explanation for that one.

Luisa stood. "I would have killed him. Thank you."

"You're welcome," George said.

"But show me up in front of my men again, and you'll go a few rounds with Marco. Do you understand?"

"I understand," George said. "But the boy goes free."

Luisa acquiesced. "He goes free."

"Thank you," George said.

"I have one more question," Luisa said. "Where is Gibson Vaughn?"

Jenn looked at George. That was a good question.

CHAPTER SIXTEEN

The van coasted gently to a halt. Gibson allowed himself to be muscled out of the back and led away from the vehicle. Hands pressed him face-first against a wall. The duffel bag with the money landed heavily at his feet. His abductors retreated back the way they had come. When Gibson couldn't hear their footfalls, he counted to ten. Not because he'd been ordered, but because he felt grateful not to be dead and didn't care to tempt fate now.

He slipped off the hood and took his bearings. They'd left him in a narrow alley by a dumpster. That felt cruelly symbolic. He tossed the hood and walked out to the street, one hundred thousand to the good. The van was long gone, but he recognized the shopfronts. It was his neighborhood. Thoughtful of them. All things considered, he'd had worse bosses. Shouldering the duffel bag, he limped double-time back to his house.

Before going inside, he hid the duffel bag behind a clump of bushes until he knew for certain the house was empty. That done, he went back inside with the bag. There was a cubbyhole in the laundry room behind the stacked washer-dryer. Gibson waggled it out from the wall and stowed the duffel bag along with his passport and the few irreplaceable artifacts from his old life—a couple of his father's books, his old

Phillies baseball cap, photos of his daughter. Even after he put money aside for his ex-wife, there would be enough left to start over again somewhere else.

Upstairs, he ran the shower and peeled off his running clothes. His bloody sock went in the trash. In the shower, the dried blood washed away to reveal an ankle turning a royal purple and black. It was a miracle that it was unbroken and he could still walk on it.

Hendricks yanked open the shower curtain. It looked like his suit had been tie-dyed with him wearing it. The swirl of color was almost comically bright. Not that Hendricks was in a laughing mood. "What the hell happened to you? Been looking all over for your sorry ass."

Gibson gaped but managed not to slip and fall. Partly surprise, mostly uncertainty as to what to tell Hendricks. The consequences for revealing Dol5 to Baltasar Alves had been made painfully clear. Gibson realized that telling Hendricks was tantamount to telling the others, and he didn't know if he could count on Jenn or George to keep it in-house. So when he opened his mouth to answer, the lie tumbled out.

He told Hendricks that he'd gone over to the café for a sandwich— that much was true. He left out the panel van, the hood, or any mention of the conversation with Dol5. Instead, he said that when the shooting started, he'd slipped out the back and made a run for it down the ravine behind the café. He wasn't sure how convincing he was being, so he let the conditioner run into his eyes as he told the story. It gave him cover to look away and rinse his face. Gibson wasn't crazy about the way the story painted him as a coward who would abandon his friends, but he didn't see another way . . . at least for now.

Hendricks took in his story in silence and let out an unimpressed whistle when it was over.

"That the story you're going with?"

Gibson suddenly felt foolish and very naked. "For now."

Hendricks rubbed at the corner of his eye and then examined his fingernails for dried paint. "I got to be worried about you?"

"People keep asking me that."

"You keep worrying people."

"No more than usual," Gibson said.

"You understand how that doesn't put my mind at ease?"

That was fair. Gibson said, "How about I let you know when you should worry more than usual?"

"All right, then," said Hendricks. "Do me a favor, though. Tighten up your story some before Luisa gets here. English ain't her first language, but even she's not going to buy it."

"Any suggestions?"

"Yeah, at least say they came after you and you had to make a run for it. That way you won't sound like such a chickenshit."

"That's not bad, thanks," Gibson said and changed the subject. "How did you get out?"

"I didn't. One second, I thought we were cooked. Those boys opened up on us with an arsenal. Turned that paint shop into a sieve." Hendricks gestured to his paint-splattered suit. "Next thing I knew, they'd stopped and pulled back. Almost like they'd got what they'd come for."

"Weird," Gibson said.

"Yeah . . . weird."

"Glad you're all right, though."

"Ruined my damned suit."

"Doesn't look so bad."

Hendricks started to retort but stopped himself. Instead, he said, "George and Jenn ran into some trouble too."

Gibson played dumb. "Are they okay?"

"They're on their way now. I'll let them know you're in one piece."

"Appreciate it."

"Whatever. I need to change clothes," Hendricks said, closing the bathroom door.

Gibson toweled off and put on clean clothes. It was a small thing, but he felt a million times better. Never underestimate the power of a long, hot shower. He limped downstairs, drawn by the smell of food. His stomach growled—Dol5 had kidnapped him before he'd eaten his sandwich. Gibson found everyone crowded into the kitchen. It was a strangely domestic scene. Jenn and Hendricks stood over the stove. Platters of food were arranged on the counter. It wasn't fancy but would do the job. Luisa's men stood around with plates held up to their chins, shoveling food robotically into their mouths. Their eyes were glassy and unfocused like a boxer between rounds who had been knocked down and saved only by a lucky bell.

It had not been a good morning for Team Alves.

Gibson asked Jenn if there was anything he could do to help. She put him on coffee detail and clapped him on the back, all tension between them forgotten momentarily at the relief that neither had been hurt.

"Had me worried there," Jenn said.

"Figured you'd have another tracker sewn into my bag."

"Not this time," she said with a smile at the inside joke. If Hendricks had told her that he didn't believe Gibson's story, she didn't let on.

"Heard you had a situation yourself."

"Well, at least I didn't ruin my suit."

Hendricks frowned. "Okay, both of you can go screw yourselves. It was a good suit."

"It's gone to a better place now," Jenn said.

Gibson put his hand over his heart somberly.

"I've never hated anyone as much as I hate the pair of you," Hendricks said and turned back to the stove.

Jenn nudged Hendricks in the back, but he ignored her resolutely. Gibson felt suddenly happy to be surrounded by his people. He had flown to Europe to join them. They'd shared a home. But for six months, they had lived parallel lives that rarely intersected. He had tried organizing dinners to bring the four of them together, but someone always found an excuse to cancel. Gibson thought he understood. They were each the other's reminder of all they'd lost. Being together made forgetting the past impossible. Or what had brought them here. So it felt appropriate that it had taken an audacious drug heist to get them all in the same room.

Gibson made a fresh pot of coffee and fixed himself a plate. At the kitchen table, George was deep in conversation with Luisa and Anibal. They beckoned Gibson to join them. Anibal watched him through venetian-blind eyes.

"Some day, huh?" Gibson said, setting down his plate and sliding into a chair opposite.

"Good to see you," George said.

Luisa asked how Gibson had escaped from the gunfight at the hardware store. He walked her through his story, embellishing it with Hendricks's editorial suggestions. Must have told it better the second time through because, when he finished, Luisa didn't have him dragged outside and pistol-whipped. It didn't hurt that Hendricks interjected color commentary, bolstering his account. Even so, he was glad Jenn was standing behind him. It always made him feel bad to lie to her face.

Luisa studied him across the table. "My uncle is waiting for me. I should have left already, but I wanted to talk to you first."

"What about?"

"I need your help."

That was ironic because Gibson needed to help her too. He knew the reason for *his* change of heart—it was hidden behind the washing machine downstairs. He was less clear as to her motives.

"Why? I thought you didn't want anything to do with us. You made that point pretty explicitly this morning. I'm the crazy one, right?"

"I apologize for my choice of words," Luisa said.

"No offense, but I don't give a damn about your choice of words. What changed?"

"My uncle is waiting for an update. I have to look him in the eye and admit that the Romanians have outmaneuvered me. At every turn. In every way. That I am failing him, and that we are running out of time," Luisa said and paused. "It will not be pleasant."

The Romanians. In Luisa's mind, they remained the obvious culprits. Gibson knew better, but he could see how she had drawn that conclusion.

George spoke up. "Luisa and I have been talking. We both agree that it is in neither of our interest that this hijacking scheme come off. Neither is it in our interest that the four of us become enmeshed in her affairs beyond that. Gibson, I know you have expressed concerns that this might happen. She has given her word that it will not."

"Oh, well, that's a monumental relief," Gibson said.

Luisa glossed over his sarcastic tone. "You saw something at the cannery. Were you able to confirm your suspicions after I left?"

"No, I need to see your uncle's computer guy. Apparently, he's at Fernando's hotel."

"That is correct. I wanted him safely out of sight until this crisis was resolved," Luisa said.

"Well, we were heading there but got sidetracked by the paint-store fiasco."

"That was his idea," Anibal said, pointing at Hendricks.

"Oh, now this shit is my idea again," Hendricks snapped. "You sure you ain't from LA?"

"*You* found the receipt on the can."

"That wasn't what you told Baltasar, now, was it?"

Anibal cursed and began to rise from his seat.

"Enough," Luisa said. "The Romanians set their traps with great cunning. We all walked into them. No one is to blame for that."

Hendricks and Anibal continued staring each other down before finally Hendricks chuckled and turned back to the stove. Reluctantly, Anibal took his seat.

"So why are you telling me all this?" asked Gibson. "I already agreed to help Baltasar this morning."

"Because I know you don't approve. That you're only going along to support your friends. But I need more than that. Especially if you saw something that might help."

It was the second time today that someone had tried to inspire him. Who knew he had so many amateur life coaches concerned about his level of motivation?

"You mean rescue your massive pile of narcotics?"

Luisa took a breath. "Did George tell you how my uncle came into power here?"

"Yeah, it's quite a story."

"I understand your cynicism. Perhaps it is self-serving that I think of my uncle as a hero, but to me he did an incredible thing. Yes, he is a criminal. So am I. But do you have any idea how much money Baltasar cost himself in choosing to protect the Algarve?"

"Come on. He looks like he's got enough money."

"Oh, he does, without question, but how often has enough ever been enough? Power is a strange thing. It is the only appetite that grows the more it is fed. Sometimes, the best we can do is to not take everything."

"You're right," Gibson said. "That is self-serving."

"I have a child's memory of how bad it was before 2001. The decision by the government to decriminalize was an experiment born of desperation. One that many, both here and abroad, predicted would end in catastrophe. Now, almost twenty years later, Portugal has among the lowest rates of addiction anywhere in Europe. But that is not the whole story here in the Algarve. My mother had cocaine in her blood when she died. Did George tell you that too?"

"No, he didn't tell me that."

"Baltasar never kept what he was from me. I sat on his knee and listened while he and George conceived the plan to remake the Algarve.

At the time, Baltasar represented only one of several competing syndicates here in the Algarve. Some saw decriminalization as an invitation to expand operations, but my uncle saw things differently. His gift has always been anticipating change before anyone else. Seeing how it will affect business. He recognized what the government's policy would do for Portugal. Rather than fight it, he proposed that we embrace it.

"It was not a popular direction among all the syndicates. We are well compensated by the Mexicans. But we are not as prosperous as we would otherwise be. Not as feared. So it required great strength and persuasion to unite the Algarve behind his vision." She put a hand on Anibal's shoulder. "Anibal was the first. He took a huge risk joining my uncle. But his example helped the others see the wisdom of avoiding open war. And to see that the protection Baltasar offered from the police was more valuable than the higher profits offered by the drug trade," Luisa said and paused, collecting herself before going on. "My uncle has held the line for over fifteen years. Kept the peace. Until this morning. This morning has put all that in jeopardy. Our arrangement with the cartel, the peace, everything. And it has happened on my watch."

It was a good story, but Gibson didn't know what she hoped to accomplish by telling it. Did she think her uncle deserved a shiny new halo for passing Portugal's drug problem on to the rest of Europe? Simply because he was the least bad criminal wasn't a good enough reason for being his stooge. Not to Gibson. Of course, it wasn't lost on him that an hour ago he had agreed to help an anonymous hacker crew iron out their ransomware operation. Was he really so naïve as to think Dol5 was a Robin Hood? Stealing only from criminals? That once their tactics were perfected, they wouldn't set their ransomware loose on a noncriminal target? Maybe not, but they weren't at the moment, so they made for better allies than Baltasar.

The irony was that, in agreeing to help the hackers, he'd be working to find a way out for Baltasar. Didn't mean he actually had to disarm the shipment if he managed to figure out how. He could always pass his report on to the hackers and leave Baltasar to face the music. That was Gibson's first choice, because then George, Jenn, and Hendricks would have no choice but to quit screwing around and move on. What he couldn't anticipate was how the fall of Baltasar Alves would affect them. Whether they would be able to extricate themselves without the blame falling on their shoulders. Push came to shove, he could trade anything he found for an exit pass. In the meantime, he would play the good soldier. Just not *too* good.

"What are you offering?"

Luisa steeled herself. "I will remember my manners, and you will have gained an ally. Help me, and afterward, if you wish to leave the Algarve, I will make it happen. And if you wish to stay on, as you are now, I will make your stay comfortable."

"I think that's a very generous offer," George said, looking directly at Gibson—malcontent number one.

Gibson thought about playing hard to get, worried that if he rolled over too quickly she would become suspicious. But Luisa Mata was desperate enough to humble herself to a crazy man. Judging by her expression, she found it incredibly humiliating. She was beyond questioning his motives.

"I can live with that," Gibson said.

Everyone breathed a sigh of relief.

Luisa said, "Good. Then tell me why you need to speak to Dani Coelho. Give me something positive to take to my uncle. Do you think he is involved?"

"Not at this point, but I do think you've been hacked. I think that's how the hijackers knew so much about your security."

"Impossible. Our internal communications are encrypted."

"Maybe, but maybe not well enough. Is that cannery the hub of your computer network?"

Luisa's eyes narrowed. "Yes. How did you know that?"

"Because otherwise Anibal wouldn't have kicked up such a fuss when I asked for access to the server closet. I need to talk to Dani Coelho, and I need him to give me access to your servers."

"How much access?" Luisa asked.

"Do you want results, or don't you?"

She nodded grudgingly. "Anibal and Tomas will take you to see him. George, would you accompany me to see my uncle?"

"Why?" Jenn asked warily.

"Because my uncle trusts George more than he currently trusts any of us. Myself included. I would appreciate his presence when I relay my lack of progress."

"Then I'm coming with him," Jenn said. "That's nonnegotiable."

"As you wish."

"I'm gonna stick with Gibson," said Hendricks. "Keep an eye on things. If that's all right with you."

"You're going to be bored," Gibson said.

"Are you kidding? Boredom's my preferred state."

CHAPTER SEVENTEEN

It was late afternoon when Gibson and Hendricks, escorted by Anibal and Tomas, arrived at the Hotel Mariana. The restaurants that circled the top of the cliff were overrun by hungry tourists, and harried waiters darted between tables. Looking over the retaining wall at the beach down below, Gibson saw that most of the debris from the storm had been cleared away. He could still trace the remnants across the beach like a scar, but the people below were too busy having a good time to notice. Sunbathers were packed together like seals. Young people played volleyball. Soccer balls whistled back and forth. Swimmers bobbed rhythmically in the surf. Farther out, parasailing boats pulled tourists across a cloudless sky. It could have been any day for the last few months. Vacationers came, vacationers went, but they all spent their days the same way. How did they know how to do that?

Hendricks strolled up. He had traded in his ruined suit for more casual clothes. "We holding you up?"

"You know, I've been here six months. Haven't once gone in the ocean."

"That is a tragedy," Hendricks deadpanned. "But I don't know if this is the time."

"Just looks nice, you know? Look at them. I've never been parasailing."

"Parasailing sucks," Hendricks said solemnly. "Get pulled around like a sucker. Just another dope on the end of a line with no control. Got enough of that in our lives already, don't you think?"

"Why'd you cover for me back there?"

"Because you've turned into a terrible liar, and you needed the help." Hendricks put a hand on Gibson's shoulder. "Seriously, you're the worst."

"I got it."

"It's like watching a toddler drive stick."

"I got it," Gibson said.

"So, my turn. Why'd I *have* to cover for you back there?"

Gibson considered how to answer the question and decided to pose one of his own instead. "Let me ask you this. Anything I tell you, you're going to tell George, right?"

"That's how it works, Vaughn."

"And then George talks to Baltasar . . ."

Hendricks's eyes narrowed and his expression soured. "Listen to me, you little shit, George is—"

Anibal interrupted with a piercing whistle and gestured impatiently toward the hotel. Hendricks tried to buy himself a minute, but Anibal strode over to get to the bottom of the delay.

"We're not done here," Hendricks told Gibson and walked toward Anibal with an apologetic grin.

The sixth floor of the Mariana Hotel was only accessible by key card. Fernando was the floor's only permanent resident and frequently its only occupant. He lived in a palatial suite fronting the ocean that had been renovated to meet his exacting tastes. The remaining rooms on the sixth floor were available only to an exclusive clientele hand-selected by Fernando himself, most of them close, personal friends. From what Gibson could tell, Fernando had nothing but close, personal friends, and a lot of them.

Gibson had been to a few of Fernando's famous sixth-floor parties, but they weren't his scene. He enjoyed the people-watching but went home when the clothes started coming off. He didn't have anything against orgies, in theory, but in real life they smacked of people trying to convince themselves they were having a good time.

Gibson smelled the cordite even before the elevator reached the sixth floor. Anibal did as well and stepped to the side and drew his gun as the doors opened. Across from the elevator, a man sat slumped in an armchair. He'd been dead only a few minutes, and his shirt gleamed wet with blood. His weapon still dangled undrawn in its shoulder holster. The dead man had a strangely excited expression, as if he'd guessed the twist in a movie before anyone else and was only waiting to see if he was right. His partner had died second and didn't have a face, much less an expression. A gun lay near his outstretched hand.

Tomas paled at the carnage, his tough-guy act draining away along with the blood from his face. He dropped to one knee and vomited into the corner of the elevator. Probably missed his shotgun, Gibson thought unkindly. Anibal hissed at him to compose himself, but the boy remained in a crouch. Gibson couldn't fault him. What did it say about them that they didn't have the same reaction to death?

The elevator doors began to close.

Anibal put out a hand to stop them and stood there, frozen with indecision. The doors began to rock back and forth, trying stubbornly to close. Gibson gestured emphatically for Anibal to let them return to the lobby for reinforcements.

Anibal shook his head. "Fernando," he said and pointed down the hall.

"Fernando's up here?" Gibson asked.

Anibal nodded grimly. There could be no waiting for help. If Anibal stood back while Fernando was killed, Baltasar would skin him. There was no other choice for him. Anibal inched forward to glance around the corner. No one shot him in the head, so that was a net win. He pushed the button for the lobby and gestured for Gibson and Hendricks to stay in the elevator. Then he made a dash for the far wall at the junction of the corridor and elevator vestibule.

The life expectancy of a single man trying to clear a hallway was brief and bloody. Judging by the resignation on Anibal's face, he knew it. Gibson looked expectantly at Hendricks, who nodded wearily and reached out to block the elevator doors.

"I thought you didn't want to get involved," Hendricks said.

"And I thought you hated this guy."

"I can't stand by while this guy gets himself killed," Hendricks said. "Even if he is a prick."

"I will never understand you."

"Right back at you." They followed Anibal, arming themselves with the dead men's guns. Behind them, the elevator closed, taking Tomas down to the lobby. Anibal glanced back at them with a mixture of surprise and contempt. The guns in their hands presented an ethical dilemma, but he didn't protest. He had a better chance of making it to the end of the hall alive with them than without them. They all knew it. Didn't mean Anibal had to like it, and the scowl on his face communicated his displeasure at fate for giving him no better option than to trust this pair to watch his back.

It wasn't a long hallway, but it took forever to work their way down its length. Anibal was overly cautious, pausing at every half sound as if hearing the word of God. It chafed at Gibson's Marine training, which preached aggression. Caution was good to a point, but it could get you killed in situations like this. Anibal stopped again, hugging the wall and using a doorframe for cover. *No, thank you.* Gibson knelt in the center of the corridor instead. Bullets had a nasty habit of skating along walls until finding somewhere soft to call home.

At the bend, they found a third body. It looked like he had been caught by surprise but had fought back at almost point-blank range. He had emptied his gun wildly into the far wall. Hitting nothing. Not a damn thing. The only blood belonged to the dead man. Gibson found that unnerving. Whoever had attacked the hotel had moved like ghosts. The question now was whether they'd gotten what they'd come for and left, or whether they were still haunting the halls of the sixth floor.

Twenty feet down from the bend, a pair of legs jutted out from an open door. One ankle was crossed casually over the other, and because there were no obvious signs of violence, it was tempting to imagine that whoever it was had needed a quick rest.

Anibal stared at the legs as if contemplating a lost Michelangelo. Gibson had had enough art appreciation for one day. At this rate, it would take another three days to cover the remaining twenty feet. Taking the lead, he moved quickly to the doorway. Hendricks came up on his six, tapped him on the shoulder to let him know he was moving past him, and crossed the open doorway. When he felt Anibal kneel immediately behind him, Gibson moved in a wide, lateral arc until he could see into the room.

It was a grisly tableau.

The legs looked a lot less peaceful from this perspective. At the back of the hotel room, yet another body lay crumpled at the foot of a desk. That brought the total to five. Gibson gave Hendricks a nod, and the ex-cop slipped into the room. Gibson followed on his shoulder, and together they moved across the space. Anibal brought up the rear and looked around in dismay. Someone had carved a dreadful path through the sixth floor of the Mariana Hotel. There was no sign of Fernando Alves.

"Maybe it wasn't a hit," Hendricks said. "Maybe they snatched him."

Whatever hope Anibal might have taken from not finding Fernando among the bodies drained away. While some people found the silver lining in any situation, Hendricks saw only the rusted zipper.

Anibal walked back into the hall to make a call. Hendricks lit a cigarette and stood between the two bodies, studying the room.

"Hendricks," Gibson said. "Come on."

"What? These boys ain't gonna die of cancer." Hendricks stepped carefully around the hotel room, eyes down like he was a sapper clearing a minefield. Gibson saw him shifting into cop mode, so he left him to it and went back out to the hall while Anibal headed toward the elevator for privacy. At the other end of the hall, an emergency exit sign flickered. Curious, Gibson walked down to the fire door and stood in the stairwell, listening. The only sound he heard was his own breathing. The attackers were long gone. Like ghosts.

Why the hell would Dol5 hit the hotel? The paint store and the bomb in the boat captain's luggage made a certain kind of sense, but this was a massacre. And to what end? Had they taken Fernando Alves alive to keep his father off-balance?

Gibson walked back toward the room to see if Hendricks had figured out what was bothering him. A thud from inside the nearby maintenance closet startled him. He flinched hard, swinging his gun up in the direction of the sound. If he'd had his finger on the trigger, he would have put a round through the door.

Flattening himself against the wall, Gibson steadied his breathing. Maybe the attackers hadn't fled. Maybe they were spread out, hiding in closets and nearby rooms, looking to take out any first responders. He turned the doorknob. Gently. Gently. When the latch clicked, he gave the door a tug and pulled his hand back, letting the door swing open on its own.

"I have a gun," a voice said from the closet.

"Prove it," Gibson said.

"Gibson?" the voice said.

"Fernando?"

"Oh, thank God."

Gibson glanced inside. Fernando was crouched in the corner behind a housekeeping cart loaded with sheets and towels. He stood up sheepishly, showed his empty hands, and stepped out into the hall. He was still wearing his tuxedo. It had seen better days.

"Where's your gun?" Gibson asked.

Fernando made a pistol with his fingers. "Intimidated?"

Gibson shook his head. "Are you all right? Were you shot?"

"No, but look what the bastards did to my jacket." Fernando held it open so Gibson could see the two holes beneath his left arm. Six inches. That was all that separated Fernando from life and death.

Anibal came back around the corner, followed by Tomas and a half dozen men. He looked so relieved to see Fernando that Gibson thought he might break into song. The men circled Fernando like a protective detail while Anibal checked him for injuries.

"You're not shot," Anibal announced.

"Yes, I know."

"We're taking you to your suite."

Fernando protested that he was fine, but the phalanx of men hustled him away down the hall. Anibal led the way, barking orders to Tomas for a floor-by-floor sweep of the hotel. It left Hendricks and Gibson alone and forgotten among the bodies.

"Housekeeping's gonna need a raise."

Gibson stared after Fernando. "Whoever did this were pros. How the hell did they let Fernando get away?"

"They weren't after him."

"What do you mean? Of course they were after him. Look at this mess."

"Come on," Hendricks said. "I'll show you." He led Gibson back into the suite, stepping over the body in the doorway like it was a puddle on a rainy day. "Look at each body. See a difference?"

Gibson did—the body by the desk looked like it had been used for target practice. The torso was pulverized.

Hendricks said, "There are five bodies from the elevator—where this started—to where we are standing now. The first four were all shot two, maybe three, times. Enough to put them down and no more. But not desk guy. Someone worked out their issues on him. This guy they wanted *dead* dead. It ended here, with him."

"Why?" Gibson asked. "Who is it?"

"Given he's unarmed? My guess is Dani Coelho."

Gibson finally caught on to the significance of what Hendricks was trying to show him. "Fernando wasn't the target."

"The question is, why was Coelho?" Hendricks said. "And why now?"

"What do you mean?" Gibson asked.

"Someone knew we were coming."

That, Gibson had not considered.

"On the bright side, it looks like you're on the right track. Someone definitely did not want you talking to this guy."

If Fernando wasn't the target, had Dol5 anticipated Gibson's next move, taking out Dani Coelho before they could speak? If that was the case, then Dol5 wasn't planning on making it easy for Gibson to complete the job they'd hired him to do. Five men were dead. Five. It made Gibson angry. That hadn't been part of their deal. Although now Gibson realized he hadn't understood the full extent of their arrangement. He'd been lulled into a false sense of security by the immature tone of Dol5. But they had almost killed Hendricks at the paint store and had been prepared to blow Jenn to hell until Gibson agreed to their terms. Looking around at the carnage in the hotel room, Gibson knew he couldn't afford to take Dol5 lightly again.

"How did they know?" Gibson asked rhetorically.

"That's our Final Jeopardy category, right there."

"Maybe our house is wired?" Gibson suggested. That was where they'd discussed coming here.

"We only got brought into this thing this morning. I'm a pretty competent surveillance guy, but that would have been moving fast."

"So how?" Gibson asked.

"I don't know. Could be electronic. Or could be we just have a good old-fashioned snitch. One of Baltasar's people. So best we don't tell anyone until we're certain."

"Well, you're nothing but good news," Gibson said.

Hendricks smiled and lit yet another cigarette. "That's me. A ray of goddamn sunshine."

CHAPTER EIGHTEEN

Jenn had been in meetings like this in the CIA.

Humiliation by debrief.

She remembered being grilled for hours after an operation had gone pear-shaped. Her decisions dissected by bureaucrats who hadn't set foot in the field in decades. She remembered the palpable condescension of their questions. The underlying assumption that nothing could ever be an accident. It was simply a matter of assigning blame. Why had she done this and not that, they would ask, as if the answer should have been obvious even without the benefit of hindsight.

Everyone was an expert after the fact.

That's how it went for Luisa now. Baltasar sitting back in his leather armchair, listening to her cascading series of setbacks, slowly strumming the scar on his chest like the last string on a broken instrument. He interrupted frequently, breaking her train of thought to ask pointed, critical questions. Forcing her back over the same ground again and again. It was enough for Jenn to feel a sense of solidarity with Luisa and to wish that she had a silver lining to offer her uncle. For all their sakes.

Off to the side, Silva and Peres listened to Luisa defend herself. Anibal's seat was conspicuously empty.

That was part of the problem.

Baltasar had summoned Anibal the same as Luisa, but she had over-ruled her uncle and sent Anibal to chaperone Gibson Vaughn instead. As Luisa talked, Baltasar kept glancing toward the vacant seat—the symbol of her defiance—while his mood darkened. Luisa had managed day-to-day operations for the last five years, but Baltasar was still the boss. So, who actually called the shots? As Baltasar picked Luisa apart, Jenn could feel him reminding his niece that there was only one answer to that question.

It was also meant as a reminder to his two lieutenants, who, truth be told, didn't look very happy to be there. They sat silently like boys in church who weren't about to allow the word of God into their hearts. It didn't surprise Jenn. For most, loyalty lasted only as long as interests aligned. Baltasar looked vulnerable, so that meant he was vulnerable. The hijacking had weakened him. Hell, allowing the Romanians to remain in the Algarve two years ago had weakened him. It was a bad look for a crime boss, and Baltasar knew it.

Jenn didn't think the lieutenants were in open rebellion. Not yet. But that didn't mean they weren't weighing their options. Most likely, all three were communicating through back channels. They would be feeling out the others' loyalty to Baltasar. None would want to be the first to broach the subject of a coup, but it was on their minds. Jenn could see it. They were already carving up the Algarve after the Mexican cartel had dealt with the Alves clan.

Baltasar could see it too. The creeping doubt. Not knowing whom to trust, needing to trust someone, but aware that choosing wrong would be catastrophic. It meant no one was above suspicion. Not even Luisa. Had his niece grown tired of playing number two? Was she making her move? Was that why she'd sent Anibal away? To signal that she was open to the idea of change?

Hence Baltasar's cruel interrogation.

"Stop." Baltasar rubbed his forehead as though the sound of Luisa's voice was giving him a headache. "This is my fault. I've done this.

Through negligence and arrogance. I thought I could step back and things would go on as they always have. That my reputation would be enough so I could put a woman in charge." He looked at his niece. "What a fool I was. Once you take away the guard dog, sooner or later the thieves return to take what is yours."

Luisa looked stricken but bore her uncle's insults stoically. Jenn had been on the receiving end of this kind of contempt too. Men never made mistakes because they were men. They made mistakes because they were stupid, incompetent, lazy—individual character flaws. But when a woman screwed up, it was a referendum on her entire gender. George Abe was the only boss she'd ever had who hadn't treated her that way. She didn't want to imagine how that would feel coming from him, but she could guess, looking at Luisa's face. Not that Jenn was convinced that any of this had been her mistake.

Then the call came in and everything went to hell.

A nervous assistant interrupted to hand Baltasar a phone. He waved her away, but she held her ground and said it was Anibal. That piqued Baltasar's curiosity. He put the phone to his ear. Whatever he heard got him up and out of his chair and pacing the room. He spoke in clipped, angry Portuguese. From what Jenn could glean, there had been an attack at the Mariana Hotel. Men had been shot and killed. She couldn't tell whom or how many, but Gibson and Hendricks had been heading there. That was enough to give her a sick feeling in the pit of her stomach. If either of them had been hurt or killed . . . She didn't like thinking about what came after that thought.

Baltasar flung the phone away, sending it skipping over the tile floor. "My son," he bellowed in Portuguese. "Someone tried to murder my son. In the middle of the afternoon. At his hotel." His finger drifted accusingly to the two lieutenants, who shrank back into the couch. "If I discover you were involved or knew anything about this . . ." He trailed off, leaving the threat implied.

Baltasar threw himself into his armchair and ran his hands through his hair. "Fortunately, Anibal arrived before the Romanians could finish the job." He looked up and found his niece's eyes. "You saved my son."

It was as close to an apology as Luisa was ever likely to hear. But it put her back in her uncle's good graces. At least until the next time he remembered she was a woman, Jenn thought cynically. It was enough for Luisa, though, who knelt beside him and took his hand. Jenn couldn't decide if that was weakness or strength. The old boss pulled her close.

"Those Romanian dogs tried to kill Fernando."

"Then we hit them," Luisa said without hesitation. "Drive them from Quarteira and back into the sea."

"That won't save the shipment."

"It doesn't make any difference now," Luisa said. "Perhaps we will get lucky before the deadline, but we can't afford to hope. We must assume the shipment is lost."

"Then *we* are lost. The cartel will come."

"Yes, they will come. But why?" Luisa asked.

"Retribution for losing their shipment."

"No, they will come to find our replacements. All they care about is their money. They need business to resume as quickly as possible."

"It amounts to the same thing for us."

"Not necessarily," Luisa said, making her case to her uncle. "What if, when they come, there is no one left to replace us? If they're forced to start from scratch, it will cost them time and money to reproduce what you have built. What if we give them no choice but to make a deal with us?"

"But the shipment?"

"They will require us to make reparations. No doubt it will be painful, perhaps even crippling for a time, but they will have no choice but to continue as before. That is all that matters. That we go on."

"Can it be done?" Baltasar asked.

"Only if there are no other options available to them when they arrive."

Baltasar realized what she was suggesting. "What about them?" He gestured to the two lieutenants.

Luisa drew her gun smoothly, trained it on the floor. From where Silva and Peres sat, they couldn't see what she'd done. Perhaps that was why they didn't fully grasp the precariousness of the moment. They sat there in their seats like boys waiting to see the principal, neither offering more than mild protestations of loyalty. It wouldn't have made any difference, though. No one named Alves or Mata was listening anymore. Luisa looked from her uncle to the lieutenants and back again. Asking the question. He looked steadily at his niece. When he nodded, it was no more than a single degree. One degree was all she needed.

Luisa shot the lieutenants where they sat. One bullet apiece. It happened with such speed that they barely had time to put up their hands. The first died instantly, but the second fell from his seat and began to crawl toward the window and the ocean. Luisa followed him unhurriedly while he sobbed and bled. She did not miss a second time.

The gunfire drew guards, who burst in with weapons drawn. All were Baltasar's men, in theory, but some worked directly for the lieutenants. At the sight of the two dead men, they stumbled to a halt as they absorbed what had happened. Shock and anger stiffened them, but Luisa headed off their emotions before they could coalesce into any kind of coherent impulse. She appealed directly to them. Gun down at her side. Assuring them they would not be harmed if they surrendered their weapons.

"These men are traitors," she said, gesturing to the dead lieutenants. "But we will know none of you are involved if you show loyalty now. Place your weapons on the ground. Do it now. Otherwise, you will never see your wives and children again."

For a moment, nothing happened. War appeared poised to break out in Baltasar's own living room. Then one of the men knelt slowly and placed his gun at his feet. He stood and showed Luisa his palms. That capitulation set off a chain reaction among the men, who one by one followed his example.

"Thank you, my friends," Luisa said and ordered them removed.

Jenn couldn't take her eyes off the two dead men. How utterly screwed were she and George? It worried her that neither Baltasar nor Luisa seemed particularly concerned that Jenn and George had seen them kill two men. But then it wasn't any harder to dispose of four bodies than two. She reckoned they were about to learn how close Baltasar and George really were.

Luisa turned to her uncle, gun still in hand.

"Anibal?" she asked.

"No, he was the first to join me. He's been loyal from the beginning," Baltasar said.

"This isn't the beginning. It's the end. The cartel would certainly consider him a viable replacement. This is the wrong time for sentiment."

"He just saved my son. I will not reward him with a bullet. Not unless he gives us reason."

"The hijacking happened in his territory. Isn't that reason enough?"

That was their prompt to remember George and Jenn. Baltasar studied them somberly like a doctor searching for the right way to deliver bad news. Luisa stood beside him, waiting for his diagnosis. Jenn had a bad feeling that the cure would hurt worse than the disease.

"I'm sorry you had to witness that," Baltasar said.

Jenn didn't care for that word. Witness.

"Nothing I haven't seen before," George said. "It reminds me of that morning in Tavira. Remember?"

Baltasar nodded somberly. "As if I could forget. Almost twenty years now, and I still see their faces."

"I see them as well," George said. "But I've never spoken of it."

"That was a hard day."

"True, but the tide turned for you as a result."

"It gave me no pleasure."

"And that is why I respect you and keep your secrets."

"You've always been a good friend," Baltasar said and seemed to noticed Luisa for the first time. He gestured for her to holster her weapon.

"*Tio?*" she said.

"It's all right. George and I understand each other."

After spending the day in her company, Jenn was getting to know Luisa's expressions. Luisa didn't like the answer, and had more to say, but the gun disappeared from sight.

"What do you think?" Baltasar asked George, meaning the two dead men.

"I think that we are not cartel material," George said, reminding Baltasar and Luisa that if the Mexicans went looking for their replacements, the Americans weren't viable replacements.

Baltasar laughed as if George had told a good joke. "No, I suppose not."

George said nothing.

"It had to be done," Baltasar said, meaning Silva and Peres. "And there is so much left to do if we are to survive this."

"Hard choices, without question," George said, neutral as a Swiss mountain.

"So, what do you say? Will you help me now before the cartel comes? As you did once before? They cannot see us as weak, and I could use your vision. I fear I have lost perspective, and no one sees the big picture quite like George Abe."

"I'll help you make the peace, my friend, but I can't help you wage a war."

"War is now the only option."

"Then the answer is no."

Jenn held her breath. She hoped George knew what he was doing. Turning Baltasar down was risky. George and Baltasar liked to dress things up in a civilized veneer, but only moments ago, Baltasar had been contemplating whether to add their bodies to the pile. It wasn't too late for second thoughts. Baltasar shifted forward in his seat. He looked none too happy. Jenn had never wanted a gun more in her life.

Baltasar said, "The Romanians started it the moment they took my shipment."

"You don't even know if it was the Romanians."

"It makes no difference now," Luisa said. "They can't be allowed to remain. The war is begun."

"It's not a war until you retaliate," George said.

"And if I don't?" said Baltasar. "What do you think they will think then?"

"That you are weak," George said. "But others have thought the same in the past. That has its advantages too."

"You don't understand the cartels. They don't care for chess. They'd prefer to burn the board and play a different game."

"Then you really don't want my help. I don't know how to play that game."

Baltasar sighed in disappointment. Luisa had the gun in her hand again.

Jenn didn't remember her drawing it.

CHAPTER NINETEEN

The brutality of the attack at the Mariana Hotel had shaken everyone. It was a tight-knit organization, a family affair that extended far beyond the Alves clan. Everyone knew the men who had died. It took hard-won experience to know how to respond. Experience that Baltasar Alves's people sorely lacked after almost two decades of peace. Gibson could see it on their faces. The anger and the accompanying frustration that came from having nowhere to put it. Gibson and Hendricks did their best to stay out of the way. They didn't belong here now, and eventually, if given no one else to focus on, the men's anger would settle on them.

It came as a relief when Tomas arrived to escort them out of the hotel. It certainly wasn't the heroes' send-off to which Hendricks felt entitled. They were disarmed brusquely and treated like potential threats. Zero appreciation for the risks they had taken on behalf of their boss's son. Tomas had rediscovered his tough-guy posture and mistaken being given a task by Anibal for actual authority. He bossed the men around as if he were an old-time movie gangster and not a green recruit. His act didn't play well with his vomit still stinking up the elevator. Hendricks waved his hand theatrically in front of his face at the smell. The men smirked. Apparently, the story had already gotten around. Tomas colored and fell silent.

The elevator opened into the parking garage beneath the hotel. Tomas tossed Gibson a set of car keys and pointed to Fernando's Porsche. Gibson smiled. He could imagine Fernando saying, "Not to keep. It just wouldn't do to have my valiant rescuers sent home in a cab. It would ruin my story." He had no doubt that Fernando's story would turn hiding in a closet into a manly act of heroism. The man had a gift for self-promotion.

Before Gibson could try out Fernando's car, Hendricks plucked the keys out of his hand and slid behind the wheel.

"Hey, I've never driven a Porsche before," Gibson said.

"All the more reason to leave it to the professionals."

Gibson rolled his eyes but got in the passenger side without argument. To be honest, he was interested to see Hendricks behind the wheel of a sports car. The ex-cop had taught at a tactical driving school in California and was the best driver that Gibson had ever been around. Riding with Hendricks was like gliding on air. He possessed an almost preternatural anticipation; even on the clogged streets of Albufeira, you felt no sense of acceleration or braking. You might even forget that you were in motion at all. Gibson sat back and enjoyed the ride.

A call came in. Hendricks fished a phone out of his jacket pocket. It was Jenn. She did most of the talking, Hendricks most of the grunting. When he hung up, he broke the news to Gibson.

"Baltasar just cut us loose."

"What the hell happened?"

"He's going to war with the Romanians. Asked George to help with his little purge. When George declined, Baltasar kind of lost his shit and gave us twenty-four to clear out of Portugal. Apparently, it was a toss-up between that or a shallow grave. The man did not see the bright side of the hit on Fernando."

"Who told him it was a hit on Fernando?" Gibson said.

"Anibal would be my guess. Probably so busy casting himself as the Portuguese John McClane that it would be the only conclusion Baltasar *could* reach. He's gearing up for war with the Romanians. Sounds like Luisa's leading the charge."

"What a clusterfuck this is turning out to be."

"People are gonna die, that's just how it'll go," Hendricks said. "The way Anibal keeps stepping on my dick? Man is auditioning for something. Luisa too. No one wants to be caught without a seat when the music stops, that much I know."

Gibson frowned. Being ejected from Portugal didn't work. It didn't work at all. He still needed access to the cannery. No access meant no penetration test. No penetration test meant no hundred thousand. Money that would come in especially handy now that they had no choice but to resume their lives on the run.

Hendricks eyed him. "What are you moping about? You got your wish. We're out. Baltasar fired us. We're on our own."

"Nothing," Gibson said without conviction, too focused on how to get back into the cannery to lie convincingly. "I just—"

"You just what?" Hendricks pulled the Porsche over to the side of the road and killed the engine. "Suddenly you want to stick around and help Baltasar? Out of the goodness of your heart? Is that it?"

"It was an interesting challenge," Gibson said, aware of how little sense he was making.

Hendricks stared at him levelly.

"What?" Gibson asked defensively.

"I think it's time."

"Time for what?"

"For you to tell me what's up with the bag of euros stashed behind the dryer."

"Oh," Gibson said lamely.

"Yeah . . . 'Oh.'"

"How did you know about that?"

"I'm a detective. I detected."

Gibson studied Hendricks. "Does Jenn know?"

"Not unless you told her yourself."

"Thank you. Let's go back to the house. I'll tell you everything."

"Tell me everything here," Hendricks said, staring straight ahead. "I don't trust that house."

"What do you want to know?"

"Let's make a deal. Just start talking, don't treat me like an idiot for once, and I'll let you know when you're done."

Sounded fair to Gibson, so they sat in the Porsche while he told the whole story—getting grabbed at the café, the stash house, the odd video-conference, and the unexpected job offer. Gibson saw no reason to hold anything back now. Although the telling of it made him acutely aware of how preposterous it all sounded. The unvarnished truth sometimes had a way of coming out like a lie. It didn't help that Hendricks listened without comment, his expression one of practiced boredom. A detective's face.

Gibson ended his story with Hendricks interrupting him in the shower. Hendricks nodded, but his expression still didn't change.

Gibson said, "That's it. That's everything."

"No, that's just the what. Still nowhere near the why."

"The why what?"

"Why you held out," Hendricks said. "Planning on cutting us out?"

"What?" Gibson said, genuinely offended. "No. That wasn't it."

Hendricks grew impatient. "Then why? Because I'm not seeing it."

"Because it's been time for us to move on. For a while now. Problem was, this place has been an easy paradise and nobody wanted to think about what came after. We've all gone soft."

"And *after* has arrived. I get it. Still doesn't tell me why you held out on us. You made this play before Baltasar stamped our exit visas."

"The money gives us options. If we had to run, which now we do. I couldn't risk jeopardizing it."

"You didn't trust us? That what you're saying?"

Gibson shrugged. "It's real nice here."

"Fuck you, boy." Hendricks started the Porsche, then cut it again. "This the same shit you been pulling since Pennsylvania."

"To be honest, I didn't need your help."

"Notice how that usually ends with me cutting you down from a rope?"

"Funny you should mention that."

Hendricks swiveled slowly and shook his head sadly at Gibson. Like a man who knew he couldn't get out of the path of that train barreling down on him.

"You know we could really use that money," Gibson said.

"And?" Hendricks said, making Gibson say it.

"And I need your help."

"You want to go back to the cannery and get me shot."

"Possibly," Gibson admitted.

"How're we even going to get in?"

"I was thinking through the front gate."

"Baltasar fired our asses, remember?"

"Yeah, but we only know that because Jenn called you."

Hendricks thought about it. "Tomas didn't know shit, did he?"

"You think we'd be in a Porsche right now if he did? I think Baltasar pitched a fit, told Jenn and George to get bent, but was too busy planning his war to actually pass word to his troops."

"So we roll up in his son's Trojan Porsche like everything's everything?"

"Something like that," Gibson said, then had a discouraging thought. "Shit. The keys. We forgot Dani Coelho's keys." Getting access to the server closet had been their whole reason for going to the Hotel Mariana, but in the chaos, he'd forgotten all about it.

Hendricks produced a thick ring of keys from his pocket and tossed them to Gibson. "You mean these keys?"

Gibson looked at them in disbelief. "How did you do that?"

"I'm a detective," Hendricks said, starting the car and throwing it in gear. "I detected."

CHAPTER TWENTY

Word of the attack at the hotel had already reached Fresco Mar Internacional. The guards at the gate met the Porsche with weapons ready. Gibson recognized the men from this morning, which was probably the only reason that they didn't shoot on sight.

A good first step.

"They'll wait 'til we get out so our blood doesn't stain Fernando's upholstery," Hendricks said, cracking a tight smile.

The guards asked them their business in Portuguese. At least that was Gibson's best guess, based on their posture and tone. He really should have learned more of the language. Hendricks explained in English that they were there to examine the server closet. It didn't translate, so Gibson did the most American thing he could think of and pointed at the cannery and said, "Server closet," loudly and slowly. As if that had ever worked once in human history. Both sides tried again. The language barrier stretched and flexed but did not break.

"Luisa Mata," Hendricks said, pointing to themselves and then the cannery.

That seemed to make an impression. The guards paused to talk among themselves. One gestured to the Porsche and said, "Fernando Alves."

"*Sim*, Fernando Alves. *Sim*." Gibson pointed agreeably toward the cannery again, holding up Dani Coelho's keys. There were probably techniques for social-engineering someone in a foreign language; Gibson didn't happen to know any of them. Hendricks joined him, and together they pointed in unison like a couple of backup dancers in a music video. The guards didn't appear to be music fans.

One held up a hand for silence and made a phone call.

"Okay, this is the part where we get properly shot," Hendricks said.

"If it goes bad, we just say we didn't get word."

"Oh, I'm sure they'll buy that."

The guard stood there on the phone in silence for what felt like an eternity. At first, Gibson thought he was listening to instructions. That wasn't it. He was on hold. Finally, someone got on the line, and the guard explained his situation for a second time. Whatever the person on the other end said caused the guard to explode in anger. A yelling match ensued. Finally, he hung up in frustration, conferred with his partner, and waved the Porsche inside.

"How the hell did that work?" Hendricks said.

Gibson shrugged. "Chaos. Baltasar is too busy going to war to take calls."

It was his first and most reliable principle—in any security setup: the human was always the weakest link. Security depended on calm, rational actors, and those were in short supply in the Algarve today. Once again, simple human error had been his ticket inside a place he wasn't supposed to be. That and a healthy dose of luck.

They parked around back. Hendricks drew a gun and popped the magazine so he could count the remaining rounds. Gibson stared at it. They'd been made to give up their weapons back at the hotel but hadn't been searched. Hendricks must have helped himself to another when he was alone in the hotel room. Hendricks caught him staring and arched one eyebrow.

"Do you have one for me?" Gibson asked.

Hendricks shook his head. "Weren't on the same side then, Mr. Hold Out on His Friends."

"We're friends?" Gibson said with honest surprise.

Hendricks looked him up and down. "Get out of the damn car before I loan you a bullet."

They went up the ramp and into the warehouse. The mountain of drugs remained undisturbed, the yellow line of paint still leading to nowhere. A lone guard sat at the security desk, shivering in a Fresco Mar parka. He must have been the low man on the totem pole to draw the unenviable task of watching a pile of narcotics wired with high explosives. They gave him a friendly wave and made a slow circuit around the shipment. Gibson wanted to make sure he hadn't missed anything, and to refresh his memory of the layout. He pointed out to Hendricks the five cables that ran up the column and disappeared into the Fresco Mar cable tray.

"We find where those terminate, and we're in business," Gibson said.

"And you're thinking the server closet?"

"Well, my first guess was the roof, but the server closet makes sense too."

They stopped at the security desk to pick up Gibson's messenger bag, which had been delivered sometime in the last few hours. The guard was friendly and bored out of his mind. He introduced himself as Filipe, and as luck would have it, he spoke decent English. He pointed them in the direction of the server closet and gave them a walkie-talkie in case they got lost or had any questions. Hendricks sat on the edge of the desk and chatted with him while Gibson made sure everything he needed was in his bag. When they left, Filipe seemed genuinely disappointed to see them go.

"Nice kid," Hendricks said as they walked away. "Dumb, but nice."

The server closet was down a carpeted hallway and through the dark, empty cubicles of the Fresco Mar offices. It was a small, windowless eight-by-eight concrete box with plywood-covered walls and a vinyl-tiled floor. Gibson had worked in a dozen exactly like it. The white noise of fans and air-conditioning greeted them at the door. From experience, Gibson knew the sound would gradually make a person lose all track of time.

At most, Gibson expected to find a switch, a firewall, and perhaps a single, older server. Plenty of juice for a business this size. What he didn't expect was a SAN or the stack of high-end servers. A SAN, or storage area network, was essentially rack after rack of hard drives linked together to manage and used to store data. Finding one in a sardine cannery was a bit like finding a smartphone on an Amish farm. There was no earthly reason a business this size would need it. He couldn't imagine what else Baltasar might be into. Digital piracy, perhaps? In any event, that wasn't why they were here. Best to stay focused.

Gibson took a moment to orient himself and visualize how everything was laid out. Overall, it looked as if Dani Coelho had done reasonably tidy work. It would make spotting anything new or hastily installed that much easier to find.

The server racks were mounted on the floor, far enough from the wall to allow access from all sides. Gibson shimmied around to the far side and began checking the cabling. Sure enough, after a few minutes of hunting, he found five network cables that came into the room along with the Fresco Mar cabling but were a different color and bundled separately.

"Found it," he said to himself.

"Cool. Can't we just unplug it and go home?"

"Sure, if you want to risk vaporizing Baltasar's shipment. If it were me, I would have programmed in a dead man's switch to interpret any tampering as a self-destruct signal."

"Great," Hendricks said. "How do people work in places like this?"

Alone, preferably. Gibson traced Dol5's cables to the core switch. What he needed now was access to the firewall between the network switch and the outside world. Problem was, it would be password protected from remote access. However, console ports often weren't—networks were designed to defend against hacks from the outside; they tended to trust anyone with physical access. Gibson hoped Dani Coelho wasn't an exception to the rule.

Fortunately, it turned out he wasn't. Once Gibson connected his laptop to the firewall, the first thing he noticed was an enormous amount of encrypted traffic originating from a single offsite IP address. Gibson felt his curiosity flare up again, but since the encrypted data wasn't in the same network range as the cannery, he disregarded it. He didn't have time to be nosing around and frankly didn't want to know any more about Baltasar's other operations than absolutely necessary. Problem was, he saw very little network traffic otherwise. It almost seemed as if the defenses around the shipment were asleep.

Something caught his eye. A short burst of encrypted data repeating itself at regular intervals. It looked very much like a "keep-alive." Back in his Marine days, when Gibson had been with the Activity, he'd worked in a SCIF—sensitive compartmented information facility—which was explicitly designed to protect classified data. One of its failsafe security precautions was a keep-alive. Rather than only sounding an alarm when something failed or was tampered with, a SCIF actively beaconed out to a monitoring team that everything was normal. Passive alarms were much easier to defeat than active defenses. Gibson timed the interval—eight seconds. The US standard. Gibson smiled as he realized what Dol5 had done. The entire hijacking had been designed like an American SCIF.

Almost.

There was a flaw in Dol5's design. An American SCIF had two keep-alive signals—a primary and a secondary—but here Gibson saw only one. Curious again, he reconfigured the Fresco Mar firewall to temporarily block the keep-alive. Moments later, a second signal beaconing out in its place along a new path. That was a serious configuration error:

Dol5's secondary path only became active if the first was compromised. That gave Gibson an idea. He had Hendricks radio out to Filipe, who answered the call eagerly.

"Hey, Filipe. Would you do us a favor and go step across that yellow line?" Hendricks asked.

Filipe didn't think that sounded like a very good idea at all. Gibson couldn't say he blamed him. Hendricks assured Filipe that he would be helping to save the shipment and that Baltasar would be very grateful. That seemed to mollify Filipe, who agreed to help. Hendricks pressed the walkie-talkie to his chest. "I almost feel guilty about this. I could just go do it."

"No, if I'm right, I don't want Dol5 to see it's us. Better for us if it's just Filipe the curious squirrel."

Filipe's voice, nervous and small, announced that he was at the yellow line and stepping over. Hendricks made the sign of the cross and rolled his eyes. A moment later they heard the alarm sound through the walkie-talkie, and Hendricks had to twist the volume way down. On his laptop, Gibson saw network traffic spike dramatically as the keep-alive became an active alarm and four new devices began streaming large chunks of data. Those would be the four cameras powering up so Dol5 could see for himself.

That was interesting.

Filipe asked nervously if it would be okay if he got out of the circle now. Hendricks told him to act afraid and to run back to the security desk.

"I don't need to pretend, *senhor*," Filipe said.

"I really like this kid," Hendricks told Gibson.

The countdown stopped and the alarm sounded the all-clear. A few minutes later, the cameras shut off too. Network traffic returned to normal. That gave Gibson several crucial insights into Dol5. First, the hacker's design wasn't fully automated. The motion sensors alerted Dol5 if anyone crossed his yellow line, only then powering on the cameras so

Dol5 could personally assess the situation. While Gibson understood the impulse, it was a bad one that left Dol5 vulnerable. Gibson couldn't prove it, but despite the countdown and all the theatrics, he had to believe that Dol5 also had manual control of the explosives.

Gibson sketched out a diagram of how he could not only deactivate the explosives, but also—if his guess was right—reconfigure the alarm to wrest away control of the cameras and explosives without Dol5 even knowing. Dol5 would keep his access to the motion detectors and the alarms, but any attempt to detonate would be greeted with a whimper, not a bang. That would be kind of sweet. Obviously, that wasn't the goal, not the main one anyway, but he would dearly enjoy pwning Dol5. The thought of taking the hacker down a peg or two made Gibson's evil little heart smile.

It took him thirty minutes of gentle probing to be sure, and another hour to circumvent Dol5's defenses, take control of the explosives, and give himself remote access and control of the explosives through the secondary path. All in all, a pretty slick piece of work, if he did say so himself. And who else would? Even if Hendricks understood what he'd done, he wasn't the impressing kind.

All the while, the huge dataflow that Gibson had chosen to ignore continued to pour into Fresco Mar. He did his best to tune it out, but his eye kept wandering back to his network mapper. He didn't want to know, but at the same time he *had* to. In his defense, there wasn't a hacker alive who, given access to a mobster's server, wouldn't feel the same itch. The same unhealthy curiosity and disregard for privacy had been getting Gibson into trouble since high school.

After all, he told himself, if you really wanted to keep a secret, you shouldn't be plugging it into the internet in the first place.

So, as he was wrapping up his hack of Dol5, Gibson took a little look-see at what was being saved to Baltasar's SAN. To his surprise, it was mostly video. Hundreds of terabytes' worth. They were grouped by date, so Gibson opened the most recent folder and clicked on the first file.

His arms went cold, as if the video playing on his laptop had reached up through the keyboard and drained the heat from his body. His hands recoiled, and he balled them into fists against his mouth, using them to shield his eyes to block part of the screen. As if that made any difference at all. He watched, throat unable to decide if it wanted to throw up or not. Gibson didn't care either way anymore.

Hendricks noticed the change and, with a puzzled expression, walked behind Gibson to see for himself. Most days, Gibson would describe Hendricks as one of the most unflappable people that he had ever known. Twenty-two years in the LAPD had given him plenty of time to build sturdy armor against the terrible things people did to one another. That armor didn't work now.

"Oh, what the fuck is that!" Hendricks said, his voice rising to a scream as he repeated the question two or three more times when the universe didn't see fit to reply.

To confirm his worst suspicions, Gibson opened other files. It was more of the same and worse. Slowly, the true nature of what they were looking at dawned on him.

"What do we do?" Gibson asked.

"We have to show this to George and Jenn. Can you copy it?"

"Not all of it; there's a thousand hours of video stored here. Maybe more."

"Get what you can," Hendricks said. "We have to get out of here. Now."

That was for damn sure. Gibson put his head down and got to work while Hendricks packed up and got ready to go.

By the time Gibson was done, the feeling of anguish that had greeted him after seeing the videos had worn away and was replaced with a much simpler emotion. Anger.

CHAPTER TWENTY-ONE

Usually after a trip to Lisbon to visit the team doctors, Sebastião returned motivated and would hunker down in his gym for hours. Good news or bad, it made no difference. The personal demons that had driven him to become one of his sport's greats wouldn't allow him rest. Not today, though. Jenn flicked on the lights and looked at all the exercise equipment. His car was parked out front, so he must be home. She walked through empty room after empty room, calling his name, feeling nostalgic for Sebastião and his big, dumb disco ball of a house.

In the dark of the living room, she sat on the bench of a grand piano. Sebastião couldn't play but had it tuned once a week. The world's largest paperweight. Jenn struck and held a key, listening as the clear tone filled and then faded to silence. She saw the flat circles of Luisa's eyes floating in the dark. Wondered again how she wasn't dead. Jenn had been in danger many times before, but she'd never thought she'd be a spectator to her own execution. It had been simple enough math for Luisa—leave no witnesses. How long had Baltasar and George stared each other down? Time had bent around them. And then the endless moment had ended. Baltasar said no.

Why had Baltasar spared them? Why was Jenn questioning miracles? With two of Baltasar's lieutenants dead and Luisa en route to

Quarteira to launch a surprise attack on the Romanians, the historic Pax Algarve was fast unraveling. She needed to find Sebastião, say her good-byes, and get the hell out of Dodge.

Out a window, she saw him on a lounge chair, staring at the ocean. It was a strangely melancholy sight. He wasn't a man ever to sit still. Even at night, in bed, he tossed and turned restlessly, as if chasing after a ball that remained just out of reach. And he was never, ever alone if he could help it. To see him doing both at once was unsettling. Where was the household staff? Jenn wondered. Where was everyone?

For a moment, she thought about following their lead and ghosting without saying good-bye. Rationalized that it would be easier on both of them. She ran her tongue over her teeth. In her experience, good-byes were overrated. All it did was prolong the inevitable, and besides, if you needed a good-bye to let someone know how you felt, then it couldn't have been that important a relationship in the first place.

She realized then how much she would miss him.

That surprised her. She thought she'd done a better job compart-mentalizing. It certainly ran counter to her philosophy about men. About all her relationships, if she was being honest. People were tempo-rary. They came. They went. To expect otherwise made you dependent on others. Dependency led to a weakness that bled you from a thousand invisible wounds. Watching her mother disintegrate after her father had been killed in Beirut had taught Jenn that lesson. In the kitchen, she filled a tall glass with vodka and splashed just enough juice to disguise it. Her mother had taught her more than one lesson, it seemed.

Looking at the glass in her hand, she felt something approximating self-disgust. She could stop drinking any time—that's what she'd been telling herself for months. Any time. Simple as that. The coldest turkey you ever saw. Baltasar Alves had almost killed her today and might still, if she were in Portugal this time tomorrow. So how was this not that time? She held the glass out over the sink but didn't pour it down the drain the way she'd meant to only a moment before. Thought about taking a drink first. A sip. Maybe two. A wave of easy rationalizations swept up and over her until all she could hear was her thirst hammering in her ears.

She emptied the glass down the drain.

It didn't make her feel better, no sense of triumph. Only a deep and abiding exhaustion. She wanted Sebastião to put his arms around her, feel the scruff of his beard on her neck. That she did made her want to throw the empty glass and see it shatter. Instead, she made another drink. Identical to the first. Maybe a touch less vodka, if you were the type to take solace in baby steps. She made the drink without meaning to do it and looked at it with surprise, unsure how it had come to be in her hand. Happy, though. Lord, was she thirsty.

Sebastião craned his neck to look at her when she slid open the patio door. He smiled sheepishly as if she'd caught him doing something shameful. Gestured at the ocean, blaming it for luring him out here against his will. He took her hand and pulled her down beside him, shifting over to make room. She bent down to kiss him, running her fingers through his beard. He growled, a low, contented rumble in the back of his throat that she felt in her knees. His skin always smelled faintly of vanilla, and she wondered if she'd forever associate ice cream with sex.

When she sat up, he licked his lips and took the glass out of her hand as if she'd made it for him. He drank half and kissed her again, then set the glass down on the ground out of her reach. On another day that might have irritated her, but today it only made her wistful. She would miss orbiting Planet Sebastião.

"How was Lisbon?"

Rather than answer, he picked up the drink again and finished it. He handed the empty glass back to her and stretched languidly.

"If you could live anywhere in the world, where would you choose?" he asked.

The question caught her off guard. Normally, he had an athlete's disdain for hypotheticals.

She said, "Right here seems pretty good."

"I'm serious. Anywhere in the world."

It wasn't a question she'd ever asked herself, so it surprised her when she had a ready answer. "Salzburg."

"Austria is a beautiful country. Have you been?"

"Two days. When I was injured in Afghanistan, they medevacked me to Germany." She had given him a sanitized version of the assault that had effectively ended her career in the CIA while making it clear that he didn't get to ask a lot of questions. He'd always been good about respecting her boundaries. It was one of the things she liked best about him. He understood that intimacy had its limits. "As I healed, they let me take a few day trips, so I got to poke around Europe a little. I liked Salzburg. Never seen so many flowers."

"You like flowers?" he teased. "You are a girl, after all."

"Don't tell anyone."

Sebastião crossed himself somberly and pointed to the heavens.

She asked, "What about you? Where would you live?"

"I don't know."

"What happened in Lisbon?"

"Nothing. There is swelling. Again."

"It will pass."

"Not in time for the start of the season. They think now the middle of October. Perhaps." Sebastião rubbed his knee thoughtfully.

"That's not so far away."

"Do you think I would like Salzburg?" he asked.

"Not really your speed. It's peaceful."

He laughed. "Maybe I am ready for peace."

"Are you all right?"

"I'm an old man. I'm allowed to dream about my retirement."

That was a forbidden word around Sebastião. Even to imply that his career might be drawing to a close could result in banishment. Sebastião demanded unwavering optimism from his inner circle, so to hear it from him was shocking.

"What are you talking about? You've got years left yet."

"Not at the top. It will take the club this season to discover that I have lost a step. I will become surplus to requirements. They will sell me to a smaller club that will use my name to sell jerseys, and after a few years they will sell me to an even smaller club, and so on, until I am playing in some league no one cares about. Maybe even America."

"You don't know that."

"I know it," he said and rubbed his knee ruefully. "I know. It's strange. I've only ever been a footballer. I don't know how to do anything else."

"I need to tell you something," Jenn said, wincing at her graceless segue.

Sebastião stood and moved toward the house. "Come to bed."

"I'm serious."

"Then be serious with me in bed."

"Sebastião . . ."

He peeled off his shirt and threw it defiantly on the ground. "In bed, serious woman. Tell me in bed."

"Like you're going to listen in bed."

He stood in the fading daylight, considering that. Finally, he shrugged. "Perhaps you are right. But I'll listen after. Can you wait that long?"

"Then we will talk?" she asked, but her feet were already following him inside.

He held the glass door open invitingly. "Yes, serious woman. Then we will talk."

Jenn woke with no memory of falling asleep. Naps rarely worked for her. Nine times out of ten, she'd wake, numb-faced and groggy. For once, though, she opened her eyes comfortable and at peace. Sebastião lay beside her, staring up at the ceiling. One of his hands cradled the back of his head, the other resting on her hip. It was a role reversal; usually Sebastião would be the one to fall asleep while Jenn lay there wired, mind buzzing.

He felt her stir and rolled onto his side to gaze at her. His hand idly caressed her stomach, which ordinarily she liked but now made her feel vulnerable. She turned to face him, pulling the sheet up to cover herself. He smiled at her. The smile that had sold soft drinks, automobiles, and about a million pairs of cleats. The smile that could unlace her best intentions.

It was time. For serious talk. She felt rotten. He seemed as low as she'd ever seen him. Spooked to be confronting his own mortality. It was a terrible time to abandon him. *Please,* she chided herself. *Don't give yourself so much credit.* The moment she left, Sebastião would invite half the Algarve to sample the wonders of his three-sink bathroom. She'd seen the way women at the clubs looked him up and down. He was probably sick to death of this one-woman routine anyway. She ran a hand down his cheek and started to speak. He beat her to it.

"Would you take me to Salzburg with you?" he asked.

She sighed. "You said we could be serious."

"I am serious."

"Well, I can't afford Salzburg."

"I can."

Jenn lifted her head off the pillow, retreating to get a better look at him. Looking for the trademark twinkle in his eye that meant he was teasing her. It wasn't there.

"What are you talking about?" she asked.

"Making this permanent."

"Permanent? Is my fugitive lifestyle a big turn-on for you?"

"I have a lot of lawyers," he said dismissively, as though she were talking about a few unpaid parking tickets. "Perhaps we get married. That will take care of the passport."

He tugged at the sheet, drawing it down while she lay there staring at him, trying to comprehend what he was saying to her. Sebastião Coval talking about marriage was like coming home to find your dog purring.

From the floor beside the bed, her phone rang once. Her head turned toward it, grateful for the distraction. After ten seconds it rang again, this time twice before it stopped. That was Hendricks letting her know that he needed to talk urgently. Given Baltasar's ultimatum, she doubted it was about the weather. She picked up as it began to ring a third time.

"What's the forecast?" she said.

"Tsunami. We need to meet. Can you bring George?"

"Where?"

"Biv."

In case of emergency, they had designated three rally points. Places that none of them frequented or might be recognized. Hendricks had named them Bell, Biv, and Devoe. Biv was a small town called Alcantarilha. They agreed on a time and hung up.

Jenn rolled out of bed and started dressing. Sebastião lay there pouting—half joking, but more than a little serious.

"I have to go," she said.

"Gibson?" Sebastião asked. She heard the edge in his voice. Neither man cared especially for the other. Both men were recovering from injuries and didn't like the competition. A couple of divas, if you asked her.

"No," Jenn said. "Hendricks."

"What's happening?"

"Baltasar gave us twenty-four hours to be out of Portugal."

"I was only in Lisbon for a few hours. What terrible thing have you done now?"

"I'm serious," Jenn said.

"Ah," he said. "Now we come to the serious talk. Was that what you needed to tell me?" When she nodded that it was, he made a pile of pillows so he could sit up in bed. "So, you and your friends are disappearing?"

"Haven't been given a choice."

"Yes," Sebastião said. "You have."

She stood staring at him. He smiled that smile.

"I have to go," she said.

"Will I see you again?"

"I don't know."

He thought about that. "Borrow my car. You know where the keys are."

"Are you sure?"

"That way you'll have to bring it back before you go," he said with a wink.

"Sebastião . . ."

He waved her away. "Then kiss me one more time in case you can't."

CHAPTER TWENTY-TWO

João Luna stirred his coffee awkwardly with his right hand. Tapping the spoon on the brim of the cup, he laid it on the saucer. He was left-handed but had to keep it balled in a fist beneath the table to stop it from shaking. Only his left hand shook, not his right. He didn't understand why. At least his head no longer felt stuffed with feathers. Whatever they'd given him felt like the anesthesia a dentist gave him to take out his wisdom teeth. With his right hand, he sipped his coffee and looked out at the ocean that he loved so much. What good was a man whose hands shook?

His body ached. When he exhaled, his breath whistled as though air was escaping through a leak somewhere inside him. His rib cage pinched like a suit he'd outgrown. There'd been no doubt in his mind that he would die. Sitting in that hotel room while that man punished him with his fists. Luisa Mata looking on with those cold, reptile eyes. Her little clock ticking off five minutes.

She had accused him of betraying her uncle, but João still didn't know what she'd meant. He didn't understand how he'd come to be in that hotel room in the first place. Or how he'd left it with his life. Two men had driven him into Faro and ordered him out of the car. Thrown his things on the sidewalk. Except his passport, which they'd kept. Acting like they had done him a favor. Which in a way, he supposed they had.

He could have called his father to pick him up, but João wasn't ready to see him. Didn't know what he would say when he did. He felt angry. Abandoned. And even though Luisa had let him go, he still feared that they would come back for him. For a moment, he felt proud that it had been him in that hotel room instead of his father. Maybe, he thought, this was what it meant to be a man.

Instead of calling his father, he'd taken the bus to Olhão and limped down to the harbor. When Luisa Mata had asked him if he had anything of value, he'd thought only of the *Alexandria*. The way Luisa had looked through him, he'd gotten it into his head that she knew everything there was to know about him. What if she'd done something to the boat? In truth, that would be worse than killing him. The *Alexandria* belonged to his family. It *was* his family in a way that neither he nor his father ever would be. Standing on her deck was the only way João would feel at ease again. Once he'd found the ship intact and checked every inch of her, he'd gone for a quiet cup of coffee so he could think.

The café sat at the corner of the old fish market. When João was a boy, his father had brought him here in the mornings after the boat had been squared away. They would drink coffee in silence while his father read the paper. It had been their tradition, and João kept it up even after his father retired. The café was where they had come the morning his father had finally admitted the family's debt to Baltasar Alves. Under the table, João flexed and clenched his hand.

"May I join you?"

Lost in thought, João flinched at the sound. He looked up to see the well-dressed man from the hotel room standing a polite distance from the table, holding a coffee. The one who had stopped Luisa's man. João's heart sank. They'd changed their minds and come back for him. The man saw his fear and took another step back.

"I'm alone," he said.

His Portuguese was good, and João was surprised that the accent was American. He gestured to the seat once occupied by his father. What alternative did he have? The man arranged his seat so that they both could look out at the boats. João watched him expectantly, waiting for him to explain why he was here. To say what he wanted. But the man sat placidly and stirred his coffee. It should have been unnerving, but João found his company strangely familiar. Comforting. They sat together like friends and drank their coffee in silence.

Up close, João saw the man's face was etched with scars. His right ear had been pummeled flat like a boxer's, and one eye drooped lower than the other, as if the foundations of his face had begun to crumble. It gave him a mournful aspect. João didn't like to imagine what could do that to a man.

"How do you feel?"

"How would you feel?" João said.

"Broken," the man answered quickly, as if he'd been thinking about the question a long time.

João nodded agreement. That was exactly how he felt.

"My name is George Abe. I owe you an apology."

"What for? Wasn't you who broke my ribs."

"I should have spoken up sooner."

"Why didn't you?"

"I was afraid."

That surprised João; the man didn't look easy to scare. Not with a face like that. It made João feel a little less ashamed of his own fear. He'd been waiting for it to fade ever since he'd been dragged out of that hotel room. But even now, out in the open air, familiar place, familiar faces, he still felt afraid. He'd never thought of himself as a coward. He'd worked the *Alexandria* in terrible conditions as waves the size of churches broke across the bow. This was something else entirely. He felt broken and unsure what to do about it. Or about the anger that he felt toward his father.

"Are you a forgiving man?" João asked.

The man considered the question carefully. It took a moment before he answered. "It depends. On what the person did."

"Say this person put you in a position where you could have died."

"Did the person know?" George asked. "That it would?"

"He should have," João said.

Something passed across the man's face. An old and grievous hurt. João realized that the sadness he saw there wasn't an illusion caused by his scars. It was real right down to the marrow.

"Were his intentions good?" George asked.

"Yes," João replied. He felt relief that he could still say that about his father.

"Then I would forgive him. If his intentions were good."

"I see," João said.

"But," George continued, "that's not the same thing as trusting him again."

João agreed with a heavy heart. This was exactly what he had been having trouble articulating to himself. He loved his father. He understood the man's choices and why he'd made them. There was nothing to say that João wouldn't have made the same choices in his father's place. But that didn't change anything. They were the wrong choices. Naïve and terrible. João could have died in that room, and the worst part was that it wasn't over. Baltasar Alves still owned the *Alexandria*, and as long as João was her captain, Baltasar Alves owned him too.

"Thank you," João said.

"One more thing," George said. "He will know if you don't."

"Don't what?"

"Don't trust him again."

"How?"

"He will feel it. You both will. Nothing will be the same between you."

João nodded. He already could. It might be that this was part of being a man as well. Taking off the blinders and learning to think for himself. He didn't know what came next. If Baltasar Alves came back and expected him to honor his father's arrangement, what would he do? Whatever he chose would have consequences, but he realized now that those consequences would be easier to bear if had no one to blame but himself.

"I have a favor to ask of you," George said.

"What do you need?"

"My friends and I are no longer welcome in Portugal. We need transportation to North Africa within the next twenty-four hours."

"There are ferries in Spain. From Algeciras you can go direct to Tangier."

George said, "The ferry is no good for us. Neither are the ports in Morocco. We will need to go ashore somewhere less . . . noticeable."

"I see." João didn't see and was quite sure he didn't want to.

"Can it be done?"

"People sneak into Europe, *senhor*. They do not sneak into Africa," João said. "Why is it you come to me? Because you stopped that *filho da puta* from killing me?"

"Yes," George said simply.

"So I owe you? Is that the idea?"

"No. You don't owe me anything."

"Then why are you asking me?" João asked.

"Because you're the only boat captain I know in Portugal, and I don't need to lie to you. We need your help. It's up to you whether you give it or not."

Automatically João wondered what his father would advise. This man could say that he didn't owe anything, but that was not how João felt. His father had always believed in paying his debts. João stopped himself. It didn't matter what his father would do. What would João do? That was the question now.

"How many friends do you have?"

"Three plus myself."

"Will this anger Baltasar Alves or his niece?"

George thought for a moment. "I don't believe so, but things are not good here. I can't say for certain. There could be some risk."

João thought about it while he finished his coffee. Despite the danger, the idea of helping someone appealed to him. He thought it might give him back some sense of control.

"I'll take you to Morocco," he said. "I know a place where no one will see you arrive."

The answer caught George by surprise, and for a moment, his sadness lifted, and João saw nothing but relief and happiness.

"I have some money but not a lot. What would it take?"

It was João's turn to be surprised. This man had risked his own life to stop Luisa Mata. "I don't want your money, *senhor*. I will take you to Morocco."

"We'll need a few hours to get ready."

"Whenever you are ready to go, but it would be better to arrive at night."

George smiled. "You're a good man, João Luna. Thank you."

João didn't know if he agreed but acknowledged the compliment. They discussed the details and made their arrangements. When it was settled, they shook hands across the table. João watched George Abe limp away and out of sight. He went back to the counter and ordered a glass of port. It didn't taste as bad as he remembered, and he found that he didn't feel so afraid anymore.

CHAPTER TWENTY-THREE

Alcantarilha was a sleepy village northwest of the thronged beaches of Albufeira. At the village's center, surrounded by a warren of narrow, medieval streets, rose the Church of Our Lady of Conception. Dating to the sixteenth century, it was an imposing, castlelike church in the Manueline style—Gibson had to Google what that meant. As the town grew over the next century, the nearby cemetery had made way in the name of progress. The disinterred bones had been relocated to a small chapel on the side of the church. More than fifteen hundred skulls and thigh bones lined the walls of the Capela dos Ossos—the Bone Chapel.

The chapel was smaller than Gibson expected. Only a few people could stand comfortably inside. Not that he'd had any sense for how many square feet fifteen hundred human skulls could tile. He'd expected it to feel claustrophobic and morbid but instead found it unexpectedly peaceful. It was no less strange, he supposed, than making up a body so that it looked alive, dressing it in a suit, and burying it under six feet of dirt.

Honoring the dead was always hard, he thought as he studied the bones of men and women that had rested here since before his own country had even been conceived. You told yourself whatever lies made sense of the senseless and did the best you could.

He wondered about his own funeral. After what he'd unearthed at Fresco Mar Internacional, it wasn't a bad time to give it some thought. Despite his repeated brushes with death, he'd never really paused to consider the aftermath. Would they allow him to come home then? He thought he'd like to be buried alongside his parents. Who would attend the service? Perhaps a few conspiracy bloggers. He smiled grimly. They would show up just to confirm that he really was dead. It would not be a packed house, that much he knew for certain. He wasn't that kind of man. He hadn't led that kind of life.

Would Ellie come to his funeral? Would she grieve her father or only curse his memory? She'd be well within her rights. He pushed the thought away. What maudlin, self-indulgent crap. Only depressed teenagers and old men on their last leg indulged thoughts of their own funerals, and he was neither. Time to get out of here before he bought an acoustic guitar and started writing sad songs. Gibson ducked through the low doorway of the chapel and stretched in the moonlight. Porsche made one hell of a sports car but not much of a bed. The brief nap he'd caught on the drive over had left him with a rude kink in his neck. Another sign he was getting older if not wiser.

Hendricks had picked Alcantarilha as one of their three rally points because, while the chapel drew a few tourists, it wasn't the kind of attraction that most came to the Algarve to see. And there certainly wasn't anything here that would interest Baltasar Alves or his people.

Hendricks smoked at an outdoor table, the duffel of money and Gibson's computer bag between his feet. They'd swung by the house after leaving the cannery. The only other customers were an elderly couple who sat silently, side by side, looking out at the dark street like a pair of stone statues guarding the entrance. The proprietor, a grumpy man with permanently pursed lips, sat inside watching soccer highlights on the television.

An electric-blue Audi R8 Spyder purred to a stop outside the café. Jenn got out and looked at the Porsche.

"Yours?" she asked.

"You like?" Gibson said.

"Hendricks let you drive it?"

Hendricks snorted.

"We're still negotiating," Gibson said.

"Like hell, white boy."

Jenn helped George from the car. He tired easily at this time of night, and it had been a long day. One that showed no indication of winding down anytime soon. Gibson looked at the two sports cars. Fernando and Sebastião shared a love of shiny, high-end toys. Not exactly ideal for keeping a low profile. Probably best to dump them.

It took some coaxing, but the proprietor eventually pried himself from the television. Coffees were ordered. Hendricks lit a fresh cigarette; he'd been trying to quit, but the stress of the day had him chainsmoking like they'd cured cancer. The elderly couple, unaccustomed to all the activity, asked for their bill. The four waited patiently for the coffees to arrive and for the couple to stroll away into the night. Once they were alone, they got down to it.

George said, "I have a boat in Olhão that will take us to North Africa. A contact in Morocco will help us from there."

"When?" Hendricks asked.

"As soon as we're ready, but I don't think we should delay longer than necessary."

"Agreed," Jenn said emphatically.

George said, "Baltasar and I go back, and that still counts for something, but given his mood and the situation in the Algarve, I wouldn't bet against him having a change of heart. Speed is essential now."

"We stopped at the house on the way here. Everything's in the car," Hendricks said, then to Jenn: "I packed you up. You're all set."

"Appreciated," she said after the briefest of hesitations.

George said, "Jenn, do you have any other stops you need to make?"

Her back stiffened. George had put it delicately enough, but they all knew what, or whom, he'd meant. Jenn was an intensely private person, and Sebastião Coval was not a topic open for discussion. It didn't help that they were all looking at her expectantly.

"No. I'm good to go," she said and shrugged with all the nonchalance she could muster. She'd make one hell of a poker player, but there was sadness behind her eyes. Gibson had written off her relationship with Sebastião as a disposable distraction. Now he wasn't so sure.

George either took Jenn at face value or chose not to linger on the question. "Good. I'll let the captain know. The sooner we're on our way, the better."

Hendricks cleared his throat, looking square at Gibson. "You telling them, or am I?"

"Telling us what?" George asked.

"Youngblood here isn't going to North Africa," Hendricks said. "At least not yet."

Jenn looked at Gibson with the same expression as when you learn your cousin has relapsed again and is back in rehab—sad but not exactly surprised either. Resigned.

"We went back to the cannery," Gibson said.

Jenn and George exchanged a look. "When?"

"After the hotel."

Incredulous, Jenn lit into Gibson. "Let me get this straight. After bitching about not wanting to get us involved with Baltasar, you wait until after he threatened to kill us if we didn't get out of Portugal to go poking around in his business? Are you out of your mind?"

"Opinions vary," Gibson said.

"Wait . . . did you say 'we'?" She turned on Hendricks. "You went along with this?"

"It's complicated," Hendricks said.

"What the hell does that mean?"

It was Hendricks's voice that turned sharp now. "Complicated means not simple. Don't talk to me like I work for you. We went back. I had my reasons."

"Which are?" Jenn said, downshifting to keep the peace.

That was Gibson's cue. For the second time, he told the story of his abduction and his delicate business arrangement with the hijackers. Jenn didn't take it half as well as Hendricks had. Maybe not even a quarter. She interrupted constantly, asking him to repeat parts, as if she couldn't believe her ears. When he was finished, George and Jenn regarded them both angrily.

"I get why you did this," she said, "but why didn't you talk to us? Tell us what was happening?"

Gibson said, "I've been trying to talk to you for three months, Jenn. Now suddenly you want a conversation?"

"That's not even the same thing, and you know it. You have no right to make decisions for all of us. What do you think Baltasar is going to do when he finds out?"

"It was worth it."

Under the table, Gibson pushed the satchel across to Jenn. She unzipped the bag. Gibson watched for their expressions to change, but it might as well have been his dirty laundry. Jenn really would make one hell of a poker player. George was no slouch himself.

"How much is here?" George asked.

"Hundred thousand," Hendricks said.

"So, after you write this report, the money is yours?" George said.

"It's ours," Gibson said firmly.

"Should make running a little easier," Hendricks said. "Don't you think?"

"That it will," George said. "I agree with Jenn that you should have discussed it with us, but this is a difference maker."

"So where's the but?" Jenn said, not ready to join in George's back-patting. "Why aren't you coming with us?"

"We have another problem," Hendricks said, stubbing out a cigarette and lighting another. "Gibson found something on the servers. It's not . . . good."

"And you intend to stay because of this discovery?" George asked.

"I have to," Gibson said.

"What is it you found?"

"It'd be easier to show you," Gibson said. He didn't mean it, though; seeing would be harder. He suggested the church across the street, the café too public for what he had to share.

Jenn gazed off down the dark, narrow road. Her tongue was playing across her teeth the way it did whenever something was bothering her.

"No," she said. "No. Whatever you've got, I don't want to know."

"You're not even going to look?" Gibson asked.

"Not even between my fingers. Whatever you've got, it's not my problem."

"It's serious, Jenn."

"I don't doubt it."

"So why not?"

"Because I don't care, and I can't afford to start."

Gibson looked at her in disbelief. "What the hell happened to you?"

Jenn paled. "You know exactly what happened to me. Same as I know what happened to you. To all of us. The four of us? We're a goddamn mobile tragedy. So why do you always have to go looking for more trouble?"

"I didn't go looking. I stumbled onto it."

"And what if you did?" Jenn said. "There's plenty of bad in the world. A lifetime's worth. So if you tell me you stumbled onto something bad, I believe you. But how about you stumble the fuck away from it again? Everything can't be on us to fix."

"Just watch the video. You'll understand."

"No," Jenn said. "Luisa all but put a gun to my head. Baltasar Alves has just gone to war with anyone he considers a threat. So far, we've managed to stay off that list. Barely. I intend to keep it that way, and that means getting my ass out of Portugal like the man said."

"Watch the video," Gibson repeated.

"And then what? What are the four of us going to do about whatever it is you've found? Hold up Baltasar at finger-point and demand he change his ways?" Jenn said. "This is a matter for the police."

"He owns the police. Isn't that the point of his 'Pax Algarve'? He keeps the drugs out. They let everything else slide."

"We're not equipped. This can't be our fight."

They argued back and forth, months of frustration between them boiling to the surface. Neither making any headway. It was impossible to win an argument if no one was really listening. Heels dug in, they were only interested in the righteousness of their position.

"Gibson," George said. His voice was low and calm.

Jenn and Gibson trailed off and slowly turned to look at George expectantly.

"I'd like to see what you found."

"Sir," Jenn said. "I don't think—"

"Then we can each decide for ourselves what we will or will not do."

And that was that. They were decided.

CHAPTER TWENTY-FOUR

Fernando Alves had a problem, and its name was Gibson Vaughn. Up in his suite at the Mariana Hotel, Fernando sat at the bar, idly stirring a gin and tonic. Not the best idea under the circumstances, but he had always thought better with a drink in his hand. Something about the clink of the ice cubes against the glass cleared his head. It would have been much more pleasant out on the balcony now that the sun had set, the breeze coming off the ocean. Anibal had forbidden it. Wouldn't even allow Fernando near the windows lest a sniper lurked on an adjacent rooftop, waiting to blow his head off.

Not exactly how he'd pictured passing his afternoon.

Ordinarily, Fernando preferred to plan ahead. Long in advance. Patiently, like a chess match. If chess weren't so suicidally boring. He'd inherited that much from his father—the vision to account for every variable. However, the hijacking of the drug shipment was a variable that no one could have predicted. The day had deteriorated so rapidly, Fernando had been forced to act before he could see how it would pan out. For one thing, he had dramatically underestimated his father's reaction. He certainly hadn't anticipated being placed in protective custody.

Since permitting himself to be rescued by Gibson Vaughn, Fernando hadn't had a moment to himself. Couldn't make a phone call without being overheard. Two of Anibal's men followed him like dogs everywhere he went. Even into the bathroom, as if assassins might slither up the drain with knives between their teeth. It was all a bit paranoid, but Anibal was only following orders. And if Anibal had one distinguishing quality, it was a blind willingness to execute Baltasar Alves's every whim to the letter. Armed guards stood watch at the front door; more waited outside in the hall. A tiny army, just for him. His father's touching concern for his safety notwithstanding, it was all incredibly inconvenient. Under the watchful eye of his new guard dogs, his hands were effectively tied. He'd become a prisoner in his own home.

Fernando didn't second-guess his decision to kill Dani Coelho. Gibson Vaughn had made it unavoidable. Coelho was a greedy cockroach of a man without a shred of personal loyalty. What had it taken to persuade Coelho to betray Baltasar? A little blackmail and some cash. He would have given up Fernando at the first hint of danger. So, the second Gibson had asked to talk to Coelho, Fernando knew what had to be done.

How hard was it to hit one jogger with a car? Fernando cursed the sloppiness of his Romanian associates. Gibson should have been safely out of the way, recuperating in a hospital. Then none of this would have been necessary. Of course, the Romanians blamed him for not allowing them to kill Gibson outright.

Fernando stirred his drink.

Perhaps they were right. Perhaps he had allowed sentiment to cloud his judgment. He'd been concerned that a hit on Gibson would only raise suspicion. But more than that, he hadn't wanted to kill him. He felt sorry for Gibson Vaughn, and killing him had seemed extreme at the time. That was before Fernando had killed five men and discovered it wasn't nearly as bad as people said. And before Gibson had stuck his nose where it didn't belong. He would almost certainly have to die now. The question was how.

The maddening part was how close he had come to pulling it off, cauterizing the threat completely. Killing Dani Coelho had fulfilled his primary goal of stymying Gibson. But the inspired part had been allowing Anibal to draw the wrong conclusions about whom the target had been. Fernando couldn't have anticipated how powerfully his father would react, but it had been beyond his wildest dreams. It had precipitated a falling-out with George Abe, who had been given twenty-four hours to leave the Algarve. That included Gibson. Problem solved.

Or so he had thought.

On his laptop, he studied the map of the Algarve. The blue dot at its center indicated the current whereabouts of his Porsche. The car had a GPS tracker installed, and he had lent it to the two Americans so that he could keep tabs on them. A good thing he had, because they'd been busy bees during the last few hours. Instead of preparing for their departure, Gibson had driven back to Fresco Mar Internacional.

Exactly the turn of events that Fernando had tried so hard to avoid. As soon as his father had involved the Americans this morning, Fernando knew that Gibson Vaughn posed an existential threat to him. Knew if Gibson got access to the servers, then he would uncover what Fernando had worked so hard to conceal. But every move he'd made had been countered or blunted as if the universe itself had made a side bet that Fernando would be discovered. In retrospect, it felt almost inevitable.

What Fernando didn't understand was why.

From the beginning, Gibson had been opposed to involving himself. And that was before Baltasar had thrown them all out of the country. So why the hell had Gibson risked returning to the cannery? Fernando couldn't make sense of it. He understood people in terms of self-interest. But even through that lens, Fernando couldn't see Gibson's angle, and that made him uneasy.

There was something he wasn't seeing, but what?

On impulse, Fernando picked up his phone. Sebastião answered on the third ring. He said nothing, but Fernando could hear him breathing, deep and slow.

"*Olá?*" Fernando said, breaking the silence, but his friend still did not speak. "Sebastião?"

"I haven't decided if I'm talking to you," Sebastião said, slurring his words slightly. He was drunk.

"What have I done?"

"Your father has sent Jenn away from me."

That surprised Fernando. Sebastião had already been with Jenn Charles far longer than he typically stayed with a woman. It wasn't like him at all. "I would have thought you'd be thanking us," he said. "I'll throw a party to announce your liberation. Women will pilgrimage to your bed to celebrate."

His attempt at levity didn't go over well.

"What do you want, Fernando?"

"It's been a bad day. A lot has happened. An attempt was made on my life."

"*Meu Deus,*" Sebastião said, sobering in a hurry. "I had no idea. I'm glad you're all right. What happened? Where are you?"

"At the hotel. Anibal is here keeping me safe like a good mother hen. I would tell you more, but it's not wise."

Sebastião said that he understood.

"I'm sorry about Jenn, my friend. I had no idea she meant so much to you."

"Neither did she. I may not be very good at sharing my feelings."

"Nor I," Fernando said, tiring of the conversation. "Is she there? I would say good-bye."

"No, she went to meet Hendricks."

Fernando ended the conversation and hung up. He didn't need to ask where, the blue dot told him that much. The Porsche was currently in Alcantarilha, a flyspeck of a town midway between Albufeira and

Lagos. Fernando had passed it a thousand times but never seen reason to stop. George Abe would be with them. No doubt about that. But what were the four Americans conspiring about? How much did Gibson know about Fernando's business with the Romanians? He should have killed his friend when he had the chance.

So now, instead of being able to sit back and enjoy his drink, Fernando had one more mess to clean up. There was nothing tying Fernando to the warehouse. Not directly. He had scrupulously covered his tracks. But if Gibson got it into his head to share what he'd discovered with Baltasar, then it would only be a matter of time before his father put the pieces together. And that could not be allowed to happen. He'd risked too much these past two years to see it undone now.

Fernando's first instinct was to reach back out to the Romanians and have them handle Gibson Vaughn. Their way this time. But that would be a mistake. He couldn't afford to look weak to the Romanians. When the time came to take the Algarve, they would need to respect him. Besides, Luisa was on her way to Quarteira. The Romanians would need every man at their disposal to survive her.

No, he would have to deal with Gibson himself.

Or would he? Maybe there was another way.

He picked up the phone and dialed his father.

CHAPTER TWENTY-FIVE

They crossed the street to the church in a solemn procession, as if going to view the body of a dear, departed friend. Jenn trailed behind, feeling very much on the outside looking in. It wasn't the first time she'd felt this way since coming to Portugal. She'd spent two years hunting for George before finally freeing him from Cold Harbor. Cold Harbor had been hunting her too. Missed her by a matter of minutes in Albany. It had been a hard, dangerous couple of years. Cold Harbor had hunted her as much as she'd hunted them. She'd relied on no one but herself. Answered to no one but herself. It had kept her alive.

Part of her preferred it that way.

Dan was right. He didn't work for her, and she had no business talking to him that way. But she was having a hard time adjusting to the idea that these people—as much as she cared for them—had a say in what she did or how she did it. The hold they had on her felt like a shackle. It made her feel unsafe. Made her crave the drink that Sebastião had taken out of her hand.

The heavy wooden door opened grudgingly and admitted them into the quiet of the church. The pews were empty, lights dimmed in case someone needed a late-night word with God.

Hendricks made a sweep to confirm that no one was having a crisis of faith. "We're alone," Hendricks told Gibson. "Floor is yours."

Gibson balanced his laptop on the back of a pew. The screen flick-ered, casting an alien glow across the church. Hendricks put a cigarette in his mouth, remembered where he was, and returned it to the pack. George sat one row back and leaned forward, fingers interlaced like a penitent awaiting absolution. Jenn stood apart from the others, arms crossed. She wished she were back in Sebastião's bed. Not standing in a musty church about to look at something terrible because Gibson Vaughn needed to save the world. The nice thing about Sebastião was that he didn't need taking care of. He had an entire staff dedicated to his upkeep. It was a very appealing lifestyle.

Then there was the matter of his retirement and the puzzle of Salzburg. His offer cast him in an unexpected light. Had he been seri-ous about marrying her? She didn't know what to make of that. From anyone else, it would have been a joke. He hadn't been kidding, though. Not that he'd given it a lot of thought, but then that wasn't Sebastião's way. She wouldn't call him an impulsive man, but once he made a deci-sion, the decision was made. Second-guessing was not in his nature. Once upon a time, she would have said the same of herself. Nowadays, though, it seemed like all she ever did was doubt herself.

Gibson finished fiddling with his laptop. He stood back and tapped the space bar. George leaned closer to see. Jenn could see just fine from where she was.

A video began to play.

Taken from above, it showed an enclosure inside a warehouse. It looked like a pen or a corral that you might find on a working farm. It didn't hold animals. Jenn felt her heart seize, but she didn't look away.

None of them did.

Jenn had always felt a visceral responsibility never to blink. To bear witness where others wouldn't. That was probably why she'd joined the Agency. It was why she had fought seeing the video at all. As long as it remained an abstraction, she could minimize whatever Gibson had found. The mind didn't allow itself to imagine certain things unless forced to see. Seeing would make it harder to argue that they shouldn't get involved. And she really believed that intervening would be suicide. Silently, she cursed Gibson for putting her in this position.

Inside the corral were two dozen boys—perhaps as young as fourteen, none older than sixteen or seventeen. She guessed they were a mixture of North African and Middle Eastern, most likely from countries like Syria and Libya. Places wracked by war and civil unrest, where human traffickers could prey on people's desperation. Slavery had reached epidemic proportions in the twenty-first century. Jenn had seen estimates as high as thirty million worldwide, with nearly a million souls trafficked internationally each year. Half of them children.

Vague promises of a new life in Europe were enough to lure them to gamble with their lives. Not realizing that there was no way out, no better life. Places like the United States and the European Union did the traffickers' work for them, creating cages without bars. Even if one of these boys managed to escape, he couldn't go to the police without being sent back to whatever hellhole he'd escaped.

The conditions in the video were deplorable. Filthy metal buckets served as toilets. No running water. The boys glistened with sweat and moved lethargically. Without ventilation, and the Portuguese sun beating down, the temperature inside the warehouse would be north of one hundred and twenty degrees during the day. She doubted nighttime brought much relief. Lights shone down mercilessly as some boys slept on cardboard, shirts wrapped around their heads. Others stared morosely through the bars, tracking something or someone beyond.

Gibson hit the space bar.

A second video began. It showed a similar enclosure. This one contained girls—similar ages, similar ethnicities. Jenn guessed that they had arrived together but had been segregated by gender. Pregnant stock would drive down prices.

"I think the pens are where they're kept before auction," Gibson said. "Wouldn't want the merchandise fraternizing before the sale."

"Auction?" Jenn said.

To answer, Gibson tabbed to another video. It showed a boy standing against a concrete wall in his underwear. His ribs stood out, but he had an athletic frame. Someone threw him a soccer ball, which he caught and held in the crook of his arm. The boy smiled despite his circumstances, a friendly, kind smile. He'd been cleaned up. Made presentable. He turned slowly in a circle. To his right, text listed his name as Kamal. Height. Weight. Education. Languages spoken. Vital statistics scrolled down the screen.

Kamal was fifteen.

Jenn ran her tongue across her teeth but did not look away.

"His file also includes a PDF of his medical records," Gibson said, his voice thick with anger. "Everything a discerning customer needs to make an informed purchase. Kamal here was sold two days ago to a buyer in France. Delivery is still pending."

Gibson tabbed again and again. A different boy, a different girl, the same concrete wall, the same nightmare. A girl with a bow in her hair. Tab. A frail boy in a frayed Nirvana T-shirt. Tab. On and on it went. Gibson cycled through a dozen more videos. The children weren't in the best shape, but Jenn saw that the boys were all handsome and the girls beautiful. These children had been handpicked with one purpose in mind. It sickened her to think what was in store for them. Especially because she could see in their eyes that they didn't yet know it themselves. Their captors' lies still kept their dreams of a better life alive. That was why every one of them smiled hopefully for the camera. Somehow, that made it all that much worse.

"How did you come by this?" George asked.

Hendricks and Gibson looked at each other and had a wordless discussion. Finally, Hendricks shrugged and said, "They're being stored and streamed through servers at the cannery. Best as I can tell, Baltasar is running a dark-web auction site."

George cast his eyes down. "This isn't the man I knew twenty years ago."

"Well, that's a huge fucking surprise," Gibson said.

"Hey, that's enough," Jenn snapped.

"No, it really isn't," Gibson said. "Benjamin Lombard. Calista Dauplaise. Now this? It is possible that you are the worst judge of character in the history of the world. Seriously, have you ever been right about anyone in your entire life?"

"Gibson," Jenn said sharply.

"What? We've been sucking at the teat of a major drug importer who turns out to be a human trafficker because George vouched for him and said he wasn't such a bad guy as all that."

"No one made you stay," Jenn said.

"You're right, there. I'm as guilty as any of us."

Jenn and Gibson stood toe to toe, neither blinking, neither backing down. She had an irrational desire to punch him in the throat and see how things went from there. But she didn't; he wasn't who she was angry with.

"He's not wrong," George said.

"It's not that simple," Jenn said.

George disagreed. "Right now, it is exactly that simple. After we deal with this, we can argue the particulars."

"Deal with it?" Jenn said. "We have to get you out of here. Out of Portugal."

"I'm not going anywhere," George said.

"Sir, you're not in any shape for us to be getting involved with this."

George struck the ground with his cane. The report startled Jenn into silence. Slowly, he rose to his feet. He trembled, whether from the effort or the emotion, she couldn't say. He looked at each of them in turn, but his eyes settled on Jenn.

"I am done being talked about like I'm on life support, Jennifer. I am not, contrary to popular opinion, an invalid who needs his diaper changed for him."

"I didn't say—"

"No, but it is implicit in every decision you make. Poor, delicate George. It stops now. I will not be an albatross to hang around all of your necks. Do I make myself understood? That stops now."

"Yes, sir."

He pointed at the laptop. "I can't allow this to go on. If you think I'm going to tuck tail and run, leaving these boys and girls in the hands of this monster, then you don't know a thing about me."

"If you stay, I stay."

"No, Jenn," George said, his expression softening. He took her hand. "Not this time. You've sacrificed so much for me already. I'll never be able to adequately thank or repay you. You certainly don't owe me any more blind loyalty. If you stay, stay for yourself."

"What about you?" Jenn said to Hendricks, who hadn't said a word. "You have to see how badly we're outgunned here."

"Maybe, but I'm with Gibson on this," Hendricks said. "Fuck slavery."

Jenn looked at him disbelievingly, then to the group. "So, do we have a plan other than pulling a Butch and Sundance?"

"We do," Gibson said.

"Well, let's hear it, then."

"We offer a trade," Hendricks said, leaning in.

Jenn looked skeptical. "What do we have that Baltasar Alves could possibly want?"

"His shipment," Gibson said.

"His shipment?" Jenn said, then did a double take. "Wait, you actually did it?"

"You don't have to act so surprised."

"You disarmed the explosives?" asked George.

"No, they're still armed, but I control them. I can disarm or detonate. And I can do either remotely."

"The kids for the drugs . . ." George said thoughtfully.

Hendricks smiled in the dark of the church. "Has a certain poetic symmetry when you think about it."

CHAPTER TWENTY-SIX

Fernando looked across the dark street at his car parked outside the café and rolled his eyes. Only Gibson Vaughn could screw up a Porsche. Did he take it to a club? Did he meet some ladies? No. He drove to a sardine cannery and then to some cheap café in the middle of nowhere. If you asked Fernando, it was a crime against precision German engineering. This also explained why Gibson hadn't been with a woman since coming to Portugal. His priorities were forever in all the wrong places. A shame. Fernando wished he could have done more to show the American a good time. It would make killing him easier.

The Audi parked beside his car was a surprise. It belonged to Sebastião, and Fernando knew it intimately. He had almost flipped it on the test drive. That it had held the road impressed Fernando so much that he'd contemplated buying one for himself. Sebastião must have leant it to Jenn. Why hadn't he mentioned it on the phone? Fernando wondered whether he needed to worry about him too. It would be disappointing if Jenn had gotten to Sebastião. There weren't many people Fernando actually liked, and he was already losing several of them.

Up in the front seat, Anibal directed Tomas to roll the car forward a few feet, lights off. He had spotted movement inside the café and wanted a better angle. In the window, an old man flipped chairs upside down onto tables. Otherwise, the café was empty. No sign of Gibson Vaughn or his friends. Up and down the street, the shops and houses were all dark. They could be inside any one of them. Watching, even now. Fernando didn't like it. Didn't like anything about the situation.

At least it had gotten him out of the hotel. It had been simple enough to let slip that Gibson Vaughn and Dan Hendricks had returned to Fresco Mar Internacional. His father's natural paranoia had done the rest. Harder had been convincing him that Fernando should accompany Anibal to Alcantarilha. Ordinarily, he wasn't permitted any involvement with his father's criminal operations. But with Luisa tied down in Quarteira dealing with the Romanians, and unanswered questions swirling about the loyalty of those inside the organization, Baltasar had a dwindling number of people he could trust.

Planting doubt in his father's mind about Gibson Vaughn had been a good first step, but it wasn't enough. His father held George Abe in the highest regard. Fernando had grown up listening to stories about the man. It would take more than circumstance to convince Baltasar that George was conspiring against him. His first instinct would be to take them alive, but that ran the risk of the truth coming out, which Fernando couldn't allow. He touched the gun beneath his jacket. It would be better for everyone if they died before then. Tonight, in Alcantarilha.

Fernando had been considering the logistics of it. How best to manipulate the outcome? Ideally, Anibal and his men could be provoked to put them down. The massacre at the hotel had had the unexpected benefit of drawing suspicion away from himself. He was a victim. Better to keep it that way for now.

Or was it?

Anibal had ambition of his own. Especially now that Silva and Peres were off the table. Did Fernando really want the bootlicker to get to play hero? Fernando could clean up his own mess and remind his father that he had value beyond managing hotels and restaurants. Luisa wasn't the only one in the family who could pull the trigger.

Anibal's phone rang. Fernando could tell from the way he sat up straight that it must be Baltasar. Such a good little soldier—a little erection bobbing hopefully in the wind. Fernando thought about putting a bullet in Anibal's head too. *Don't get greedy,* he told himself. *Unless the opportunity presents itself.*

Two vehicles approached slowly from the opposite direction—a sedan followed by an SUV—stopping at the far corner from the café. Anibal told Tomas to pull alongside the sedan so that the rear windows aligned. When the two windows opened, Baltasar greeted his son across the narrow divide.

"Pai?" Fernando said, scarcely able to conceal his fury. His hand balled into a white-knuckled fist. This ruined everything. Disposing of the Americans would be impossible with his father overseeing things. Fernando saw his opportunity evaporating and, for a long second, feared that his father knew everything. Baltasar rarely left the safe confines of the compound. That he'd done so tonight, with war raging across the Algarve, was unfathomable unless he knew his son's intentions. Sweat trickled down Fernando's rib cage. It was an unfamiliar sensation, and it took him a moment to identify what he was feeling. Fear.

"Are they here?" Baltasar asked.

"The car is here. There's no sign of them."

"Have you asked the café owner?"

"Not yet."

A look of irritation crossed his father's face. Fernando saw the truth. His father wasn't here to confront him. Baltasar Alves had driven to Alcantarilha in the middle of the night because he didn't trust Anibal to handle the situation. It was as simple as that. Had he traveled to Quarteira to supervise Luisa as she dealt with the Romanians? Of course not. Luisa was above reproach. This morning's hijacking had happened in Anibal's territory, a major liability in his ledger.

Fernando realized he had misread the terrain. Anibal didn't see the death of Silva and Peres as an opportunity. He wasn't looking to climb the ladder; he was simply trying not to wind up in a box beside them. After all, he was an endangered species now. The last of his kind. That's why he'd been peacocking in front of Baltasar all day. Trying to prove himself. Fernando thought there might be an opportunity there. Anibal had always been loyal to Baltasar, but a man's loyalty to his own neck usually took precedence. Anibal's uncertainty about where he stood might be exploited under the right circumstances.

Baltasar's car moved up and parked across the bumpers of the two sports cars, blocking them in. When Baltasar got out, all the vehicles emptied in unison. Anibal strode forward, barking orders and gesturing imperiously to his men, who fanned out, searching for the Americans. Quite a commanding figure the lieutenant cut, Fernando thought mockingly. With Anibal protecting him, his father had nothing to fear from the dirt and dog shit.

The café proprietor stopped working and leaned on his mop in the doorway, watching the show with interest. Fernando hurried to keep up with his father. For a reformed reprobate with a pacemaker, the old man could still move. Hard to believe that his father had only months to live.

Turning Dani Coelho had been a boon on many levels. His father's organization relied heavily on encrypted e-mails. Control of the servers had given Fernando access to all of them. They made for fascinating reading. He probably had a more complete picture of the inner workings of the organization than anyone. His father's health included.

Baltasar hadn't told anyone what the doctor had found on the CT scan in February. The language in his e-mails painted a hard picture: inoperable, degenerative, lymph nodes, spreading. His father had masked it so far, but in another month, it would be impossible to hide the truth. Then the question of who would succeed him would finally have to be addressed. Fernando knew that his father meant for things to go on as they had before—Luisa running the criminal arm, his only child fetching clean sheets for tourists.

Baltasar had always had a soft spot for Luisa. Ever since she and Fernando were children. Knowing her as he did, Fernando though Luisa might make a good soldier, but she lacked the personal authority to keep the peace in the Algarve. Not without Baltasar Alves standing behind her. The peace endured because his father lived. When he died, it would die with him if Luisa were allowed to take over. Fernando had seen no choice but to act. The Algarve had been unified by an Alves man, and that's how it would remain.

He'd been laying the groundwork for two years. Forging ties to the Romanians had been an unsavory but necessary step to preparing for that eventuality. They weren't the allies he would have chosen, but respect for your allies wasn't always possible. The Baltasar Alves of twenty years ago had understood that. His arrangement with the Mexicans wasn't born from respect but necessity. The younger Baltasar certainly wouldn't have killed Silva and Peres but left Anibal alive. Sloppy and sentimental. The latest in a long list of missteps that his father had made since his heart attack had turned him philosophical. Fernando didn't recognize the nostalgic shambles of a man his father had become.

"We're closed," the proprietor said as Baltasar came up the steps.

"Of course. I only need a brief word. My name is Baltasar Alves."

Recognition sparked in the proprietor's face. Apologizing profusely, he put away the mop and arranged the chairs at his best table. Baltasar thanked him graciously, sitting on the warped metal chair like it was a throne. His father asked the proprietor to join him. He did not offer his son a seat, so Fernando stood there awkwardly like a simple waiter.

Despite that, he was grateful not to be the center of attention. It gave him time to compose himself and suppress his anger and fear. If there was one thing he was good at, it was looking like he didn't care. Most of the time he didn't, but on those rare occasions when something mattered to him, he was practiced at the art of defiant neutrality.

Baltasar said, "When I was a boy, my father conducted business from a small café like this one. I've always liked the smell and the noise. The talk. The regular faces. You know what I mean?"

The proprietor nodded in agreement. "Community."

"Exactly," Baltasar said, pointing at the proprietor as though he had said something profound.

Fernando rolled his eyes at his father's man-of-the-people act. He had seen it too many times before.

"What's your name?" Baltasar asked.

"Hagen, *senhor*."

"Hagen, it's good to meet you. I apologize for keeping you here late, but I need your help."

"Anything, Senhor Alves. I know what you have done for the Algarve," Hagen said. "My sister's daughter would not be alive today if it were not for you. Heroin. Today she has a husband, two children of her own."

"I'm happy to hear that."

"What can I do?"

"The cars outside your shop. Did you see the drivers?"

Hagen nodded, relieved to be asked a question he could answer. He described three men and a woman—one Asian, one black, two white—who had drunk coffee and argued. "But they left," he said and pointed to an empty table on the patio as if to corroborate his story.

"What did they argue about?"

"They talked in English, Senhor Alves. I don't know."

Baltasar smiled. "Of course, I understand. Did you see where they went?"

"Into the church. They were there a long time. Then they came out, took bags from the trunk of their car, and walked south."

"When?" Baltasar asked.

Hagen looked at his watch. "Perhaps fifteen minutes ago."

Fifteen minutes ago, Fernando would have been furious at the news, but now he felt only sweet relief. It didn't save him, but it bought time to find a way out. He was now rooting for the Americans to stay one step ahead of his father.

Baltasar asked for a cup of coffee.

"Of course, Senhor Alves," Hagen said, rising from the table.

Baltasar's phone rang. It was Luisa. Her men were in Quarteira.

"How long?" Baltasar asked.

Fernando didn't hear her answer. Baltasar chewed at his lip thoughtfully. Planning his next five moves, unless Fernando missed the mark. Fernando hated the sallow, loose folds of excess skin that made his father look like an old, deflated balloon. Ironically, he'd looked far healthier when he'd been fat. Only the eyes were the same—bright and full of calculating intelligence.

"Call me when you're in position," Baltasar said and disconnected the call.

"How are things in Quarteira?" Fernando asked.

"The Romanians are tough. But their numbers are small. Luisa will break their backs and send them scurrying into the ocean."

Fernando nodded, although he didn't agree with his father's assessment. His impression of the Romanians was that they might occasionally lose battles but rarely lost wars. They took the long view. Even if somehow Luisa beat them now, they would never concede defeat. They would regroup and return stronger, and when they did, they'd look to their longtime ally. It would play out in his favor so long as Gibson Vaughn could be contained. That was the only way he could lose.

Baltasar said, "Tell Anibal to send a car after George. Perhaps we'll finally have some luck."

"It's strange that they would leave the Porsche here. Why do you think they did that?" Fernando knew that his father had been wondering the same thing, but the old man wasn't ready to hear that George Abe had betrayed him. Fernando knew better than to be the one to suggest it openly.

"That's something we'll have to ask when we find him."

"Yes, *Pai*." Merely the thought of his father talking to George was enough to bring the taste of bile into his mouth.

"And, Fernando?" His father turned his head to look his son in the eyes. "You did well to recognize what the Americans were doing. I won't forget."

Baltasar patted his son's arm affectionately. Fernando felt a spreading warmth at the praise. Was it pride? Love? It didn't matter. Whatever the name of his misguided emotion, it made him feel like a child. He hated that his father could still affect him with a few words. After so many years. What a fool he was.

"Of course, *Pai*. I'm glad I caught it in time. We have to put a stop to this."

Hagen returned with the coffee and a pastry. Baltasar held out money. Hagen refused it, and Baltasar managed to appear both humble and surprised.

Fernando switched to English. "Should Anibal search the place? Question him again? I don't trust the owner."

His father looked Hagen up and down. "Do you have any reason?"

"I just want to be thorough."

"No," Baltasar said. "That's no reason to make an enemy. Treat people like animals, they will become an animal. How many times do I have to tell you and Luisa? Force is a tool that feels good in our hands but bad in our memory. Be careful how you wield it. Do you understand?"

"Yes, *Pai*." Fernando excused himself to convey his father's order to Anibal.

What sanctimonious nonsense, he thought. Silva and Peres weren't even cold, and his father was giving speeches about restraint. Perhaps if he'd been a little less restrained all along, no one would have dared to go after the shipment. Then they wouldn't all be in this awful situation.

CHAPTER TWENTY-SEVEN

Fernando found Anibal on the steps of the church.

"Quite a day," Fernando said. "Peres. Silva. Who would have thought it?"

Anibal stared out at the street from under the brim of his sombrero and spat into the dirt. "They should have been smarter."

"Would that have saved them?"

Anibal grimaced but said nothing.

"It's unfortunate what happened at the cannery," Fernando said, testing the knife to see how far it would twist. "Bad luck."

"What do you want?" Anibal asked.

"We should talk."

"About what?"

"About not joining Silva and Peres," Fernando said. "To be honest, I'm surprised you aren't with them now. The hijacking was in your territory, after all."

Anibal was grim-faced and silent.

Fernando had a good grip on the knife now and hunted for a nerve. "And that's not all that's happened in your territory lately."

For the first time, Anibal turned to look at Fernando. "Are you threatening me?" A condescending smile played across his mouth. Fernando looked forward to wiping it off his smug face.

"I just want us to understand each other," Fernando said.

Anibal straightened his hat resolutely. "I let you run whores. As a favor. What are you playing at?"

"You still think I'm running a brothel?" Fernando made an exaggerated face to express his surprise. He had Anibal's undivided attention now.

"What have you done, boy?"

Fernando laid out the entire operation to him in lurid Technicolor. At the mention of the Romanians, Anibal paled.

"Baltasar forbade it."

When the Romanians had arrived two years ago and suggested a business arrangement, Baltasar had made it bluntly clear what he thought of human trafficking. If he found out that his only son had gone behind his back to go into business with the Romanians . . . Well, there would be no coming back from that.

"Yes," Fernando said patiently. "He did."

"If your father finds out, we're both—"

"Yes, *my* father. I imagine he will be very disappointed with me. Remind me what you are to him?"

"What do you want?" Anibal asked for the second time.

"Nothing for now. I only wish to point out that it is best for both of us if my father never knows," Fernando said. "But especially you."

Anibal glared at him with loathing. This was how they always looked when Fernando gave them the stick. It was a necessary part of blackmail. Anibal would come around when it came time for the carrot.

"Oh," Fernando said. "My father wants you to send a car south after the Americans. They have a fifteen-minute head start." Fernando glanced at his watch. "Twenty now."

Anibal cursed. "Why didn't you tell me that immediately?"

"We needed to understand each other first."

Fernando watched Anibal scurry across the street, his thoughts returning to Gibson Vaughn. Ditching the Porsche had been smart. How Gibson knew he was being tracked, Fernando had no idea. Clearly, he'd underestimated him. When Gibson had first arrived in Portugal, he'd seemed lost and broken. Fernando realized that his first impression had stuck, clouding his judgment about the man. He couldn't afford for it to happen again. If even half of what the conspiracy blogs said about him was true, a long line of people had underestimated Gibson Vaughn and paid the price for it. Fernando did not intend to join their ranks. Hopefully, he had bought Gibson a little more time to get away.

A thought occurred to him. Maybe he was looking at this whole thing the wrong way. Since the morning, he'd been playing defense. Trying to prevent his father from learning the truth. His intention had always been to wait until after his father's funeral before moving against Luisa. But what if, instead of a threat, today was an opportunity? All of his plans these past two years were based on the reality that he was, at best, fifth in line to follow his father. The deaths of Silva and Peres had cleared the board of two rivals. That left only Luisa and Anibal.

It was risky, but Fernando liked those odds.

He slipped inside the dark church. Not to pray—he hoped never to be that desperate. He needed to make a call that required absolute privacy. What better place than a church? Fernando typed in a phone number that was not in his contacts. Constantin Funar picked up on the second ring. They had only met once and had not spoken directly in almost two years, until early this morning.

"Fernando. Twice in one day," he said in heavily accented English. Fernando didn't speak Romanian, and Constantin didn't speak Portuguese—English bridged the gap. "You're not still having problems with your American friend? I told you we should have dealt with him more permanently."

"No, I have that under control."

"Good. That is good. So, what is it I can do for you?"

"Luisa Mata is in Quarteira," Fernando said.

A silence followed. Fernando listened to Constantin breathe slowly.

"Why is she here?"

"For you. For all of you."

"I see." Constantin sounded entirely disinterested in the news. "So why are you telling me this?"

"Because we are friends, Constantin. A show of good faith."

"And what do you want?"

"Only that she never leave."

Constantin said something in Romanian and hung up. If the Romanians were as tough as their reputation, that should be enough. Fernando crossed himself with exaggerated, ironic motions. In a few hours, he should have only one challenger remaining in the Algarve. Anibal would fall in line or be buried under it.

From the doorway, Anibal called for Fernando to hurry. Baltasar had finally gotten his luck. The car he'd sent after the Americans had found them. They were in a blue Fiat heading west on N123. Fernando gritted his teeth. Why couldn't anything go smoothly?

CHAPTER TWENTY-EIGHT

There it was again. The same yellow car. Gibson had seen it a few miles ago, and it had stayed with them ever since.

"We're being followed," he said.

"We're not being followed," Hendricks said without looking back. He was still grumpy about dumping the Porsche and Audi in Alcantarilha. They'd hot-wired an old Fiat with a sun-damaged hood and the horsepower of a glorified golf cart. He was in no mood for Gibson's amateur tradecraft.

Gibson was notoriously awful at spotting a tail. He wasn't much better at following someone, and it had bitten him in the ass on more than one occasion. Their exile in the Algarve had seemed like an ideal time to correct that weakness. Especially since a retired LAPD detective and tactical-driving instructor slept down the hall. It had taken two weeks of pestering before Hendricks relented and agreed to teach him the fundamentals. Gibson had expected Hendricks to give him a lot of stick about it, but to his surprise, Hendricks had proven to be an excellent instructor. Once the lesson started, his natural irritability was replaced by a very un-Hendricks-like equanimity.

Even so, the results had been mixed, Hendricks grading him out at a C-plus. Gibson had gone from not being able to pick up a tail to seeing them everywhere. Anyone behind him for more than a block became immediately suspect. If nothing else, it gave him plenty of opportunity to practice losing someone—even if they weren't following him to begin with. Hendricks assured him that it was a natural over-reaction and that once it became second nature, Gibson would relax. But in the meantime, he was like a faulty car alarm that went off if the wind changed direction.

The yellow car dropped back behind a truck. Gibson slouched down in his seat and watched for it in his side mirror. Every minute or so, it peeked out from behind the truck, pulling onto the shoulder long enough to keep tabs on them.

"Stop it," Hendricks said. "We're not being followed."

"I really think we're being followed."

"We're not . . ." Hendricks drifted off, reconsidering. "Which car?"

"The yellow one."

Hendricks scanned the rearview mirror. "What yellow one?"

"Behind the truck. It'll stick its head out in a minute. On our right. There!"

"Got it," Hendricks said. He drove with his eyes on the rearview mirror and accelerated gradually, putting distance between them and the truck. Seconds later, the yellow car pulled out and passed the truck. Gradually, it closed the distance until it was fifty meters back and matched their speed.

"Huh," Hendricks said. He drew the gun he'd taken from the hotel and handed it and a spare magazine to Jenn in the seat behind him.

"Are you sure?" Jenn asked, ejecting the magazine and counting the remaining rounds. She replaced it and handed the spare magazine to George next to her.

"No, but I will be," Hendricks said, accelerating.

The yellow car maintained its cushion like it was attached to an invisible string. When he took his foot off the gas, the yellow car fell back. The dance went on for a few miles.

"I'm sure," Hendricks said. "Which side do you want them on?"

"This side, if it works out." She and George rolled down their windows. "But I'll manage," she said, unbuckling her seat belt and shifting around to test the most comfortable and effective firing positions. "George, if they wind up on our right, I'll need you to get down in the seat well."

"I'll be ready," he said and unbuckled his own seat belt.

Gibson marveled at the transformation. Six months of rust falling away in an instant. The old Jenn emerging—alert, poised. Her clear eyes taking it all in, missing nothing.

Hendricks slowed as they approached a roundabout. It had no traffic lights, and right-of-way belonged to the car already in the circle. Hendricks let the yellow car come up on their bumper before accelerating out in front of a minivan that had to slam on its brakes to avoid a collision. It honked angrily in protest. The yellow car tried to follow, but the minivan wasn't having it and edged ahead stubbornly, daring the yellow car to hit it.

"Hold on," Hendricks said as the Fiat leapt into the circle. It skidded into the turn, the back drifting away while the front tires clung stubbornly to the inside lane. Instead of using that momentum to launch the Fiat out of the circle, Hendricks held its orbit and let it slingshot them around the circle back toward the yellow car.

"What the hell are you doing?" Gibson said.

"Well, if I was driving a Porsche, I could outrun them," Hendricks said bitterly. "But no, you got me tooling around Portugal in a fucking Fiat."

The yellow car had finally gotten itself into the circle just as Hendricks roared up behind them. Hendricks tried to take the inside lane, but the yellow car swerved sharply to cut them off. Hendricks grinned in the dark, cocking the wheel back the other way. The Fiat swung wide and beat the yellow car to the outside. Jenn braced herself as they came up alongside. She fired twice, paused, then fired twice more.

Both tires on the right side of the yellow car exploded. It fishtailed wildly and went into a spin, crossing three lanes and going broadside into an ancient stone wall. The wall won.

Gibson had to crane his head back to see it, though, because they were already past the circle and accelerating away smoothly by the time the yellow car came to a rest in a cloud of dust and burnt rubber.

They drove on in silence, Gibson's ears ringing from the gunfire. Jenn fastened her seat belt and switched magazines. Gibson watched the road behind them but saw no one keeping pace. Hendricks made a series of random turns, killed the lights, and pulled off behind an abandoned house with a partially collapsed roof. Graffiti covered the walls. They sat there in the dark and waited. Gibson worked his jaw to coax hearing back into his ears.

"How the hell did they find us?" Hendricks demanded. "We just stole this damn car."

"Could be a tracker in our go-bags," Gibson suggested. "And everyone needs to power off their phones."

"Great," Hendricks said. "That's great."

Jenn said, "Maybe this is just their home turf, and they have more eyes than we know about."

"I think the more pressing issue is not how they found us but why they were looking for us at all," George said.

"They must know we went back to the cannery," Hendricks said. "Shit."

"Well, they were going to know that sooner or later," Gibson said.

"Would have been nice to be the one to tell Baltasar, though," George said. "There are a lot of ways to interpret what we've done. Most of them bad."

"Don't expect we'll be getting the benefit of the doubt," Hendricks said.

"Silva and Peres sure didn't," Jenn said.

CHAPTER TWENTY-NINE

The Guarda Nacional Republicana was already on the scene. Crimson road flares closed the outside lane of the circle while an officer directed traffic around the accident with brusque, efficient hand motions. Desperate tire marks showed where the yellow car had spun out of control and slammed into a low stone wall. A miracle no one had died. Its occupants sat handcuffed against the car in the dirt.

Anibal leapt from his car even before Tomas brought it to a complete stop. He strode purposefully over to the most senior officer to make clear who was now in charge.

Fernando watched from the cool comfort of his Porsche—Gibson had been considerate enough to leave the keys in the center console. The rituals when dealing with the GNR were endlessly fascinating to him. Although the GNR had been eager to take Baltasar's deal and had profited handsomely from it both financially and politically, they nevertheless found the arrangement distasteful. Everyone had to bend over backward to maintain the illusion that it was the GNR who still gave the orders. That required a time-consuming choreography—everything phrased as a question rather than a command, which the GNR then took time to consider. To Fernando, it was an unnecessary courtship—money had already traded hands, and it ought to be clear by now who would be loosening their belts and grabbing their ankles.

Anibal was in no mood for romance. He cut off the officer before the dance had even begun. The disregard of protocol didn't sit well with the officer, who attempted vainly to remind Anibal of how things worked. It went poorly.

With a snarl of contempt, Anibal gestured to Baltasar's sedan and read the officer an operatic riot act. Realizing who was inside the sedan, the officer wilted and fell over himself trying to answer Anibal's questions. Fernando enjoyed the predictable reversal. When Anibal was satisfied, he demanded that the officer release the prisoners. Grudgingly, they uncuffed his men and retreated back into their vehicles, peeling out, sirens wailing plaintively. Announcing their authority to the disinterested night.

When the GNR was gone, the two men followed Anibal sheepishly to Baltasar's sedan. Fernando joined them to hear what had happened. He was torn. Part of him felt his interests were best served here at his father's side where he could spin any unfavorable reports. But another part of him knew that he was shackled as long as he was under his father's watchful eye. Wouldn't he be more effective on his own? A lot hung on that calculation.

Both of his father's men were badly shaken from the accident and swayed on their feet like stalks of dying grass. One had blood in his hair that had dripped down the left side of his face. Baltasar did not invite any of them into his car, so they all stood next to the open window while telling their story in faulty stereo. The gist of it was that they had followed the blue Fiat at a respectful distance as they'd been ordered. When they'd come to the traffic circle, the Americans had ambushed them, unprovoked, shooting out their tires and sending them into the wall.

"The Americans are armed?" Fernando asked, sensing an opportunity. "How did they get guns?"

The question hung between the men like a glass tumbling to the ground just out of reach. Baltasar dismissed the two men to see to their injuries. The men made their apologies and backed away. When they were alone, Anibal echoed the question: Why *were* the Americans armed?

Baltasar had the look of a man who had made a wrong turn and saw no safe place to turn around. Despite the mounting evidence, openly suggesting that George Abe had betrayed him had been off-limits up until now. Fernando's father clung to the notion that this had to be a misunderstanding, but now the Americans were shooting at his men. Fernando didn't know their intentions yet, but whatever Gibson knew, or thought he knew, his father was becoming less and less likely to listen. Fernando appreciated that they were doing his work for him.

Even so, he couldn't afford to wait any longer. The Americans had been heading west. Olhão was to the west. The warehouse was to the west. He had no proof, but Fernando felt in his gut that he knew their destination. He still didn't know why. He had too many leaks and too few fingers to plug them all. When the Americans made their move, his father couldn't still be on the fence about George Abe. He'd hoped that his father would say it first, but time was against him. It was a dangerous play, but he didn't see any other way forward.

"The attack at the hotel," Fernando said. "Was I really the target?"

That caught Anibal and Baltasar's attention.

"Who else could it be?" Anibal asked.

"Who was Gibson Vaughn on the way to see?" Fernando said. He let the implications of that sink in.

"The American asked to see Dani Coelho," Anibal said. "But why go through the charade if he intended to kill him?"

"How did the attackers find Coelho at the hotel? Someone had to tell them," Fernando said. "We hid Coelho there only this morning."

"You think it was Vaughn?" Anibal asked.

"Who else?" Fernando was curious to see if Anibal would work with him or try to counter his theory. "How many times did he demand to meet with Coelho?"

"Too many," Baltasar said. He'd been silent up until now, but was sitting forward, deep in thought. Fernando grinned inwardly. His father had taken the bait, leading the conversation rather than following Fernando's bread crumbs. The wheels were turning now. All he had to do was keep the gears well oiled.

"So they went through the charade of helping Anibal clear the hotel, knowing the attackers were already gone," Fernando said. "I feel foolish for lending them my Porsche."

Anibal nodded in agreement, obviously happy to support any theory that didn't make him a suspect. "It was Hendricks who found the receipt on the can. He led us into the ambush at the paint shop. Putting himself above suspicion."

"Could the Americans really be behind it?" Fernando asked, pretending to play devil's advocate now that the idea had taken root. "They don't seem capable of such a thing."

"I know what they look like," Baltasar said. "But they are more formidable than they appear. Trust me on this."

"Yes, *Pai*," Fernando said, voice dripping with respect.

Anibal agreed with Baltasar. "Our operation has worked smoothly for more than fifteen years. Then six months after they arrive, this happens? It is quite a coincidence."

"So has this been the Americans' game all along, or did they hatch the plan after they arrived here?" Fernando asked.

"Does it matter?" Anibal said.

Baltasar's phone rang. He looked at the number, frowned to himself, and answered. "Hello, George. We were just discussing you."

Right on schedule, Fernando thought to himself grimly. Now the game got serious. He strained to hear the other side of the conversation, but the passing traffic drowned it out.

"Yes," Baltasar said. "I'm there now. Both men are alive." The tinted window of the sedan slid closed, cutting Baltasar off midsentence. It left Fernando and Anibal to stare uneasily at their own reflections. Fernando had always wondered what it felt like to be one of those poor bastards stuck waiting in line outside of his nightclubs. Now he knew.

Anibal glanced at Fernando, who arched a sympathetic eyebrow his way. Fernando didn't know which of them Baltasar didn't trust to listen in to his conversation. Most likely both, but the fear in Anibal's face told Fernando that Anibal didn't think he was long for this world.

Good. That left him in desperate need of an ally. A port to ride out the storm. Anibal would latch on to the first friendly hand extended to him. Fernando would offer that hand. As it turned out, he was in the market for an ally himself. He had an errand to run and needed Anibal to keep tabs on his father while he was gone. Fernando liked the symmetry of it. Anibal had been with his father from the beginning. How appropriate if he were there for the beginning of Baltasar's son's rule too.

Together they would remake the Algarve.

"We should talk again," Fernando said.

Anibal nodded with all the enthusiasm of a patient agreeing to an experimental, untested surgery that would either save or kill him.

Fernando winked at him. "Don't worry, I'll be gentle."

CHAPTER THIRTY

George hung up the call and powered off his phone.

"How did he sound?" Jenn asked.

"Remarkably civil and reasonable."

That raised Jenn's eyebrow about four degrees above top dead center. "Even after I shot up his men's car?"

"Exactly," George replied. "And he agreed to a meeting—our time, our location, our conditions. No strings attached."

"Well, that's not good," Hendricks said.

"No. No, it is not," George agreed.

The four of them sat in the dark of the car, brooding over the implications. The irony was that their plan depended on Baltasar to be reasonable, but it was reasonable that he be angry. That he wasn't, or was hiding it, gave them all cause for concern.

"Gibson, how certain are you that you can detonate remotely?" George asked.

"Ninety-five percent."

"What would get us to one hundred?" Hendricks muttered.

"You trust a car you've never driven?"

Hendricks acknowledged the truth of the statement with a drawn-out curse.

Gibson said, "I didn't build their gear. Won't be one hundred until after I detonate."

"Well, then ninety-five will just have to do," George conceded. "We can all agree that I should be the one to talk to Baltasar at the meet? I think it will go better coming from me."

Everyone could.

"Jenn, is it too much to hope that you'll let me go in alone?"

"It is," she said simply.

George didn't bother to argue. It would take an asteroid strike to keep her away. George laid out the bones of a plan, and the other three filled in the blanks. Or as many of the blanks as they could from inside a stolen Fiat behind an abandoned house. It made for an uninspiring command center.

When they were as done as they were going to get, George gave them his bottom line. "I give us no better than a fifty-fifty chance. There are too many variables we can't account for. Everyone willing to accept that?"

"Fuck slavery," Hendricks said.

"Agreed," Jenn said.

No one asked Gibson. "Come on, it's a no-brainer. We have his shipment. If he doesn't get it back, the Mexican cartel he fronts for will clean house in the Algarve and start from scratch. Luisa told us as much. How can Baltasar not go for it?"

George said, "Under normal circumstances, I would agree. But he is under enormous pressure. His back is already up against the wall, and we shouldn't count on him to make rational decisions."

"So what happens if we're on the wrong side of fifty?" Hendricks asked.

"Plan B," George said.

"Which is?" Jenn asked.

"I have no idea." George paused. "But we should probably have one."

For some reason that struck Jenn as funny. An uncharacteristic snicker escaped from behind the fist she put to her lips. A moment later she was cackling. Hendricks tried to stifle himself, but Jenn had set off a chain reaction throughout the car. Soon they were all howling with laughter at the absurdity of the situation. It had been a long day and night, and none of them was thinking exactly clearly. Exhaustion had stamped itself across all their faces. The meeting with Baltasar was set for eight in the morning. George suggested adjourning for a few hours to get some sleep. They would still have time to come up with plan B after they got some rest. No one argued.

Gibson volunteered to take first watch; he'd dozed on the way to Alcantarilha and felt decent. Hendricks handed him the gun and said to wake him up in a couple of hours, then disappeared into the abandoned house to find a flat surface to call a bed. George reclined the passenger seat of the Fiat and was asleep in a matter of seconds. Gibson left the back seat to Jenn and fished his laptop out of the trunk.

He found a window at the front of the house with a view of the road. The panes had long ago been smashed, leaving little more than a rectangular gash in the house. Gibson found a three-legged chair. A stack of bricks made a passable fourth. He opened his laptop on the windowsill and scanned for available Wi-Fi networks. Not a damn thing. He shut his laptop and stared out at the dark road.

"Some view," Jenn said, straddling the windowsill, one leg in, one leg out of the house.

"You should get some sleep."

"Caught a nap earlier. I'm good." She stared out at the dark, empty road.

"What's up with you and Sebastião?" Gibson asked.

She gave him a hard look. "How do you do that?"

He shrugged. "It's cool if it's none of my—"

"He asked me to marry him," she said.

Gibson had been prepared for a lot of different answers, but that left him speechless for a long minute. "When?"

"Couple of hours ago."

"He asked you tonight?"

"Nice timing, right?" she said with a sad laugh.

"I didn't know it was that serious."

"You and me both."

"What did you tell him?"

"I told him I had to go, and he lent me his car."

"That was nice of him."

"No one knows how to break up anymore."

"I'm sorry I got you involved with this."

"No, you're not," Jenn said. "You wanted me involved, I'm involved. Don't walk it back now. *That* would piss me off."

"Fair enough."

"Anyway, I would have done the same thing."

He looked up at her silhouetted against the starlight. "So why'd you fight me so hard?"

Jenn shrugged. "Habit?"

They both laughed. Gibson felt very close to her in that moment. Now that they weren't bullshitting each other anymore. He wished he knew the right thing to tell her and searched for words that would reflect all they'd been through together. Whatever those words were, he didn't know them. Wasn't sure he'd recognize them even if he did.

"So, what are you going to do?" he asked instead.

"Thinking about marrying him, to be honest," she said but couldn't meet Gibson's eyes.

Marrying Sebastião Coval would mean parting ways, and Gibson could hear the guilt in her voice. It had no reason to be there as far as he was concerned. They all owed her, not the other way around, but Gibson thought that abandoning George might kill her. Thing was, though, staying with him might kill her another way.

Jenn stood. She'd reached her threshold for sharing. "Anyway, you're definitely not invited."

"That's cool. I hate weddings."

She looked down at him, her eyes shining like the shattered glass on the floor. "Gibson," she began, then stopped. "Don't get yourself killed trying to put things right."

"I was just thinking the same thing about you."

"I know, and I'm trying. I'm trying real hard. Just need to know you are too."

"I can't leave those kids like that," he said.

"That's not what I mean." She put a hand on his shoulder. "A person shouldn't be defined by their worst moment. I mean, who would that leave? Best we can do is learn from our mistakes, not kill ourselves over them. Penance is overrated."

She squeezed his neck affectionately and left him alone with his thoughts. He sat there for more than an hour, staring out the window, thinking about penance. The penance he'd done, the penance he continued to do. Who it was for and whether any of it made a damn bit of difference. In all that time, not a car passed, and the night grew so still that Gibson swore he could feel the turning of the planet beneath him. A quiet hum filled his ears. He thought he'd drifted off and sat up straight to wake himself. The humming grew louder.

Outside the window, a drone descended on a cushion of air. It stopped at eye level and hung there. Gibson stared back neutrally and reached for the gun. The drone floated forward and landed on the windowsill where Jenn had sat. From inside the drone, an ominous click. Gibson flinched. The three bricks propping up his chair flinched too. It sent him sprawling onto the floor. From his back, he watched the drone lift off again. It hovered in the window a moment as if saying good-bye before buzzing away into the night.

Gibson climbed to his feet and brushed himself off. The fall had cost his chair a second leg, and he left it there amid the broken glass.

His ankle, which hadn't bothered him in hours, throbbed irritably. On the windowsill, a box sat where the drone had been. Gibson limped over and studied it. What did he think he was going to find? Up close, it still looked like a plain cardboard box. The unthreatening kind. He decided, spontaneously, to open it. If the aim had been to blow him up, he figured it would have cut to the chase by now.

Inside, he found a brand-new air card, a small device that provided a cellular connection to the internet when Wi-Fi was unavailable. Kind of like now. Interesting. Printed on a white index card was an http address and password. He opened his laptop and plugged in the air card to his USB port. On his screen, a window popped up, warning him explicitly not to connect this unknown device to the laptop. Gibson did it anyway. There was nothing on the laptop he cared about, and if this was some elaborate social-engineering hack to tempt him into a stupid mistake, well, then it was working.

The http address led to a blank page with a simple log-in box. He entered the password. A chat window appeared.

Dol5: This wasn't part of our deal.

Vaughn: It's not not part of our deal.

Dol5: Are you actively trying to get yourself killed?

Vaughn: It's not my primary motivation.

Dol5: We've made a sizeable investment in you.

Vaughn: I solved your little puzzle box.

Dol5: And yet, no report.

Vaughn: I've got to take care of something first.

Dol5: Like I said, that was not part of the deal.

Vaughn: Neither were those kids. Do you know what's going on in that warehouse?

Dol5: We're aware.

Vaughn: If you're that worried about my well-being, you could take care of it for me. You have the resources here to do it.

Dol5: Now that's definitely not part of the deal.

Vaughn: I'll give you the money back. Write the report for free. Just get those kids out of there.

Dol5: You're a principled guy. I admire that.

Vaughn: And you're not?

Dol5: I am. Different principles. We're not getting involved with this sideshow.

Vaughn: So what now?

Dol5: Hypothetically—what would you say if we threatened to kill Jenn Charles unless you backed off?

Vaughn: I'd say send a lot of guys.

Dol5: Christ, you're a pain in the ass, you know that? Have you really broken our hijack?

Vaughn: Try detonating. See what happens.

There was a pause. For several minutes, Gibson sat there waiting. He began to worry that he'd crossed some invisible line. Somehow, his new employers didn't strike Gibson as the types who liked to be shown up. This despite the fact they'd hired him to do exactly that. Better not to stir the pot, no matter how much Gibson would enjoy letting Dol5 know exactly where he stood in the grand scheme of things.

Dol5: How did you do it?

Vaughn: It will be in my report.

Dol5: Which you haven't written yet.

Vaughn: I'm working on it.

Dol5: If you get yourself killed, the deal's off.

Vaughn: That's okay, I don't think they take euros in hell.

Dol5: If Baltasar catches you, don't even think about trading us for your life.

Vaughn: What do I really know?

Dol5: We will nuke you from orbit just to be sure. Just saying.

There was a second pause, longer than the first, and Gibson came away with the impression that he was being discussed. Something about this guy rubbed him wrong, and he was glad they couldn't see his face this time. As soon as he thought it, he realized what an absurd assumption that was to make. He was hiding in an abandoned house, and Dol5 had still managed to land a drone in his lap. Perhaps best to assume they had eyes on him, no matter what.

Dol5: I'm sending you two files.

Gibson clicked on the link and let the files download. One was a text file with hundreds of lines of code. The second was a PDF containing installation and configuration instructions for the code. Gibson scanned it. He had heard talk of this security vulnerability going back at least a decade. Plenty of time to address the problem. Theoretically. But vulnerabilities had a way of going unpatched until it cost someone money. To his knowledge, this exploit had never been used outside of the movies, so he wasn't surprised that nothing had been done about it.

Vaughn: Is this for Baltasar Alves?

Dol5: Who else?

Vaughn: Does it actually work?

Dol5: If you install it correctly. The internet of things is a beautiful place.

Vaughn: I mean, has it been field tested?

Dol5: On an identical model. It works.

Vaughn: So why? I thought you weren't getting involved.

Dol5: We're not. Not directly. But we want that report. And since you're too stubborn to walk away from Baltasar Alves, maybe this will help level the playing field.

Vaughn: You know what would really level the playing field? A weapons drop.

Dol5: LMFAO. This ain't *Call of Duty*, Gibson.

Vaughn: Just thought I'd ask.

Dol5: You're not what I thought you'd be.

Vaughn: I get that a lot.

Dol5: This is why they say never meet your heroes.

Vaughn: Get better heroes.

The chat window closed. Obviously, the hijacking hadn't been a one-person job, but Gibson guessed that Dol5 was American, white, and male. His syntax and pop-culture references had an unmistakable ring to them. Gibson was thirty-one. If he had been Dol5's hero, then the hacker was probably under twenty-five; people didn't typically choose heroes who were their juniors. Hopefully this would be the last of their friendly little chats. Gibson really couldn't stand the guy.

It was time to wake Hendricks, but Gibson didn't think he could sleep now if he tried. Instead, he spent the next few hours studying Dol5's malware backward and forward. Coding had never been his strongest suit, but he knew enough to recognize top-shelf work. It was a clean, impressive exploit.

Using the back door he'd installed in the servers at Fresco Mar Internacional, Gibson installed the malware. Baltasar's estate had a secure connection to the servers, which meant Gibson now had a secure connection to Baltasar's estate. Once installed, he would be able to execute the malware from his phone. He had no way to confirm that it would perform as advertised, but he was willing to trust Dol5 on this, at least. It was a Hail Mary anyway. If it came down to using it, he was probably as good as dead.

It was a little after five when Gibson finally closed his laptop. He stood and stretched. About time to wake everyone and get ready to meet the morning. George stood in the doorway, leaning on his cane.

"All quiet on the western front?" he asked.

"A car passed an hour ago. I decided not to sound general quarters." He omitted the drone, although he couldn't say why.

"Did you take the whole watch?" George asked.

"People needed to sleep."

"So did you. We need sharp minds, not martyrs, today."

"I appreciate what you said in the church."

"It has to be done," George said.

"Just can't believe that, in the twenty-first century, we haven't evolved beyond slavery."

"That's not what evolution is," George said.

"You don't think?"

"No. I don't know when 'evolved' became synonymous with better. Probably some self-help guru thought it sounded good in the seventies. When a species adapts to survive in its environment, that's evolution. That's all it is. We're not evolving into something better, more enlightened. Or worse. We evolve to survive. Nothing more. And survival is amoral. It is not an enlightened state."

"That's pretty cynical."

"Only because you're a righteous man, Gibson."

"Thank you, I guess."

"It wasn't a compliment."

"Ah," Gibson said.

"It wasn't an insult either. Simply the reality of who you are—an idealist in an unideal world. It makes you dangerous. To us as well as them."

"There was also a drone," Gibson blurted out, much to his own surprise. He figured that he'd fought so hard to make them a team again that the least he could do was to start acting like it. But Jenn was right; it was hard to break old habits.

"A drone?"

"It landed right there." He pointed to the windowsill.

"I see," George said. "What did it want?"

"It came bearing gifts from Dol5."

"A little early for Christmas," George said. "I hope it didn't bring lumps of coal."

"Only for Baltasar Alves. I may have our plan B."

CHAPTER THIRTY-ONE

After the little shoot-out at the traffic circle, the Americans had vanished from the face of the earth. Despite his best efforts, Fernando had been unable to sway his father or prevent him from agreeing to a meeting with George Abe. Even more confounding, Fernando still had no idea what Abe intended to say. His best guess was that the Americans meant to trade what they had found at Fresco Mar Internacional for a payday.

Fernando had driven Sebastião's Audi across the Algarve like a maniac. He couldn't quite talk himself out of the notion that Jenn had involved Sebastião somehow. If so, his house would make an ideal place for the Americans to lie low. It was the best lead he had, and anything was better than sitting idly by while the clock ran out on him.

He checked his phone. Anibal was with Baltasar and would let him know if there were any developments. Fernando was still hoping for good news from the Romanians, but Quarteira had gone dark shortly after Baltasar had given Luisa the green light. All he could do was cross his fingers and hope the Romanians lived up to their reputations.

Fernando parked in front of Sebastião's house and killed the engine. Inside, all the lights blazed. Not unusual for Sebastião, even at this hour, but it didn't put Fernando's mind at ease. He slipped the gun into the hollow of his back the way he'd seen his father's men do. It felt uncomfortable there. He took it out again, checked the safety a third time, and slid it back in place. He liked his ass too much to shoot it off.

The front door was unlocked, the house silent. He didn't like it but resisted the urge to draw his gun. Better to come in peace. For now. He would know the score when he saw Sebastião. His friend had never been a good liar in person and had always proven a bit gullible. It had provided Fernando endless entertainment when they were children. If Sebastião was truly heartbroken, as he'd sounded on the phone, he would be drowning his sorrows, lost in a forest of empty champagne bottles.

Like many kids who had grown up achingly poor before making something of themselves, Sebastião spent money not out of need but to reassure himself that he had escaped. Fernando remembered the exact moment when Sebastião's obsession with champagne had begun. Fernando had been fifteen, Sebastião fourteen, and Baltasar had thrown a lavish wedding at his home for a beloved cousin. The happy couple had been married on the cliffs overlooking the ocean. An octet of musicians played in the background. Ninety-nine doves released when they were pronounced husband and wife. Fernando had thought it was the tackiest thing he'd ever seen. Sebastião, who had been invited as Fernando's guest, had been entranced.

At the reception, Baltasar had given a toast, champagne poured specially for the occasion. No ordinary champagne would do, of course: the newlyweds were toasted with Dom Pérignon 2004 rosé. Fernando did the math later and estimated that the toast alone had cost twenty thousand. Even the children were permitted a small glass. It had made quite an impression on teenage Sebastião Coval. Years later, when he signed his first big contract, Sebastião had celebrated with the same Dom Pérignon 2004 rosé. Fernando's only surprise was that no doves had exploded out of the cake. After that, Dom had become Sebastião's signature drink. His bar tabs routinely ran into the thousands of euros. Fernando should know—Sebastião was one of his best customers.

Fernando found Sebastião alone by the pool, not a champagne bottle in sight. He looked dressed for a night out on the town, and in the moonlight, his hair shone like a brilliant black wave. It was after two a.m., but he had showered and shaved recently. Fernando had taught him that trick. Nothing better than a postmidnight shower to revive a flagging soul and give it a new lease on the evening. Although it didn't look as though partying was in the cards. So, what was he doing? Why were a cup of coffee and two large bottles of water his only companions?

Fernando decided to play the concerned friend, but the weight of the gun against his back felt reassuring. "What are you doing out here all alone? This is a tragic scene."

Sebastião turned around and grinned half a smile, the other corner of his mouth tumbling away like a lonely invalid down a flight of stairs. Fernando felt himself relax—it was no act. What could make a man look that way? Jenn Charles was a beautiful woman, no doubt, but beautiful women were nothing new to Sebastião. She must be spectacular in bed to put such an expression on his friend's face. That was the only reasonable explanation. Although Fernando knew better than to put it in those terms. At least not while his friend was in such a sensitive state.

"I'm waiting for her," Sebastião said.

"Is she coming back?" Fernando asked, hope rising.

Sebastião smiled his crooked smile again. "I don't know. I hope so."

"I prefer it when women wait for me," Fernando said.

"I asked her to marry me."

Fernando mostly hid his surprise. "Did you mean it?"

"I did."

"And you're still hoping she comes back?" Fernando said, unable to resist needling him.

Sebastião ignored it and changed the subject. "How are things with you? What's it like to almost die?"

"It makes you question your priorities," Fernando said. "But it passes."

Sebastião laughed. "It would take more than a brush with death for Fernando Alves to change his ways."

"I drink in the face of death," Fernando said with mock bravado.

"Has Baltasar dealt with the trouble?"

"No, not yet."

In that moment, Fernando decided Sebastião would be coming with him. Assuming Jenn Charles felt something similar, this simpering Romeo would be useful leverage. His first instinct was to draw the gun and make Sebastião his prisoner. But how much simpler it would be if the prisoner didn't know he was one.

Fernando struck a worried expression. "That's why I'm here, I'm afraid."

"What's going on?"

"We found your car abandoned in Alcantarilha. I brought it back for you."

"Alcantarilha?" Sebastião stood up. "Where is Jenn now?"

"We don't know. I was hoping you might have some idea."

Sebastião fumbled for his phone and dialed Jenn. The call went straight to voice mail, as Fernando expected it would. The Americans' phones had all been off since setting the meeting. Sebastião hung up and looked accusingly at Fernando.

"What did you get Jenn involved with?"

"Me?" Fernando protested. "That was Baltasar."

"Your father, Fernando. *Your* father. He ordered them out of Portugal."

"Yes, and they didn't go. My father is very angry."

"What aren't you telling me?" Sebastião asked.

"I just have to find them." Fernando turned to leave. "Let me know if you hear from her."

He made it ten paces before Sebastião stopped him.

"Wait," Sebastião said. "I'm coming with you."

Fernando suppressed a smile before turning back. "Good, because I need to borrow your car."

"I'm driving," Sebastião said. "That is nonnegotiable."

Fernando said, "Absolutely. Lead the way."

CHAPTER THIRTY-TWO

A private stairway set into the cliff face led down from the Hotel Mariana to the beach below. The sand was a rippling golden pond from this height. Fernando could see where the meet with George Abe was set, a rocky outcropping that separated Albufeira Beach from Fisherman's Beach to the east. He followed his father and Anibal down the curved steps. It was a little past seven in the morning, and the rising sun was in their eyes. This time yesterday, he had been on a bench waiting for Gibson Vaughn, wondering how badly he'd trapped himself. Hard to believe how much had happened in only twenty-four hours.

Hard to believe how close he was to turning piss to gold.

The finish line was almost in sight. This meeting would decide how he crossed it—in the lead or on a stretcher. It would decide his future, the future of the entire Algarve. That made it imperative that Fernando be there to hear firsthand what George Abe had to say and to spin it in his favor. Anticipating that his father would reject the idea, Fernando had prepped for an argument, even going so far as to enlist Anibal to press his case. But in the end, none of that had proved necessary. His father had personally asked him to attend. "It's important that you see how things work," he had told his son with an intimate confidentiality.

Something had changed between them. After Fernando had brought Sebastião to Baltasar and told him what he had in mind, his father had looked at him differently. With respect. Fernando could feel it. George Abe couldn't be allowed to jeopardize that either.

While they descended to the beach, Fernando listened to his father and Anibal review the security arrangements for what seemed the hundredth time. That George had proposed the beach for the meeting had spooked his father. The Americans couldn't have made a more foolish choice. Hemmed in to the west by cliffs and the ocean to the south, the beach had only one escape route: into town. That concerned Baltasar. George Abe wasn't the kind of man to leave himself no outs. So the question of the morning had been what they were missing.

They'd been over it from every angle. The Hotel Mariana presided over one end of the beach and offered a commanding vantage. Spotters on the roof would see George coming, and more importantly, they would see him go. This early in the morning, he wouldn't even be able to disappear into the crowd, and Anibal's men lurked at all the choke points leading off the beach. A speedboat prowled a hundred meters offshore, on the off chance that George Abe had himself a submarine. Fernando had told his father that the only way George was getting off that beach was by spaceship. Baltasar did not share his optimism. He had too much respect for George's abilities.

Fernando thought his father was allowing his fury to affect his judgment. After all that Baltasar had done for George, he was taking his betrayal personally. It had been festering all night. Almost as soon as his father had begun to calm down, he would discover some new way that George was the Antichrist and begin to rant all over again. It had been incredibly irritating to listen to, but Fernando couldn't help but smile at the irony. This was what kindness brought you—betrayal and ruin. He was, after all, exhibit A. Still, there was time for Fernando to make it up to his father. He wouldn't let George Abe take the Algarve from them.

"Any word from Luisa?" Baltasar asked, interrupting Anibal's recitation. No one had heard from her in hours, and that was also weighing heavily on him.

"No, but they will let us know the moment she checks in," Anibal said.

The Romanians had also gone radio silent, but Fernando didn't share that piece of information. Whatever was happening in Quarteira must be heavy.

Anibal stopped and cupped a hand over his ear. The observation post on the roof of the hotel was reporting in—the Americans had arrived.

"How many?" Baltasar asked.

Only two had been identified so far: George and Jenn Charles.

"The others will be nearby. Find them," Baltasar said.

Clever. Of course the ones who'd broken into Fresco Mar hadn't shown up. Their knowledge was the bargaining chip.

At the bottom of the cliff, Anibal readjusted the straps on Baltasar's lightweight Kevlar until he was satisfied. For once, his father's ugly, billowing shirts served a purpose. The vest was virtually undetectable.

"The men are in place at Fresco Mar?" Baltasar asked.

"Ready to go, the moment we free the shipment," Anibal confirmed.

"They work around the clock. There will be bonuses if it departs on schedule."

"Very generous, I'll tell them."

"Tell them also that their lives depend on it," Baltasar said, his voice weighing down with emotion. "Tell them the Algarve depends on it. We will not go back to the way it was before. Nothing else matters."

"Nothing else matters," Anibal echoed.

"We might survive this yet. With luck, the cartel will never know what happened," Baltasar said.

Anibal went to adjust Fernando's Kevlar, but Baltasar stopped him and did it himself.

"You know your part?" Baltasar asked his son.

"Of course." Fernando powered up the tablet and showed his father the screen. "I know what to do."

"Good boy," his father said and clapped his shoulders warmly. "After this is over, you and I will talk."

"I'm ready," Fernando said, catching Anibal's eye to make sure he understood the implications.

"All right, then, good. Let us see what George wants."

The three set out, Anibal leading the way across the wooden walkway that bisected the wide beach. Down by the water, an older couple strolled past in the other direction. Fernando waved, but the couple, sensing something amiss about three men in suits on a beach at dawn, hurried away. What must they think? Fernando felt a vague thrill that they'd been frightened of him. His phone buzzed. Not the default vibration but the one he'd assigned to Constantin Funar. *Word from Quarteira, at last.* Fernando slipped it out of his pocket and read the message against his thigh:

Done.

Fernando felt the news in his spine. His cousin was dead. One step closer to his destiny. He and Luisa might not have been on the same side anymore, but he didn't revel in her downfall. If he blamed anyone, it was his father for pitting them against each other since they were children. He would give her a heartfelt eulogy at the funeral. She deserved no less.

At the outcrop that divided the two beaches, they saw George limping in their direction. Jenn trailed behind, eyes hidden behind mirrored sunglasses. As they neared, she moved laterally. A subtle thing, adjusting her position to keep a clear line of sight with Baltasar. It unnerved Fernando for some reason. He had always thought of Jenn Charles as a frivolous party girl, but now he wasn't so sure. If the shooting started, he suddenly felt quite sure that he wouldn't want any part of her.

"Hello, George," Baltasar said, as if they'd bumped into each other by chance.

George came to a halt, five slim meters separating them. "Thank you for meeting with us," George said. "I'm sorry it's come to this."

"That makes two of us. I must say, I'm surprised at you choosing this for a meeting place."

"I wanted you to have the high ground, as it were."

"You're giving up a lot to put me at ease."

"Let me worry about that."

"It's a public beach, so you're most likely safe here. But how will you get out? I've looked and looked, but I don't see it."

"Perhaps I've lost my touch," George said. "Is that what you think?"

"I know your woman is very good, but I have snipers on the rooftops. She'll be dead before she clears her holster. If I don't get what I want, you'll never make it off this beach alive."

"Then Gibson will detonate your shipment, and I will miss the cartel carving your family into steaks."

What little blood remained in Baltasar's worn-out body drained from his face. Fernando had to give George points. That was cold-blooded. Two or three sharp retorts came to mind—there was little Fernando enjoyed more than trading insults—but he kept them to himself. It was still his father's show. At least for a little while yet.

"Is that supposed to intimidate me?" Baltasar asked.

"No, the Mexicans don't need me for that."

Damn.

Baltasar said, "You asked for my help, and I gave it gladly. I asked for your help, and you betrayed me, George. Let's not forget that."

"Is that the way you see it?"

"There's no other way to see it. You sent your people back to Fresco Mar after I told you to leave Portugal."

"I did," George said.

"Why?"

"To finish what we started."

"Were there ever really hijackers?" Baltasar asked.

"Not to get philosophical, but you can't have a hijacking without hijackers. The good news is that they no longer control your shipment."

"And you do?" Baltasar said.

"Yes."

"So, you're here to profit, is that the idea? How much do you want?"

For a moment, Fernando allowed himself to get his hopes up that Gibson hadn't found his secret after all. He'd only disarmed the booby-trapped shipment; the Americans were simply looking for traveling money before leaving Portugal. If so, Fernando was home free. The Algarve would be his.

"We don't want your money," George said.

Fernando's body stiffened. He held his breath.

"Then what is it you do want?" Baltasar asked.

"We want the children."

Fernando sighed. There it was.

Baltasar tried to hide it, but Jenn thought the old gangster looked genuinely surprised. As if he really had no idea what George was talking about. It was a strange play. What did Baltasar think he had to gain by bluffing now? He had to know Gibson had him dead to rights.

"I give up," he said. "What children?"

"Haven't we known each other long enough not to lie to each other?" George asked.

Outrage flashed across Baltasar's face. "You lived in my home for six months. I paid for your surgeries. Your recovery. Everything. Don't lecture me about integrity."

"I know you did. That's why this is so hard." George held out a phone to Baltasar.

"I'm sure it is," Baltasar said. He took the phone and looked at the screen, falling silent while the video played. Fernando couldn't see the video, but judging from his father's expression, he could guess easily enough.

"What is this supposed to be?" Baltasar asked.

"Exactly what it appears to be. My only question is whether you are in business with the Romanians, or whether you stole their idea and cut them out?"

Baltasar exploded. "You think this is *me*?"

"It was on your servers," George fired back. "This and much, much more."

"Then why didn't you bring it to me?" Baltasar asked.

"Because it was on *your* servers."

Jenn winced. This meeting depended on a rational Baltasar Alves. That was how they would get off this beach alive. On paper, trading the shipment for the children was the only choice. Especially with the threat of the Mexicans hanging over his head. But this was personal for Baltasar. Jenn could see that. This was about loyalty and trust and the history between these two men. There was nothing so ugly as the loss of trust between friends. She hoped George saw that too. But it was personal for him as well; she hadn't fully grasped that until now. The two old friends looked ready to take a swing at each other. Then where would they be?

Baltasar turned on Anibal, holding up the phone. "What do you know about this?"

His lieutenant had turned seasick pale.

"What?" Baltasar demanded. "Speak up, goddamn you."

"Luisa," Anibal said like a wounded man on a lonely battlefield making his last confession to God.

"Impossible!"

"She has a warehouse in Olhão. I didn't know what it was for."

"How could you not have known?"

"She's the boss."

"I am the boss," Baltasar snarled.

Anibal took a step back and made more stuttering excuses, his mouth backfiring like an old car engine.

Fernando stared intently at Anibal. "Could Luisa have had Dani Coelho killed?"

Baltasar had the look of a man working a complex math problem that had too many variables and not enough constants. It was clear he didn't like the answer he kept reaching.

"What a day this has been," Baltasar said. "It appears I am surrounded by snakes." He turned back to George. "Give me my shipment. I will deal with Luisa and get to the bottom of what is happening here. I will put a stop to this." He shook the phone in disgust. "You have my word."

"I'm sorry," George said. "We're long past that. Release the children, then I'll release your shipment."

"I need my shipment *now*. It takes time for my people to divide it up, pack it, and transport it to the cartel's customers. Time I can't spare. If you won't give it to me now, then you may as well destroy it. The outcome will be the same for me. I will take care of the children, I promise you this, but give me my shipment now. If not for me, then for the Algarve," he said, appealing to what they had built together.

George wasn't having it. "The youngest of those children is maybe fourteen. Boys and girls. There are dozens and dozens of them. Kept and sold like animals."

"Please, George. I had nothing to do with it. You must know that."

"For your sake, I hope that's true. But it changes nothing. As you said, you're the boss here. You allowed this to happen. You want your shipment, set those children free."

A dark look passed across Baltasar's face. It made Jenn swallow hard. She'd made that expression herself once or twice. It only came when you stopped giving a damn about the consequences of your actions. The breaking point when the delicate seesaw between rational and animal tilted too far the wrong way. That was where atrocity lived. Afterward, people always said that they'd been out of their minds, but in the moment, Jenn knew how sane it felt. Baltasar had that look now. She understood that George didn't dare give up their only leverage, not yet, but he'd pushed Baltasar too far. When the bullets came, there wouldn't be a damn thing to stop it.

CHAPTER THIRTY-THREE

Jenn was wrong. The bullets didn't come. It was so much worse than that.

To Jenn, laughter had always been an expression of happiness. Probably because it didn't come easily to her people. Her grandmother had rarely smiled and had laughed like she'd owe heavy interest on it. It had always taken something joyous to coax laughter out of her grandmother—Jenn could count the times on one hand. Hearing that laugh had always made Jenn feel hopeful. Even as she knew that the next few weeks would be that much harder while her grandmother settled up with the universe.

There was no joy in Baltasar's laugh, only low resignation. He turned to her now. "I make you the same offer, Jenn. Return my shipment now, and I will take care of these children. I will make things right and punish those responsible."

She glanced at George. "He speaks for me," she said with far less assurance than she'd intended.

"Yes, but I'm giving you the chance to think for yourself. We all want the same thing here. It's only the sequence that we don't agree on, and I'm telling you seriously that I cannot wait any longer."

"George speaks for me," she repeated. It didn't sound any more confident with practice.

"And your position is nonnegotiable?"

She shrugged, tired of being asked the same question like a child.

"That is a shame," he said. "So is mine."

Baltasar gestured at Fernando, who came forward and held out a tablet to Jenn. She took it but didn't like that he wouldn't meet her eyes. Not one bit.

"What's that?" George asked.

"You have videos. I have a video of my own," Baltasar said. He dialed a number and put the phone to his ear.

With the sun to her back, Jenn had to shade the screen to see what was on the tablet. Gradually she made out a man in an upright wooden chair. As her eyes adjusted to the glare, she saw his arms were tied behind his back. His head was not in frame, but a taut rope tied around his right ankle pulled the leg outstretched. Jenn felt a hand reach into her chest and twist her heart cruelly in its fist. She knew those scars.

A golf club came into frame. A driver. It lowered slowly until the oversized titanium head kissed Sebastião's knee. The club drew back and repeated the motion three or four times as though preparing to tee off at the Masters. She saw Sebastião strain against his ropes. There was no sound, but imagining the anguish in his voice made her sick.

"What do you want?" she said.

"I've told you," Baltasar said. "But it's too late now. Hand Anibal your gun."

"I can't do that."

"Gibson *will* detonate," George said, trying to regain control of the negotiation. He raised his right hand—his signal to Dan, who watched from a building behind them.

"Then get on with it. I am done enduring threats," Baltasar said. "But make your peace with God before you do."

When things got down to life or death, most people panicked. Jenn did something more akin to a brownout—all nonessential parts of her brain went dark. The world went quiet and syrup slow. Everything shone with painful clarity, as if the beach had just gone high definition: Fernando's downturned eyes, the subtle shame at the corners of Anibal's mouth, Baltasar seizing the initiative, George losing the page. The range from here to the roof of the Hotel Mariana, calculating how long a bullet would take to travel from the barrel to the bridge of her nose. The three seagulls dancing with the surf by the water's edge.

But at the same time, it all moved too quickly for her to think through. That wasn't how it usually worked. Usually she knew what to do before she understood all the options, the answer glaring like a forty-foot billboard in her face. Today, thinking felt like trying to read Sanskrit on a roller coaster. Nausea spilled up her throat. This was Sebastião's fault. Her feelings for him making the right answer suddenly wrong. Muddying the water. Not caring had its tactical advantages.

"What is it?" George asked.

"They have Sebastião," she said.

"Hand Anibal your gun, Jenn," Baltasar said.

"Wait," she pleaded, playing for time she wasn't going to get.

"Do it," Baltasar said into the phone.

In a blur too fast for her eye to follow, the golf club vanished and then whipped down into the knee. Sebastião's leg buckled sideways, his entire body arching silently as the pain hunted for a way out.

Jenn felt the cold grip of the gun in her hand. Improbably, it was still holstered but seemed determined to jump out and do the talking for her. She ran her tongue across the fake front teeth that had replaced the two she'd swallowed in Afghanistan along with a quart of her own blood. She knew one thing, though:

Baltasar was wrong.

She would clear her holster.

She could see it. Two in Baltasar, move, two for Anibal. If she wasn't dead by then, Fernando could kiss his ass good-bye as well. It wouldn't give Sebastião his knee back, but—

George closed his hand around her wrist. It felt like a cork going back into a bottle, and it stopped her from finishing her thought, or from acting on it. She took a breath, then another.

"Let go of me," she said to George.

"You sure?" he asked.

"I'm good." That was the furthest thing from what she was; she only meant that the urge to go out in a hail of bullets had temporarily passed. George took his hand off her wrist, and she thrust the tablet into it so he could see for himself. With two fingers, Jenn drew her gun and held it out to Anibal. He darted forward and took it with all the confidence of a rat smelling a trap.

George looked at the tablet and then up at Baltasar. "What have you done?"

"The Algarve comes first, George. It always has. Sebastião understands that."

"Is that what understanding looks like?"

"Today it does."

"What happens now?" Jenn asked.

"Now you call your friends," Baltasar said. "Tell them to meet us at Fresco Mar."

"And nothing else will happen to Sebastião?"

"Of course not," Baltasar said. "I love that boy."

CHAPTER THIRTY-FOUR

Most of the customers ate breakfast outside in the morning sunshine. The restaurant was one of eight on this block, and competition was fierce. A young Portuguese man with a bright smile stood on the sidewalk with menus, hoping to wrangle tourists inside. His task was complicated by the table of British men laughing uproariously and telling tall tales about the drunken Irish birds they'd come this close to shagging the night before. None wore shirts, and their sunburned bellies rippled like dancing hams. They were enjoying the second beer of the morning along with their eggs.

Gibson thought about sending them another round. A small price to pay for such effective tourist repellant. The restaurant was well away from the beach, but this was still Albufeira; the fewer eyes looking this way the better. To be on the safe side, Gibson lurked at a table just inside the threshold of the restaurant. It was cool and dark in a peaceful sort of way. He kept his cap pulled low and his eyes on his breakfast.

He felt guilty eating while Jenn and George were off risking their lives meeting with Baltasar, but he'd rationalized that he couldn't just sit there for hours without ordering. The moment the food had arrived, he'd wolfed it down hungrily. He'd been beyond famished. It had taken a second full breakfast to really take the edge off. Now he was nursing a cup of coffee and watching his phone.

Hendricks had dropped Gibson off at the restaurant before moving into his position overlooking the beach. His role was to spot for Jenn and George during the meet with Baltasar; Gibson was the triggerman. If they gave the signal or things went sideways, Hendricks would relay word to detonate. Gibson spun his phone idly on his closed laptop. Blowing up the shipment was only a last resort. It would likely get Jenn and George killed. They all knew that. But a deterrent only deterred if the other side believed you crazy enough to follow through. And if the other side wasn't crazy enough to test your resolve.

His phone vibrated under his hand. He put down his coffee and took a steadying breath before lifting his palm a few inches like a gambler shielding his hole cards from prying eyes. It was a text from Hendricks.

Outside in 5. Piece of shit green Peugeot.

Better than an order to detonate, but it didn't tell Gibson much. Even though he understood the wisdom of the plan, he hated being the safest of the four. He'd put them in this position, so the risks should be his, not theirs. Not knowing what was happening down on the beach was unbearable. It felt like being assigned to a missile silo, contact with the outside world cut off, hoping not to get the call that the war had begun. He texted back asking Hendricks for an update. No reply.

He packed the laptop into his messenger bag, left money for the bill, and went out into the sunshine. The British table had finished breakfast and were taking turns slapping each other on their sunburned backs to see who could leave the biggest handprint. A lanky, pockmarked blond with a sunken chest and a Manchester United tattoo on his shoulder looked to be the unexpected champion. He had broad paddles for hands and wound up like Juan Marichal pitching strike three.

His next victim was built like an enormous concrete pylon. Gibson couldn't tell where his head ended and his body began, but the pylon had to weigh at least three hundred pounds. He looked intent on proving himself more of a man than his friends. He straddled his chair bravely, presenting the vast terrain of his raw, peeling, Nagasaki back as target. "Ken ye no hit hard, ye wee nob?" he taunted, taking a sloppy drink. The table cheered, but the lanky blond, standing behind him, glared down with payback eyes. He set his feet and lined up his attack. Gibson got the distinct feeling the two men had history going back to grade school.

A two-door, algae-green Peugeot pulled up to the curb. Hendricks hadn't done it justice. It was little more than a ball of crumpled tinfoil with wheels. Gibson lifted the long strap of his messenger bag over his neck and hurried out to the car. As luck would have it, that gave him a box seat to witness Juan Marichal bring the heat.

The slap thundered up and down the street, flat and wet like a tuna hitting pavement from twenty stories. A rude, affronting silence followed, lasting perhaps a full second. It took that long for news of the war crime to travel from the pylon's outraged back to his confused, belligerent cerebellum. He dropped his beer and let out a primordial shriek—he had impressive range for a man that size.

Everything on the street stopped. Heads turned to see who was dying. Everyone watched the enormous sunburned man writhe and holler. Everyone except for the pair of men on the sidewalk who were staring at *him*, not the howling Brit. Gibson didn't recognize them, but they clearly knew who he was. Already moving toward him. Gibson kept his eyes from glancing toward the Peugeot. The two men hadn't made Hendricks yet, and Gibson wanted to keep it that way. No sense in both of them going down. He turned and ran back into the restaurant. The men gave chase.

Gibson danced through the maze of tables and chairs inside the restaurant. At the kitchen door, he collided with a waitress coming out from behind the bar. Impressively, she managed not to drop her tray while simultaneously cursing him in Portuguese. The manager told him he couldn't go back there. Gibson apologized but didn't stop. As he spun off the waitress, he saw the two men chasing him had closed the distance, flinging tables out of their way as they came.

Gibson backed through the swinging door into the cramped kitchen. The strap of his messenger bag caught on a random hook protruding from the wall. It brought him to a sudden, inauspicious halt. His legs kicked out from under him, and his momentum sent him sprawling across the floor. The cooks stopped to stare and laugh at what they assumed was another drunk tourist lost on the way to the bathroom. Shouting from the restaurant got Gibson moving again. He found his feet, put his cap back on, and disentangled the messenger bag from the hook.

No longer amused by his intrusion, the cooks slapped and hit him as he tried to force his way through. The last chef grabbed a pot off the range and swung it at him. Gibson blocked the pot with his forearm, feeling it burn. Baked beans flew everywhere, further enraging the cooks, and reminding Gibson how much he hated English breakfasts. A rack of knives caught his eye, but by the time it occurred to Gibson to take one, he was already at the back door. The two men chasing him burst into the kitchen. The time to go was now.

The back of the restaurant opened into an alley. Gibson looked left and right, neither way a dead end, and chose left, running for it. Behind him, the restaurant door crashed open. Voices yelled for him to stop. Gibson broke into a sprint, or at least the best version of a sprint he could manage on his swollen ankle. Advanced hobbling might have been a more honest description. It was a hundred yards to the street. Eighty. Seventy. He could see people. Perhaps he could blend in and disappear. If he could make it in time, which he couldn't. Anyway, it was a terrible plan. He hoped they wanted him alive and didn't just shoot him in the back.

Behind him—a thump, a scream, and a crash. Then a second set of rolling thuds. Gibson didn't look back and pushed himself to run faster. He didn't. A car came up on his heels, honking. Gibson hugged the wall, and the green Peugeot pulled alongside. Hendricks had circled the block and plowed down Baltasar's men. One had been thrown against a dumpster. The other had rolled up and over the hood and lay motionless in the alley.

The Peugeot wrenched to a stop. It didn't look any the worse for wear, or maybe it was more accurate to say that it couldn't look any the worse for wear.

Gibson got in and said, "I take it Baltasar didn't go for the deal?"

"What gave it away?" Hendricks said and stepped on the gas before Gibson could shut his door. They shot up the alley. The Peugeot at least had more pep than the Fiat, but even with the seat all the way back, Gibson's knees were still crammed against the dashboard. As a car thief, Hendricks was nothing if not a bargain hunter. The Peugeot turned out of the alley onto the street, merging with traffic, and immediately slowed to a normal speed.

"Roll your window down and put your arm on the sill," Hendricks said.

Gibson did as he was told, doing his best to look casual even though he still had enough adrenaline in his system to launch a satellite.

"Why the hell didn't he take the deal? It was a good trade," Gibson said.

"I do not know. Guess it wasn't as straightforward as you thought."

"*I* thought . . . ?" Gibson didn't like the direction Hendricks was heading with that.

"All I'm saying is we're on the wrong side of George's fifty-fifty. Baltasar has them. I saw Jenn surrender her weapon."

"She did what?" Gibson said. That didn't sound like the Jenn Charles he knew. "What happened down on that beach?"

"Wish I knew."

"George didn't give the signal?"

"Did you get a call from me?" Hendricks said irritably. "Then no, he didn't."

"We should have had ears on them," Gibson said.

"We should have a lot of things. For this kind of operation? Come on, man, this is *Gilligan's Island*. We're making shit out of coconuts here. Got one gun between the four of us." Hendricks corrected himself. "*Had* one gun. All I know is Baltasar's calling the plays now."

"So, what does he want?"

"He wants his shipment. So that means you."

"Where are Jenn and George now? Do we know?"

"Headed for Fresco Mar."

"And Baltasar will be there?" Gibson asked.

Hendricks shot him a dirty look. "You're going all *Rain Man* on me again, aren't you? Yeah, he wants us to meet him there in an hour. Or else."

"Or else what?" Gibson said.

"Man, what do you think?" Hendricks said. "Time for that good plan B."

"Yeah."

"So . . . ? Do we have one?"

"Part of one," Gibson admitted.

Hendricks grimaced. "Is that like part of a condom?"

"It's gonna have to do."

Hendricks yanked hard on the steering wheel. The little car skidded off the road and into the parking lot of a gas station. They stopped hard beside one of the pumps.

"What is wrong with you?" Hendricks said. "Why you always so fired up to get yourself killed? I'm not saying we don't meet him—I want those kids freed as bad as you—but we go in without a solid plan, we're all gonna get ground into sardine pâté."

Gibson didn't have a solid plan; he had part of a condom. He got out of the car.

"Where're you going?" Hendricks asked.

"I got to hit the head. I had about six cups of coffee waiting for you."

Hendricks shot him a dirty look. "You ate?"

"What else was I supposed to do in a restaurant?"

"I am starving here, and you're eating breakfast."

Gibson held up two fingers. "Two, actually."

"That is not cool."

Gibson handed him the bacon and toast that he'd wrapped in a napkin. It was a little the worse for wear, but Hendricks wasn't complaining.

"Still not cool," Hendricks said. "What's that on your shirt?"

Gibson looked down. "Baked beans." Apparently, he hadn't completely escaped the blast radius of the cook's pot.

"Oh," Hendricks said as if that required no further explanation. "Get me a Coke."

In the bathroom, Gibson scrubbed the baked beans off his shirt with a wet paper towel. A solitary bean fell out of his beard. Gibson picked it up to look at it, then dropped it back into the sink. It was a bean. Nothing special about it. He ran cold water over the burn on his forearm and gave his ankle a once-over to confirm it was still attached. It gave him time to work the situation over in his head. Baltasar hadn't taken the deal, and now he had Jenn and George. He'd think he had the upper hand. Good. Let him think it.

Gibson bought a Coke from the cashier and went out to the pumps, where Hendricks was meticulously cleaning the car's windows and topping off the gas tank. There was something on his mind.

"Look, I got to ask," Hendricks said. "Your mind is clear, right? This isn't some suicide by gangster thing? 'Cause if this is some kind of kamikaze thing, I'm not getting in the plane."

"I don't want to die," Gibson said. He needed to reassure Hendricks, but it was a relief to realize that it was also the truth. "I just can't leave these kids. The second I saw them, I knew I'd do what I had to do."

Hendricks didn't look exactly happy, but he looked less unhappy. "So, if it comes down to it, what's your priority? Our lives or the kids?"

"What's yours?"

"That it not come down to that," Hendricks said. "But that may be wishful thinking."

"Yeah," Gibson said. Neither one had answered the question. Neither one had an answer. All they'd done was acknowledge the tightrope they were walking.

"If it does, though . . . I just want the chance to make up my own mind. Know what I'm saying? Can you do that for me?" Hendricks screwed the cap back onto the gas tank and hung up the pump handle. They got back into the car. Hendricks turned the engine over.

"I'll try, but what if you had to make up your mind right now?" Gibson asked. "May not be time later."

Hendricks pulled the car away from the pumps and rolled to a stop at the street corner. Gibson could see him thinking it through. When a break in traffic came, he turned west in the direction of Fresco Mar.

"Then I guess you better tell me about plan B before we get there."

CHAPTER THIRTY-FIVE

Fresco Mar looked much as Jenn remembered it. The paint cans had been removed, a little more trash had accumulated around the improvised security desk, but the monument to Mexican industriousness still dominated the warehouse like a solitary, unclimbable mountain on an otherwise dreary and empty plain.

George, not moving fast enough for the guard's liking, caught a hard shove in the back. He stumbled forward, losing his balance, but Jenn caught him by the elbow, helping him to keep his feet. She spun back to suggest the guard try that with her, but George pulled her away and quietly urged her to let it go.

The golf club came down on Sebastião's knee, his back arching in agony. It had been playing on a loop in her mind ever since the beach. Made letting anything go a tall order, but she acknowledged grudgingly that this wasn't the time. That didn't stop her from adding the guard to the running tally of people who would answer for their choices if the opportunity presented itself.

After the furnace of the Portuguese sun, the chill inside Fresco Mar had felt refreshing. Only for the first few minutes, though; the cold was already working its way into their bones. George stood shivering, arms folded tightly against himself. The temperature didn't agree with

Baltasar either, who gave orders for the refrigeration to be shut off. One of the guards trotted away to find the controls while Anibal helped his boss on with a heavy coat emblazoned with a Fresco Mar logo. Together the two men walked to the edge of the yellow circle to survey the shipment. It was the first time Baltasar was seeing it firsthand, so Anibal took care pointing out the explosives and cameras.

The two men stood there a long time, locked in intense discussion. Jenn couldn't make it out, but it was clear that Baltasar was suggesting the same ideas that they'd considered and rejected yesterday. Anibal's body language was of a man trying to applaud his boss's ingenuity while delicately explaining why it wouldn't work. Being a sycophant must burn a lot of calories, Jenn thought. It would have been comical had the stakes not been so high.

Jenn and George huddled in place, trying to keep warm. With nothing else to do, the guards circled Jenn and George and awaited instructions. She was flattered, but it didn't take four of them to watch her unarmed. To a man, they were miserable and on edge. They all had the look of people who woke up knowing where they stood with the world, only to discover the world had walked away.

A lurching mechanical sound boomed through the warehouse. It was only the air handlers shutting down, but the guards all flinched in the direction of the shipment. Jenn wouldn't mind it if they'd keep their fingers off the trigger if they were going to be this jumpy. Things were tense enough as it was without adding automatic-weapons fire to the already-combustible mix. The noise also signaled the end of Baltasar's patience for Anibal's patter. He silenced Anibal with a hand and returned to the desk where his son waited.

Fernando had always struck Jenn as a man trying hard not to care about anything. Up until now, she'd credited him for succeeding spectacularly. He was charming enough in small doses, and Sebastião loved him like a brother, so she tolerated him. But she had always suspected that Fernando Alves was probably a bit of a sociopath. There were more of them around than people thought, and most weren't what the movies made them out to be. Most weren't even dangerous, not in a basement-dungeon kind of way, at least. Many tended to gravitate toward, and excel in, fields in which a lack of empathy was an asset—politics, medicine, finance . . . you couldn't throw a rock in Langley without hitting two.

But watching Fernando now, she saw that that was anything but true in his case. When he'd moved to follow his father and Anibal over to the shipment, Baltasar had rebuffed him and told him to wait behind. To look at Fernando, it would be easy to think he'd been relieved. With a one-shoulder shrug, as if he couldn't be bothered to lift both, he'd wandered over to the desk and leaned against it. Ankles crossed, he'd become engrossed in his cuticles and even stifled a yawn. But it was all for show. Jenn saw the way he'd angled his body so that, although it looked like he wasn't paying attention, his eyes never once left his father. The pain in his expression when he thought no one was watching would have been heartbreaking if Jenn weren't so preoccupied with ripping it out of his chest.

Still, Fernando barely acknowledged his father's return. Kept his back turned even when Baltasar sat down behind him. Fernando pointed to the shipment and asked a question. Judging by Baltasar's alarmed reaction, it was a good one that neither Baltasar nor Anibal had anticipated. Fernando turned his head but kept his back to his father, said something further, and pointed a manicured finger in Jenn and George's direction. Whatever he suggested met with Baltasar's approval.

That didn't give Jenn the warm and fuzzies.

Fernando strolled over and conferred with the guards, then turned to her. "You two. Come with me."

He led Jenn and George to the edge of the yellow circle and ordered them to sit. She realized they were being used as human shields in case Gibson got a mind to detonate the shipment. The refrigeration might be off, but the floor felt like a block of ice through their summer clothes.

"Could we get some blankets? Or maybe a stool?" Jenn asked, worried about how much George could take.

"You'll survive until Gibson arrives," Fernando answered. "Provided he's on time."

"Why'd you do it?" Jenn said, meaning Sebastião. The question caught Fernando off guard, and his eyes stuttered out of focus for a half second.

"What?" he asked.

When she'd been stationed in DC early in her career, Jenn had briefly dated a meathead with the Secret Service who lied the same way. The same vacant expression, the same telltale pause, and the same playing for time by asking for the question to be repeated as if he'd gone momentarily deaf. She didn't want to say it was genetic, but a lot of men simply lied more slowly than women. Suddenly, she understood that Baltasar's attempt to keep Fernando away from a life of crime had failed long ago.

"What have you done?"

Fernando recovered his poise and gave her a crooked smile. "You wouldn't understand."

"You know when people say that, it's because they're ashamed of why."

Fernando straightened, smile falling away. For a moment, in between, Jenn saw the face he kept so carefully hidden. As if Fernando's whole life was a play and the curtain had accidentally reopened too soon, revealing the barren, undressed stage.

"I'm not ashamed of anything," Fernando said.

Maybe he was a sociopath after all.

Jenn beckoned him closer. Unafraid with the guards nearby, Fernando squatted down to look her in the eye. She leaned in close, her voice the raw hiss of steam escaping a cracked nuclear cooling tower. "No way your dad or Anibal would have known how to get to me. Only you. Only you, Fernando. You might not have swung the club, but you put it in their hands."

"Don't be ridiculous. He'll be fine," Fernando said, dropping the pretense that he didn't know what she meant. "Providing."

"Providing what?"

"Providing I check in with Tomas regularly. You remember Tomas? The boy has a natural swing. And he doesn't care for our dear Sebastião. Not. One. Bit. But as long as I keep calling him and telling him that you're cooperating—"

"We're cooperating," Jenn cut in.

"Then he'll be fine."

"He'd better be." Jenn didn't hold out any hope for herself. On the beach, she'd accepted what surrendering her weapon meant, how it was likely to end for her. It had been a desperate act, but she'd known that Baltasar wouldn't stop at the knee. She'd seen it in his face. The exact moment when "desperate times call for desperate measures" went from abstract to literal. Her choice was either to watch Sebastião die or to take his place. She hoped it had counted for something. He was an innocent in all this. A loyalist too. Even after all this, he would still keep Baltasar's secrets. There was no reason not to let him go. None but pure spite. "Please, Fernando," Jenn said, changing tack. Begging didn't come naturally to her, but she'd do it if that's what it took. "Let me see him."

"I'm afraid Sebastião is at my father's house enjoying his hospitality." Fernando's face softened. "As long as Gibson shows up and does exactly what my father says, then no further harm will come to Sebastião. However, if he doesn't, and I don't check in, well . . . Tomas will practice his long game." Fernando stared into her eyes. "The club's in Gibson's hands now."

"Fernando. Sebastião's not a part of this. He loves you like family."

"Yes," Fernando agreed, his outward cool returning. "But he's not. There's a difference."

Baltasar was calling him. Fernando took that as an opportunity to have the last word. Jenn watched him go, wondering whether she'd gotten through to him at all.

She took off her jacket, light as it was, and draped it over George's shoulders. His teeth were clenched, but she could see the muscles in his jaw working.

"I'm going to freeze to death in August," George said with a thin smile. "There's a metaphor here somewhere."

"It's Fernando," Jenn said.

"Yes," George agreed. "It is. It would appear I owe Baltasar an apology of some kind."

"May be a little late for that now."

George chuckled. "Yes, I think that ship may have sailed. No pun intended."

"I'm sorry," Jenn said. "This is my fault. I shouldn't have—"

George cut her off. "No. I'm sorry we got Sebastião dragged into this."

"He asked me to marry him yesterday. Can you believe that?"

George took her hands in his. "He's a wise man."

"I don't know about all that."

"I do, and he is. Unless loyalty, strength, smarts, and toughness don't count for anything anymore."

"You forgot looks and charm." She smirked.

"No, no, I didn't."

Jenn rested her head on his shoulder for a moment. "Hey, here's a weird question, but would you walk me down the aisle? Is that still a thing?"

"It is if you want it to be."

She looked around them, at their situation. "Well, it's kind of a moot point now. I just hope Gibson and Dan get to the boat and get away from this mess."

"They're coming."

His certainty dismayed her. One of her only silver linings was the thought of them getting away. Under his breath, George laid out plan B—the drone and the exploit it had delivered.

"You can't be serious," she said when he was finished. It was the most Gibson thing she'd ever heard. And, no, that wasn't a compliment. Even if it were feasible, it was the kind of operation that would take months of planning, not one that could be thrown together overnight.

"He thinks it will work. So he'll come," George said.

"If it works, why doesn't he just do it where he's safe?"

"Unfortunately, he has to be on the same Wi-Fi network. He needs to be in the building."

"Christ. Well, I hope at least Dan's smart enough to sit this one out."

George gave her a disapproving look. "Of course Daniel will come."

"Why?" Jenn said. "If all four of us are here, and Gibson is wrong, then we're all as good as dead."

"If it were you, would you stay where it was safe? This is who we are, Jennifer. This is why I hired you and Daniel in the first place."

"Well, you hired a couple of idiots," she said with a bitter laugh. "Gibson fits right in."

"Yes, he does," George said. "Yes, he does."

CHAPTER THIRTY-SIX

The clock in the Peugeot's dashboard read 10:48 when Gibson and Hendricks arrived back in Olhão. A little over an hour until the hijackers' original deadline.

Hendricks was in a nostalgic mood. He'd talked the entire drive, telling stories from his childhood. As if his memories were heirlooms that he was wrapping in gentle cloth and passing on to Gibson for safekeeping ahead of a coming hurricane. Without prompting, he reminisced about growing up in Oakland, his father working as a studio engineer across the bay at the Wally Heider Studio in the Tenderloin. Hendricks rattled off the names of some of the artists his father had helped record: Jefferson Airplane, Creedence Clearwater Revival, Santana.

"I met Van Morrison in '71. He was working on a couple tracks for *Saint Dominic's Preview*. I must've been seven, eight? Pops said I could stay in the studio as long as I kept quiet and did my homework. Van sits down beside me on the couch with a guitar, working out a piece of 'Jackie Wilson Said.' You know that song?" Hendricks sang the chorus in his sandpaper baritone. "Turns to me serious and says in his thick Belfast accent, *Whaddaya think, little brother?* Swear that man thought he was black. Carried it like that anyway. Van the Man. Kind of an asshole if we're being honest, but then they all were once they'd been in the studio long enough."

"What did you tell him?" Gibson asked.

"Said it sounded cool. What else I'm going to say to the man paying my dad?"

Hendricks explained that Wally Heider Studio had changed hands in 1980, becoming Hyde Street Studio. Robert Hendricks had been forced to look elsewhere for employment. He'd moved the family south back to Los Angeles, closer to his parents and siblings, where he'd gotten steady work in the punk scene with SST and Slash Records, recording bands like Black Flag, Minutemen, Hüsker Dü.

"Pops worked on *I Against I* with Bad Brains. You believe that? Those guys were incredible."

Gibson said he couldn't.

"Anyway, Pops died in '92, month after the riots. June 27," Hendricks said wistfully.

"What of?" Gibson asked.

"Emphysema," Hendricks said, tapping his chest and plucking the last cigarette from the pack. "Don't ever let them say that Hendricks men don't know the score. Although, I wouldn't bet on emphysema getting me at this point.

"Those were strange days," Hendricks said, drifting back to the riots. "Almost quit the department over some of that shit. Still went to Pops's service in my dress blues. Was not the most popular man at the funeral, I can tell you that. Too stubborn to change, I guess. But what else did I know how to do?"

Hendricks fell silent and smoked his cigarette, blowing the smoke out his window. It was the most Gibson had ever heard Hendricks talk about himself. Getting personal information out of the normally recalcitrant Dan Hendricks was like hacking the NSA, but something about the long odds facing them had turned the key in the lock. Gibson, sensing the door might not open again, asked a question that had been on his mind for months.

"Why are you here? I mean, Jenn and I are wanted by the FBI. The man who broke George is still out there. We don't have any choice but to hide. But nobody's after you. You could have gone home anytime you wanted. Why did you stay? Why are you staying now?"

Hendricks flicked his cigarette out the window and reached for a fresh pack. "I don't know. And that's the truth. I was only going to stay a couple of weeks. Maybe it was the weather? We don't get much sun out in California."

"In California?"

"Nothing but gray skies. How could I leave all this? Course, if I'd known you were going to go full white savior, I might've made other arrangements." He caught Gibson's expression. "Man, I'm kidding you. I'm kidding. I'm with you. Jenn and George too. We all are."

Hendricks parked near the docks where the fishing trawlers bobbed lazily in the sunshine. Across the harbor, the white rooftops of Fresco Mar Internacional stood out among the older industrial buildings. That would be their next stop, but first they needed to drop off their things. Showing up to meet Baltasar Alves with one hundred thousand euros was a good way to wind up one hundred thousand euros the poorer.

Hendricks popped the trunk, which opened only halfway before grinding stubbornly to a halt. "I hate this car." They wrestled it the rest of the way open and divided the bags between them.

"You sure we can trust this guy?" Gibson asked. "This is a lot of money."

"George said he's cool."

"Imagine my relief."

Hendricks shot him an exasperated look. "You know, I'm not real comfortable being the voice of reason, but you might want to think about giving that shit a rest."

The docks were deserted at this time of day. The boats had all been squared away, and the crews had long since dispersed to their beds. The *Alexandria*, moored at the far end, was painted a weathered green and red to match the Portuguese flag. Her size surprised Gibson; the Atlantic was an awfully big ocean for such a small boat. A young man no older than twenty sat on deck, repairing a net. He stopped when he saw them. Wincing when he stood, gingerly, like an old man who had exercised hard for the first time in years.

"João Luna?" Hendricks asked.

"Sim," the young man said warily.

It took some pointing and blank faces to establish that they didn't share a common language.

"George Abe?" João asked.

Hendricks and Gibson both nodded vigorously, and both said "George Abe" in unison as though it were the basis of a new language. João relaxed visibly now that he knew they weren't there to kill him. He welcomed them on board and took them below to stow their bags. Back up on deck, João pointed to his watch and looked at them quizzically. They didn't have an answer for him, and even if they did, Gibson didn't think that "George Abe" was enough to communicate it. João pointed at the sun and then pointed at the horizon, his message simple—*hurry*.

Walking back to the car, Hendricks looked out across the water toward Fresco Mar. "Can't believe we're going back in there again. Three times is kind of asking for it."

Gibson agreed. They were pushing their luck.

"Enough to put me off sardines for life," Hendricks said.

"You eat sardines?"

"Yeah, I tried the spread. It's good on a little bread."

"No, thanks," Gibson said.

"Expand your horizons before the horizon expands you."

Gibson thought about it. "What does that even mean?"

"I don't know. Just made it up. Sounds good, though."

Back in the car, Gibson opened his laptop.

"What are you doing?" Hendricks asked.

"Getting the lay of the land."

Using Dol5's air card, Gibson opened his back door into Baltasar's network. Now that he knew where Baltasar would be, he modified the firmware on Fresco Mar's Wi-Fi access points using Dol5's malware. Effectively weaponizing it against Baltasar Alves. Assuming, of course, that Dol5 knew his or her business.

In addition to the explosives, Gibson had also seized control of Dol5's cameras inside Fresco Mar. Powering them up now, Gibson angled the laptop so Hendricks could see what he saw.

"Oh, that's pretty slick," Hendricks said.

"Why is everyone always so surprised?"

Gibson scrolled through the four camera feeds that gave Dol5 three-sixty coverage of the warehouse. There was even one pointed straight up to cover the roof. Everyone was clustered in the northeast corner around the security desk. Gibson enlarged the video to fill the screen. Jenn and George sat cross-legged on the ground but didn't look injured. That was something anyway. Their backs were up against the yellow line that marked the beginning of the no-fly zone. If the shipment blew, they'd catch the brunt of it. Gibson had entertained a vague hope of catching Baltasar napping and blowing him and his goons to heroin Valhalla. So much for that.

Hendricks read his mind. "You didn't think Baltasar Alves would be that easy?"

"A man can dream."

Baltasar sat at the makeshift security desk. Anibal stood nearby. Both looked anxious and checked the time with reflexive urgency. A man squatting by Jenn and George stood.

Fernando.

"What the hell is he doing there?" Gibson asked.

"Don't know. He was at the beach too."

That meant something. Gibson didn't know what, though. Before today, Fernando would never have been allowed anywhere near the shipments. Either they had been misled from the beginning or else things were changing in the Alves organization. Maybe the murders of Silva and Peres had created a job opening.

"Can we hear what they're saying?" Hendricks said.

"Oh, right." Gibson had forgotten he had audio and tabbed up the volume on the microphones. It was indistinct, but they could just about make out the conversation happening around the desk.

"Where are they?" Baltasar asked.

Gibson didn't get why they were speaking in English until he realized that Baltasar didn't want to be understood by his own men.

"They'll be here," Fernando said. "Gibson would do anything for Jenn."

"I thought she was Sebastião's woman," Baltasar said, checking his watch again.

"Yes, but Gibson carries a torch. You can hear it the way he talks about her. It's in his voice even when he doesn't mean it to be," Fernando said. "He'll show."

"*Cabrão,*" Baltasar said, causing Anibal to snort in agreement.

Gibson didn't know what it meant, but it didn't sound like a compliment.

"Luisa?" Baltasar asked.

"Nothing yet," Anibal said.

"I want her found and brought to me."

Anibal and Fernando both agreed.

"I mean it," Baltasar said. "Nothing happens to her until I talk to her face-to-face."

"Where *is* Luisa?" Gibson asked, muting the laptop. She didn't seem like someone who should go unaccounted for.

"Good damn question. She wasn't at the beach either. Jenn said she was taking men to Quarteira to deal with the Romanians."

"Sounds like she's fallen out of favor in the meantime."

"One less we have to reckon with, then," Hendricks said. "Frankly, she scares me more than those other three put together."

They counted only five armed men in the Fresco Mar warehouse. That didn't mean there weren't more, but that was all they could see. Gibson held out hope that, with everything that had happened, Baltasar had spread himself too thin. Luisa would have taken their best to confront the Romanians. Perhaps that had left Baltasar vulnerable. Not that they were shooting their way out. Even if they had guns, which they didn't.

Gibson watched Fernando on-screen for another minute. From the moment the Alves scion had met him on the beach yesterday morning, Gibson had felt that he was seeing only about half the picture. So far, he'd made the best decisions he could, but seeing Jenn and George in harm's way, he worried that it was the wrong half.

———

Driving alongside the chain-link fence outside Fresco Mar, Gibson didn't see any signs of life. Under the relentless sun, the facility looked like the bleached bones of an animal long dead. Hendricks turned in at the gate and stopped. A solitary man squatted on a milk crate in the shade of the guardhouse. He stood as they pulled up and crushed a cigarette under his heel. Unarmed so far as Gibson could tell, the man had the kind of gentle, open face that you would trust to watch your kids. He was about as intimidating as a shih tzu. That he had been posted here, weaponless, was a sign of how little Baltasar feared them. The man opened Hendricks's door like a valet and motioned that he intended to search them.

"Like hell. I'm not armed," Hendricks said without moving.

Apologetically, the man shrugged that he didn't understand and gestured again for them to exit the vehicle. Hendricks still didn't move. Gibson shook him gently by the shoulder. It was hard to tell when something would rub Hendricks wrong, and once he dug in his heels there was no moving him.

"We don't have time for this," Gibson said.

Hendricks grunted.

Gibson got out of the car and raised his arms to allow the man to pat him down. Hoping to set a good example. Gibson gave him his messenger bag to search. To make it simpler, the man took out the laptop and handed it back to Gibson without a second glance. No one ever thought of computers as dangerous until they'd been attacked by one. Gibson intended to remind everyone exactly how foolish that was.

Grudgingly, Hendricks followed Gibson's lead and got out of the car too. The retired cop looked none too happy at being frisked. "You know you missed about three different places I could have a small pistol?" Hendricks asked pleasantly. "Fucking amateurs."

When the man was satisfied that neither Hendricks nor Gibson were concealing bazookas, he pointed toward the warehouse and made it clear that they'd be walking from here.

"In this heat?" Hendricks said. "That ain't even Christian."

The man gave Hendricks a blankly agreeable smile and held out a hand for the keys.

"All right, but I just gassed her up, and I know the mileage, so no joyrides, youngster," Hendricks said.

Gibson and Hendricks squeezed around the gate and set out across the dusty lot toward the back of the warehouse. The sun high in the cloudless sky, scorching everything it touched. It had to be a hundred degrees. Gibson was sweating after thirty feet.

"At least it's a dry heat," Gibson said.

"Shut the hell up."

They circled the corner of the main building. Against the back fence, a row of vehicles was parked so as not to be visible from the road. A motley assortment of old trucks, cars, and even a few motorbikes. They hadn't been there yesterday.

252

"What's that all about?" Gibson said.

"That's about Baltasar planning on getting his drugs back," Hendricks said. "They'll break the shipment down and pack it into the vehicles and send it north. Same game they play at the Mexican border. Nice thing about the European Union, though, is that once you're in, you're in everywhere. But to be safe, Baltasar will spread the shipment out among all these vehicles so there's no chance of losing the whole thing to one overzealous customs official."

"That's good," Gibson said.

"How you figure?"

"We still have something he wants."

"Yeah, same thing we had down at the beach," Hendricks reminded him.

And there was the bottom line. The deal George had offered to Baltasar Alves should have been an easy one to strike. Instead, here they were walking into a hostage situation that should never have happened. It only emphasized that Baltasar Alves and his organization were in chaos—Silva and Peres dead, Luisa missing. How realistic was it to think Gibson or Hendricks could negotiate with Baltasar where George had already tried and failed? Gibson saw the faces of the children who had been sold into slavery. He saw the face of Kamal, hopeful and kind, smiling for the camera. How many had gone before him? How many would follow if it wasn't stopped now? Gibson's anger, which had been smoldering, caught and roared back into flames. Baltasar would see reason or he would die. Gibson was done playing nice.

Hendricks read his mind again. "It comes down to it, blow the shipment."

"Even if we're in the blast radius?"

"Even if," Hendricks said. "But do me a favor, yeah?"

"Name it."

"Make it count for something. Let's get those kids free first."

CHAPTER THIRTY-SEVEN

Anibal came strolling down the ramp from the loading dock like a man without a care in the world. Hendricks stopped to let him come to them. A peculiar casualness seemed to have fallen over the day, as if admitting the previous urgency on both sides was tantamount to disaster. It seemed pointless gamesmanship to Gibson, but he waited with Hendricks. Still, he wondered, if Alves's people were going to posture, couldn't they at least do it in the shade?

"Enjoy the sunshine," Hendricks said with typical clairvoyance. "It might be our last."

"You are King Pep Talk, you know that?"

It made Gibson uneasy to see Anibal alone and unarmed. But glancing up, he spotted two black rifle barrels poking out from among the white air handlers on the roof. For whatever reason, that settled him. That he was in trouble was a given; all Gibson wanted now was to be able to anticipate from what direction that trouble would come.

The flat brim of Anibal's sombrero shaded his eyes, but when he tilted his head up, Gibson saw how weary he looked. No one had seen much sleep since this thing had begun. Another factor that decreased the odds of a peaceful resolution.

"Been a long couple of days," Hendricks said.

Anibal grunted in agreement and told them to turn around. He frisked Hendricks despite his protestations.

"We went through this out at the gate," Hendricks said, hands above his head. "What you think? I stumbled over a Glock on the walk over here?"

Anibal, unswayed, took a knee and searched Hendricks's legs. Thoroughly. "Did I miss three places too?" he asked when he finished, making the point that he'd been listening over an open radio.

"No," Hendricks conceded, readjusting his pants. "Think you found one or two I didn't know I had."

Anibal smiled at that, then searched Gibson. He took the messenger bag and rifled through it. When satisfied, he slung the bag over his own shoulder as if doing Gibson a favor. That sparked a moment of frustration that Gibson hoped didn't show. Anibal couldn't know how badly he needed the laptop. For now, having it in Anibal's possession worked to Gibson's advantage, psychologically. If Baltasar wanted the shipment disarmed, then he would have to choose to return the laptop. That appearance of choice would give Baltasar the illusion of control, and the illusion of control had a funny way of lowering one's guard. Gibson would only need an inch or two.

They followed Anibal up the stairs to the top of the loading dock, where the retractable door rolled open like it was hungry and could smell dinner. Two guards stepped out of the gloom to greet them, hands on the pistol grips of their bullpup compact rifles. Gibson recognized them from the video feed. Including the guy at the front gate and the two on the roof, that made at least eight. The odds of getting out of here alive kept sliding in the wrong direction. The two guards ushered everyone inside, and one of them pressed a button set into the wall. The door rumbled ominously closed, and that sense of being swallowed whole redoubled.

"This way," Anibal said, as if there was anywhere else for them to go. It wasn't a long corridor, but he kept glancing back to reassure himself that they were still following. The guards fell in behind but left a buffer in case Gibson or Hendricks decided to try anything. Gibson thought that was giving them entirely too much credit.

Emerging into the warehouse, they took their bearings. Not much had changed from the video feed. There were still five guards; Baltasar was still holding court at the security desk; and Jenn and George still sat on the floor by the edge of the circle. Hendricks took a few tentative steps in that direction, but the guards barred the way and funneled them toward the desk. Jenn caught Gibson's eye and mouthed something to him. He didn't catch it the first time, so she repeated it, slowly this time: "Fer-nan-do." Beside her, George brought his chin down with the finality of a judge's gavel. The implication was plain, but it was hard for Gibson to wrap his head around. *Fernando*, not Baltasar? Could that even be possible? Gibson suddenly became aware of how unnaturally still it felt in the warehouse. The refrigeration had been shut off. His footfalls echoed cavernously in his ears.

Cocooned in a thick white coat, Baltasar offered them seats across the desk. Gibson sat; Hendricks stood—stubborn streak at eleven. At a sign from Anibal, one of the guards forced Hendricks down into the seat. Baltasar sipped from a coffee cup balanced on a saucer. It all seemed so civilized. Gibson wondered if he should have printed out his résumé. Anibal put Gibson's messenger bag next to the desk where Fernando was leaning. Fernando seemed otherwise engaged and was slow to look Gibson's way, but when he did, his familiar, cocksure smile played on his lips.

"Gibson," Fernando said. "I looked for you at the beach this morning."

"Sorry, I wasn't up for a run. Did you find your car okay?" Gibson looked for any hint in Fernando's eyes of what Jenn and George were trying to say about him. He saw nothing.

"I did, thank you. I don't have much reason to visit Alcantarilha ordinarily. We were sorry to miss you there."

"So, I thought you didn't have anything to do with all this," Gibson said. "Or was that just bullshit?"

"Amusingly," Fernando said, "I was about to ask you the same question."

"Enough," Baltasar rumbled. "It appears I should have been talking to you from the beginning, Gibson. Am I saying that right?" He didn't wait for an answer. "Or perhaps I have been? Perhaps there never were any hijackers? How do I know you four haven't been behind this from the beginning?"

Gibson chuckled at the preposterousness of the idea. "Mr. Alves, with all due respect, if we had the resources to do that . . ." He pointed at the mountain of drugs behind him. "Do you think we'd have let you take George and Jenn?"

Baltasar acknowledged the point with a grumbling sound. "I'm told you control my shipment. What does that mean, exactly?"

"It means your noon deadline is off. You're welcome, by the way. But if you or your people go anywhere near it, it's going to rain heroin for twenty miles."

Baltasar grunted at the threat. "If you were able to take control of it, what's to stop me from having someone else do the same?"

"Time," Hendricks said. "You don't have any."

"And how do I know you control the shipment? This could all be an elaborate deception."

"What time do you have?" Gibson asked.

"Five of," Anibal said. He'd taken off his watch and stood beside Baltasar, nervously watching the second hand orbit the dial. Gibson smirked. Only guys over a certain age used a watch when they wanted to know the time.

"You'll know in six minutes when we're not all on fire," Gibson said. "Or we can go wait outside if that would make you feel safer."

They sat there in silence as time ticked by, reading each other over the desk. Baltasar's men had begun drifting toward the exits.

"If it detonates, George and Jenn will take the worst of it," Baltasar said.

"Not going to detonate."

Baltasar studied Gibson for any tremor of fear or doubt. Seeing none, he told Anibal to control the men. Anibal barked orders and gestured for them to return. There was a pause. A moment's flickering indecision when Gibson thought the men would bolt. It would only take one to start a stampede. Gibson prayed, but it wasn't to be. The men still feared their boss more than a quick death, but none took his eyes off the shipment. They looked like villagers on a tiny island gazing up at a volcano threatening to erupt.

"Three minutes," Anibal announced.

"Then we will wait and we will see," Baltasar said.

"Can I get some coffee while we wait?" Hendricks asked. He didn't seem overly surprised when no one offered him any.

The minutes dragged by.

Anibal kept a steely eye on his men. Baltasar and Fernando switched into rapid-fire Portuguese, and Gibson regretted again how careless he'd been these past few months not to learn the language. Not that he'd be able to keep up, but at least he wouldn't feel like such an American.

When Anibal called out the last minute, Baltasar and Fernando went silent. Baltasar's knuckles were white on the armrests of his chair. Even Fernando's practiced nonchalance looked in jeopardy; Gibson caught his eye and winked at him. Fernando colored ever so slightly and sneered back. It was childish, but Gibson needed the morale boost. Besides, it felt good for once to be more certain of a situation than his dapper friend.

As the clock ticked down, Gibson half expected Hendricks to begin counting down from ten like an MC at a New Year's Eve party. The retired detective loved nothing so much as an excuse to twist the knife if he thought you were an asshole. But Hendricks had turned still and serious too. That irked Gibson—he was wrong about a lot of things, but when was the last time he'd gotten a hack wrong? He cuffed Hendricks on the leg and mouthed the words "What the hell?"

"That's it," Anibal said, the relief clear in his voice. "It is the afternoon."

Baltasar relaxed visibly. Gibson turned in his chair and gave George and Jenn a thumbs-up. Neither looked overly reassured.

"Satisfied?" Gibson asked.

Fernando didn't look satisfied. "I think it was already deactivated and this is all for show."

"Take a walk and find out," Gibson said.

Fernando did not take him up on the suggestion.

Baltasar cleared his throat. "To answer your question, I will be satisfied when the explosives are disarmed. Not before. Now, do I need to make threats or will you see reason where your friends have not?"

Before Gibson could reply, the radio at Anibal's hip squawked. Baltasar glared at it for interrupting his negotiations. With an apology, Anibal walked away and put it to his ear. The warehouse appeared to be playing havoc with the signal. He asked for the message to be repeated and moved toward the exit, trying to improve the signal, but it only seemed to make it worse.

From the corridor, a rumble of motors filled the warehouse. The loading dock door was opening again. Anibal snapped his fingers twice, and two of the guards sprinted up the corridor to see what was happening. Anibal must have found a pocket of clear air, because he told the voice at the other end to repeat the message.

Gibson only made out one word—"Luisa."

Luisa Mata was here.

The warehouse descended into chaos. Judging by the reaction, her arrival had not been on the menu. Baltasar was up and on his feet, red-faced, demanding answers no one seemed to have. Meanwhile, Anibal attempted to marshal and organize the men, who didn't look happy about what they were being ordered to do. Gibson didn't get the impression Luisa was being welcomed back with open arms. Fernando, on the other hand, had gone absolutely white, as if he'd been hung on a hook to bleed out. It was so out of character that Gibson couldn't take his eyes off him. Fernando glanced his way, but this time there was no sly smile, no arrogance. Only fear.

A commotion preceded Luisa's arrival. Angry, elevated voices echoed out into the warehouse. Gibson got a tingle of anticipation at the base of his neck. It reminded him of the time his squad mates had dragged him along to a WrestleMania event in Charlotte. He'd rolled his eyes at wrestling, but when they'd gotten in there and the music started, with the audience whipped into a frenzy, Gibson had been caught up in the energy and spectacle and screamed along with his squaddies as the wrestlers came out of the tunnel. It felt like that now, although this time he wasn't safely in the audience; they were all part of this show.

The two guards reemerged, walking in reverse. Their weapons were down but at the ready. They looked unsure what to do and glanced over to Anibal for direction, who looked to Baltasar. The old man had stopped yelling and stood watching like everyone else.

Following the guards came Marco Zava, Luisa's personal tank. He steered a man in a torn, bloodstained T-shirt before him like a shield. The man's arms were bound behind him, and he looked like he'd been in three different car crashes. His head was battered and misshapen. One eye was swollen shut, the other barely more than a slit.

Luisa followed after. Grim determination was the only way Gibson could think of to describe her expression. If the apocalypse wore a face, it would look much like that.

She was flanked by two of the men who had accompanied her to Quarteira. They both had the blank, middle-distance stares of soldiers who'd survived a long night against all odds. Their weapons were also down but ready. Everything seemed to hang in an uneasy balance, but Gibson didn't like the odds of it staying that way.

Marco Zava reached Baltasar and yoked back on his prisoner's arms, bringing him to a clattering stop. With a well-placed boot, he took the man's legs out from under him, dropping him to his knees. The man grunted but did not cry out or make any other sound. Either he was a tough son of a bitch, or else he'd already absorbed all the pain his body could process for one day.

"Welcome back, Luisa," Baltasar said. "No one has heard from you. I've been worried."

Luisa looked around at the way the men had surrounded her and her team. "Thank you, *Tio*. What have I missed?"

Instead of answering, Baltasar asked the name of the bleeding man at his feet. "Who is this man, Luisa?"

"Constantin Funar."

The name meant nothing to Gibson, but judging by Baltasar's reaction, he knew the man well.

"Really? I barely recognize him." Baltasar leaned in for a better look. "Hello, Constantin."

The man gave no answer. Gibson guessed that this was a wise move on his part. If things went badly here in the next few minutes, Gibson would be smart to heed the lesson.

"Why is he here? You were sent to deliver a message to the Romanians, not to take them prisoner."

"This one has an interesting story to tell," Luisa said and looked her cousin dead in the eyes. "Doesn't he, Fernando?"

CHAPTER THIRTY-EIGHT

In the commotion surrounding Luisa's arrival, Fernando had been able to steal a moment to compose himself for what would come next. The shock of seeing her alive had badly rattled him and thrown his plans into disarray. He understood now that the text from Constantin Funar's phone had been a trap to buy Luisa time. In his eagerness for good news, Fernando had stumbled into it like a clumsy child. It also meant that Luisa knew everything—to assume anything less would be suicide. The only question remaining was how to respond to her accusations.

Fernando drew a deep, turpentine breath, made his face a blank canvas, and considered what to paint on it—indignant and falsely accused? Perplexed and hurt? Dismissive and mocking? Should he play defense or launch an offensive? He tried to gauge his father's reaction to each tactic. Doubt had already been sown in his father's mind about Luisa. How best to harvest it? The important thing was to keep his cool. What gave most accused people away was reacting out of character. Who was going to believe righteousness coming from Fernando Alves? Certainly not his father. Besides, Luisa was already white-hot with anger, and Fernando had no prayer of matching it. Contrary to popular opinion, people who fought fire with fire usually wound up with an inferno.

"Do you want to tell them, or should I?" Luisa asked him, her contempt like salt in the earth.

Fernando shrugged and made himself comfortable on the edge of the desk. "I do like a good story. Please. Regale us."

Luisa turned to Baltasar. "The Romanians have been smuggling enslaved refugee children into the Algarve. Almost from the instant you rejected their offer two years ago. Selling them to the highest bidder and transporting them north. This Romanian dog admitted everything."

"Yes, we know," Baltasar said.

That caught Luisa off guard. "How?"

Baltasar gestured dismissively toward Gibson Vaughn and Dan Hendricks. Luisa looked over as if seeing them there for the first time, pieces falling into place. "Then you know that our network has been compromised? That the auctions have been conducted from our servers so that if the authorities ever discovered it, everything would point back to you."

Fernando saw his father's anger building as the old man realized the degree of the betrayal. Now, with the shipment safe, his normal focus had returned.

"Say what you mean to say," Baltasar said, his voice glacial and unyielding.

"Fernando's their partner. It was his brainchild."

Fernando laughed and pointed at Zava. "How long did your psychopath torture the Romanian before he agreed to tell that story?"

For a moment Fernando thought Luisa might lunge for him. Zava too; hatred burned in his eyes like two incandescent bulbs. How perfect that would be. Growing up, all their arguments had ended with her losing her temper. The less he gave a damn, the angrier it made her. Fernando rolled his eyes and puffed out his cheeks dismissively. Luisa teetered on the edge but checked herself, cursed him, and spat on the ground. Baltasar hadn't moved a muscle.

Fernando broke the silence. "What are you going to do? Beat me like you did him? Until I confess to whatever you want? We all know your methods, cousin."

Luisa smiled then, a cruel, knowing smile. In her hand was a phone that she held out to Baltasar. Fernando's confidence fell away. Even before she spoke, he knew what she would say.

"I don't need your confession, *cousin*," Luisa said. "I already have it."

"What is this?" Baltasar asked, taking the phone reluctantly.

"It belongs to Constantin Funar. His text messages with Fernando will tell you everything you need to know. They go back years."

Fernando felt the brass ring slipping from his fingers and a bottomless pit opening up beneath him. He had thought to get another phone, one that didn't trace back to him, but carrying two phones had felt excessive. He didn't even like to carry the one since it ruined the lines of his clothes. It had seemed sufficient to delete his texts to and from the Romanians. He'd reassured himself that no one would ever see Constantin Funar's phone. Watching his father scroll through the text messages, he thought of all the ways this moment should have been impossible.

"Anibal already told us about the warehouse," Fernando told his father in desperation, even as he saw how flimsy his framing of Luisa looked now. "You must be desperate to go to such lengths to pin this on me," he said to Luisa, then looked to Anibal for support, but the man didn't leap to his defense. Didn't he realize that his neck was on the block as well? Anibal had lied to Baltasar's face to help frame Luisa.

"There was never any attack at the hotel," Luisa said. "Not from the outside anyway. That was Fernando covering his tracks. Dani Coelho has been in his pocket for two years, ripping holes in our security for Fernando to exploit. That's probably why it was so easy for the hijackers to compromise our network—Fernando had already done it. He couldn't risk the Americans finding out, so he murdered four of our men to silence Coelho. The Romanians were never there."

"You expect anyone to believe I killed five men single-handedly?" Fernando scoffed at the idea. "It's absurd."

"We all underestimated you," Luisa replied. "No one more than me." A gun appeared in her hand.

"You're pathetic," Fernando said, hoping to transmute fear to exasperation. It didn't sound convincing, even to him. His mouth was as dry as a Portuguese summer.

At last, Baltasar looked up at his son. His face was heartbroken and scored with deep lines that Fernando had never seen before. Looking from Luisa to Fernando and back again to his niece, Baltasar let his gaze fall to the gun she held. He crossed the space between himself and his son—slowly, like a man approaching the open casket of a dear friend. When they stood eye to eye, Baltasar took his son's shoulders in his hands, turning him this way and that as if studying him for defects. Then he took Constantin Funar's phone in one hand and typed a simple text message. Hit send. Fernando's phone buzzed in his pocket.

"*Pai . . .*" Fernando said and trailed off, his gift for words failing him.

His father slapped him hard across the face. Fernando stumbled, his knees buckling as the hope drained out of him. His father caught his son and hugged him fiercely. "Goddamn you for what you make me do," he whispered in his ear.

Turning back to face Luisa, Baltasar positioned himself between his niece and his son. "You and your men, lay your weapons on the ground," he said to Luisa.

She looked at Baltasar in disbelief. "You can't mean it."

"Do as I say, Luisa."

"You saw the texts. How can you not believe me?" The gun in Luisa's hand inched upward.

"I do believe you, but he is my son. Tell your men to put down their weapons. No one has to die."

When Luisa didn't do as she was ordered, Baltasar spoke directly to the men, urging them to listen to reason. To think of their families.

Fernando could see the many competing loyalties on their faces. Baltasar was the boss, yes, but Luisa had been running things for four years. And then there were the local ties some shared with Anibal; they considered the men who had died in the hotel brothers. The two men behind Luisa fingered their weapons nervously before unslinging them and placing them carefully at their feet. They stepped away from Luisa, hands raised. Only Zava stood by her. He never wavered.

The smart move here would be for Luisa to follow the example of her men. Allow herself to be disarmed and give Baltasar time to think. Fernando saw a dozen ways that this could all still work out in her favor. Her problem was that she was a true believer. So blindly loyal to Baltasar and the Algarve that her outrage at what Fernando had done made it impossible for her to be pragmatic. If Fernando had told her once, he'd told her a thousand times—caring would be the death of her.

"Your *son*," she began, the words dripping with disdain, "has betrayed us. Threatened everything you've built." In her fury, she raised her gun in Fernando's direction, and unfortunately, Baltasar Alves himself. Shouts and warnings echoed through the warehouse as weapons rose in a flurry, like a flock of birds taking to the sky.

Zava reacted first, drawing his own weapon and stepping in front of Luisa. A single, booming shot. Fernando couldn't tell who had pulled the trigger or whether it had been intentional or the inevitable outcome of so many anxious fingers on so many triggers. It made no difference to Zava now. He died midstep and pitched forward, deadweight, only his face there to break his fall.

Luisa screamed in rage and pain. She knelt beside the body of the man known as the Beast and placed a hand on Zava's shoulder. The silence stretched out in every direction. Fernando marveled at the true chaos inherent in a moment like this. All the possible outcomes. So many factors no one could control. Luisa looked around, realizing how alone she really was. To his surprise, he didn't see any fear in her eyes, only resignation. He thought for a moment that she was about to choose the most violent outcome at her disposal.

Then Anibal pressed a gun to her ear. It snapped her out of whatever fugue state she had fallen into. She froze in place and let the gun fall from her hand. Anibal forced her down onto her stomach and knelt on her back. They both looked up at Baltasar questioningly. Ironically, it was the same question.

Baltasar shook his head. "No, not here. Not like this. She deserves better."

Fernando felt a wave of disappointment. Not that he particularly wanted to witness her death, but this needed to be over and done with. It never would be so long as Luisa still breathed. Two of Anibal's men rushed forward and pulled her aside to where her men were kneeling.

"And get that out of here," Baltasar said, meaning Constantin Funar.

Anibal ran a thumb across his own throat, asking an ancient question. Baltasar inclined his head, and the Romanian was hauled unceremoniously to his feet and led away. Marco Zava's body was dragged by the ankles toward the exit, leaving a wide, greasy smear in its wake. Fernando watched it with morbid fascination. It was only the sixth dead body that he had ever seen. All in the last twenty-four hours. He wondered if it would be his last.

Baltasar turned his attention back to Gibson Vaughn and Dan Hendricks, who still sat in their seats like good students waiting for teacher to return. Fernando trailed after his father, but Baltasar stopped and cast a disgusted look at him.

"Stay there," Baltasar muttered. "Say nothing while I clean up your mess."

"Yes, *Pai*," Fernando said as dutifully as he could manage.

Baltasar started to say more, but then thought better of it and turned his back on his son. He switched to English and spoke directly to Gibson.

"I've had time to think. Mr. Hendricks will die first. Since he's right here. I will use a knife so you can listen to him being gutted. Smell it. Then I will move on to George and finish with Jenn Charles. Unless you give me back control of my shipment. Now."

Gibson paled. "If I do . . . what happens after?"

"After is an eternity from now. Let's take this one thing at a time."

"All right," Gibson said. Seeing Marco Zava die appeared to have finally knocked some sense into him. He seemed to understand that he didn't have a choice.

"Perhaps you would like to see the knife?"

"No, I don't need to see the goddamn knife," Gibson said angrily. "You don't have to do any of that."

"Good. So get to it."

"Whatever you want," Gibson said. "I just need my laptop."

CHAPTER THIRTY-NINE

Pacemakers were remarkable devices when you really stopped to think about it. Fortunately, as a healthy thirty-one-year-old, Gibson had never had any reason to. In his head, pacemakers were grotesque Frankenstein boxes of wires and dials jutting out of your chest. But after his unscheduled summit with Dol5 early this morning, he'd taken time to read up on the principles behind them. Gibson had been impressed. Modern pacemakers were miniature technological marvels.

Take Baltasar Alves, for instance. His coronary five years ago had left his heart severely weakened and vulnerable. Without the surgically implanted pacemaker, there would be no prayer of him surviving all the stress and strain he had been under the past two days. It monitored Baltasar's breathing, sinus node rate, and blood temperature to determine his activity level and then set his heart rate accordingly. Even more remarkably, his pacemaker was remote manageable so that his doctor could monitor his history and, if necessary, tweak the settings—no password, no firewall, nothing. Whose bright idea was that? Gibson wondered.

He opened his laptop on the desk, conscious of Anibal looming over his shoulder and of the gun in his hand. The odds were small that Anibal was secretly tech savvy, but to be safe, Gibson opened four or five programs that all looked important but mostly monitored the laptop's background processes. All he needed was to create enough clutter on his desktop to distract and confuse Anibal should he get overly curious. In actuality, shutting down the defenses around the shipment could be accomplished with a few keystrokes, but Gibson needed to play for time. He didn't know how long it would take for Dol5's exploit to take effect. It wasn't like he had ever hacked anyone's heart before. Not literally anyway.

"I need the Wi-Fi password," Gibson said.

"Why?" Baltasar asked.

"Well, the explosives don't respond to voice commands."

Grudgingly, Baltasar agreed. Anibal leaned in to enter the password, shielding his hands. Gibson didn't know what that was supposed to accomplish.

An interesting tidbit that Dol5 had shared last night was that Fresco Mar and Baltasar's home were both part of the same network and relied on the same Wi-Fi credentials. That way the senior team and their devices could move from location to location seamlessly. Not an uncommon design, although extending it to multiple sites was a foolish measure in Gibson's estimation, one that emphasized convenience over network security. It also meant that Baltasar's pacemaker had connected to the Fresco Mar Wi-Fi the moment he entered the warehouse. Gibson saw it listed now on his network mapper among all the other connected devices.

"How long is this going to take?" Baltasar demanded, taking his seat across the desk and pulling his coat tight around him.

"A few minutes," Gibson said. "It has to be shut down in the correct sequence, or we'll get a cascading kernel failure, and then, you know . . . boom."

Gibson was afraid that might be laying it on a bit thick, but Baltasar nodded in agreement as though "cascading kernel failure" wasn't utter gibberish. If there were a single rule of human nature that Gibson could depend on, it was that people would rather bluff than admit ignorance.

Baltasar growled at Gibson to get on with it. With a mock salute, he opened the interface for Dol5's exploit and triggered the firmware update. It would take about three minutes to reconfigure Baltasar's pacemaker. To look busy while waiting, Gibson tabbed around among his open windows and started defragmenting his hard drive.

When the update was complete, Gibson input the sequence of commands that he'd memorized last night. When sent, they would instruct the pacemaker to gradually increase Baltasar's heart rate to dangerous levels. It would be unpleasant at first, terrifying by the end. Especially for a man who had already suffered one heart attack. But terrified suited Gibson, it suited him fine. There would be plenty of time to reset the pacemaker once Baltasar found himself in a more compliant frame of mind. Gibson opened a text file, began to write code in a babel of Python, C++, and Java, waiting for Baltasar to begin to feel the effects.

It didn't take long to realize that something had gone badly wrong. Baltasar made a slurping, throttled sound like a man trying to drink a thick milkshake through a narrow straw. Unable to draw a clean breath, his face went the blackened red of an overripe cherry. Baltasar locked eyes with Gibson. It was impossible, but for a moment Gibson felt certain that he knew. But there was no accusation in the old man's panicked stare, only helplessness. He knew he was dying and only needed to believe he wouldn't be alone.

Well, Gibson had been in Baltasar's place, and he knew better. Dying was something that you had to do alone.

As soon as he realized how quickly it was happening, Gibson swore and hurriedly switched back to Dol5's exploit interface to send a cancel command. It was too late, though. Baltasar clawed at his chest as if trying to dig out his own heart. His eyes fluttered coquettishly, and he slumped sideways out of his chair. Fernando was the first to react, leaping forward to catch his father. No one else moved. The guards, mouths agape, hovered purposelessly in place like drones that had flown out of range.

Fernando lowered his father gently onto the ground, looked around at all the stunned faces, and screamed for an ambulance. That shocked everyone out of their torpor; Anibal was the first to find his phone.

Fernando started CPR but didn't look like he knew what he was doing beyond mimicking what he'd seen in movies. Ignoring the guards, Luisa rose and went to Fernando. She knelt opposite him, on the far side of Baltasar, and told him how to do chest compressions. She counted to thirty as he worked, told him to pause, and delivered two deep breaths into Baltasar's mouth. Then Fernando began again. Together they fought to resuscitate the man who had raised them. Anibal, who had known them both since they were babies, stood over them, a gun in one hand, a phone in the other, describing the situation to emergency services.

For a moment, Gibson saw them as the children they'd once been. Luisa, the elder of the two, gently taking charge and telling Fernando what to do and when. Fernando kneeling over his father and doing exactly as she said without question. It was a surreal and strangely touching scene. Despite everything Gibson knew about them, he felt a strange solidarity with the pair. But this was how people were—at each other's throats until an emergency reminded them of what was really important.

Minutes ticked by. Luisa's face was a taut, expressionless mask, but Gibson could see the swell of emotions beneath the surface struggling to get free. Her cousin was having no such luck controlling his feelings. Tears streaked his face, and with each round of compressions, he became more frantic. By the fourth round, Fernando was sweating from the exertion. Luisa stopped counting and looked away. Fernando picked up where she left off, but when he reached thirty, Luisa only shook her head. Baltasar Alves was gone, and all the amateur CPR in the world wouldn't bring him back.

She reached across the no-man's-land of Baltasar's body to take Fernando's hand. Tried to anyway. Fernando slapped it away and said something sharp in Portuguese. Gibson might not have understood the words, but he understood the change in her expression well enough. Whatever truce had existed between them, however brief, was over. Unless Gibson badly missed his guess, Fernando was laying the blame at her feet. Gibson didn't see that it was in his interests to disabuse Fernando of the notion.

Hendricks leaned in to Gibson and whispered, "Did you really just kill a motherfucker with a laptop?"

Yes. He hadn't meant to, but that's exactly what he'd done. Somehow the distinction did little to make him feel any better about it. Glancing back, he caught George's eye—plan B had gone off the rails. They would need to improvise a plan C or wind up beside Baltasar Alves.

On the other side of the desk, the argument between the two cousins continued to escalate. It was plain that they were fighting for control of Baltasar's kingdom. From his knees, Fernando gestured angrily at his dead father. Then he looked up at Anibal and spoke to him in a calm, hate-filled voice. It had the imperious tone of an order. The gun twitched in Anibal's hand but stayed at his side. His mouth formed a tight, straight line. Fernando said it again, more forcefully.

The gun came up this time. Anibal shot Fernando in the chest, casting his vote for who he thought should run the Algarve. The impact drove the losing candidate backward and down, his legs twisting awkwardly beneath him. He lay there motionless. From that range, Gibson thought he must be dead. But then Fernando's hands twitched and came together over his wound. Anibal shook his head, irritated with himself, and stepped forward to finish the job. Luisa stopped him with a single word. She rose to her feet and held out her hand for the gun, never taking her eyes from Fernando. You'd lived the wrong sort of life when people lined up to put you out of your misery.

Anibal nodded, turned the gun around in his hand, and held it out for her to take.

"Obrigada," she said, one of the only words Gibson knew in Portuguese, even though he'd been saying it wrong for months: *thank you.*

Weighing the gun in her hand, Luisa stepped over Baltasar so she could better look down into Fernando's eyes. Gibson didn't want to watch but couldn't bring himself to look away.

"Bad shit got a half-life to it," Hendricks muttered under his breath. "You watch."

Luisa said something quietly to Fernando, spat on the floor at his feet, then turned smoothly and shot Anibal in the head. His sombrero spun away prettily as he dropped to his knees and flopped onto Baltasar's ankles. As the gunshot echoed away and dissolved into silence, Luisa stood at the center of the three bodies and surveyed the carnage with archeological detachment. As if she had stumbled upon the ruins of a long-dead civilization and was trying to reconstruct how they must have lived their lives.

Across the warehouse, two men loyal to Anibal backed slowly away and then turned and ran. Those who remained lowered their weapons in a sign that the king was dead, long live the queen.

"Oh, shit," Gibson said.

"Exactly," Hendricks said.

They weren't talking about the same thing.

Without considering the consequences, Gibson leapt out of his seat and rushed to Fernando. Luisa barked at him to stop, but he ignored her. More than likely it would get him killed, but with Anibal lying dead and Fernando not far behind, Gibson couldn't afford to wait.

Fernando's eyes were closed. There was no tension in his face. No pain. He wasn't dead, not yet; Gibson could still see his breath curling faintly up into the cool air. If he didn't look below the neck, Fernando might be mistaken for someone taking a siesta. One glance down shattered that illusion. Through Fernando's tented fingers, his suit had turned black with his own blood.

"What the hell are you doing?" Luisa said, pressing the muzzle of her gun to Gibson's ear.

Slowly, Gibson looked back at her. "Anibal is dead. Fernando is the only one left who knows where the children are."

"The slaves?"

"Who else?" he said angrily.

"Is that what this has all been about for you?"

"Why else would I still be in Portugal?"

Luisa didn't have an answer to that. Her stern expression softened, and she pointed the gun away from him. "Fine, ask him, then. Find out if you can."

"Really?" Not what Gibson had expected from Luisa Mata, but people had been surprising him all day.

Luisa looked at the bodies all around her and said, "Do I look like I need any more bad karma?"

Gibson understood that impulse. Subconsciously—or, hell, maybe consciously—he'd been seeking some way to redeem himself since arriving in Portugal. What a foolish notion it was, this vain hope that if he saved a few children it might ease his guilt for all those other things he'd done. Maybe it worked that way for some, maybe Luisa Mata was one of them, but for him, he knew that even if he saved every child in the world who needed saving, his mind would still find ways to remind him why it wasn't enough. Why it would never be enough.

Nodding his thanks, he turned back to Fernando, who still hadn't stirred. Gibson tried calling his name a few times, no response. Then he resorted to slapping him, lightly at first, then harder and harder.

"Hello," Fernando rasped wetly. "What have I missed?"

"Anibal is dead."

"Oh," Fernando said, taking in the news. "Understandable." He tried to raise his head to see the hole in his chest but couldn't muster the strength. "How does it look?"

"An ambulance is on the way." No one had cancelled Baltasar's ambulance, so that was technically true. Although Gibson doubted it would make any difference.

"That's very thoughtful." Fernando was laboring now for breath. "You were always a good friend."

"Tell me where the children are," Gibson said. "Would you do that for me?"

"Why? It's empty," Fernando said.

"What do you mean? Where are the children?"

"Never going to get the blood out now," Fernando said, feeling the lapel of his jacket. "I think it's ruined."

"Where are the children, Fernando?"

It took a moment before Fernando's eyes focused. "Being loaded onto a bus, most likely. Couldn't risk leaving them where they could be found with you sniffing around." Fernando coughed thickly. "Had to move up the delivery."

"What bus?" Gibson demanded, but Fernando had slipped out of consciousness as his body prepared itself to die. There would be no last words, no heartfelt confessions. Even if the ambulance arrived miraculously in time, what were the odds of Fernando Alves growing a conscience in his dying moments?

There had to be another way. Gibson wracked his brain but couldn't see it. The frustrating thing was that Fresco Mar was connected to Fernando's slave warehouse, but while Gibson could see the data that flowed back and forth, it didn't give him a real-world address; he couldn't see the source. It wasn't like . . . The thought trailed off into space as another idea muscled its way into his mind. It was a big one, and it seemed generally pissed off at Gibson for taking this long to think it.

CHAPTER FORTY

"I want to make a deal," Gibson said too loudly. To his dismay, his voice boomed through the quiet of the warehouse.

Luisa turned back to him. "A deal? I don't know that you're in a position to bargain."

"I still have the shipment, assuming you want it."

"And I still have your friends, assuming you want them."

And like that, they were back to the original standoff. Some of the players had exited the game, but the stakes hadn't changed.

"What do you say we lay off threatening each other," Gibson said, standing up and stepping toward her and away from Fernando. It felt like bad luck having this conversation so near his body.

"What else is there?" Luisa asked, with only a trace of sarcasm in her voice.

"It just hasn't gotten us very far," Gibson said, sweeping his hand across the three dead bodies like a model on a game show displaying the prizes.

"Did he tell you where the children were?"

"No, he seemed more concerned about his suit."

"There's something admirable about a man who sticks to his principles until the bitter end."

"But I think I know how I can find them."

"So what is it you want?" Luisa asked.

"The kids. I want them taken care of."

That was clearly not what Luisa had anticipated. "Define 'taken care of.'"

"Taken care of," Hendricks interrupted. "They don't get shipped back to whatever war zone they were trying to escape. They don't get turned over to Interpol."

"They get what they thought they were coming for," Gibson said. "Safety. Jobs. A chance."

"How many are we talking about?" Luisa asked.

"Forty-some," Hendricks said.

Luisa considered it. "And what do I get?"

"A whole lot of good karma," Gibson said.

Luisa almost cracked a smile. "That is certainly enticing. And when will I get the shipment?"

"Right now," Gibson said.

Her eyes narrowed. "The shipment is your only bargaining chip. What's your angle?"

"No angle. But Fernando's having those kids transported as we speak. Time's up. One of us has to give first, or else we'll just wind up back at threatening each other. So, I figure, why not me? Besides, I don't get the impression you're exactly good with what Fernando did."

"No, I am not."

"So, do we have a deal?" Gibson put out his hand. "I give you the shipment, and you make sure these kids get a fair shake?"

Luisa did the same, then hesitated. "And then you will get the hell out of Portugal?"

"With pleasure."

They shook on their hastily negotiated arrangement. It felt good. Gibson even gave it a fifty-fifty chance that he hadn't just gotten them all killed. Luisa had accumulated quite a body count in the last twenty-four hours, and it wasn't impossible that once she had what she wanted she'd simply kill them. But Gibson didn't think so. That wasn't the read he had on Luisa. He guessed he would see how good his hunch was in a few minutes.

Disarming the shipment proved anticlimactic, especially after the life-and-death struggle that had preceded it. A few keystrokes and it was done. The most dramatic moment came when Gibson stepped across the painted yellow line and the Klaxon didn't scream its warning and a countdown didn't begin. He turned back with a grin. Everyone had moved away to a safe distance except for Luisa, George, Jenn, and Hendricks, who stood at the edge of the circle.

"See?" Gibson said.

"Never a doubt in my mind," Hendricks said.

Screwdriver in hand, Gibson approached the shipment. From a distance it had looked large, but up close and personal, Gibson was stunned by the size of the pile. It had to be ten feet high. And this was only one of four annual shipments? It boggled his mind to imagine the sheer scope of the operation in those terms. He thought about all the lives it would affect. The damage it would do. Weighed against the lives of several dozen children, had he done any good, or was he simply trading one evil for another? Was that all life was? Choosing the grenade you hoped would cost you the fewest fingers?

Carefully, he detached one of the tightly wrapped bundles of explosives. A show of good faith. He brought it back and handed it to Luisa. She turned it over in her hands.

"If it's a fake, it's a damn good one," Jenn said.

"I'd have bet real money it was all a bluff," Hendricks said. "I'll be damned."

"So, are we square?" Gibson asked Luisa. All four looked at her expectantly. This was the proverbial moment of truth.

"We are," she said. "Find the children. Bring them back. I will see they have a home here. My uncle would've wanted that."

"Thank you," Gibson said.

"Where will you start looking?" Luisa asked.

Gibson pointed straight up. "The roof. I have an idea. Hendricks, will you be a second set of eyes?"

For once, Hendricks didn't ask any questions. "Yeah, I can do that."

"Okay, then," Gibson said. "We'll be right back."

Together they took off at a trot. Gibson felt good. Reinvigorated. Not being dead had really put a smile on his face. Even his ankle didn't hurt so much. Outside, he climbed the ladder fixed to the outside of the warehouse, followed by Hendricks.

On the roof, Gibson took a moment to orient himself. He flinched at the sight of the two snipers. They sat side by side in the shade, backs against one of the massive air-conditioning units. The men passed a cigarette back and forth between them like two ex-lovers who had sworn this would be the last time. They stared at Gibson and Hendricks sullenly. Like their compatriots below, they seemed unable to process the death of Baltasar Alves or what it meant for the Algarve. Neither reached for the rifles set across their legs, so Gibson took off at a slow jog, feeling reasonably certain that he wasn't going to get shot in the back.

"What are we looking for?" Hendricks asked.

They came around a corner, and Gibson saw it. The laser bridge that had seemed so out of place yesterday. At the time, Gibson hadn't yet discovered the gigabytes of video stashed away on the Fresco Mar servers, so he had put it out of his mind. But now it all made sense— Fernando and Dani Coelho had installed the laser bridge to create a secure, high-speed link between here and their child-trafficking warehouse. The genius had been putting it in plain sight and trusting it to blend into its surroundings. After a few months, no one would have even looked at it twice, much less thought to ask questions.

Gibson pointed his arm along the laser bridge. "What direction is this?"

"Northeast? I think. Do I look like a damn Boy Scout? Soon as I'm back down on the ground, I'll have no idea."

"Well, it's gotta be that way. No more than a couple of miles. A laser bridge needs line of sight, so the warehouse is literally straight that way."

"Hold that thought. I'll be right back," Hendricks said and then disappeared back the way they had come. He returned with one of the sniper rifles.

"They just gave you a rifle?" Gibson said.

"I think those boys might be a touch depressed," Hendricks said and sighted the rifle along the top of the laser bridge. Adjusting the scope, Hendricks surveyed the landscape until he brought something into focus. Then he stood back and held the rifle steady so Gibson could see for himself.

A little more than a mile to the northeast stood a cluster of three industrial buildings with blue rooftops. Gibson pressed his eye to the scope, then looked over the top of the rifle. Nothing significant stood between here and there, and the three buildings blocked any line of sight beyond—one of them had to be where the children were being held. *Had been held,* Gibson corrected himself.

"If they've left already, they could be anywhere," he said.

"Only so many ways north from here," Hendricks said, unusually optimistic now that they'd finally caught a break. "Don't overthink it. We go there and figure it out."

"Okay, but we'll need a car."

Hendricks grinned at him. "Don't think Fernando will be needing that Porsche no more."

He had a point.

CHAPTER FORTY-ONE

Jenn watched Gibson and Hendricks head for the roof. There was something a little bit sweet about seeing the two of them working together after all their differences. Who'd have thought it? There'd been times in Pennsylvania when she'd been afraid one would kill the other. And while there were still vestiges of that old antagonism, it had softened and morphed into something else. It made her smile for some dumb reason.

Luisa signaled the crews standing by that it was safe to begin repackaging the shipment for transport. In minutes, the warehouse would be overrun with workers on a frantic scramble drill to do in hours what usually took three days. It gave Jenn a moment to say good-bye to George.

"I'm not going with you."

George nodded thoughtfully. "I know. Why didn't you say good-bye to the others?"

She swallowed a phantom knot that had become lodged in her throat. "Because I'm chickenshit."

George embraced her firmly and held her there a long while. "I'll let them know."

"Thank you, sir."

"Hush with that. Thank you, Jennifer. I owe you my life many times over."

"The least I could do," she said because she wasn't good with the kind of words he deserved to hear.

"I wish you good luck. Make a life."

She kissed his cheek and felt him let her go. She ran to where Fernando lay. A sinking feeling told her the bullet that had killed him had probably also destroyed his phone. That was the kind of luck she'd been having lately. But when she dug the phone out of his jacket pocket, it was in one piece and working fine. For all the good it did her. Jenn didn't know his passcode, and he'd been careful to turn off notifications to his lock screen. There was no way to tell how long it had been since Fernando had spoken to Tomas, or how much time she had left.

Before he'd died, Fernando had made it abundantly clear that his regular calls to Tomas were the only thing keeping Sebastião alive. Well, there wouldn't be any more of those, so the clock was ticking now. Fernando had been dead almost fifteen minutes—how long did that leave? It was at least an hour to Lagos. No way she would make it in time.

She found Luisa out on the loading dock, directing traffic and organizing teams for the impossible task ahead of them. Jenn butted in and cut right to the chase. "I need a car and a weapon."

To her credit, Luisa barely blinked an eye. It was possible that the last two days had pushed her past the point of surprise.

"Tell me why."

Jenn gave her the abridged version—Tomas, golf club, Sebastião, Fernando's call-ins. That got Luisa's undivided attention. She cursed and strode away from Jenn and the workers, who frankly looked relieved to see her go.

Jenn followed Luisa's beeline for a black SUV.

"Where are you going?" Jenn asked, hurrying to keep up.

"With you. Apparently, I'm not done killing today. Get in."

"Why don't you just call over there and tell Tomas to stand down?" Jenn asked.

"Because in the last day, I've killed Carlito Peres, Branca Silva, and Anibal Ferro. Word has no doubt spread that Baltasar and Fernando are dead—how long before the rumors begin that I killed them too? So I don't know yet who is with me and who will come for my head. But Anibal was Tomas's uncle. I think I can guess which side he will be on."

Luisa's two guards sprinted up to the SUV. They'd rearmed themselves and tried to get in the back, determined to accompany their boss. But Luisa locked the doors on them and ordered them to stay behind.

"You're in charge now. Protect the warehouse and keep the men working. The shipment leaves on schedule. Everything else depends on that."

Grudgingly, the men nodded and stepped back from the SUV. You couldn't buy the kind of loyalty Jenn saw in their faces. If Luisa could bring the rest of her uncle's organization under her control, it boded well for the future of the Algarve. In the short term, though, Jenn imagined she would miss that loyalty when they got to Baltasar's estate.

Luisa drove like hell, both hands on the wheel and a grim expression on her face. Jenn didn't know how fast 190 kph was in miles, but it felt too fucking fast. Especially given how busy the highway was. It didn't seem to bother Luisa, though. If a car blocked her way, she drove up on its bumper and leaned on the horn until it got right with God. Two times a car moved too slow to suit Luisa, and she nudged it with her bumper like she was asking to squeeze past in a tight supermarket aisle. Jenn, accustomed to Dan's smooth, almost effortless driving, clutched the grab handle for dear life and remembered why she hated being a passenger.

"So, you really care for Sebastião?" Luisa asked out of nowhere.

Jenn didn't answer, conditioned to expect something biting from Luisa. When it didn't come, she realized Luisa was asking sincerely.

"It seems so," Jenn said.

Luisa appeared to give that answer its due. "Good, then."

And that was it. Question answered and apparently satisfactorily, Luisa finished their white-knuckle drive in silence. Jenn had thought

Luisa's animosity was personal, but she realized now that Luisa had her own feelings for Sebastião. It gave Jenn a different perspective on the woman and also encouraged her. She'd seen firsthand what Luisa was capable of when angry—that might come in handy shortly.

When they pulled up to Baltasar's estate, it was clear that something was wrong. The gate stood conspicuously open. Not a soul in sight. Luisa stopped the car as if the gate had been closed and sat in the idling vehicle, staring over the steering wheel, up the road toward the house.

"It looks like you were right about word spreading," Jenn said.

"So it would seem."

"I don't want to toot my own horn here, but this will go better if I'm armed."

Luisa threw the SUV into park and popped the hatch. They walked around to the back, where she unzipped two bulky canvas bags filled with rifles and assorted pistols. Luisa had not gone to Quarteira unprepared. She told Jenn to help herself.

"Damn. I like how you shop," Jenn said.

Luisa selected a black combat shotgun and set to loading it. To complement it, Jenn picked a compact bullpup rifle that she knew and was qualified on. There were a lot to choose from, but she was a firm believer in going with what you knew, especially into combat. She was also happy to see the familiar grip of a Sig Sauer P226 peering up at her from its holster. It even had a suppressor already fitted. Checking the magazine was full, she slipped the holster onto her belt. She had felt naked without it.

"Good choice," Luisa said approvingly.

Compliments now. What a weird day it had been.

Jenn felt Fernando's phone buzz in her pocket. The screen showed an incoming call from Tomas Ferro. Was that a good sign, or only Tomas confirming that Sebastião was dead? She showed the phone to Luisa, who shook her head and said not to answer.

"Question—is this your car?" Jenn asked.

"Yes, why?"

"'Yes,' it's a car you use, or 'yes,' they'll know it's you coming?"

Luisa realized what Jenn was asking. "Know it's me coming."

"It wouldn't happen to be bulletproof, would it?"

Luisa shook her head as they got back in the vehicle.

"Well, you can't have everything," Jenn said.

They went slowly up the long, curving driveway to the house. Jenn rested her rifle on the windowsill, but the only motion she saw was a cluster of birds feeding in the lush green grass of the rolling lawns. Otherwise, she saw no one and nothing. After the heavily armed presence around the property yesterday, it was more than a little disconcerting. It had the eerie vibe of one of those postapocalyptic movies in which survivors wandered through abandoned buildings that had once been teeming with activity. It bothered Luisa as well, who muttered in hushed Portuguese.

Rounding the last bend, Jenn saw a score of men at the front door of the house. They were all armed, and Jenn wouldn't have described their reaction to the SUV's arrival as exactly friendly. The men fanned out, taking intelligent positions behind parked cars that took good advantage of their numbers. Nevertheless, Jenn felt a jolt of hope. One of those cars was Sebastião's electric-blue Audi R8 Spyder.

Luisa pulled over sharply, bringing the SUV to a lurching halt inches from a tree. She was thinking hard, and Jenn saw her reach a hard, lonely conclusion. "If Sebastião's alive, he will be in the greenhouse along the cliffs."

"What are you going to do?"

"Talk to the men. I have to invite them to join me."

"They don't look to be in a joining mood," Jenn said.

Luisa took a deep breath. "No, but I have to try. The Algarve can't afford a civil war."

"I can back you up."

Luisa looked surprised by the offer, then smiled gratefully. "Thank you, Jennifer, but there are too many. Even for us," she said, summoning all her bravado. "If they mean to kill me, they will kill me. I won't need your help for that."

"Are you sure?"

Luisa pointed along the side of the house. "Give me ten seconds to draw their attention, then go that way. They won't see you from this angle."

Luisa eased slowly out of the car, hands in plain sight, leaving the shotgun across her seat. She gave it a lingering last look before shutting the door.

"Tell Sebastião that I am ashamed at what my family has done and that I am truly sorry," Luisa said. "If you hear gunfire, send flowers. And be careful on your way out."

Jenn wished her luck and watched Luisa walk up the driveway toward the house. At the count of ten, she slipped out of the SUV and made a low run to the edge of the house. She knelt and listened. No gunfire yet. That Luisa hadn't been shot on sight was a promising sign. Working her way quickly to the far corner of Baltasar's enormous mansion, Jenn encountered no resistance. Beyond the pool and clay tennis court, the roof of the greenhouse rose above the hedge that mostly hid it from view.

Taking a steadying breath, she sprinted across the open space by the pool and disappeared down a flight of steps that split the hedge. At the bottom of the stairs, the low murmur of men's voices brought her up short. The voices were coming from around the corner hedge from the direction of the greenhouse. Crouching, she propped the rifle against the hedge and drew the Sig Sauer with its suppressor. She would have killed for a tactical mirror to give her some sense of what lay around this corner, but she'd left her SWAT gear in her other pants. Going in blind against an unknown number of hostiles was a lousy option. Going in blind and alone verged on suicidal. There had to be another way. Could she negotiate with Tomas?

A bellow of pain rendered the question irrelevant. It was Sebastião. He was alive. He was in agony. Her tongue snaked across her front teeth. *The hell with this,* she thought. Maybe George could have found a peaceful resolution, but she didn't have his way with words. She wanted the fight. An old, familiar coldness descended over her. As far as she was concerned, anyone near this greenhouse had made their choice; they would all have to live and die with it.

Jenn came around the corner, gun raised, rising out of her crouch. Two men stood guard at the door. They both saw her at the same time. The first panicked and struggled to draw his pistol; Jenn shot him twice center mass and sent him tumbling over a crude wooden bench. He lay there, unmoving.

The second man didn't panic. He had the eyes of someone who had been shot at before and knew there was nothing to be gained in hurrying. Calmly, he shouldered his rifle and brought it up, trying to bring it to bear on the intruder. Fortunately for Jenn, it had a long barrel that wasn't designed for close quarters. In the time it took him to train it on her, Jenn fired twice. And missed twice. Both to his right. She overadjusted and missed a third time, this time to his left. Behind him, panes of glass to either side shattered, along with the element of surprise. This was what six months of rust won you—the terrifying ability to miss water from the end of a pier. That and the parting gift of a large-caliber bullet in the head.

Her fourth shot coincided with his first. He missed. She didn't. Shouldn't have been possible, but he did. She had no idea by how much—could have been an inch or a mile—only that she was alive by sheer, dumb luck. She'd done everything to get herself killed, and then an experienced killer had pointed a cannon squarely at her and simply missed. She shot him a second time as he staggered back, trying to catch the blossom of blood flowering from his clavicle. He took a weak step to his right, stumbled, lost his feet, and went down.

Confirming that her mind hadn't deceived her into believing she was uninjured, she fought adrenaline's whispering lie that she was unkillable. But it was so seductive, and she felt the rising euphoria that only came after surviving a brush with death. She willed herself to focus. Sebastião was inside. He was alive. She could still save him. Her magazine was only half empty, but she ejected it and slapped a fresh one into place. Then she kicked in the greenhouse door.

Sebastião sat lashed to the same chair from the video they had shown her on the beach this morning. Had he been here all day? The mottled scrum of his sweat- and blood-soaked clothes spoke to his barbaric treatment. His surgically repaired leg had been stretched out and bound by a taut length of rope. And it looked as if Tomas had been getting himself a workout, because the knee itself was purple and grotesquely deformed. When Sebastião looked up at her, she wasn't sure if he even recognized her. There was nothing in his eyes but anguish.

Tomas Ferro crouched behind Sebastião, using him as a shield. He'd traded his golf club for a pistol that he pressed to Sebastião's temple. Only the top of Tomas's head was clearly visible. Six months ago, Jenn would have shot him without a second thought. The idea of accidentally hitting Sebastião wouldn't have entered her mind. It was all she could imagine now. But she'd left all faith in her aim outside.

In a shaky voice, Tomas threatened to kill Sebastião if she didn't drop her weapon. He said it in Portuguese, though, so by the time her brain translated and reacted, Jenn had already taken three more steps. And after those three steps, Tomas still hadn't made good on his threat to kill Sebastião. That he hadn't told her everything she needed to know.

Don't give him time to think.

The longer this played out, the more likely it ended with Sebastião dead. Her mind went quiet, and she took a single step toward Tomas. He repeated his threat even as she took another and another and another. A confused and terrified expression crept onto his face, as if even though he knew what was happening, he was paralyzed from stopping it. When she reached Sebastião, she stopped and in one easy motion put the gun to Tomas's forehead like she was brushing away a strand of his hair. Even she couldn't miss from this range.

She didn't.

CHAPTER FORTY-TWO

The red Porsche slalomed in and out of traffic as if the other cars were bolted to the roadway. It was a beautiful, nimble automobile, but it was a tight squeeze for three. With Hendricks driving and George in the passenger seat, Gibson had been left to wedge himself into the back. He snorted. Porsche had a lot of nerve calling this padded coffin a back seat. To fit, Gibson had to turn sideways with his knees up against his chest. Hendricks had made about three different sardine jokes in the five minutes since they'd left Fresco Mar. It was his way of not dwelling on Jenn's absence. They were all in shock at her decision. Even as crowded as it was, the car felt strangely empty to Gibson.

The three blue roofs came up fast on their left. Hendricks eased off the gas as they made a drive-by. All three buildings were part of a single complex that had once been a medium-size construction-supply business. Judging from the condition of the exterior, it had been closed a long time. Closed but not abandoned. The exterior fences that circled the property were well maintained, and Gibson saw several places that had been repaired and reinforced. Coils of razor wire snaked along the top of the fence. From down on the road, Gibson couldn't spot a laser bridge on any of the roofs, but that didn't mean one wasn't up there.

Something about this place gave him a bad feeling.

"A lot of security for a bankrupt construction company," George observed.

"Almost like they're more interested in keeping people in than keeping them out," Hendricks said.

After they'd driven the length of the property, the Porsche made a looping U-turn and went back for another pass. The main gate was open. A pickup blocked the way. Its doors were ajar, and four men stood staring at the buildings expectantly.

"Pull in," George said, laying a pistol across his thigh that he'd taken out of Anibal's hand. "Nice and easy. Let's see what they do."

Hendricks slowed and turned into the driveway. One of the men by the pickup turned to see who had arrived. A flash of recognition crossed his face at the sight of the Porsche, and he raised a hand in surprised greeting. There was only one reason the man would know this car, or its former owner. Gibson didn't need to check the roof now; this was definitely the right place. The only thing he didn't understand was what the four men were doing there. They were facing the wrong way to be guarding the place. There was a sense of anticipation, as if they were waiting. But for what?

When the men at the pickup truck went back to what they were doing, Gibson realized they'd caught a lucky break with the time of day. The angle of the sun, and the way it reflected off the windshield, made it impossible to see inside the Porsche. That bought them a moment to assess the situation in relative safety. No one saw any weapons. That was something. But they were still outnumbered, and for all they knew the cab of the pickup might have an arsenal inside. Still, the Porsche had provided a Trojan-horse edge that should give them advantage enough if they used it right.

A cheer went up from among the men, who slapped the hood of the pickup and pointed up at the top of the nearest building. Smoke curled out of slats in the roof, growing thicker and darker by the second. In another minute, a black cloud began to billow from a second building.

Somewhere a window exploded and fire rippled out, licking up the corrugated siding of the third building.

Gibson understood now. The men at the pickup were the demolition crew. There to scrub any evidence and close up shop, permanently. At Fresco Mar, Fernando had told Gibson that the children were being moved ahead of schedule. Had that been another lie? Were they inside, being cleaned up too? His stomach pitched horribly at the thought. Hendricks had the same idea and was out of the car before either George or Gibson could stop him. George didn't move as fast as he used to but did his best to follow. Gibson, pinned in the back seat, could only watch helplessly.

The men, expecting Fernando Alves, gaped in confusion at the African American man walking sternly toward them. Hendricks raised his gun and shouted for them to freeze—in English.

It didn't inspire the desired result.

Instead, the men shouted in alarm and scrambled for the pickup. Hendricks put three bullets through the windshield. That seemed to help overcome the language barrier, and the men stopped where they were.

"Give me a reason," Hendricks said. "Give me a goddamn reason."

George came up alongside and translated from Hendricks to Portuguese. Hands floated up into the air. Behind them, the three buildings burned angry and hot, and a plume of smoke rose into the sky that would be seen for fifty miles.

———

Speed was such a relative thing. Gibson had ridden in planes traveling five hundred miles an hour and slept like a baby. He'd flown in helicopters screaming over treetops while daydreaming about home. But there was something about doing 220 on a Portuguese highway that really brought the reality of pure speed into harsh perspective. Gibson waited for a caption to float across his eyeline, warning him not to attempt this, that the driver was a professional on a closed course. Except this highway was anything but closed, and the sound of the wind as they passed other vehicles felt like a collision inside the fragile sports car. If anyone but Hendricks had been behind the wheel, Gibson would have started drawing up his will.

The children hadn't been inside when the fires started. Fernando had been telling the truth about that much. They were being transported in a motor coach. Hundreds like it choked the roads in the summer months, bringing tourists to and from the Algarve. The bus they were looking for was silver and green, and it had an hour head start. Its route had it traveling east on the A22 until it crossed into Spain. At Seville it would merge onto one of two major highways and make its way north to the French border.

None of the men from the pickup truck knew which major Spanish highway, though. They'd sworn on their mother's lives that Fernando had been careful not to share that information with them. Hendricks had worked them pretty hard without getting anything else out of them, and Gibson had been inclined to believe them—that kind of secrecy sounded like Fernando. Hence the breakneck drive across the Algarve. They had to catch the bus before it reached Seville. To keep the men from alerting the bus, Hendricks had emptied his gun into the engine block of the pickup truck. Back in the Porsche, George had powered off the phones they'd confiscated from the men. After a few miles, he began slipping them through a crack in the window, letting them shatter on the pavement.

At the Spanish border, they caught up to the bus, which was keeping just below the speed limit, no doubt to avoid attracting attention. Hendricks took his foot off the gas and let their momentum bring them up alongside the bus. It raised the philosophical question of how to stop a fifty-ton bus with a fifteen-hundred-pound Porsche. All the scenarios Gibson envisioned ended with the Porsche being scraped off the highway with a spatula. He suggested shooting out the wheels, but Hendricks thought that would put the kids at one hell of a risk.

"Honk," George said. "Just honk."

Hendricks pulled level with the driver and got his attention with the horn. George rolled down his window just far enough that he could stick his hand out and point for the bus to pull over. To everyone's surprise but George's, the bus did just that. The power of Fernando's red Porsche appeared to know no bounds. Hendricks pulled over and then backed up until his bumper almost kissed the front of the bus. It wouldn't stop a bus, but it might buy them a few seconds if the driver got antsy.

The bus door swung open. Two men stepped down and ambled up to the Porsche. They looked confused and shook their heads in irritation at this unscheduled stop. At the car, one squatted down and rapped on George's window, asking in German what the hell was going on. George slid the window open and put a gun in his face. The man's mouth snapped open and closed. An inarticulate warble rose out of his throat as he lost his balance and fell backward into the dirt.

His companion wheeled away and dashed for the bus, shouting as he ran. George tried to follow, but his door only opened as far as the fallen man's forehead, which absorbed the impact with a dull thwack. Hendricks was up and out on his side of the car. He put his thumb and pinkie in his mouth and whistled. The fleeing man looked back, and Hendricks shot him, catching him in the shoulder. Remarkably, the man didn't fall but spun like a top, then threw himself forward into the bus, his legs scrabbling in the dirt to push himself the rest of the way inside.

From the back seat, Gibson felt the Porsche shudder violently, then lurch forward. The bus driver was trying to make a getaway. The impact threw George out of his seat and into the dirt. Hendricks, who was circling the front of the car, was tossed onto the hood, where he rolled once and fell off onto the shoulder.

Frantically, Gibson tried to climb out of the back seat. In his mind, the bus would ride up the back of the Porsche and flatten it like a pancake. Out the window, he saw Hendricks yelling. Gibson squeezed himself between the two front seats, learning how toothpaste must feel. He fell forward as the bus began to accelerate, driving the Porsche before it, and he struggled in the tight confines to roll over so he could jump out before the bus picked up too much speed. His foot caught in the steering wheel, and he kicked at it, trying to free himself. Then, as suddenly as it began, the bus shuddered, air brakes hissing, and came to a gentle stop, half in and half out of traffic.

Gibson rolled out of the car and flopped onto his back like a sailor gratefully reaching dry land after a shipwreck. He crab-walked a safe distance away before standing up. He wanted to be well out of harm's way if the bus started moving again. He looked back down the highway, surveying the damage. All told, the bus had taken him for one hell of a joyride. Bits and pieces of Porsche littered the road as if the bus had eaten, digested, and shat it out. He spotted George limping and Hendricks running in his direction. They were perhaps a hundred yards away. But if they hadn't stopped the bus, what had?

In answer to his question, a man tumbled out of the bus and landed hard on the ground at the foot of the stairs. Gibson took a step toward him when a cheer went up from inside the bus. Young boys and girls began streaming out. They'd taken matters into their hands and stopped the bus on their own. For so many reasons, that was the coolest thing Gibson had ever seen. He wished he shared a common language with them so he could tell them how proud he was, but it didn't look as if they needed his encouragement.

He leaned against Fernando's ruined car and watched the children dance in the sunshine. How long had it been since they'd been outside? Their joy was infectious. When George and Hendricks arrived, the children cheered and circled them. Hendricks was grinning like a damn fool. Who could blame him? It was a beautiful sight. Gibson felt better than he had in . . . he couldn't remember how long. The only thing to improve it would be if Jenn were here to see it too.

A boy who might be Kamal raised his hands to the sky in thanks. Gibson looked up as well. He saw it then. Perhaps fifty feet up—a familiar black drone hovering above the bus. It waggled its wings at Gibson. *Hello, I see you.* Then it buzzed away to the south.

Gibson's phone vibrated in his pocket. The message cut right to the chase:

Don't make us come looking for you in Morocco. We want that report.

So much for his good feeling.

CHAPTER FORTY-THREE

Jenn pulled the Audi up to the front door. Sebastião's garage was underground, and she didn't want him climbing any more stairs than absolutely necessary. The knee was already a purple you only saw in a sunset sky over certain kinds of industrial accidents. After leaving Baltasar's estate, she'd begged to take him to the hospital, but he'd refused. *Home. Please,* he'd said over and over, his face turned to the window. The harder he fought to hide the heartbreak in his voice, the closer it brought her to tears of her own. She didn't like that invulnerable men made vulnerable might be her kryptonite.

"We're here," she said but got no reply.

She went around and opened his door. Sebastião lay back on the fully reclined passenger seat, his battered leg stretched out like a broken wing. Supporting his ankle with both hands, Jenn guided the foot onto the ground. Arm around her shoulder, he hoisted himself into a standing position. The pain made his eyes water, and his brow knitted in concentration. She heard a near-silent groan from somewhere deep in his chest.

Together they limped into the house. He took one look at the staircase up to his bedroom and suggested the pool instead. Out on the lanai, Jenn eased him into a lounge chair and elevated the leg with pillows from the house. She brought ice for his knee and raised an umbrella for shade.

"All better," he said.

"How is it?" she asked.

He shook his head. His playing days were over. Walking without a limp would be the priority now, and he knew it. He just wasn't ready to think about it yet. There would be plenty of time for that in the days and weeks ahead. Still, she knew how much he loved the game, and the thought that it was over was hard for her to bear.

"I'm so sorry. I should have—"

Sebastião took her hand and held it firmly. When he spoke, his voice was full of anger, but low and serious. "You saved my life. This is not your fault. Tell me you understand that."

She told him she understood. He pretended he believed her. Kissed the back of her hand, rubbed it against his cheek, and told her again. She freed her hand and asked if she could bring him anything. Something to eat. He shook his head at the notion.

"Champagne. Bring us a bottle of champagne. The good stuff."

"What are we celebrating?"

"The end," Sebastião said. "And a beginning."

In the kitchen, she knelt to open the wine refrigerator. Before meeting Sebastião, she wouldn't have thought anyone could need eighteen bottles of chilled Dom Pérignon. The only champagne he would drink, although she secretly doubted he knew the difference. On the bottom shelf of the refrigerator were three bottles of Dom Pérignon 2004 rosé that he saved for special occasions. *The good stuff.* At two hundred and fifty a bottle, it ought to be.

Tomorrow, if Sebastião was still in a stubborn mood, she would threaten to call Luisa. Sebastião usually steered clear of crossing Luisa. It would be a bluff, though. Between getting the shipment away on schedule and corralling the renegade factions that had splintered off since Baltasar's death, Luisa had problems of her own. But Jenn had a feeling she would solve them. The way Luisa had won over the men at Baltasar's house had been inspired. If she could make it through the next forty-eight hours, then Luisa and the Algarve stood a chance.

Before Jenn had left to take Sebastião home, Luisa had let her know that a busload of hungry children had been delivered to Fresco Mar— another tangled mess for Luisa to unravel. But she was already on top of it and appeared to have every intention of honoring their deal. That meant George, Dan, and Gibson were on the way to the boat by now. Getting ready to depart for North Africa. Jenn felt bad for ghosting the way she had. It wasn't her finest moment. Dan would get over it, of course, but Gibson would hold a mean grudge. She didn't want to leave things that way and thought briefly about calling to say good-bye while their phones still worked.

Instead, she chose a bottle of champagne, placed it on the counter, and took down two flutes from a cabinet. Then she peeled the tin-foil away from the wire cage over the cork but didn't open the bottle. Sebastião liked to do that himself. He could take the cork off with his hand so smoothly that it hardly made a sound, water vapor smoking from the mouth of the bottle. Then he would wink and bestow the cork upon her like a trophy.

He was a ridiculous man. She smiled and looked around at his house. It was quite the life he led. Sebastião Coval—he of the three-sink bathroom and bottomless champagne. A life he wanted to share with her. It was a miracle. No more running. The chance to breathe and to live. It wasn't a life she'd ever imagined for herself. Dream weddings and happily ever afters didn't run in her family. For the first time in a long time, she felt lucky. Leaning against the counter, she allowed herself a moment to daydream about the future. Would they really live in Salzburg? It didn't matter to her. Whatever he wanted. After all, beggars couldn't be choosers . . . She stifled a sob that came out of nowhere like a rogue wave, dark and miles wide.

It had been a long time since she'd cried, but she sensed that if she started now, it would be hell stopping again. She gripped the counter's edge and took short, hitched breaths, fighting for control. Her shoulders shook violently once before she was able to swallow it all down. Lock it back in the place that she kept the things she couldn't kill. She dried her eyes, dabbing at the corners so she didn't look like a raccoon. Then she fixed a smile on her face, took the glasses, the champagne, and went out to say good-bye to Sebastião.

He smiled back at her and held out a hand for the champagne. Struggling into a sitting position, he opened it with a flourish, sending the cork arcing into the pool. Champagne flowed onto the lanai, and he hurried to pour two glasses before spilling any more.

"What a waste," he said, shaking champagne off his hands and licking his fingers. "Remind me never to do that again."

He held out a glass to her. His shoulders sagged slightly. Watching him, the smile had slipped from her face. She saw that he knew.

"Why?" he asked.

She thought—*Because I have nothing, and if I stay, I will rely on you for everything. Money. Safety. Because nothing lasts forever, and my life would depend on you never getting tired of me. We will never be equals, and I can't live that way. Dependent. Deferring to you. Afraid to rock the boat. You will come to despise me for it. While I come to resent you.*

She said, "Because it's not safe. For either of us."

"We can figure all that out."

"Can we? Look at your knee."

"That wasn't your fault," he said. "I told you that."

"Haven't you noticed the way people around me wind up beaten to a pulp?"

"Is it Gibson?" he asked.

"This has nothing to do with him."

Sebastião sighed and looked away before he said, "I'm sorry that I did not let you know how I felt sooner."

"Neither of us is any good at that."

He laughed. "No, I suppose not."

"I feel the same way," she said, dancing around the word neither of them had ever said to the other.

"Then stay."

"I can't. Not now, not like this."

He thought about it while he searched her eyes. "Perhaps in the future, things will be different."

"Sebastião . . . ," she said, not knowing what to say to that.

He held up his glass. "A toast." Somehow there wasn't a trace of bitterness in his voice. What an unexpected man he had turned out to be. "To the future."

She touched her glass to his and watched him drink his glass dry. What was she doing? She put the glass to her lips but did no more than smell the bubbles. For the first time in months, the thought of drinking made her sick.

CHAPTER FORTY-FOUR

João showed the time to George Abe. They would really want to get under way soon. One hundred and twenty-five nautical miles separated Olhão and Tangier. A minimum twelve hours of travel time, which didn't include finding a quiet place for the Americans to go ashore. João didn't know the coast of North Africa, so that would take time too. If they waited much longer, they would arrive after dawn and lose the cover of darkness.

"How soon?" George asked.

João shrugged apologetically. "Now, *senhor*."

George said that he understood and patted him on the arm appreciatively.

They left the wheelhouse and went out on deck of the *Alexandria*. The sun sparkled across the water of the harbor. The man George called Daniel sat on the coaming, chain-smoking. He hadn't moved in an hour, gazing away across the harbor toward Fresco Mar Internacional with a tired scowl that wore him like an old and familiar friend. The two men exchanged a look, Daniel asking a question with his eyes. George nodded reluctantly. A decision was reached. Daniel stood and flicked his cigarette into the water.

Not a word had been spoken, but there had been a conversation nonetheless. It reminded João of his crew. How the men could pass long nights working the nets without speaking more than a dozen words between them. Everything communicated through a glance or a gesture or a simple action.

Such an understanding didn't come without a price, João knew. It took years on the open ocean. Far out beyond the edge of the world. It was closer than anyone wanted to believe. That place where no help would come in time. When you were on your own with only your crew to watch your back for that wave that would drag you overboard. Knowing the person to your left and to your right better even than their own families because all your lives depended on it. There wasn't always time for words out there in the dark. João had always thought it was unique to sailors, but he realized that was naïve. There were other oceans, other kinds of waves.

Daniel went up the gangway to the dock, where the third man waited. He stood looking down the dock toward the roadway, a red baseball cap pulled low over his eyes. Unmoving. No acknowledgment that Daniel was standing beside him. The two men stood there together and stared down the dock.

Daniel said something under his breath that caused his companion to laugh. The kind of laugh that's like a pipe bursting. It faded as quickly as it had come, and once again the two men stood in silence.

Despite the flecks of gray in his thick beard, the man in the cap was the youngest of the three. The closest in age to João, yet he had a feeling they would not have much in common. There was something haunted in the man's face that João was only too happy to know nothing about. The man had been almost superstitious about keeping his distance from the *Alexandria*. Some people were afraid of the ocean, but João didn't believe that was it.

The only reason they hadn't departed for Tangier was because the Americans were waiting for the woman. The fourth member of their crew. João hoped she came so that he could thank her personally for saving his life. However, there seemed to be disagreement about whether she would show up at all. The Americans had already argued once. João only spoke a few words of English but got the sense that the man on the dock was the lone holdout. He wouldn't come aboard because that would be admitting she wasn't coming.

Up on the dock, the argument began anew.

Daniel remained calmer this time and pointed repeatedly to the time. That only made the third man angrier. He gestured down the dock.

They both froze.

At the end of the dock, a blue sports car skidded to a stop, throwing up a scrim of dust. A woman with dark hair got out. Daniel looked back at George. João couldn't tell what it meant. He wasn't a part of them.

The bearded man took off his red cap and held it straight up in the air as if she might not see him otherwise.

George turned to João with a smile equal parts relief and regret. "We're all here now. We can go."

ACKNOWLEDGMENTS

Until *Debris Line*, all of my books have been set in the familiar, comfortable confines of the American Northeast. It's my home; I know it. Relocating the setting to Portugal was necessary, but it came with no small amount of trepidation. I would never claim to have insight into Portuguese life, but it was important to me that I represent it accurately to the best of my ability. To that end, I want to thank my father, Tom FitzSimmons, who drove me back and forth across Portugal during the summer of '17 so that I could visit the towns that figure in the story and meet a few of the people who call the Algarve home. Hopefully, I have not made too much of a hash of it.

I also want to thank my mother, Marcia Feldhaus, and stepfather, Steve Feldhaus, for giving me a respite from a gloomy DC February to take up residency on their Florida patio. I've finished three of my four books at that table, and it doesn't feel like a book is well and truly complete until I type "The End" and throw myself into your pool.

And if anyone is starting to get the impression that I'm never actually at home, a hearty thanks to Jaz, Laura, and Ishmael at Jacob's Coffee for giving me an office away from office and for never thinking it weird (or at least never saying it was weird) that a guy who doesn't drink coffee could spend so much time working at a coffee shop.

My thanks to author Kate Moretti (*The Blackbird Season*, *The Vanishing Year*) for putting me in contact with Anabela Araujo, who cleaned up my clunky Portuguese. Angela Hofmann for her insights into the modern-day face of slavery and the especially terrible toll it takes on children. Nathan and Patrick Hughes for always steering me straight on all things USMC. Drew Hughes for answering my annual creepy medical questions without once calling the cops. Eric Schwerin and Katherine Manougian for reading bits and pieces of *Debris Line* and listening while I improvised plotlines that never made it to the page.

To say that Gibson Vaughn and his stories would have turned out differently without my friend Mike Tyner is a feckless understatement. I can't count the number of times I have sat down to dinner with him, scratching my head, and left with a notebook full of new ideas. *Debris Line* is no exception to the rule. Thank you.

The same is true of Vanessa Brimner—my first reader, my sounding board, and canary in the coal mine for every lunatic idea that comes into my head. She probably reads these books more than I do, and during the inevitable period in each book when I think I've lost my way, she points me in the right direction.

Ed Stackler has edited all of the Gibson Vaughn novels and somehow keeps coming back for more. It's been a great relationship since book one, but to work with someone who knows the characters as well as I do is a real gift.

As is my partnership with the Glorious DHS—David Hale Smith. A great agent, a better friend, and an all-around great night on the town.

My eternal thanks to the wonderful team at Thomas & Mercer who work tirelessly to bring these books into the world. I have to begin with my editor, Gracie Doyle, who has always been a champion of

Gibson Vaughn. But, I also need to thank Dennelle Catlett and Ashley Vanicek, who spearhead PR; Gabrielle Guarnero, Kyla Pigoni, and Laura Costantino in marketing; Sarah Shaw, who takes such good care of all the authors; Oisin O'Malley, Thomas & Mercer's art director; Rex Bonomelli, who has designed all of the wonderful covers for the series; and Laura Barrett, the production manager. Finally, I want to thank Jeff Belle, Mikyla Bruder, and Galen Maynard, who have done a world-class job building Amazon Publishing and making it such a wonderful home for authors such as myself.

ABOUT THE AUTHOR

Photo © 2017 Douglas Sonders

Matthew FitzSimmons is the author of the *Wall Street Journal* bestselling Gibson Vaughn series, which includes *The Short Drop*, *Poisonfeather*, and *Cold Harbor*. Born in Illinois and raised in London, England, he now lives in Washington, DC, where he taught English literature and theater at a private high school for more than a decade. Visit him at www.matthewfitzsimmons.com.